i    *Gutter*

iii    **Editorial**

1    Street Maw
     Philip Murnin
5    Flygirl
     R A Martens
8    Great Long Story
     Paula Morris
13    For Anyone Who Wants To Be Friends With Me
     Anneliese Mackintosh
17    Extract from the novel *Articles of Faith*
     Michael Cannon
20    The National Ghost
     Andrew C Ferguson
21    Gerontocracy
     Ryan van Winkle
22    Autograph
     Brian Docherty
23    Abusive Language
     John Brewster
23    Probabilities
     Robert Marsland
24    Poetry
     Robert Marsland
24    Pilgrim
     William Bonar
25    The Man with the Cross-sectioned Heart
     Brian McCabe
30    Extract from the novel
     *The Trees Aren't Sad So Why Am I?*
     Tracey Emerson
34    Muddy Water
     Joe McInnes
39    Fuck You Too, Pixie Meat
     Kirsty Logan
42    Cliff
     Eleanor Thom
45    The Bower
     Judith Taylor
46    Incomer
     Judith Taylor
48    Bride from Lahore
     Rizwan Akhtar
49    In the Flood
     Brian Johnstone
49    What the young films of Man Ray dream about
     Sarah Neeley
50    Four Poems from *Anderson's Piano*
     Sally Evans
53    The Wedding Flowers
     Wayne Price
62    Hello! Hello!
     Rodge Glass
66    The Minotaur of Pollokshields
     R.W. Mosses
68    GAP
     Ewan Morrison
77    Hive
     Jim Stewart
79    A Raincoat, A Spell of Rain Ago
     Ryan van Winkle
80    St Anthony's Fire
     John Brewster

81    Light
     Leel...
81    Desc...
     El G...
83    Pray
     Iya...
88    Sol...
     Ano...
90    Against the Grain
     Jim Carruth
90    Twins
     Jim Carruth
91    Held And Held In Place
     Gordon McInnes
91    The Black Art
     Marion McCready
92    Vision
     William Bonar
92    A Surplus of Possible Reintegrations
     Dorothy Alexander
93    Extract from a memoir in progress
     Fiona Montgomery
101    Pleasureland
     Anna Stewart
106    William John MacDonald
     Carl MacDougall
110    Toothless Towards the Grave
     Steve Cashell
115    The Custodian
     J David Simons
121    The Whip Hand
     Brian Johnstone
121    Parable
     Owen Gallagher
122    The Pope & Saint Marx
     Owen Gallagher
122    The Bitter Fruits
     Brian Johnstone
123    Art School 1 & 2
     Allan Harkness
124    Unthanks
     Andrew F Giles
125    Far Field
     Jim Carruth
127    Husbandry
     Jim Carruth
128    Laidlaw
     Jim Carruth

128    **Reviews**

144    World Enough and Time
     Andrea Mullaney
145    The Mast
     Kathrine Sowerby
148    The Mothers
     Sandra Alland
149    Mind Furniture
     Jim Ferguson
151    A Visit
     Natasha Soobramanien
153    The Weight
     Craig Lamont
156    Translation
     Chris Wardhaugh

Contents

157 Fragment 2, translated by Donal McLaughlin
   Arno Camenisch
161 Walk With Me, Anne
   Ginna Wilkerson
162 Helen Doing the Crossword in Bed
   Graham Fulton
163 Construction/Togail, translated by Kevin McNeil
   Tom Petsinis
164 Now That We Are Parting/Agus sinn a-nis ri
   dealachadh, translated by Kevin McNeil
   Lidija Šimkutė
166 A Celebration
   Allan Wilson
171 Beat Versus Benoit
   Toni Davidson
175 Here Before
   Stephanie Brown
179 Yellow Polka Dot Dress
   Dilys Rose
180 The M8 Gantry's Lament
   JoAnne McKay
181 Sitzpinkler
   Colin Will
181 Small Countries of Mother-of-Pearl
   Olga Wojtas

182 **Contributor Biographies**

# Editorial

Welcome to *Gutter* 05, your cultural pilot through unfamiliar waters. With the SNP administration re-installed with a staggering majority, they have the mandate to do pretty much what they like. Wouldn't it be nice if they paved the way for their independence referendum with a re-awakening of national identity through a massive increase in investment in Scotland's arts and culture? We're not holding our breath.

This issue sees a number of *Gutter* debuts, but we are particularly glad to present a significant amount of poetry in translation. From Donal McLaughlin, we have an interpretation of contemporary Swiss poet Arno Camenisch's long and playful 'Fragment 2'. Tessa Ransford and Scottish-Palestinian poet Iyad Hyatleh have engaged in a fruitful co-translation of each other's work in English and Arabic based around the five pillars of Islam. We are also glad to have, from Kevin MacNeil, translations into Gaelic of fascinating poems by Tom Petsinis and Lidja Šimkuté, naturalised Australians of respectively, Macedonian and Lithuanian birth.

It is a rare treat when *Gutter* receives translated submissions from or into Gaelic and while we've published some great pieces in Scots over these last five issues, the number of submissions that make the grade is disappointing. By Scots we don't just mean references to puddocks and nichts, but language that represents the way people speak that's distinct to Scotland, present and past, regardless of geography.

Here lies a problem. With an SNP Government and the recent census question on the current state of Scotland's two surviving ancient languages, the future for Scots and Gaelic has never looked brighter. Yet, from over five hundred submissions to this issue, only a small proportion was in Scots and a smaller proportion of that

was of publishable standard. This may be a problem of perception – there are other literary magazines that exist specifically for those languages (including the venerable *Lallans*, which recently lost its Creative Scotland funding) – but it's our opinion that the problem is a more fundamental, demographic one: the majority of our readership and writership are under forty-five years old, and people under forty-five are less likely to write in Scots or Gaelic.

Aha, you say, that's because publishers don't want books in Scots. While there's a well-documented perception in London publishing that Scots is commercially toxic, and a dislike amongst some reviewers (we remember one reviewer complaining in a *Scottish* broadsheet about the use of Scots in Alan Bissett's *The Incredible Adam Spark* – not how he used it but that he used it at all), the success of Bissett, Anne Donovan, Matthew Fitt, Irvine Welsh and the granddaddy of contemporary Scots, James Kelman, amongst so many others, contradicts this. Sometimes, work in Scots is rejected because it's just not good enough. Good writing in Scots is not a matter of changing was to wiz. Reading any of the writers just mentioned will demonstrate the subtleties involved.

Writing in Scots can also be about preservation as much as cultural assertiveness. But what value old words in our vibrant, cosmopolitan, interconnected future? Let's write as we speak today, you say. Well, while here at *Gutter* we embrace internationalism and would be the first to defend the notion that 'all living language is sacred' (Tom Leonard) – and agree that there is little merit in a return to the entrenched, factional infighting over dialect, register, spelling and orthography which dominated 20th century Scots and Gaelic letters – the world is culturally and psychologically impoverished every day by the loss of native speakers and writers. In 2009 UNESCO estimated that 2500 of the world's 6000 languages were in danger of complete extinction. Imagine the outcry were the

⇥

world about to lose almost half its native tree or bird species? Or if half Scotland's listed buildings were bulldozed? And yet we are all complicit in the demise of the very essence of the human.

To expand on the notion that we should write as we speak today: the hard evidence is that we don't. The Scottish Government's 2010 survey on *Public Attitudes Towards the Scots Language* found that 80–90% of those interviewed felt that Scots was an important, valuable part of Scotland's heritage, culture and identity; 67% felt that it was important that Scots continued to be used in contemporary Scotland; and although 85% spoke Scots (of whom 43% did so 'often' or 'a lot'), only 51% and 35% respectively read and wrote in the language. To reiterate, people are not engaging in written form with the language they speak on a daily basis.

The reasons are complex and encompass class issues, demographic shifts, social prejudice, educational policy and notions of relative cultural worth. Interestingly, 52% of children and 16–34 year-olds spoke Scots, compared to only 44% of 35–44 year olds, so perhaps there is a glimmer of hope for the future – but there is also evidence of severe attrition and vocabulary loss (that is, *anglicisation*) amongst the 1.6 million people who speak some Scots. Gaelic literature fares better within a smaller number of speakers, and is protected to an extent by its linguistic 'distance' from Scots' nearest neighbour, English.

Some might accuse older Scots and Gaelic writing of lacking engagement with the contemporary global zeitgeist. But there are several successful examples of reversal of linguistic demise, for example Catalan, Welsh and Basque. All of these were accompanied by an outpouring of contemporary creative activity (literary and musical) by a confident young generation of artists, with the support of state cultural organisations and broadcasters. Compare and contrast with couthy BBC2 programmes about 'Wurds yer Granny used', bombastic 1980s Gaelic rock bands with dirges about fog and loss, and

Glasgow indie bands who sing with a fey, slightly Scottish accent.

We should accept that there are two valuable languages – Scots and Gaelic – in this country that are in desperate need of a jumpstart. From our current position, cultural globalisation seems unstoppable, but much of that is a mirage. The way to humanise globalisation, to subvert or mitigate its effects, is to engage with it robustly on our own cultural terms. *Gutter* is a magazine to give our languages a platform. Just make sure it is well-written and above all has contemporary relevance and urgency. So send us your slices of life in Scots, your ambisexual ennui in Gaelic/English, and while you're at it, some experimental poetry translated from Urdu would be great.

As well as the translations mentioned above, Issue 05 also features new poetry by Dilys Rose, Brian Johnstone and Graham Fulton. We are particularly pleased that Jim Carruth chose to send us his long poems 'Laidlaw' and 'Far Field' along with three shorter poems which further establish his reputation as the true bard of modern Scottish rural life. Other major sequences in this issue are Jim Stewart's *Hive*, and a selection from Sally Evans's work in progress *Anderson's Piano* – about the Cruachan train derailment and the Victorian wire landslide detector that was meant to prevent it. Further notable inclusions are two new poems each from Ryan van Winkle and Owen Gallagher, plus contributions from Dorothy Alexander, John Brewster and William Bonar.

There is cracking new fiction from previous *Gutter* contributors Joe McInnes and Anneliese Macintosh and *Gutter* debuts for Katharine Sowerby, Michael Cannon and Tracy Emerson. We are delighted to present an extract from Rodge Glass's forthcoming and tabloid-timely novel *Bring Me the Head of Ryan Giggs*, a new short story from Brian McCabe, an unsettling piece by author of *The Credit Draper* and *The Liberation of Célia Kahn*, J David Simons, and an extract from a Toni Davidson novel-in-progress. Hot off the back of her selection as one of *The Culture Show's* top debut novelists, we also have a new story by *Tin Kin* author and Saltire First Book Award winner, Eleanor Thom.

Life in the *Gutter* can be addictive. Having immersed ourselves in contemporary Scottish writing over the last two and a half years, Freight, publisher of the magazine, has developed something of a habit and decided to add publishing novels, collections of stories and poetry to its list of activities. So on August 28th this year Freight Books was/will be born. Although Freight has something of a history with the anthologies *The Hope That Kills Us*, *The Knuckle End* and *Let's Pretend*, amongst others, the time was right to start mainlining.

At this year's Edinburgh International Book Festival, in addition to an event for our other recent publishing project, the graphic novel *Dougie's War*, and a late-night *Unbound* event on stimulant inspired writing, we will be launching Christopher Wallace's *Killing the Messenger*. Reviewed in this issue (by someone totally independent...), it's a smart political conspiracy thriller and biting satire of the Blair Years. Also planned for Spring 2012 is a debut story collection by the outstanding Wayne Price, previously runner up in the Macallan Short Story Competition, runner up twice in the Bridport, winner of the US Carver story competition and winner of the Edwin Morgan Prize. We're delighted to include *The Wedding Flowers* in this issue, Wayne's homage to one of the greatest 20th century American short story writers, Paul Bowles, and a fabulous story in its own right.

In mid-2012 Freight Books will also publish Elizabeth Reeder's remarkable debut novel *Ramshackle*, a funny, charming and deeply moving story of losing and finding set in suburban Chicago. We're also working on a debut poetry collection by Patricia Ace, *Fabulous Beast*, whose elegant, insightful and often uproarious work can be found in *Gutter 01* and *04*. And, as well as a number of other projects currently in negotiation, we're excited to be bringing to a wider readership a neglected little masterpiece *All the Little Animals*, by Airdrie's very own Walker Hamilton. He tragically died shortly after its publication in 1968 and despite a film of the book in the late 1990s, starring Christian Bale and John Hurt, the work remains unjustifiably obscure, particularly in Scotland. We have our Editorial Board member Alan Warner to thank for drawing our attention to this forgotten classic of life on the run and road kill.

We hope you'll join us in toasting the launch of Freight Books and take an interest in the great work we publish.

# Street Maw
## Philip Murnin

MAW'S MAN CAME round to the flat when the baby was crying – her ugly man with his yellow teeth. She said to go away and give her some peace and quiet and take that fucking wean. She'd a sore head. Take that fucking girning wean away from me, girl, and don't come back for a good while. And take Davie and all is what Maw said. The baby cried and cried all the fucking time and it was doing her box in. Maw said it cried because of its teeth but that wasn't right because I checked and it didn't have any teeth. It was a gumsy baby. It was Kelly's wean but Maw was looking after it for a few weeks until she was back. Now it was my shot.

Me and Davie stuck the baby in the pram and shoogled it to keep it quiet. The pram was from olden days, like out of a black and white film, except it was dark green. It squeaked on its springs and was big enough to put Davie and the baby in it. Davie had to stand on his tiptoes just to look in. When you walked, it always wanted to go left. If you let it, you'd go round and round in circles.

We stayed at the top of Phoenix Heights nearly. We always used the stairs but the pram was bigger than me and Davie put together so we checked out the lift. There was chewing gum on the button and a pish smell when the door gaped open. Davie said no fucking way. He was right, I'd rather us jamp off the side. I told Davie he was a wee gayboy anyway.

Davie took the front end and we lifted the pram down thirteen sets of stairs. Bounce bounce bounce. The baby stopped crying and rolled from side to side laughing. Davie complained that I was pushing too fast and he

would deck it if I didn't stop. I told him I'd kill him if he dropped the pram.

There was no one at all in the court. Just concrete and sky.

'Right, I'm the maw, you're the da,' I told him.

'What does the da do?'

I was quiet for a second while I thought of an answer. 'He does what he's told.'

We took a peek at the baby in the pram. It was in a wee blue suit and its arms stuck out like it was flexing its muscles. It looked tiny in that empty pram. Maybe babies were bigger in olden days.

We'd forgot the baby's blanket.

'You'll need to give him your trackie top, Davie.'

'Like fuck.'

So Davie got hit and he shouted but in the end he took off his top and I wrapped it round the baby. We put the head in the hood and zipped it up and folded the arms over it to keep it warm. It was a lime green baby. Baby Sponsored by Nike. Just do it.

'Tracey, now I'm cold,' Davie said.

'Well you're just the da so it doesn't matter. It only matters that the baby's cold.'

I put on the baby voice Maw used when she talked to it. I reached in and gave the baby's belly a wee shake. Cootchi cootchi coo just like Maw did. The baby squeaked.

'Alright. Shut up,' I told it. 'It's no wonder Maw can't be arsed.'

Tina lived in Bell Court only three floors up so we wheeled the pram round there to shout her out.

'Tiinnaa!' I shouted at the building. 'Tina! TINA!'

I shouted loud enough to wake the deaf. Tina's name bounced off the building until it sounded as if I was on every floor of Phoenix Heights at once – an angry me on every floor. The balcony door opened but it wasn't Tina that came out but Tina's mum. She was fat.

'Beat it Tracey. You stay away from Tina. She's still got bruises,' Tina's maw shouted. She leaned over the balcony and pointed her finger.

'Was I shouting for you, you cow? I'm looking for Tina. TINATINATINA!' Noise and commotion came from inside the flat and Tina's maw disappeared. There was shouting and then a door slamming and running feet pittering pattering downstairs. Then Tina ran out of the close. Her maw on the balcony was raging and she wobbled as she shouted after her. 'TINA! Get back here now!'

But we were running away, over to the left because of the pram. I gave her the finger. She wouldn't chase us because it was her who ate all the pies.

When we stopped to get our breath Tina asked how come we had a baby. I told her that Maw said we should look after it.

'We're not old enough!' Tina said.

'Am so. I'm two months older than you. If you don't want to play you can fuck off.'

Tina peeked into the pram at the baby and asked his name. I shrugged and told her that he was just the Nike baby. She told me that the baby must have a name. 'When Jamie was born we got a book out of the library and picked a name from that.'

So I decided that it was time we checked out the library and named the baby.

You could ride the pram when there was a hill. Davie rode on the bottom part and I leaned on top with the baby. Tina ran along beside us saying careful careful careful. But we forgot the pram wanted to go left. We fell into the stank and Davie fell out. Me and Davie laughed but Tina didn't.

'Yous are stupid! Yous have got to look after the baby! Yous are going to hurt him!'

she shouted. But the baby gurgled away in the pram.

'See the baby's laughing,' I told her. 'He pure loved it.'

The Nike baby gurgled again and put its hands in its mouth.

'Babies need to get looked after properly!' Tina shouted. 'You've got to watch them otherwise you'll hurt them! Give him here!' Tina tried to push me out of the way and take the pram but I pushed her back harder – much harder.

'NO!' I shoved her again and she fell over. 'It's our baby, not yours. We're its family and you're a stranger. The baby loves me and it hates you. You're trying to take it away from its family!'

Tina lay on the pavement and looked at me. 'I won't touch but let's walk and not ride the pram.'

We walked the rest of the way but took a shortcut across the Empty place. Once there was Falcon Tower there but one day they knocked it down and everyone came to see it. We walked across the empty Empty place to the library on the other side. It was all bits of Falcon Tower and mud and grass. The pram tyres got stuck and we needed to lift it.

The library was an old building with pillars and books inside and computers. It had a swirly orange carpet. Everyone in there growled at us when we went in just because I told Davie to hold the fucking door open. Tut tut tut tut, like insects they went – the sound of shaking heads.

A woman bustled over from behind the counter. 'You must be a bit quieter in the library and you can't swear,' she hissed.

I held my tongue.

'Where's the baby's mummy?' the woman asked.

'She's parking the car outside,' I told her.

'We're sorry,' whispered Tina. 'We're just in to find a name book to pick one for the baby.'

The woman looked at the pram. 'Surely the baby must have a name by now!' she said.

'Aye but we're playing a game,' said Tina.

The lady let out a big sigh, huffing and puffing as if she would like to blow us away.

➤➤

She bustled behind the counter and came back with a brown book for us. She told us to look at it over on the table. Quietly.

The book was brown and full of all the names in the world. So Tina said. Tina did the looking up because she knew how it worked. Every name had a meaning, Tina tried to tell us.

'How? Mines doesn't,' I told her.

'Aye it does.'

'Well mines doesn't and neithers does Davie's.'

The woman came out from behind the counter with a glower all over her face and told us we were being too loud again. What was the matter? Tina told her that I didn't believe that names had meanings and the woman said that yes they did. She asked my name. I told her mine was Julie because I wanted it to be. Tina and Davie both gave me a look.

The woman looked it up and held the book away from her while she read it aloud. 'Julie – of Latin origin from the noble Roman name Julius originally meaning short-bearded.'

Tina and Davie snorted.

'Well my name isn't Julie anyway. It's Tracey,' I told her.

'Well, why did you tell me it was Julie?' the woman asked.

I shrugged. The woman huffed and puffed again and fucked off behind the counter. Tina looked up the rest of our names. Tina meant follower of Chris. 'Who's Chris?' I asked but she didn't know and we didn't want to ask the woman and make her huff again. Davie meant beloved. I laughed at him. 'See I told you you were a gayboy,' I said.

'Beloved,' he said. 'Maw couldn't have known that names have meanings either.'

The book showed that names were a lot of shite. I didn't let Tina look up my name in case it meant something stupid. What if Tracey meant hoor or something. There'd be no going back.

The baby started crying. I rocked the pram but he wouldn't stop. It cried and cried. The woman came over again to speak to us. 'Where is the baby's mother? The baby must be hungry. Is he being breast fed?' She poked her big nose in the pram and wrinkled it. 'The boy needs his nappy changed. There's a terrible pong!'

'No it doesn't,' I told her. 'It's not him. It must be your library that smells of shite.'

'Where is your mother?' said the lady. 'She's not coming at all, is she? Why on earth are you in charge of this baby? This baby is not being looked after properly.'

'It fucking is so.' I got her told.

She bustled over to the phone on the counter. 'Now wait there a minute.'

'That'll be right,' I said and we ran for it. The woman dropped the phone and tried to stop us. She grabbed Davie's arm but Davie called her a paedo and kicked her. The woman screamed and then we were out on the street running and laughing. We ran and ran with the pram always going left, until we reached the swing park.

The sky was now pinky purple with wisps of cigarette smoke and the moon and the sun were both out at the same time. People that walked past us stared. Greet greet greet was all that the baby did. Its eyes were screwed up and its face was red and wrinkled like an old party balloon. Tina wanted to pick it up but I wouldn't let her. I lifted it and rested it on my shoulder but it wouldn't stop crying as if I'd hurt it. Deep sobs and loud and I felt as if I'd hurt it. 'Shush!' I said.

'It's hungry and it's dirty and it needs its real mammy,' cried Tina.

'You shush! Maw doesn't want it! We look after it. Why won't it shut up? SHUT UP! SHUT THE FUCK UP!'

I gave it a shake but it wouldn't be quiet. It would never ever be quiet.

'YOU'RE A BAD BABY! STOP BEING BAD! BAD STINKING BABY!'

Tina started crying too. 'Don't shout at the baby! Don't shout at the baby! It needs looked after. It won't stop crying until it's fed and its nappy is changed and it's warm.'

Tina's face was red and wet with crying. I wanted to belt her and get her to shut up. 'You shut it and all you boot!'

'Let's go get the baby some milk then,' said Davie. 'Let's go get some milk then he'll be quiet.'

'Fine then!' I said.

We wheeled the crying pram to Phoenix Heights. We couldn't all go back to the flat. Maw would be raging. Tina stayed at the bottom of the stairs with the greeting baby. She crossed her heart and hoped to die that she wouldn't touch him.

We ran up the stairs touching only every second stair. I put the key into the lock as quiet as possible. I told it not to make any noise. Door do not squeak, I said in my head. The door of the TV room was shut. There was the smell of smoke – sweet and plasticky. Sweet and plasticky smoke that clung to Maw and her man with the yellow teeth. It got into their clothes and into their heads. I smelt it and knew it was safe to make noise. We went into the kitchen to get the baby bottle. We took the baby's blanket. We took some milk from the carton in the fridge and heated it up in the microwave for thirty seconds and we got a nappy for it. We were looking after the baby properly now like real maws and das. It made me warm like the baby's bottle and I smiled at Davie.

'Come on Da. Let's go fix the wee one.'

'What?' said Davie.

'Never mind.'

We looked over the railing to shout to Tina in the court beneath. I couldn't hear the baby crying anymore. I couldn't hear Tina shushing it. The court was just grey concrete. She'd fucking stolen the baby! They were away in the distance hurrying across the empty Empty place back towards the library lights.

I howled across the city at Tina. 'TINA! TINA! Come back or I'm going to fucking kill you! I'm going to fucking kill you Tina!'

She stopped and looked back. She saw me up on Phoenix Heights. My howl had frozen her on the spot and she looked at me. She shouted something but we couldn't hear. I couldn't make out her face. Then she turned and hurried to the library.

She was too far away to chase. Davie asked what we should do. Fuck knows, Davie. Fuck knows.

'She's away with my trackie top,' Davie said.

We stood and watched the pram going towards the library. There was us in our tower block with the concrete below. There was the crying pram carrying the Nike baby across the empty Emptiness and the sky – the pinky purple sky where there was the sun and the moon both at once.

# Flygirl
## R A Martens

IT CAME TO the time when Momma died, and my brother Walt already away with a family of his own, so I went to work in Miller's restaurant in town and to stay in a small room nearby, the house having been taken for Momma's debts. There was a new waitress at Miller's around the same time I started there, named Joan. She was from England, and she never spoke of family, nor expected such talk from me, so we got along very well. She was a good deal older than me, and called me Rabbit, as she said I reminded her of someone back home who she'd called by that name.

I was let go from Miller's, soon enough. I had just set down dishes before two of our regular diners, and one of the little angels came to sit at my shoulder, right close by my ear, to sing to me. I could not help but sing back, just like the first time, and soon the windows were black with angels. Later, I could only praise the Lord that all the windows and doors were shut, that they could not come in and make us all sick to death. It was Joan who pinched my arm to wake me, saying, this is you Rabbit, isn't it? I think you'd better make them go away now my sweet. So I thought of the first time, of all those hundreds of little angels falling and dying around the house as Momma sprayed them. The sadness brought the smell about in me, and the windows cleared. Only Joan knew that it was my doing, but I was let go all the same, for ignoring diners in the midst of a calamity.

Joan said that Miller's was no good anyway, that she knew of a house that was taking on, and would I come with her to there, so I went. The owner of the house was a fat man,

sleek like a seal, very pleased with everything about himself and his house. He treated his staff well, and Joan and I were not unhappy in our shared room there. In our second summer, an illusionist came to town from Europe – the great something, he was called, I don't remember any longer – and Joan, who earned a good sum more than me due to her being experienced, took me to see him on my birthday. He was quite wonderful, and performed such magnificent feats that I took the small amount of money I had saved that summer, and bought a second ticket.

Would you like to come with me Joan, I asked her. I was sure that she would want to; his being, like her, a stranger here, I had the idea that she might take some kind of comfort from his presence. She looked at me in her kindly way and she said oh Rabbit, we are all strangers on this earth, every one of us. She seemed so sad, then, that I took her hand, and said that she was no stranger to me, and was as good a mother to me as I might have wished my own had been, at which she cried a great deal. Wishing to distract her, I told her about the first time the angels sang to me.

I had been only six years old or so, alone in my room and wishing as I often did that I might be as light and small as the little black creatures that flew lazily about the windows; that I might fly away with them. I believe I may even have shed a tear or two, when I felt something, and looked down to see one of them stopped on the back of my hand. I lifted the hand closer to my face to see his thousand glittering eyes and his fine, delicate wings as they caught the sun, and he sat quite calmly, wiping his face with his thin and nimble legs. Then he lifted up on his wings, and he sang to me. And I sang back. I had not known until then that I could sing like that, but soon there were a thousand other angels at the window, and it grew as dark as night, their joined buzzing drowning out all other sounds. I was about to open the window to let them in, when I heard Momma shrieking from below, and went to the stairs to see what was the matter. She was swatting about her head, and spraying furiously from a can as she shrieked. I could see all the angels jerking and falling to the ground, and I cried out and begged her to stop, but she would not. And then the smell came about me, with the great sadness, and they ceased to stream through the door.

Later, as I shovelled up the tiny dead to take outside, Momma told me about the angels being dirty, diseased things. She said that their feet and their tongues were in the worst kind of dirt, and that if they had set upon my brother Walt in his crib, they could have made him sick to death. Of course, I did not want any harm to come to Walt, who I loved with all my heart – but it seemed sad beyond bearing, that the little angels had fallen and died so many about me. How could they help where their natures took their feet and tongues? Of course, after that I was most careful never to sing to them with doors or windows open, as I had no wish to be made sick to death myself.

Joan said only, see, you are a stranger too. And I could not deny that it seemed true, after what I had said.

The following night, when I was returned, glowing with excitement, from my second visit to the great man's show, Joan greeted me with even greater fervour than I felt myself. Rabbit, she said, you won't believe it. What do you think? And it took me a good while to stop her teasing and have her tell me the news. The great man himself, Rabbit – he is coming here tomorrow, after the show! It was hard to tell whether my own excitement was greater than Joan's on my behalf. Oh, but will we have to serve him dinner? I asked, my legs gone all to water. I was relieved when she assured me that his visit would come at the price of what, even for her, was a half-year's wages, and the master had said that he'd be blowed if the great man was to get his dinner as well.

When it came to it, I was shaking so badly in serving the master and his family their meal before the visit that I was banished before I should cause someone an injury, and sat in the kitchen whilst Joan did the work of both of us. Eventually, with a great smile, she came and took my hand to lead me to a corner of the dining room, where we would stand quiet as mice. She whispered to me before we entered that if I felt myself likely to faint in his presence, I should look at him plainly, and remember that he shat just the same as any of us. I could have died, and it took some time before I was composed enough to enter quietly.

He performed some illusions for the family – again, I fail to remember what they were, now – and he was about to take his leave when Joan stood forward and said to him that this was all very good, but that her friend here could do something even better, and would he wish to see it? She looked around the room to see that the windows and doors were closed. Although I was fit to pass out with embarrassment, I must confess that I had been entertaining a notion myself before she ever spoke. My hope was that somehow the great man would chance to see my ability, and that he would wish to learn it from me. Of course, I would not know how to teach it, and we would be forced to spend quite some time together to see if such a thing were possible. Nevertheless, faced with having to perform like this, I shook my head and simpered like a child. The master and his family, far from being affronted by Joan's behaviour, looked to the great man for a reaction. He gave little indication, and so the mistress said very well, let us see your parlour trick.

I simpered again, and shook my head. The great man came forward and placed a hand on my shoulder, standing opposite me, and leaned in so that I could almost swear I was to be kissed. Putting his mouth by my ear so that I could feel the tickle of his great moustaches, he whispered, come, little mouse, let us see your trick, and I resolved not to disappoint him. There were none of the little black angels in the room at that time, but I was able to conjure their song for myself, and began to sing. Soon enough, the windows grew dark, and the buzzing of the angels grew fiercely loud. I could scarcely hear when the mistress cried out that she must have some air, and rushed to open the door, pushing Joan out of the way. We heard her footsteps along the hallway, and then the creak of the heavy front door opening, and a scream.

Almost immediately, the room was filled with shoals of the tiny creatures, and they were all coming straight to me. I felt the caress of their many tiny legs about me as they moved and sang. It was truly heaven, even when the song quieted as they began to settle. I was head to toe in them, and I closed my eyes that I might better feel the thrum and warmth of the blanket they made to cover me.

Dear God, said the great man, and I did not need to open my eyes to know his disgust. I could hear, too, the master blustering wordlessly as his wife returned to the room to provide us with more of her screams. Happily the angels were unperturbed.

Can she – can she make them leave? said the master, and I made to answer. I could feel my sweet companions around the edges of my open mouth, tickling my lips, and I wanted to giggle, to purse my lips and send them kisses.

I had not yet replied when Joan said, why of course she can. What would it be worth to you good people to have her bring this about?

And well, that was the way things went from then.

# Great Long Story
## Paula Morris

AT THE GRAVESIDE of Robert Johnson, I was stung on the neck by a bee. Before he died Robert Johnson was living in Greenwood, Mississippi. Greenwood still calls itself the Cotton Capital of the World, though nowadays Greenwood farmers prefer to grow corn and soybeans and catfish. The Amtrak train called City of New Orleans stops there en route to Chicago. At Greenwood, two rivers – the Tallahatchie and the Yalobusha – become the Yazoo and run through Vicksburg to the Mississippi. Some people say that Yazoo is a Choctaw word for 'river of death'.

Nobody knows exactly where Robert Johnson died.

We drove along Johnson Street in Greenwood, looking for the place in Baptist Town where Robert Johnson may or may not have lived. Johnson Street is not named after Robert Johnson. We were looking for a building on the corner of Young and Pelican, where Robert Johnson may or may not have died. There's no building there anymore, just a historic marker. Residents of Baptist Town were out in the street, eating barbecue. It was Saturday afternoon, Halloween. A local hospital had set up some kind of information tent. We read the marker without getting out of the car. The neighbourhood was like New Orleans, but smaller and shabbier. Some of the houses were falling down. People looked at us, sitting in our car. We looked at the historic marker.

Nobody knows exactly where Robert Johnson died. Some people say he died out at the Star of the West plantation, north of Greenwood. There is no plantation house

out there anymore. Paige at the Greenwood Convention and Visitors Bureau thinks it fell down, or was torn down, many years ago.

The Star of the West plantation was named after a Union steamship captured by the Confederates and sunk in the Tallahatchie river. Some people say it was sunk to avoid recapture. Some say it was sunk to block a Union flotilla headed for Vicksburg.

Nobody knows anymore exactly where Robert Johnson is buried. His death certificate said he was buried at Zion Church. Someone erected a grave marker near Payne Chapel Missionary Baptist Church in Quito, south of Greenwood. Some people say that the last place he performed was at Three Forks in Quito.

Some people say that the Three Forks where Robert Johnson performed for the last time was a club west of Greenwood, not south. We drove to the intersection of Route 49 East and Route 82 where the juke joint once stood. It's very close to Walmart. Some people say it wasn't called Three Forks. It was just a juke joint around the back of Schaeffer's Store, and probably destroyed, along with the store, by a storm in 1942.

In 1991 Columbia Records placed a marker at Mt Zion Missionary Baptist Church on the road between Quito and Morgan City. They thought this was the Zion Church listed on the death certificate. But in 2000 an old woman named Rosie Eskridge said her husband was the person who dug Robert Johnson's grave. He was a field hand on the Star of the West plantation. She said he dug it under the pecan tree near

➵

the Little Zion Missionary Baptist Church. This cemetery is just north of Greenwood, across the Tallahatchie river.

At the graveside of Robert Johnson, I was stung on the neck by a bee.

Hallowe'en. I stood reading the historic marker at the cemetery just north of Greenwood. On the other side of the road: a field of stubby cotton. The ground was muddy, waterlogged around the pecan tree. It had poured with rain the night before, when I was doing a book-signing in Oxford. I wore a long chain around my neck – silver, dangling a silver globe. Something touched my throat, something that wasn't the chain. I reached up with one hand to brush it away. A piece of fuzz, I thought, until I registered the pain of the sting. The red welt kept growing and throbbing. I was having an allergic reaction. We had to drive to Walmart, on the west side of town, to get antihistamine cream. Robert Johnson sent a bee to sting you, said my husband. You stood too close to his grave.

Nobody knows anymore exactly where Robert Johnson is buried.

At Walmart, a woman approached my husband and asked him the kind of question someone asks a pharmacist. He is a white man, like the pharmacist. At that moment, in the pharmacy section of Walmart, he was the only white man anywhere in sight. She seemed to think he was the actual pharmacist. I wondered when the red welt on my neck would stop growing and itching and hurting. We had to drive to Jackson for another book-signing at four. My book is a ghost story. It was Hallowe'en.

The gravestone at the cemetery just outside Greenwood may not mark the spot where Robert Johnson is buried. Even if he is buried in that cemetery, he may not be buried under the pecan tree. He may be buried near the historic marker where a bee stung me on the neck.

At Walmart, my husband approached the pharmacist behind the counter and asked if we were buying the right kind of antihistamine cream. The pharmacist said that we could buy meat tenderiser instead and make it into a paste. This would draw out the sting. But we had lingered at the cemetery where Robert Johnson may or may not be buried, and then we'd driven around looking for a pharmacy. It was too late for the paste to work. We had waited too long.

Robert Johnson lay dying for three days.

Nobody knows exactly where Robert Johnson died. Some people say that he was carried from Three Forks to a house in Baptist Town and that he died there. Some people say that he was carried from Three Forks to a house on the Star of the West plantation and that he died there. Some people say that he was carried from Three Forks to the house in Baptist Town and later to a house on the Star of the West plantation. His death certificate reads: Greenwood (outside).

Robert Johnson lay dying for two or three or four days. He died on August 16, a Tuesday. Elvis Presley also died on August 16, a Tuesday, thirty-nine years later. Like Robert Johnson, Elvis Presley was born in Mississippi. He was three years old when Robert Johnson died.

There is no birth certificate for Robert Johnson. His half-sister said he was born in 1911. The State of Mississippi was not required to keep birth or death certificates until 1912.

Robert Johnson was born in Hazlehurst, Mississippi. Hazlehurst is the county seat of Copiah County, once the Tomato Capital of America. Like Greenwood, it used to have an opera house. Without realising it, we have driven past his birth site many times. The house was moved to accommodate a ramp leading to I-55, on the east side of the highway. The house had to be moved in the '60s, when the highway was built. In 2009 it was moved again, into downtown Hazlehurst. The house was falling down. Trees and vines were growing in it. The roof has collapsed. Only two original rooms are left.

Things I wrote in my notebook at the graveside of Robert Johnson: pale blue sky. Muddy hollow. Scattered graveyard. Puddles of water. Pine trees. Pecan tree, rusty leaves. Water in the grooved ridges of the field. It hurts to get stung in the neck by a bee.

Nobody knows exactly where Robert Johnson died. It was August. It was hot. He had to stop playing at the juke joint because he was violently ill. He'd drunk bootleg whiskey, the same as everyone else there. He wouldn't have been carried to the big house on the Star of the West plantation. He would have been taken to one of the shacks, where someone he knew lived. Some people say it was a shotgun house. Some people say the man living in the shack was known as Tush Hog.

The gravestone in the cemetery outside Greenwood quotes Robert Johnson's song 'Four Until Late': When I leave this town/ I'm 'on bid you fare ... farewell/And when I return again/ You'll have a great long story to tell.

On the other side of the gravestone the engraver has reproduced the handwriting of Robert Johnson. These lines are not song lyrics. They are words Robert Johnson wrote down on a piece of paper 'shortly before his death'. They read: Jesus of Nazareth King of/Jerusalem. I know that my/Redeemer liveth and that/He will call me from the grave. Some people say that the piece of paper was found in the shack where Tush Hog lived.

Paige at the Greenwood Convention and Visitors Bureau says Miss Rosie Eskridge's house is still there, on what used to be the Star of the West plantation. But nobody can go there anymore, because it's private land.

At the graveside of Robert Johnson, I was stung on the neck by a bee.

The road to the cemetery north of Greenwood is called Money Road. We passed a small white house on the edge of the cotton fields. A sign on the house read WABG 960 KH. We tuned the radio. The station was playing the blues.

Money, Mississippi is eight miles north of Greenwood. It used to be the Woodstock plantation. It still had a cotton mill in the 1950s, but now so few people live there it's not a town. Its official designation is Populated Place. In 1955 Emmett Till, a black teenager from Chicago, was there visiting his uncle. It was August. It was hot. At Bryant's Grocery he whistled or said something to a white woman. Several days later her husband and another man took Emmett away from his uncle's house. They beat him up, fracturing his skull and his legs and his arms. They gouged out one of his eyes. They shot him. They used barbed wire to fasten a cotton-gin fan around his neck. They threw him into the Tallahatchie river. When his body was fished up three days later, Emmett Till could only be identified by the ring on his finger.

In 'Hellhound on My Trail', Robert Johnson sang: I got to keep moving/Blues falling down like hail.

Nobody knows exactly how Robert Johnson died. Some people say it was strychnine poisoning. But strychnine is hard to disguise, and it wouldn't have taken days to kill him. The poison might have been made from boiled moth balls. It might have been made from arsenic. He was poisoned by a jealous lover, or – more likely – by the husband of a jealous lover. Maybe the husband didn't mean to kill him. He just wanted Robert Johnson to leave town.

Robert Johnson got sick at the juke joint. He had stomach cramps and then maybe he got pneumonia. Maybe he had some underlying condition that was triggered by the poison. Some people say that Robert Johnson had Marfan Syndrome, a genetic disorder. No cause is listed on his death certificate. The only thing written in that column is: No Doctor.

In 'Preachin' Blues', Robert Johnson sang: The blues is a low-down achin' heart disease/ Like consumption, killing me by degrees.

At the graveside of Robert Johnson, I was stung on the neck by a bee. The bee flew onto my neck because it was attracted by the sun glinting off the silver chain. It stung me because I tried to brush it away.

Robert Johnson may have sent a bee to sting me on the neck because I stood too close to his grave.

Robert Johnson may have been called from his grave and transformed into a bee. When I brushed him away, he stung me, and then he died. I may have killed Robert Johnson.

During his lifetime, Robert Johnson was not diagnosed with Marfan Syndrome. Signs have been deduced by examining one of the three extant photographs. One of his eyelids seems to droop; his fingers are very long and thin. Another sign is joint flexibility. Maybe this is why his playing could sound like two performers, two guitars. Some people think that the violin virtuoso Paganini had Marfan Syndrome as well. It can result in aortic dissection. One of the symptoms of aortic dissection is severe, stabbing pain.

Nobody knows if Robert Johnson made a pact with the devil. People said that about him, because he played so well. The same thing was said of Paganini. The Archbishop of Nice wouldn't allow Paganini a church burial. Paganini's embalmed body lay in his house for several months before city officials insisted that it be moved. For a while the body was on public display. Paganini wasn't buried in Parma cemetery until 1876, thirty-six years after his death. Some people say Paganini was poisoned.

Some people say that Robert Johnson sold his soul to the devil at the crossroads of Highways 61 and 49 in Clarksdale, Mississippi. Some people say that this intersection did not exist during Robert Johnson's lifetime. Some people say that the crossroads in question is in Rosedale, where Highways Eight and One meet, or further south on old Highway Eight, where it crosses Dockery Road, or somewhere south of Tunica, known as the cross-town road, or somewhere else in the old cotton fields outside Greenwood, or any number of other roads in the lush green Mississippi Delta.

The juke joint where Robert Johnson performed for the last time was on the crossroads of Route 49 East and Route 82. It's very close to Walmart. In Greenwood these roads cross in more than one place. Even if you're at the right crossroads, the crossroads have changed. These are big roads now, highways. They're not the same as the roads in the 1930s. We pulled over and wandered the grass verge where the juke joint may or may not have stood.

Robert Johnson wrote a song called 'Cross Road Blues' but it does not mention selling his soul to the devil. Robert Johnson wrote a song called 'Me and the Devil Blues' but it does not mention a crossroads.

Some people say that the reason that Robert Johnson is so desperate in 'Cross Road Blues' to flag a ride is that it was dangerous for a black man in Mississippi to be out alone at night.

Another Johnson, Tommy Johnson, born around 1896, claimed to have sold his soul to the devil in return for the ability to play any song. Another Johnson, Robert Johnson, born around 1582, wrote the music for a song in Shakespeare's play The Tempest. The song was 'When the Bee Sucks'.

Crystal Springs, Mississippi is ten miles north of Hazlehurst. Crystal Springs was once known as the Tomato Capital of the World. It is the home of the Robert Johnson Blues Museum, although Robert Johnson was from Hazlehurst, not Crystal Springs. Tommy Johnson, the blues musician who said he sold his soul to the devil, lived in Crystal Springs. He died in 1956. He is buried in a cemetery outside Crystal Springs, but nobody can go there anymore, because it's private land. He has no gravestone.

Robert Johnson had two known recording sessions, the first in San Antonio and the second in Dallas. Robert Johnson had two known marriages, the first to Virginia Travis and the second to Calletta Craft. There are two known photographs of Robert Johnson, one taken in a photo booth and the second in a studio. He may have made another recording, an audition record. There may be another photo, of Robert Johnson and Johnny Shines. There may be three or four or five photos of Robert Johnson. There were many other women in Robert Johnson's life, but no more wives.

Even if Robert Johnson is buried in that cemetery, he may not be buried under the pecan tree. Rosie Eskridge was 85 or 86 years old when she told that story. It was 2000. Robert Johnson died in 1938. She says that Noah Wade, who owned the Star of the West plantation, told her husband to dig the grave. Rosie went to the cemetery to take her husband some water. She pointed out the spot in 2000, when she was 85 or 86 years old. She may have remembered the correct spot. She may have been confused.

I can't remember things that happened

last year. I can't remember if we drove around Baptist Town before we went to Walmart or afterwards. Maybe this was why we were too late to make a paste with the meat tenderiser. My husband had to remind me about the pharmacist suggesting meat tenderiser. I had forgotten this part completely. I didn't write it down in my notebook.

Things I wrote in my notebook at the graveside of Robert Johnson: empty whiskey bottles, crushed can of Red Bull, Howard County library card, condom packet, Mardi Gras beads, rain-soaked flattened straw hat.

In 'Me and the Devil Blues', Robert Johnson says: Baby I don't care where you bury my body.

Nobody knows exactly how Robert Johnson died. He was married twice, but he moved around a lot – Mississippi, Arkansas, and Texas; Memphis and Chicago – and had liaisons with a lot of women. He may have been poisoned by a jealous husband. The night he was taken ill at the juke joint, the jealous husband was Ralph Davis, known as Snake. His wife, the one Robert Johnson was sleeping with, was named Bea.

Everything in this story is true, apart from the things that are wrong, and the things that are lies, and the things that are misremembered.

Hallowe'en in Mississippi. Cemetery on the road to Money. Pale blue sky, stubby cotton fields. I lingered too long at the graveside of Robert Johnson, and Bea stung me on the neck. She didn't want to kill me. She wanted me to leave town.

# For Anyone Who Wants To Be Friends With Me

Anneliese Mackintosh

IF YOU ARE considering being friends with me, there are a few things you ought to know.

> I like springtime, dancing, blueberries and linguistics.
> I don't like frogs, polystyrene balls, hairdressers or lies.
> Once, I won a trophy for excellence in music.

Another time, this happened.

It was Christmas Eve. I worked in Our Price (remember it?). One day I got graded 27% by a secret shopper. The report said: 'friendly but ignorant'. I was fine with that.

So anyway, Christmas Eve. We had to listen to festive songs all day, and answer questions from grannies holding long lists of band names they didn't know. 'Napalm Death? For your grandson?' I'd say to some old dear. 'Certainly, Madam. Right this way.' And she and her Zimmer frame would follow close behind, while Noddy Holder blared from the speakers above me.

*Are you hanging up a stocking on your wall?*

After an exhausting day's work, I went back to a friend's house. We'd been talking about lesbianism for some time now (it all started with a drunken heart-to-heart in the Wetherspoon's toilets) and I wondered if tonight might be the night I'd finally kiss her. Didn't fancy her or anything, but there comes a time when you've talked about something for so long you start to think you actually want it.

In her bedroom we drank vodka. We peeled off our red Our Price sweaters, taking small sideways glances at each other's underwear, and we put on our party gear. I wore a miniskirt, fishnet tights, and a black shirt covered in homemade glitter-glue slogans. Scrawled in silver across my shoulder blades was 'broken wings'.

I gelled my electric pink hair into perfect spikes, applied even more black eye make-up than I wore to work, tightened my piercings (they often came loose), and away we went into the night.

I was barely eighteen; still too young to wear a coat. It was absolutely freezing outside, but the drink helped.

We went to a pub in our small local town and drank a lot of whisky. After that we went to another pub and drank a lot more. Now I don't know if you've ever been to Buckingham, but it's not exactly known for its cultural diversity. It's all ferrets, 4x4s and jodhpurs. The 'punk look' tends to stand out. It wasn't uncommon for people to throw things at me or spit in my face or shout obscenities as I passed. Anyway, in this particular pub, we started getting comments off a group of people by the pool table, so we went somewhere else. And drank more whisky.

It was getting pretty late and we were getting pretty drunk, but we still hadn't kissed. I decided to bring it up. 'What do you think would happen if we started kissing, right now, at this table?'

She looked hazily around the room: at the

guys fiddling with their phones, at the girls rifling through their handbags, and at the impatient throng, red-faced at the bar. She eyed the men in rugby shirts, stinking of beer and sweat and aftershave.

Then she eyed me.

I have to say, kissing her wasn't as exciting as I hoped it would be. It was small and wet and like any other mouth I'd ever stuck my tongue in. Couldn't even feel her lip piercing, and I doubt whether she could feel mine.

Seconds into the kiss, I felt a tap on my shoulder.

'Hey girls,' slurred someone whose face has, in my memory, all but vanished. 'You should come with us.' He motioned towards the rugby-shirted guy beside him.

Drunk and intrigued, we got up from our table. Holding hands, we followed this man and his friend.

There was only one cubicle in the men's loos. (I remember thinking that was weird, but I guess men aren't shy unless they're taking a shit.) The four of us bundled in, and the men locked the door and told us to kiss again. As we did, we felt their hands run over us, sliding beneath our tops, kneading our breasts and grabbing our crotches.

I could hear Noddy Holder in the room next door. The same song I'd been listening to all day at work.

*So here it is, Merry Christmas,*
*Everybody's having fun...*

With one sharp tug, my tights were pulled down, and I felt a hard, wet cock being squeezed into me. 'Bend over,' said a gruff voice, pushing me hard over the cistern. I grasped the toilet seat to steady myself while he thrust at me, grabbing me by the glitter glue and ripping apart my 'broken wings'. From the sound of things, my friend was getting banged up against the cubicle door.

It's about this point that my memory gets very, very cloudy indeed.

I can remember thinking I didn't want to be here, and I can just about remember the sea of faces hanging over the top of the cubicle: at least half a dozen of them, all sweating and stinking of beer and sweat and aftershave. Cheering.

Meanwhile, the cock inside me came.

Then another cock came inside me.

Then another.

The faces hanging over the top of the cubicle changed places, and we were fucked and fucked and fucked by man after man. My clothes got ripped. My thighs dripped with semen.

'Get out!' screamed a sudden voice, somewhere outside the cubicle, and I jumped back to hyperconsciousness. 'What the fuck do you think you're doing? Get the fuck out of here! You're barred.'

I wasn't sure who was barred exactly, because there had been so many of us in there, but I knew I wouldn't be going back into that pub ever again. I kept my eyes on the carpet as I walked back through the busy bar and then out into the street.

I could feel the cold more than ever now. The whole of me was stinging. My friend and I didn't say a word. We gripped each other's hands, zigzagging the pavement back towards her house.

'Hey, wait!' someone called out. 'Don't you want to come back with us for a Christmas drink?'

We stopped.

There were two men behind us. It was hard to tell whether they had come from the loos with us or not. I was having trouble remembering anything at that point to be honest.

My friend let go of my hand. 'I could do with a drink,' she said.

While she walked ahead with one of the guys, the other took his place beside me. They led us down an alleyway.

'Stop,' urged the guy with me. He pushed me up against a wheelie bin. It was a quick and awkward fuck, and he didn't utter a thing until afterwards, when he called me a 'dirty bitch'.

We caught up with the others.

'This is my car,' said one of them. 'Let's

get in.'

We all got in the car. My friend and her guy in the front, me and mine in the back. There isn't really a polite way to say what happened next.

They fucked. We fucked.

The guys swapped seats and we swapped fucks.

Then my friend crawled into the back with me and the men told us to lick each other out. She sat down on the seat and – I don't know how I did it, I was so drunk – but somehow I went upside down, and sucked on her pussy while she sucked on mine, vertical.

Then we went into a house, God knows where.

I ended up in bed, in a different room to my friend. I lay in complete silence for a while, becoming increasingly aware that it was Christmas Eve and I really shouldn't be here. I called a taxi.

'Where are you going?' asked the guy.

'Home,' I murmured, wondering what on earth was going on.

About twenty minutes later I stumbled out of the taxi and stood swaying at my front gate.

At the gate was my mother.

'Hi,' I said.

'Where the hell have you been?' she screamed. 'I've called the police!'

'Just out. I'm fine.'

'Why are your tights around your neck?'

I looked down and noticed my legs were bare. My fishnets were wrapped around my neck. 'I fell in a puddle,' I slurred.

'Get inside.'

I slumped into my bed, and the last thing I remember thinking before I fell asleep is that I had lost my knickers.

My sister ran into my room at 6 am. 'It's Christmas!'

I pulled the duvet over my face.

We sat in the lounge to unwrap our presents: me, my sister, my mum and my dad. Mum looked at me disapprovingly as I opened my gifts. I alternated between saying thank you and running upstairs to be sick, too groggy to register the hair slides, socks, pyjamas and perfume I'd been given.

An hour later, at 7 am, we got into the car and started the two-hour drive to my uncle's. We were spending Christmas with him this year because he was alone and had MS. The whole journey I tried not to listen to Slade on the stereo as I held in the vomit.

*Look to the future now,*
*It's only just begu-u-un...*

When we arrived, I ran into the bathroom and threw up. Then I went to bed and missed Christmas dinner.

My grandparents were at my uncle's too. 'Your mother tells me you had fun last night,' Grandpa laughed. I smiled sheepishly, running my hands through my fluffy pink hair, hoping that my Deftones hoodie hid the bruises.

I went into the kitchen for a glass of water and a cry. I wondered if anyone could sense what I'd done.

We sat in the living room watching old re-runs of *Only Fools and Horses*, eating cheese and biscuits. My uncle drank his wine through a straw because only a quarter of his face was working. I sat beside him.

At some point that evening the guy texted me. How he got my number I don't know.

merry xmas from paul

When Paul asked me out on a date a few days later, I said yes. I thought it might normalise things. Cancel out the other night, if we could manage to have a nice time. We went to the cinema then back to his. I had to run up the stairs so his mum wouldn't see me. We had sex. Dry, difficult, miserable sex, and then I got up to leave. Before leaving, I asked if he had my knickers.

He took them out of his bedside drawer, and said that he wanted to keep them.

'Why?' I asked.

'To smell.'

I grabbed them off him. Back at home, I took them out of my coat pocket and stared at them in horror. Black satin covered in silver hearts and white stains. I pushed them deep inside the kitchen bin. Then I deleted Paul's number from my phone. Finally I felt a bit better.

As for my friend, the surprising thing is that I can't remember what happened to her. I guess we must have texted each other, maybe even worked another shift together, but I've honestly forgotten all about it. In fact, I'd forgotten about the whole thing until a couple of years later, when it came back to me violently and aggressively and I could hardly breathe.

After that Christmas Eve, I did other things.

I fucked someone who professed to be a Nazi, I fucked someone in hospital, I fucked someone on the bathroom floor while he told me he'd 'deflowered a thirteen-year-old', I fucked a guy while he told me about his two lovely children, I was held down and raped by a guy who'd just dumped me, I pissed all over a guy while I fucked him, I fucked someone I met on the Internet, I sucked off a rock star backstage, I fucked someone whose dad fed me cocaine, I fucked someone who later published a novel in which I was the cruel heroine, I fucked someone who gave me chlamydia, and I fucked plenty of people who might have given me AIDS, but thankfully never did.

Nowadays, my hair is brown and I have tiny pinpricks where my piercings used to be.

There is no glitter glue in my wardrobe. I grow my own herbs and listen to jazz music and drink peppermint tea and read books about the universe and work hard in academia and laugh at puns and dream about owning a house and kittens and learning to use a sewing machine and travelling to beautiful places. And I like dancing and blueberries and springtime.

If you become my friend, I will cook you a meal using my herbs. I'll play you jazz and offer you a peppermint tea. I'll talk to you about kittens and the universe. I'll tell you about the link between blueberries and memory loss, if you ask nicely.

But I probably won't tell you any of the other stuff.

Every now and then, though, we'll be sitting in the sunshine, and I'll be in the middle of laughing at your puns, or telling you about all the beautiful places I want to run away to, and I'll stop

to look down at my bare legs.

And I'll feel the fishnets still coiled around my neck.

I just thought you should know.

# Extract from the novel *Articles of Faith*
## Michael Cannon

WHEN HE IS three years old Michael Neavie is treated to the optical illusion of a ship sailing down a street. Thirty thousand tonnes of blunt keel and angular superstructure slides across his vision, interrupted by skeletal cranes and gingerbread tenements. He sits, balanced on his mother's jutting hip. She, with one arm around him, the other braced against the sandstone for purchase, stands in the pose of a capital K, buttressing the block. Her skirt is pulled taut against her splayed calves in a ladder of horizontal folds like corrugated tin. The hand against the wall intermittently detaches itself and flattens in a casual salute, as she shades her eyes against the mid-morning glare. She is standing at the close entrance to the terrace which slopes steeply, perpendicular to the river. The red sandstone drinks in the morning light, windows flashing in a string of descending suns to merge with the glare at the foot of the hill. Alternately bracing herself and shading her eyes, Deborah Neavie follows the ship's path as it glides on the scarcely glimpsed river, a streak of molten tin behind the intervening buildings.

Waves of sound float up from the launch: the indistinct fog horn of a distantly amplified voice; the detonation of the bottle against the hull, more imagined than felt; the roar; the displacement of metal and dragging chains.

Dotted at close entrances down the street other young mothers, similarly burdened, hold their children up, point, exhort, explain. This is one of the calibrations in their allotted history.

In her classroom above the tenement terraces, aloof from the beano, Miss Aherne sits with a pile of corrections. She is putting the solitude to good use. Mr Gilchrist, the Headmaster, with what Miss Aherne would consider questionable judgement, has subscribed to the local propaganda and permitted the children to bear witness to their history. Postponing her disdain, Miss Aherne watched her children file out in the company of the delegated assistant. From her window she watches the buoyant crocodile, scarves flying, join the tributaries of other classes as the mass of the school tramps down the hill in an air of infectious hilarity. At the first outrolling of sound Miss Aherne's lips twitch, and again, and again, until she becomes more irritated at herself for this repeated spasm than at its cause. A boom, that sounds more like artillery, causes the glass to creak. She puts down her pen and gazes into the vacant sky and wonders at the herd mentality that compels them to club together and exult over an iron hulk obeying the laws of gravity. To see the activity would require her to stand up, cross the room and gaze down the hill. But she will not, because she feels this voyeurism is a kind of participation. Secular crowds disturb her. Church congregations above a certain size also give her a sense of disquiet, the silent cacophony of all those felt intentions, wanting and wanting, like a clamorous butcher's queue, compromising her intimacy with God.

Miss Aherne has eschewed the launch just as, in two years to come, she will eschew the safety of the Anderson shelter, as the Luftwaffe endeavours to level Clydebank. That piece of allotted history will find her kneeling on the floor of her first floor tenement, black out blinds agape to admit the pulsed light of the incendiary bombs. While others cower she will kneel before the crucifix, praying with fierce joy, steepled fingers at right angles to horizontal forearms, bony elbows gleaming as phosphorescent flashes starkly illuminate the room. This young-old woman gazing up in adoration at the tortured sagging body, the sibilance of her whispered prayers drowned out by the maelstrom beyond the window; an old-young woman, worshipping His pain, daring the detonations as they approach.

But the day of the launch holds no clues for the happy crowd of the inferno that will one day be visited on them. Shading her eyes again, Deborah turns to look at Michael. His eyes swivel, as if trying to locate the source of the sound. Finding the task beyond his means he buries his face in her neck. She strokes the fine filaments of his hair, murmurs to him, and turns her head to stare down the hill. She wonders how much, if anything, he will retain of this moment. He will not know himself until, many years later, approaching Suez, he is confronted with the majestic passage of superstructure between sand dunes and casts back to a half-grasped image of a descending terrace, sliding bulk and a sense of euphoria, billowing, like smoke, up from the river.

Looking at him she decides his age will not disqualify him in future. He will join the school, balanced on her hip or his father's shoulders, watching the Clyde spawn giants. And in fact he is there at the next launch, and the one after that, and the one after that, until he confuses sequence with consequence. 'Heavy,' he says to his father, imitating the gesture of smashing the bottle, and his father grasps his meaning and laughs.

'Heavy,' his father repeats, and repeats the gesture.

Stephen Neavie is delighted with the error, and repeats it among his workmates, in the lee of these hulks. He fosters it, embroiders it, so it will become the stuff of family folklore: the bottle that moves the ship. He comes home from work with stories of the vigilance of him and his workmates, to preserve this precarious equilibrium. Imagine the disaster of an accidental launch. What if someone were to lean against the hull?

Stephen is a man who, as far as Michael can tell, descends the hill every morning to spend his day among metal and smoke and comes back every night smelling of both. What about an inopportune flock of starlings? Stephen is amused by his own invention. What about a particularly violent sneeze? His good-humoured baritone laugh resounds off the kitchen pans. Michael seeks Deborah's skirts and hears her admonish Stephen in a voice on the edge of laughter.

Compared to others they have space, but it's still a cramped household, eventually destined to become more so, and Michael is used to the muffled sound of their strident coupling before ever he understands what it is.

In this bright sunny morning, staring down the hill, Deborah Neavie can't conceive of any of this coming to an end. The shipyards will ring and flash, and when necessity demands glow in the dark, and these hallmarked works of pride will sail down the estuary into posterity. Clyde Built. Her eyes film in uncharacteristic nostalgia, for a time not yet gone, and she is caught up in the euphoria of the moment. Even the boy feels it, like oxygen. A mote swims into the corner of her eye. She wipes it with a pulled sleeve and watches it resolve into the figure of Father Delaney making his arthritic progress up the hill. Even at this distance his complexion is visible. He is a series of unresolved dots, topped and tailed by the dark smudge of a suit and trilby, his florid face a purple wobble balanced on the white speck of his dog collar. The gradient is testing, as is his habit. There are rumours about Father Delaney in the parish. There are rumours about everything in the parish. Stephen, exposed to brutalities at work she can only guess at, has taught her to suspend her judgement. 'Fucking women', she has heard him breathe, believing himself out of earshot because he never swears in her presence.

The persuasion of the women Father Delaney passes can be guessed at, even from this distance. Mrs MacGregor, a devout Episcopalian, greets him civilly. Mrs Beith, an inflexible Calvinist, nods to him with the glacial condescension of one of the elect. As he puffs past her each comforts themselves in their separate ways: he reminds himself to pray for her in her error, one of these numerous mental notes he makes a dozen times a day, consigned immediately to the oblivion of trivial intentions; she reflects that he will have an eternity of regret in which to contemplate the error of his choice. The Catholics are more effusive. Each relaxes as he passes, grateful not to be the subject of his attentions. Deborah knows her odds are narrowing. He did not haul his liver up this gradient in the windy sunshine to enjoy the view. She shades her eyes once more and affects not to see him until he passes at the base of her steps, bowed, one hand on the iron railings, their greeting delayed by the fit of tartarean coughing that subsides as he gradually cranks himself erect. He raises his hat. The wind catches his hair, scant and unruly, and lifts it like a lid until he forces the brim down upon it.

'Deborah.'

'Father Delaney.'

'And how is young...' he waves his hand in a rolling gesture, as if flicking out benedictions, '...Peter?'

'And who might he be, Father Delaney?' The hand continues to roll until she is obliged to supply 'Michael'.

'Young Michael.'

'He's grand, Father.' Michael has embedded his face in his mother's neck at the prospect of this dark figure standing at the bottom of their stairs. She is contemplating her meagre quota of biscuits. 'Would you like to come in for a cup of tea?'

'Very kind, Deborah, but I can't just now.'

She does her best not to look relieved. Another roar from the river brings a welcome distraction.

'You were at the launch then, Father, blessing the ship perhaps?'

'Launch?' He looks momentarily perplexed. She is now re-evaluating the situation. This isn't, as she hoped, co-incidental. He's not wandered up from the church and the river buoyed by an excess of good will he's anxious to distribute. 'Yes, the launch.' He sketches another casual benediction in the direction of the river. 'There were other clergy...'

She is thinking the more the merrier, some ecumenical blessing that covers all contingencies, when he suddenly stops in his distracted movements and stares directly at her. His colour has begun to subside, with the exception of his nose, a roseate blob in the centre of his face. If she half-closes her eyes, as she used to do during bored moments at church, it becomes the sole distinguishing feature in his face, a conical red jelly in the vague pastry flan above the dark mouth, droning out orthodoxies. She's half minded to try it again, after all this time, when she realises she's not according him the respect his office demands.

'Will your husband be in tomorrow evening?'

'We are in most evenings, Father.'

'Is eight o'clock convenient?'

No one from the parish has ever refused him. No one ever would. He knows this and is showing unusual circumspection. Eight o'clock will give them time to get the tea out the way and for her to make the necessary preparations.

'Eight o'clock would be fine, Father.'

# The National Ghost
Andrew C Ferguson

No wonder Scotland's so haunted.
We stand by our ancestors
cheek by death's head jowl;
they stand, we stand,
spirit and corporeal, the damned
united in this nation's claymation
of God's own mud.

In Madrid, on the other hand,
death is a social activity.
You can pay your respects on an evening out
to the newly dead, in the *tanatorio*:
there's a restaurant, and bar,
TV monitor,
cash machines and pre-paid phone cards.

In the Valley of the Fallen
El Caudillo has 40,000 dead for company.
You approach through dog roses, thyme,
stands of ilex, oak, and poplar
to Franco's tomb.
You can see the granite cross
from Madrid on a clear day.

On Spanish roadsides,
out of every village
the verges burst each spring now:
buds of bone,
like white asparagus.

# Gerontocracy
Ryan van Winkle

I never put my foot down or even tried
to govern and I never pushed a boat out
or offered straw for a hat and my mother
sometimes screamed so loud our neighbours
pretended to water their lawns and my father
would drink so much he'd lose his hearing –
my old man with his tv channels on yell
and my mother shouting to turn it down
so that there was only ever silence
below noise. That was our government `
and still I do not think government is evil

or that conspiracy is anything but silence
and maybe you and I needed papers
like the old boys on capitol hill, maybe
we needed debate, gavel bangs, and lashings
of a whip. But I couldn't call that government
to order because all I'd ever learned
of government was from father's hand
across mom's face and all I ever learned
of talking was from the tv so loud
it drowned out everything honest
so I could not tell what was puppet
and what was shadow. So, when my mother
finally took to the lawn and threw her eyes
at her own home I think I understood
the single government of my father

like the night you came home drunk,
your feet wet from the walk and I spied
your new congress and wished
my own government wasn't owned
by the same old ghosts of old men,
who only listened to their lawns
and cashed their checks and kept up
the monosyllabic megaphone
till the garage door opened,
the engine turned, and we were left
with only noise and the cold majority
of silence below noise.

# Autograph
## Brian Docherty

'As a teenager, I went to poetry readings like pop concerts:
I heard Norma MacCaig, Peter Porter, Adrian Mitchéll when I was 15, 16.'
(Carol Ann Duffy, Guardian Weekend, 25th September '99, P22)

Norma MacCaig spoke Gaelic very loud and very fast.
She wrote very quietly and very slowly in English
and Gaelic, in invisible ink; sang the Metrical Psalms.

For many years a printer's error made Norma
the only published Gaelic woman poet in Scotland.
Edinburgh's literary elite found this amusing.

On learning she wasn't Iain Crichton Smith's muse,
they decided she was a lesbian and spat in her sherry.
Exiled from Edinburgh, airbrushed out of photographs.

By the time women her granddaughter's age
were writing and publishing in either tongue,
Norma was silent in her writing and in real life.

She was a schoolteacher 40 years in Wester Ross,
taught generations of girls to love both languages,
sent them out into the world with her blessing.

In 1982 she produced her best creative work;
Visa application accepted, she spent two days
revising her autograph: Miss Normanon MacCaig.

Train to Glasgow, taxi to Wylie & Lochhead,
four Laura Ashleys, six pairs of shoes,
an Astrakhan coat, a Kathleen Ferrier box-set.

Norma appeared in Court once, and print twice more:
the Daily Record and an obituary in the West Highland
Free Press. Neither mentioned her poetry.

## Abusive Language
John Brewster

It took me
a silent afternoon
in your company
to know what ogres poets are.

Here was I thinking
you were a virgin
awaiting an experienced lance,
or, as the mood changed,
a blank potentiality
dependent on a catalytic line.

Trust you
to be a frightened black
upon a white sheet.

Trust me
to write a poem
about it.


## Probabilities
Robert Marsland

must I define
the thing I am

I am

whatever that
may be
and
its possibility
opens with
desire

## Poetry
Robert Marsland

heavy with
breathed cognitions,
white broth
power


## Pilgrim
William Bonar

I peaked early in piety, forswore
swearing at nine, learned texts by heart,
*amened* aloud, hymned in a tone-deaf roar:
hobgoblins nor foul fiends would daunt my spirit!
I was Joseph, David, Christ in the Temple
in short-trousered, shoe-shined, Protestant best,
on burnished pews, in filtered, reasonable,
Presbyterian light, on Christian's quest.

Now inside Kilmory Knap, grave-slabs boast,
after their fashion, of sword, birlinn, hound.
I close the door on their blether and walk
down to the bay – Jura set in crystal,
plovers and oystercatchers probe glazed sand,
wavelets froth and relent, froth and relent.

# The Man with the Cross-sectioned Heart
Brian McCabe

HE IS WALKING at a steady pace but not a leisurely one – it's more purposeful than that, it's hardly what you'd call a stroll in the park. If he was in a park – the Meadows, say – he might be striding across it on the way to the office, checking his watch to make sure he wasn't going to be late. That's the kind of steady pace the treadmill is making him keep up now, holding with both hands on to a chrome bar in front of him a bit like the bar of a turnstile – maybe it will let him through, maybe it won't – and the regular thwacking noises the soles of his trainers are making on the mat of the conveyor belt as it travels under his feet sound almost mechanical, as if he is becoming part of the machine. The jiggling of the tiny wires and electrodes fastened to his chest adds to this robotic feeling and when he glances over to the desk where the young nurse is standing, he can see all the dials and monitors the wires from his chest connect to, measuring his performance in flickering needles and pulses of light. Below them a printer is doing its job with a strident, intermittent screech, and a print-out is emerging a centimetre at a time, showing the graph which the nurse is leaning over the desk to study and which must be his results. *Thwack, thwack, thwack.* He wonders if he is passing the test.

The nurse moves away from the desk and comes over to him. When he looks at her she smiles and nods slightly as if to encourage him – she has wide-open blue eyes, a freckled nose and wears her red hair pulled back and tucked up – then she lays her hand on his shoulder and asks, 'Feeling all right there, James?'

'Fine!'

He says it with a bit of a gasp, and when he takes one hand from the chrome bar, he misses his stride and has to grab hold of it again quickly before he loses his footing altogether and is swept to the back of the treadmill.

'You keep hold of that now. You're doing fine, James.'

She goes back over to the desk and looks at the print-out, then adds some figures to a column she has been writing – his heart-rate, maybe?

On the wall a few feet in front of him there are various posters. One shows part of a box of chocolates, except that instead of assorted chocolates in the fluted paper cases there are apples, oranges, tomatoes, brussel sprouts... The caption above the box reads *Take five!* Another poster does a spoof on a fizzy-drink advert: *You've been mangoed!* Then there is one with a diagram of a man, showing the cross-sectioned heart and the vascular system, with tiny red arrows moving through the arteries and veins, in and out of the heart's chambers – what were they called again, ventricles? He tries not to think of his own vascular system, but can't help imagining thousands of miniature red arrows racing around his body, up and down his legs and his arms and in and out of his heart. It's like watching traffic from an aeroplane, all the tiny cars speeding along a complex system of roads... Is he taking off or coming in to land? *Thwack, thwack, thwack...*

'Now James –' The nurse comes over to the treadmill again and reaches for a dial. '–We're going to speed you up a bit, if you feel OK. Just tell me if it's too much for you and we'll take it back down...'

It was a cold, crisp, sunny morning when he drove to the hospital for the first meeting of the 'Back to Health' group, which met on Wednesday mornings in a small hospital on the edge of the town. It felt good to be going to something new – almost like starting school or university again. He'd gone for a sort of interview with one of the nurses the previous week and he'd signed up for a six-week 'course' of exercise classes followed by 'health education seminars'. He'd been given an 'achievement sheet' which had a section for each day for 'goals' and 'achievements'. It included daily exercises (in his case walking or swimming), intake of fruit and vegetables and fish, cigarettes smoked, timed breathing exercises and alcohol consumption. It was meant to give him a way to monitor his own progress. So far he'd resisted the temptation to cheat, though he hadn't always counted the cigarettes.

The traffic moved forward, then slowed and stopped. His route happened to coincide with one of the main commuter paths out of town, and it was that time in the morning. He made a mental note to plan another route next Wednesday. He found himself automatically reaching into his pocket for his cigarette packet, then he left it there.

Getting caught in slow-moving traffic was the kind of situation, he realized, which would cause him stress in the past. He remembered how he would swear and thump the dashboard and say 'Come on, come on, get a move on!' to the cars in front of him, looking at his watch again and again even though he knew the time. Then he would smoke, just for something to do. Now he tried to let go of the stress. He probably wouldn't be late anyway and even if he was – what would it matter? It was just a voluntary exercise class with a 'health education seminar' thrown in afterwards. No one was going to give him a row for being late. He kept the window half-open and tried to practice the breathing technique he had been taught by the nurse who'd interviewed him last

week. A deep, measured breath in. Hold it in a moment, then let it out slowly and evenly. He had been surprised at how this technique had been helping him to get to sleep at night – even without the use of alcohol.

He reached the hospital with a few minutes to spare but couldn't find a parking space in the car park – again a situation, he realised, which would sometimes have made him blow a gasket in the past. Now he just waited near the gate until he saw someone leaving.

After the aerobics there were other exercises – it was a bit like circuit-training for the elderly, to music. You moved round the various stations performing the necessary exercises, which were drawn as diagrams on big sheets of coloured card. There was a bench you stood up on then got down from twenty times. A station for sit-ups, another for knee-bends, another for lifting weights. The nurse who'd interviewed him – maybe she wasn't a nurse at all but a fitness instructor – went round making sure everyone was doing what they should.

As he moved around he caught glimpses of the others. He was probably the youngest, and he was surprised that there seemed to be as many women as men in the group. By co-incidence, there was also someone he knew, or had met before at least – a guy called Malcolm who worked in typesetting the paper. He'd spoken to him once or twice, usually to make last-minute changes to his copy before it went into print.

Then they went on to the exercise bikes. A nurse came round raising and lowering the gears and setting a dial to so many minutes. It showed the time you had to go as you pedalled in a certain gear, counting the seconds down like an old-fashioned oven-timer. He had to admit that he was glad to lie flat on the floor at the end of the session and do the controlled breathing with all the others.

During the tea-break, he compared heart-attacks with Malcolm. This had been Malcolm's second, and he was trying to kick the fags. He'd been a forty-a-day man, he said, but now he hadn't had a cigarette for a month.

➤→

'I'm still choking for a smoke,' he admitted.

He didn't like to admit to the guy that he'd probably be lighting one up himself as soon as he got out of the hospital grounds.

*Thwack-thwack-thwack...* The higher speed of the treadmill gives his steps an edge of fear, like someone in a hurry to get somewhere or get away from somewhere. He isn't quite running but he's walking much faster than he would ever walk normally. The wires and electrodes on his chest are jiggling frantically and there is something almost comical about their tinny rattling.

'Are you doing OK there, James?'

'Uh-huh!' he gasps between breaths. 'Fine!'

'I'll just do your blood pressure again.'

She wraps the rubber cuff around his arm and pumps it up. He feels it getting tighter and tighter as he runs, until she deflates it.

'Thank you, you're doing really well – and your blood pressure's fine and dandy.' She goes over to the desk and writes it down, below two other readings she has taken.

Fine and dandy, fine and dandy. He repeats it like a mantra in his head, to the rhythm of his steps on the treadmill. But now the man with the cross-sectioned heart on the wall has begun to jump up and down with each step, and he almost laughs aloud as the thought pops into his head that maybe the man is on a trampoline and he's building up to do an extra-high bounce, then a mid-air somersault – but can all that exercise be good for a man with a cross-sectioned heart? And the fruit-and-vegetable chocolates have started jumping out of their box, crying, 'Eat us, eat us now, before you die! Five of us a day, or it's pie in the sky!'

The nurse comes back from the printout, which is now a long narrow strip showing the graph of his heart-rate – at least, he supposes that's what it signifies, but maybe it shows other things too like the regularity or irregularity of its beats – and she places her hand on his arm. Her hand feels cooler than before – no doubt because his own temperature has gone up. He can feel the sweat trickling from under his arms and running over his ribs.

'Now James, how d'you feel about trying the highest speed, just for a few minutes? Just say if you don't think you can manage it.'

'OK,' he gasps, 'I'll try it.'

'Hold tight to the bar. Here we go –'

And now he's running, not jogging but really running. Maybe he's trying to catch a bus and it's getting ready to pull out from the stop and it's the last bus and if he doesn't catch it he'll have to walk all the way from the bottom of Leith Walk to Marchmont, and he can't even raise his arm to hail a taxi because if he does the force of the treadmill will throw him off and he'll fall into the gutter...

He searched his face in the toilet mirror, checking for any signs of anxiety or stress apart from the usual worry lines you couldn't do anything about. He tried a relaxed smile, but if anything it made him look a bit too relaxed, as if he'd stopped caring about anything much and he didn't want the Editor to think that. He tried to do a certain kind of frown – a hardworking, concerned frown, not one that would make him seem worried or ill – but that didn't work either: he looked like someone who was ready to start an argument and he certainly didn't want to walk into the boss's office looking like that. In the end he gave up on the face and checked his appearance. He was smart enough but not too buttoned-up looking, and casual enough without looking untidy or careless. He would do.

It was his first day back at work. The Editor, Harry McGuire – or Guffy, as he was known among the reporters – had called him a few days ago and asked him to look into the office when he came in. This could be taken as a compliment or a threat and he wasn't sure which the invitation was. Already he'd got tired of people asking him in a concerned way how he was, and telling people the story of his heart attack, but no doubt there would be more of it to come from his colleagues. He wanted to forget it and move on, if other people would only let him. He'd completed the 'Back to Health' course and the nurse had given him a special pass for the local gym, which meant that he could use it more cheaply. He had arranged to go for an induction session tonight after work. He stopped a moment outside the Editor's door – in reality it was his secretary's door, since her office acted as a kind of filter.

He knocked and waited until the secretary called him in. She was busy with something on the computer and she went on typing as she looked up.

'Hello there, take a seat and I'll see if he's free.'

He sat down on the couch just inside the door and waited. Though he'd been working on the paper for several years he had been here only a handful of times, usually when he'd made a mistake that might have legal implications, according to the Editor, like the time he'd said something about a murder suspect that could be construed as implying guilt. Maybe being ill was also considered a misdemeanour. He crossed his legs and started jiggling his foot up and down and drumming his fingers on the arm of the couch, then he stopped himself. The secretary was on the phone. He took a deep breath, held it in. Let it out slowly and evenly. Another.

'You can go in now.'

Guffy was a tall, heavily built man in his late fifties. Everything about him seemed pugnacious. Even the way he sat at his desk, his huge hands balled into fists on either side of his laptop, like a boxer waiting for the bell when he would rise from his corner and go for the knock-out. His bald scalp was pitted and slightly misshapen in places, like a helmet dented in battle. He sweated a lot – hence his nickname – and his skin had a leathery appearance. His shirt always had dark stains under the arms, the sleeves rolled up carelessly and his tie was always loose and yanked to one side. He wore broad, coloured braces – 'his power braces' as the reporters referred to them – which were usually bright red.

He had just answered the phone as James entered the room. He raised his eyebrows as if surprised to see him – even although he'd asked him to come and even although the secretary had just phoned through to announce him – then he gestured with his free hand for him to take a seat.

He sat down and tried to do the breathing while Guffy went on talking loudly, as if he was having to cover the distance between him and the person he was disagreeing with, or as if he was having to make something very clear to a difficult child.

'No, no, that isn't what I'm saying. I'm not saying you *shouldn't* say that. I'm saying you *can't* say that – got it? Good. I'll look it over when you've finished. Bye.' He barely paused in his speech as he hung up. 'James, you're back with us, back in the land of the living dead, eh? Among the zombies of tomorrow's news today!'

He nodded and did his best to laugh a little. The Editor leaned back in his chair and pawed at his chin with a hand.

'So how are you feeling?'

'Fine, back to normal in fact.'

'That's good. You had the angioplasty?'

'Yes.'

'How many stents?'

'Stents?'

'Isn't that what they call them – the tubes they put in the arteries?'

'Oh, yeah... just the one.'

Guffy thumped his own chest with one hand then another, for all the world like a gorilla – the alpha male, sending a message to a rival. 'I've got four of the bastards in there. Be a by-pass next.'

'Oh, don't say that.'

'Anyway, I thought maybe it was time you had a change, which is why I asked you to call in.'

'Oh?'

'I'm taking you off hard news and putting you on Features. It'll be good for you – less stress, more fun. You can generate your own ideas, but we're doing a whole series on diet and health, so you can maybe start with a feature on heart disease – bring in your personal experience if you want, but don't forget the stats. Oh, and Lorrimer goes on holiday next week for three weeks, damn him, so how d'you like to do the TV column?'

'I'd... like that.'

The TV column was generally regarded as a piece of cake, and a plum job.

'Great stuff.' Guffy leaned over the desk

➥

and winked at him. 'Between you and me I'm thinking of bumping Lorrimer off it – he's too nice about everything, his copy doesn't have teeth. So we'll see what you can come up with, eh? But keep it zipped about Lorrimer.'

Guffy made a zipping gesture across his mouth, then went into more detail about what he expected of him in features, threw a few deadlines at him and told him that Brewster, the features editor, would firm everything up with him.

As he left he wondered if he had been promoted or demoted. Was it a prelude to something else – making him a Cinderella before the 'I've decided to let you go' speech?

*Thwackety-thwackety-thwackety-thwackety-thwackety...* Now he is part of the machine and it is driving him; he has no choice about the rate he runs at because to keep up with the treadmill he has to run as fast as he can. The wires and electrodes are bouncing on his chest with a constant clatter. The fruit-and-vegetable chocolates are leaping in and out of focus and the man with the cross-sectioned heart is pogo-sticking for all his worth and the tiny red arrows are zooming in and out of his heart and the cars have become a blur of light through the tangle of night highways.

'All right there, James?'

The hand feels so cool on his skin. He can barely nod in reply.

'You've done so well – now I'm going to slow it down by stages then stop it altogether. Ready?'

He has never felt more ready for anything. The nurse turns the dial and he slows his pace, then she turns it down again and he sees the man with the cross-sectioned heart slowing down, hardly jumping at all, and the fruit-and-vegetable chocolates are settling back into their little paper cups. When the treadmill stops altogether it is as if his legs want to keep going and he staggers as he steps off so that the nurse has to catch him with both her arms.

'Ready for a dance now, eh? Let's get you unhooked.'

She unfastens the wires one by one. At one point she accidentally brushes against his nipple with her hand and he jumps away from her as if he's been tickled.

'Oh my, you're awful sensitive – down, tiger! Now come over here and have a seat. Want a cup of tea? Milk and sugar?' He nods and gasps, 'Uh-huh.' It feels like a strange kind of dance as she guides him to a chair by the door. She waits until he is seated before going along the corridor to the tea machine.

He closes his eyes and starts to regain his breath slowly, but although he knows he's sitting in a chair he still feels that he is on the treadmill, his whole body like an after-image of walking. He looks up at the posters on the wall. The fruit-and-vegetable chocolates in their little paper cups look strange, like little Magrittes, and he can't imagine ever eating them. He feels sorry for the vascular man who can never sit down and take a break, his arteries and veins always buzzing with tiny red arrows, in and out of his cross-sectioned heart.

# Extract from the novel *The Trees Aren't Sad So Why Am I?*
Tracey Emerson

'YOU WANT TO know about your conception?' Grace said.

'Yes.'

Grace pulled her knees into her chest and touched the long, crusted scab on her cheek. The room was too dark to see Anna's face or to check if her daughter carried anything in her hands. The curette. The gun.

'Where's Jack?' she asked.

The mattress dipped as Anna settled at the other end of the bed. 'Gone for a walk.'

Jack had stopped this same conversation yesterday but now Anna had chosen to disobey him. Should she see this as a sign of hope?

'You really want to know?' she said.

'Yes.'

Her daughter had already heard about the day she was aborted and now she wanted to hear about the day she was conceived. Of course she did. It was the story that began all stories. Her genesis.

'I need to hear it all.' Anna said. 'From the beginning.'

Grace was glad of the dark. Glad they were just two disembodied voices. 'You were conceived in August 1994.'

'I worked that out myself.'

'We called it the Summer of Three Dares.'

'Why?'

'Your... Ben called it that.' He'd named it as they lay side by side on the musty bed, panting. The Summer of Three Dares.

'Why?'

'You'll see.' Grace closed her eyes. 'It was just after we finished University. We were living in Beeston near Leeds.'

'What kind of house?'

'A two-up two-down, end of terrace.'

'Can you remember the street name?'

'West Grove Avenue.' A piece of information she wasn't aware of retaining. It must have lodged inside her, waiting.

'Go on,' Anna said.

'We'd both signed on and were living off credit cards.' A lazy summer. Sleeping, sex, too much wine.

'What about the dares?'

Grace's legs tingled. She could almost feel the rough, rotting blankets against the back of her thighs, almost smell the damp stink of the room in which her tale would end.

'The gasman was first,' she said. 'He came one morning in June to fix the meter in the cellar. We were having breakfast in the kitchen while he was down there and Ben dared me to have sex with him.'

'With the gasman?'

'No.' Grace opened her eyes. 'With him.'

'Why?'

She explained Ben's love of risk. She surprised herself with the details she remembered as she talked. The pink and white-spotted dressing gown Ben had opened before pushing her legs apart and going down on her. The half-eaten white toast with honey lying on a blue plate that she looked down on as she straddled Ben on his chair and fucked him like he told her to. The way she had to put her hand over his mouth at the end to stop him crying out. The look of approval he treated her to, the one reserved for when she surprised him, when

➤➤

she went further than he thought she would.

The sheets shifted as her daughter changed position. 'You didn't have to do everything he said.'

Grace sighed. She should warn Anna that some people have that power. They can make you do what you never wanted or intended to do. 'The way he looked at me,' she said. 'I lived for that look.'

'That's lame. I'd never let a guy treat me like that.'

You're doing it now, Grace wanted to shout. With Jack. I've seen you. You've signed yourself over to him and you don't even know it.

Bit late for motherly advice.

Anna's head turned towards the blacked out, padlocked window. 'Keep going.'

'July was hot,' Grace said. 'Really hot. We bought a second-hand barbecue and ate outside most nights. One evening we started drinking at five.' Three bottles of chardonnay for the price of two. She'd often wondered what it would be like to be the third bottle, added on for free, worth nothing. 'He asked me if I wanted to play a game. I said yes so he went inside and brought out a gun.'

'A gun?'

'An air rifle. I didn't know he had it. He got an empty coke can from the bin and put it on the wall at the end of the garden. He hit it on the second shot. I said I didn't want a go but he insisted. My hand was shaking but I got it first time.'

'What was the dare?'

'He got bored of shooting cans so he picked up one of the tin plates we used for the barbecue. It was white with a blue rim, we got a set cheap from Leeds market. He asked me to hold it and then he started getting undressed. Took everything off.'

'Everything?' Anna's tone, light and girlish. As if she was listening to any old story. As if she'd forgotten this was about her.

'Everything. Then he stood in front of the wall and put the plate... he covered himself with it. Go on, he said. I dare you.

'So you did it?'

'I remember hearing a bee hum as I stretched my arm out. Really loud. Then I shot him.'

'Did you hit the plate?'

'It chimed like a bell.' She'd laughed as Ben jumped around the garden. Fuckfuckfuck. 'Then it was my turn so I stripped off and stood in front of the wall with the plate over me.'

'Were you scared?'

'Yes.'

'Did you trust him?'

Ben had asked the same question as he swigged from the third bottle of wine, weapon dangling at his side.

'Not really.' *Point Break*. That's what she'd thought about as Ben lifted the rifle. She'd watched the film the night before. Keanu Reeves was an undercover FBI agent posing as a surfer to get close to a bank-robbing Patrick Swayze. Towards the end, Reeves dived from a plane onto a freefalling Swayze and they clung together, rushing towards the ground, each refusing to pull their parachute cord and chicken out.

'He hit the plate?' Anna said.

'Yes.' Her whole body had vibrated with the impact. Ben followed the pellet with a Told You to Trust Me look.

Silence.

Grace listened out for the warning scuttle of stones, the crunch of Jack's boots.

'August,' Anna said. 'What about August?' Her tone heavy now, forceful. She'd remembered what this tale was about.

Grace reached across to the bedside table and picked up the plastic cup. Empty. She didn't dare ask for more water.

August. Packing up clothes, books, records and CDs into boxes and black bin liners. Deciding which credit card companies to do a runner from.

'It was the week before we moved to London,' she said. 'We went to get milk from the twenty-four hour garage. There was an abandoned house near the other end of the street, we passed it every day.'

'What number?'

Grace waited for the digits to emerge. She could see the door – brown, flaking paint, tarnished brass knocker.

'Come on,' Anna said.

The 2 under the knocker, the 3 next to it, upside-down, one screw missing.

'Twenty-three,' she said. 'The curtains were shut but if you looked through the gap you could see a mouldy plate on the floor. Whenever we walked past the house, we'd make up stupid theories about what had happened. An old man had lived there but aliens abducted him or he'd been murdered in his bed. That sort of thing. This time Ben stopped and said we should go inside. We climbed over the gate into the backyard. There was an orange and green striped deckchair on the patio and a pint glass, full of leaves and water. The back door was locked. That scared me. I wondered why no one else had broken in. Ben put his shoulder to the door and pushed. It gave way third time.'

Everything in threes. Just like a story. She'd thought that then as the door flew open. We're making a story here.

'What did you find?'

'The kitchen curtains were closed and it was really cold. There was a yellow Formica table with a jar of jam on it. The lid was off, and it was all furry inside.'

If only she could provide a better setting. *We were in Venice, the Caribbean, the Maldives.* But who did get to start life's journey in such surroundings? Most humans were just impulses, whims, fancies, accidents. Urges fulfilled in the backs of cars, against rough, cold walls, on sofas in advert breaks.

She shivered. 'We went into the living room. There were photographs of an old man and his wife everywhere and some of their son with his wife and kids. I didn't understand how the son could let his parents' house rot away like that.'

Now she did. Now she understood that homes betray nothing of the cruelties that pass between one generation and the next.

'We went into the hall. There were coats hanging up, a man's raincoat and a suit jacket. We both stood there. I looked at the stairs and when I looked back, Ben was pressed against the coats. He was scared, he was actually scared. So I put my foot on the bottom stair and said, I dare you.'

'Did he do it?'

'He had to. He held my hand the whole way. At the top I had to keep going, I was winning. All the doors were shut. I guessed which one was the bedroom but when I touched the handle I couldn't do it. That's when he took over.'

'He opened the door?'

'Yes. His whole body relaxed when he looked inside so I knew there wasn't a corpse in there. I still felt sick though.'

'What was the room like?'

'The bed wasn't made. There was a blue sheet and two brown blankets, all messed up. The pillow had a dent in the middle of it.'

'Do you think the old man died in there?'

'I don't know. The curtains were yellow. The sun was coming through them, it made everything yellow.'

'It must have smelled awful?'

'Yes.' The reek of old age and regret. 'I wanted to leave. Ben was white. I knew he wanted out too but he wouldn't say it. He kissed me instead.'

The two of them tangled in freefall, neither wanting to pull the cord first.

'I sat on the edge of the bed,' Grace said. 'I looked at Ben and I said, come on then. He looked surprised, just for a second, then he pushed me back on the bed and undid his belt. He said... what was it? You're something else. That's right. You're something else. I was angry that I felt so pleased. I thought maybe I'd won.'

The blankets against her skin, death-riddled fibres.

'Keep going.' Anna urgent now, nearly there, nearly at the instant when all of her was decided – hair colour, eye colour, height, sex.

'I was wearing a blue dress. He lifted it up and pulled my pants down. Then he was inside me. It was sore but we both knew we'd have to be quick. He was staring right into me, looking for a sign of weakness so I wrapped my legs around him and told him to fuck me.'

'You could have told him to stop.'

Grace swallowed. 'I thought he'd pull out.'

'You should have reminded him.'

'I know.' Grace's heart raced around her chest, looking for the emergency exit. 'He was speeding up, I knew he was about to–'

'What did you do?'

'I closed my eyes.'

The hot stream of him as he ejaculated inside her.

Two tangled bodies in freefall hit the ground.

# Muddy Water
Joe McInnes

BEFORE I SLIP beneath the water I see you walk away. I don't care, I'd rather drown than call out to you for help. As I sink my skirt balloons and my hair spreads out like seaweed. I hold my breath for ages-and-ages, like that time we drove through the tunnel. It feels good to drop all the way to the bottom. My feet hit the riverbed and the water muddies. I cannot see anymore.

In the darkness someone has reached out and taken hold of my hand. I feel myself pulled upward and my body goes limp. As we rise I'm aware of the sunlight penetrating the surface of the water. I black out.

I remember the day we met. I stand outside the university library smoking a cigarette and you knock on the glass wall. When I turn around you wave and I give you the finger. You cross your arms over your body as if someone has stabbed you in the heart. I smile.

We become lovers and you say it's love at first sight.

You're in your third year of a literature degree. I'm a first year studying the history of art. We skip lectures on wet afternoons when I drag you round city galleries. At night, after we make love, you read me sixteenth-century romantic poetry.

Now we walk to the university library hand-in-hand and ride the elevator to the top floor. We sit together to study and when we get bored we look out across the sprawling city. Sometimes I feel you stare at me and when I look up you turn away and you are blushing.

It's my birthday and you bring round a framed print of Jacob Lawrence's *The Lovers* and we hang it above the fireplace of my flat. The next morning I get up early and wander round second-hand book stores hidden down west end side streets where I find a copy of *The Poetry of Alexander Montgomerie*. You're still asleep when I return and I make two mugs of coffee which I carry into the bedroom. You awake slowly and when you go to drink your coffee notice the book on the bedside table. You're elated and try to kiss me and spill your coffee on the quilt cover. We end up making love anyway, your hot hands all over me, your tongue halfway down my throat.

You roll me over and I think you want to take me from behind but instead you wrap your arms around me tightly and perform the Heimlich manoeuvre. I begin to throw-up what seems like gallon after gallon of water. You turn me around and give mouth-to-mouth resuscitation. The next thing I know I'm being carried on a stretcher into an ambulance. A paramedic places a respirator over my face and says, 'You have beautiful eyes.'

'You have beautiful eyes,' you say, as we lie on top of my bed after our love making.

'Read me a poem,' I say, and turn my back on you.

You need to lean over me to pick the poetry book off the floor and already I feel you hard against me.

I hear you flick through pages and say, 'How about, "The Perversitie of his Inclinations throu Love."'

'Sounds kinky,' I say, and press my bottom into you.

We stay in bed all afternoon and rise in the dark November dusk. You order takeaway and we sit it on the floor beneath the print of Lawrence's lovers, feeding each other slices of mozzarella pizza. We get ready to go out and I have to insist on separate showers.

You've bought tickets for the Comedy Club but we end up sitting in the pub all night getting smashed on Pernod and pretending it's absinthe. Someone keeps playing the Beautiful South on the jukebox and we stagger from the pub to the sound of 'And I love you till my fountain pen runs dry'.

Outside you put your arm around me and we stroll through the park. We take the path along the edge of the river. It's cold and you wrap your scarf around your head until I can't see your face. I laugh and do the same. You take my hand and as we walk along the pathway blindfold you try to kiss me through the cloth.

'Imagine if someone was watching us,' I say.

We come out on the other side of the park and an ambulance zooms past us along Argyle Street, its siren wailing as it turns into the Western. Eventually we reach the entrance of your close and climb three flights of stairs to your flat.

You go straight over to your vinyl collection and begin to sift through stacks of LPs piled up in the corner. I head for the kitchen to search for more alcohol and escape another lecture on the merit of vinyl. I come across a half-full bottle of Bacardi beneath the sink, grab two glasses from the dish-rack and return to the living room where the jagged rhythm of Muddy Waters crackles on the turntable, 'Baby I can never be satisfied'.

We sit on the couch listening to the blues and drink rum between booze fuelled clinches. Our passion ratchets up a gear and we end up on the floor. Sex is so fierce we break the coffee table.

But that doesn't stop us, and when I come my back arches with such ferocity it feels like a bolt of electricity going through my body.

'Early CPR ineffective,' you say. 'Patient responding to automated external defibrillator.'

I go into a fit of convulsions and can't stop shaking. The last thing I hear before I pass out is the sound of a siren.

I wake up on the floor with you beside me.

It's dark outside, but not enough. I can make out the busted table, a bottle of rum next to a table leg unbroken but empty. A pain shoots through my chest and my head feels dull and groggy. I stumble to the bathroom and throw up. I drape my arms around the toilet bowl and retch into the pan. My stomach is wracked and empty and no sick comes. I stare into the off-white enamel which reveals thousands of minuscule lines running through it. I gag, but still no vomit. I totter into the bedroom and fall upon the bed.

The morning light blazes into the room as you pull back the curtain. I push my head under the pillow and groan. You jump on the bed and try to pull the bedclothes off me until I start yelling. You change tactics and slip beneath the covers and slide your hand on to my breast. I elbow you in the ribs and tell you to, 'Fuck off.'

You storm out of the bedroom and slam the door but not before shouting at me, 'You weren't the one left sleeping on the floor all fucking night.'

This is our first argument.

I get dressed and leave. As I close the outside door I catch sight of you inspecting the damage to the coffee table. It's early Sunday morning and I wander along Argyle Street. I don't want to go home and decide to go into Kelvingrove Art Gallery. Downstairs the museum is full of stuffed wild beasts but upstairs in the gallery the sensual colour of Matisse's *Pink Tablecloth* and Andre Derain's *Blackfriars Bridge* helps soothe my thumping head.

I come out the revolving door to find you sitting on the steps.

'How did you know I'd come out this way?' I ask.

'I knew you couldn't resist the revolving door,' you reply.

You stand and we walk down the steps together.

'I'm sorry,' you try to say, but I kiss you before you can get it out.

We hold hands as we walk along the riverbank in the opposite direction from how we came last night. In daylight the river seems less romantic and the water brown and muddy. Once across Kelvin Way we sit on a park bench and you put your arm around me and I snuggle into you to keep warm. You're wearing jeans and I'm wearing yellow tights and blue stilettos and our legs look matchstick-thin in the cold. The park is quiet and we watch a woman with a child in a stroller approach along the path. As she passes we see she has a bandaged nose and someone has spat on her arm.

It's the holiday now and you go home and leave me in the city alone. Then on Christmas Eve you phone and say you wish you didn't have to spend Christmas with your family. In the background I hear voices competing to be heard above dodgy festive music.

'Remember not to open my present until tomorrow.'

'I won't,' I say, and think back to our exchange of gifts at the train station, our promise not to open them till Christmas day.

'I love you,' you say, before you hang up the phone.

This is the first time the word has been mentioned since you joked about it when we first started dating. I look across at your present which sits unopened alongside my Norman Rockwell Christmas tree. Whatever it is, you've disguised it with padding. I think about my gift to you. The brick-like two volume *Norton Anthology of American Literature*. You'd have worked out what it was before your train even left the station.

I go into the bathroom and run a bath, then the kitchen to make tea. Tomorrow's salmon fillet defrosts on the unit and looks like a still life painting. I place a floret of broccoli and two sweet potatoes beside it, but the moment has passed.

In the bath I sip tea and flick through a book of Alison Watt paintings but my mind keeps going back to what you said on the phone. So much so I get goose bumps before I realise

the water has become lukewarm. Placing the book on the bathroom floor I turn on the hot water and thick brown sludge spurts out the tap. The water quickly runs clean but the bath is polluted. When I step out the bathtub I drip muddy water onto the book and leave mucky footprints on the floor.

I dry myself sitting on the armchair in the living room. The television is garbage and, feeling sorry for myself, I decide on an early night. But I can't sleep and lie awake with the covers drawn up around my chin. Out in the street it sounds like the weekend and whenever I'm about to doze off the close door opens and I'm woken by footsteps going up the stair.

Sometimes the voices in the stairwell are audible and I listen to the conversations. I hear Mum's voice and feel happy she's flown over here to be with me. Then I hear your voice and you keep saying, 'I love you.' But this time when you say it you sound sad. I try to ask if you liked your present but it's one of those dreams where I can't speak or move. A nurse comes into my room and tells you and Mum she needs to roll me over on my side. When she turns me she tucks the covers tight beneath the mattress.

I wake on Christmas morning but feel so sluggish it takes everything I have just to get out of bed. Once up I make instant coffee and go into the living room. I lift your present from beside the tree and shake it around a bit. But I'm still none the wiser.

I rip the expensive wrapper only to reveal paper shreds and more packaging. I begin to think it's one of these gifts with layer upon layer of wrapping and I start to tense up. What if it's a ring? I imagine this kind of thing to be just like you. But I needn't worry. Because when I tear the second layer open I find a pair of pink fluffy slippers, which I throw at the wall.

'I thought you'd like them,' you say when you call later that afternoon. 'You're always walking around in your bare feet.'

'So you're my mother now,' I say.

'Don't be like that,' you plead.

'I wouldn't be seen dead in them,' I say and

➡

hang up the phone.

After that I refuse to take your phone calls and all week you keep sending soppy text messages. So far I've been able to resist calling you back. But on New Year's Eve I flag down a taxi on Byres Road and give the driver your address. As I climb the stairs I can hear music and when I reach your landing the door of your flat is lying wide open. I step inside and push open the living room door where you stand in the middle of the floor doing a bad reggae impression, clutching a bottle of red wine and singing along to the record on your turntable.

'There never was a better time
For trying to set the words to rhyme
Of when a golden love turns blue
And dreams of dreams that won't come
    true.'

You see me and point an accusing finger. I take hold of your hand and we dance together and I join in on the chorus.

I wake up and a nurse is placing a bouquet of roses in a vase on my bedside locker.

'Take them away,' I say.

'But your mother brought them,' says the nurse. 'She's just popped along to the coffee machine. Wait till she sees you're awake.'

Mum cries when she sees me. She goes through a full packet of tissues till eventually she tells me how at first you'd come to visit. You'd been distraught, according to Mum, inconsolable. Then after a while you stopped coming. The last she heard you had left uni and gone back home.

On the day I'm discharged from hospital I return to my flat. I run a bath and go into the kitchen to make tea. I go back through to the living room to wait for the kettle to boil. I sit in the armchair listening to the bath fill when I notice the empty space above the fireplace.

It's Valentine's Day and we cross the river to the Gorbals to see the remains of the saint in the Church of the Blessed Duns Scotus. The bones are in a wooden casket and because it's the saint's day the friars have adorned a statue of Valentine with dozens of roses and placed it next to the relic.

Afterward you take me around the corner to a rose garden where you tell me you played as a child before your family moved out of the city. Originally a cemetery, we walk around looking at some of the old headstones. We sit on a bench next to a memorial sculpture of a giant metal rose. You seem nervous and say you need to talk to me. You look sad and I reach across to take hold of your hand. But you say I might not like what you have to tell me.

This gets my attention. The next thing you produce two silver rings and tell me not to be afraid.

'They're friendship rings,' you say.

'They're beautiful,' I say. And they are. Inside there's an inscription but I can't make it out. 'What does it say?'

'Anam cara,' you tell me. 'It's Gaelic for soul mates.'

We face together holding each other's hands. It feels scary and we squeeze tight as if afraid to let go.

'Don't look so worried,' I say. 'I love it.'

'I have to tell you something,' you say.

'What is it?' I ask, and release your hands.

'Do you remember I went home for Christmas?' When you speak you won't look at me. 'Well there's this girl I used to go out with.'

'Please stop.'

'Before I came to university,' you continue. 'I suppose you could call her my first love.'

'Fucking stop.'

'I'm sorry,' you say.

'Fuck off,' I say and get up and walk away.

'That's why I bought the rings.' You follow after me. 'I want us to have a fresh start.'

'A fresh start,' I turn to you and spit with rage. 'I didn't even know anything had ended.'

I run out the rose garden away from you. I reach the main road but don't stop and a car has to swerve to avoid hitting me. You try to follow but get pinned on the other side by traffic. I continue running through the high flats and don't look back. I come out at the river and run along the walkway behind the distillery. One of my shoes has slipped from my feet and is held by the strap around my ankle. When I look up I see you coming along the walkway. By the time you catch up I've got my breath back and duck beneath the railing and walk to the edge of the river.

'What are you doing?'

I ignore you and pull the friendship ring from my finger.

'Be careful,' you shout.

I go to throw the ring in the water but my shoe gets tangled in reeds and when I try to pull free I trip and fall in the river. I thrash around but the current is strong and pulls me under. Before I slip beneath the water I see you walk away. I don't care, I'd rather drown than call out to you for help.

# Fuck You Too, Pixie Meat

(After Hole's 'Rock Star')

Kirsty Logan

IT WENT LIKE this: the sky was glittering, the dancefloor was throbbing, and every single goddess there was looking at the way –

Once upon a time there was a girl, and one star-strewn night she met a boy who was a bite of perfection, all lipstick and bones, and they lived happily –

Fuck it. This is how it really was: Wednesday night at the Olympia and everyone looked the same. Some girl was up on stage doing her thing, standing on her tiptoes to sing because it hadn't occurred to anyone to lower the mic after the boys had played. Her band was Bitches on Acid, or Cuntfight, or Slit, and they had red glitter drumskins and Hello Kitty stickers on the bass. You know exactly how they looked: pink hair, smeared lipstick, and muffin-tops anchored over the waists of their jeans. There was even a plastic unicorn standing guard at the front of the stage. You know exactly how they sounded too, but who needs more than three chords anyway?

I was lurking near the back with a couple of girls I barely knew, girls I wish I'd known in high school but I was too much of a loserfreak then so I had to be friends with them now, when they only talked to me because I bleached my hair and always had pills to share. A few months ago they'd seen me holding a baggie in a bathroom and called out a name that wasn't mine, but I pretended it was and fake-remembered all the things they were talking about. School, classes, graduation. As if I could have gone to that school. They hadn't caught me out yet. I'd done some research and dropped some names at the right time, and they were too stoned or

self-involved to notice if something was off.

They were both whining over some guy, some dickweed with artfully tousled hair and hipbones that could cut glass. He hadn't shown up yet, but every girl's eyes were pointing straight at the door so they didn't miss a second of his performance. Him just walking in is a performance, him ordering his drink and paying for it and slouching to the corner of the room and watching us from the hooded arch of his eyelids: all a performance. All just total fucking bullshit.

The next band is up: shoeless, tights torn, vintage dresses taut over their little pot bellies. The singer pulls the mic off its stand and wraps it around her arm so tight the flesh puckers out, drowned white against the leech-black wire. I sigh and flip my empty beer bottle into the corner, sneaky-like so the bar guy doesn't yell at me.

Jennifer's pulling on my elbow, whining *they're gonna be on soon* as if we actually came here to see Do It For The Kids and not just stalk some chunk of pixie meat, and I don't know why I never noticed before that Jennifer's got on so much eyeliner that it looks like her eyes are wearing mourning veils. I know what she wants, and I link my arm with hers and stick out my other arm elbow-first so that Tabitha can hook onto me, and I lead them into the girls' bathrooms.

We spend a few moments playing with lipstick and eyeliner – red, black, sex and death – then cram into a cubicle. The door won't close right around Jennifer's arse, and Tabitha and I swap glances over Jennifer's bright-red tangle of hair. We don't get to eat cherry-nut sundaes, but we can slip into the smallest of cubicles. Jennifer breathes in until her ribs stick out and she can get the door shut; I slip my hand into my boot and pull out a tiny plastic bag. I count pills into their waiting palms, saying *one pink, one blue, one for me, one for you*, and they never take their eyes off the bag, and my rhyme falters when I realise that I don't know when we last met each other's gaze.

Back out by the stage the loserfreak pixie meat has arrived. He's leaning one elbow on the bar, eyelids at half-mast, plastic cup of something in one hand. If Tabitha and Jennifer didn't already have pupils the size of pennies, they would have widened at the sight of his t-shirt-draped bones. They hold my arms tight enough to bruise. I glance over to Tabitha and I swear to christ I can see her left tit vibrating with the pressure of her heartbeat. Fuck this shit.

*Hey* I yell across the floor *hey you goddamnit* and the pixie meat looks up and puts down his drink and stands there staring at me and before I can think I unhook myself from those bruise-tight grips and I march over to him, feeling fifty feet tall in my torn babydoll and untied boots.

Now that I'm so close to him I don't know what to say. I wait for him to call me out on cussing at him but he doesn't.

*I'll have one of those*, I say, nodding at the plastic cup, and he turns to the barman and points at the cup, then takes the new cup off the bar and puts it in my hand. It's that quick, that smooth, all one motion like a bird opening its wings. I take a sip even though I don't really want it because I don't know what else to do and I'm scared that he knows somehow, that the lies I told to be here are written on my clavicles for him to read. He just stares at me with his eyelids so lazy-low that he barely has to move them to blink.

*I'm a rockstar* he says and keeps staring at me like I'm the doll inside a snowglobe, like I'm the angel on top of a Christmas tree, like I'm fascinating. Like I'm someone.

*Bullshit* I say *I never heard of you.*

*Well I'm practically a rockstar* and I can't

even tell when he's blinking and when he's looking; and then he says *any day now* and normally shit like that would make me laugh and move on to the next guy but there's something there, something I can't even say, and it's not just that he stares. It might be the pink pill talking or maybe the blue one but he makes me feel like I'm the girl with the most cake. If he can fake it this good then maybe it's not faking.

The band has come out by now – *We are Doing It For the Kids!* – they whine into the mic before the drummer taps them in and it doesn't make sense to mangle their name like that but whatever, what the fuck ever, because now my heart is thumping so hard that I bet my own left tit is vibrating.

I think the pixie meat can probably see the vibration so I lean away from him, just a little bit, because I can't see whether he's looking down my dress or not. He just leans closer.

I don't know why but I glance up then, across the floor to where I left Tabitha and Jennifer, and I guess I thought they'd be flinging their limbs about to the band by now but they're not. They're looking at me. At us.

And Tabitha has never looked more like what she is, which is a beauty queen gone bad, all honey-smooth vowels and a blowjob mouth, and I know she is going to fuck me up. Oh mother mary, she is going to fuck me up good because she knows what I am. She's always known, but she didn't care because I had baggies in my boots and I was always there when she called.

*I have to*, I say to the hood-eyed boy, *I have to*, and he knows because he's looking over at Tabitha too. At least I think he is, it's hard to tell if there are even eyeballs under those lids. He takes my drink and says *I'll hold this till you get back*, like I'm coming back, like I'll ever be in one piece ever again, and I head straight for the door. Do It For the Kids are playing some whine-rock and the crowd are swaying like the lungs of a beast, a mass of hair and cloth and scar-shining limbs. I wish I'd laced up my boots because those motherfuckers feel heavier than coal.

➤

As I elbow through the crowd I think, there was never going to be a revolution. There can never be a girl-revolution because we're too busy arguing over who gets to be the queen. This thought makes a hell of a lot more sense to me than that slice of boy who can't even lift his goddamn eyelids.

Outside, the air tastes like gin. Everything is a tangle and the stars are blurring but I finally feel like I can put my boots flat on the ground. I know the shape of my feet, the thump of my heart.

I am.

I am.

I am.

I take a lungful of the thickening city air and I go to shout out my own real name but before I can remember it the stars have flickered to black and there's grit on my cheek and my boots are up above my head and it's Tabitha, that goddamn fucking cunting oh –

and I'm over again, the kerb by my jaw, and I'm up on my feet and I can see the smear of her face so I put my shoulder into it. There's an oooof of breath and I catch the scent of her skin, booze and sex and sugar, and a shiver runs through me. I hold out my arms until I can get my balance, and I look over at the tangle of Tabitha on the ground. She's perfect. She's a goddess. I want her oh god oh fuck I want to be inside her and I want to be her and –

Why are we even fighting? What the fuck are we fighting over? Some slab of pixie meat who can't even open his goddamn eyes, just a t-shirt full of bones and fingers on guitar strings? Which girl is the thinnest, which girl has more sugarpills, which girl swallows more, which girl is *the* girl, the best girl, the one with the most cake boys tits pills love love love and it's stupid, it's so stupid, I never wanted to do it. I put one boot in front of the other and I walk. I walk as fast as I can without falling over.

*Goodbye!* I yell over my shoulder. *Goodbye, motherfuckers!* and I keep walking because I don't know how to come back.

# Cliff
## Eleanor Thom

THE MORNING'S TEABAGS are lumpy, squeezed shapes. They are weeping onto the worktop. It's the nicotine colour the gauze takes on and their cold liveriness in my fingers. I nip the bags by the edges and drop them into the black throat of the bin.

The dishes have to be done before bed. I've been keeping busy. I wash them with bare hands because I hate the feel of Marigolds, the way those rubbery grains of dirt get inside each elastic finger and roll under my nails. They're like eraser shavings and dry snotters. Human things: skin, hair, sweat from palms.

I can sympathise with hands. For most people it's eyes isn't it? They will be watching a programme about gorillas and they'll say look at those big sad eyes. But for me it's always the hands, the tarry black palms crisscrossed with paths of wrinkles. They're strong and fleshy, but oddly slim at the tips. A pianist's fingertips. There are even nails. Fingernails!

My hands guide me as they key their way, doh-ray-me, through octaves of light and shade. Supple. Maybe that's why I have a feel for hands. Music is a conjuring trick, I tell my students. Magic for the senses. It's different for everyone, but for me, *Maestoso* is Indigo blue, *Staccato* is hiccups, and *Glissando,* liquorice!

Every afternoon between lessons I take the dog out and walk along the high coastal path. That's how I relax. I thumb thoughts into my palms like coins, nestle my mind in jacket pockets. I think of stepping and of keeping a check on Petra, who is getting old now but she still wants to run.

It was here that I saw the man. He had a black terrier, a yappy little thing. We got talking one day while we sat on a bench. He did most of the talking. He had an accent. He was from abroad but he'd been here a long time. You could tell. I studied the bare fingers of his right hand. He held them splayed across his thigh and they were the hands of an old man, thick and marbled, knotty knuckles. His nails were strong, rooted looking. A wedding band. In my head I counted his fingers once and then set to counting again. I counted them gently this time because I'd noticed his eyes, wet like a beachcomber's treasures. Not really crying. It could have been the wind or the salty air, or just a look he had. I've always been bad at emotion. I didn't know what to say so I kept counting. I had a stupid thought that somehow he'd know what I was doing, registering each of his fingers as kindly as I could, like a girl in an old song wishing five sailors home from sea.

Above us a bank of cloud made a strange shape, a cube. It actually looked like a box. The man blinked away the weather in his eyes and we spoke about the sky. A change of subject. I heard it in his voice though, a herring bone trapped in the throat. It wouldn't disperse. He put a hand out to the terrier and let her lick salt off his palm.

The man always held his dog on a long lead and whenever we met, Petra would flaunt her freedom. I've never carried a lead. She would close in on the terrier, wagging and sniffing before leaping up, mantis-like on her whippet's limbs, and just when the terrier thought she'd get a chance to chase, Petra would go belting out

➡

of reach, racing the shrieking gulls.

'Petra! Come ya! Come ya!' I yell through the wind. I don't shout because she hears or obeys. I just enjoy feeling the words blown sideways from my mouth, the sea sloshing out the shells of my ears.

'That dog's a maniac,' the man used to say. He tempted her with heart-shaped treats from his pocket.

When the dishes are set to drain I go to bed. I've already brushed my teeth and washed my face, and all that's left to do is hook my dressing gown behind the door. I sleep naked between the sheets, pink in the darkness like a mussel in a shell. I brace myself for cold cotton covers. The washing-up liquid is sticky on my arms. I reach for the lamp. Waiting for sleep, I wonder about the man.

He held out the treats for the dogs on a wide flattened palm. Hands like floured muffins. The last time I saw him the tide was out and there were rocks. It was a weekend and the path was busier than usual. It's popular with couples who walk arm in arm against the wind, smiles glossy with shared fish and chips. The man came and sat beside me on the bench, and the terrier lay down by his shoes.

It was cold and I was wearing gloves. They were dark pink, but he called them beetroot. He said I like your beetroot gloves, and he told me about the town where he was born. I just let him speak, and the way he described it you could picture the bar on the square, those bright umbrellas and a grey church tower. There was a beetroot factory in my town, he said. The stench of soured wine hung over it on a warm day. Imagine these women, he said, lines of them up to their elbows for ten hours at a stretch. No wonder they stained. Mothers and lovers with beetroot gloves. He told me he wanted to go back. It was a beautiful place. I got the feeling he had left someone there, a girl or maybe a child.

He would have had to reach down to pat the terrier and release her from the lead. Or maybe he tied the lead round the leg of the bench, knowing that someone would miss the dog and that here she would be found. Maybe he was thinking of someone else when he left the terrier.

A woman walks it now. She wears a beige cagoule and a chenille scarf, and she often needs to pull a hanky from her sleeve. The rest of the time she keeps her hands stuffed in her pockets and glances to the horizon, and I wonder if she's remembering the man and the days when he travelled in his lorry, delivering prawns and shellfish.

There was one column and a small photograph in the local paper, but never a follow up. People waited. They said that at the very least, a shoe would tumble ashore or a wallet would slap open on the sand. But despite all the souls who daily walk along the high path, nothing has turned up.

The woman passed me today. The wind was up again, a storm on its way, and she was pushing flyaway strands of hair behind her ears. She made me think of my mother at the piano. My mother had wild hair but always held it neatly off her face when she played.

I have not slept well here. My house sits right on the sea and in a few years it will be slowly engulfed like the hulk of a grounded ship or it will fall like a deck of cards. Outside the waves are busy, bleaching, digging, shifting shingles, folding the shoreline like tireless housekeepers. They exhaust me. I'm afraid of what they might turn up in the night and dump on my doorstep.

I dream of the woman with the dog. In the dream she is living in the house where my mother lived before she died. I know the flaky blue paint on the windowsills and the bay tree by the gate. Her fingers are cold and she warms them on the radiators as she moves from room to room. Her hands peel an orange with great care, turn on a tap, draw curtains, unbutton her clothes and apply cream. She switches off the light at her side of the bed. Her skin is smooth as wax and her fingers are swollen. Her knuckles are polished pebbles. She is waiting for the man, like my mother waited, still keeping things clean. She remembers him as a good man. I try to shout, but my voice makes a pathetic sound, breath blown over a bottle, and I change my mind. I look down and my hands are beetroot red.

The storm wakes me at dawn. I find the sea's residue in my hair, in my belly button, between my toes. The bedsheets are salty. In the corner the curve of the piano is huge and dark, and in the half light it could be something else altogether, a tug, a whale, an ocean liner's anchor. I stare at its lovely form till I remember myself.

Outside the sea is crashing a relentless *rondo*. People long to live on islands and coastlines but now I have tried it I can't say I understand. I stay awake listening to the sea. It's conducting its fingertip search, unpicking us, scaling its way up the beach.

# The Bower

Judith Taylor

The story was, the Queen of Scotland
loved this boxwood bower on Inchmahome –

but how much love would you feel, really,
for a gaggle of shrubs on a cold, windswept island
where you were kept waiting
three weeks, at the age of six
to be taken somewhere better?

Somewhere better's the thing, of course.
We'd like to believe a tenderness for Scotland
– or a portion of it –
hung about the heart of that young girl
at the glittering court of France.

We'd like that
in the face of all the evidence

that to her, Scotland was lumber, nothing more:
her oldest family heirloom,
awkward, dark, and crudely made.
That it wouldn't have broken her heart
if she had lost it. That she wasn't glad to find it

all she was left with
when the husband died, and the big prize
slid from her pale, finely-manicured hands.
But kings and queens
had always worked that way: the story was
they loved their people better than anyone else did.
And people who think they're loved
will wait around through almost anything;
will allow themselves to be traded on,
traded away, like chips in a game.

At any rate, the bower you see
is Victorian, no earlier.

A few old trees could not sustain the onslaught
of Romanticism – all that love
that came on the boat
in the early nineteenth century, needing souvenirs.
Step in, then, to imitation shade,

you lonely visitor.
Rest on the park bench
so thoughtfully provided.
And consider how the love is divided out
between the one who leaves – at least
until there is nowhere better left to go –

and the one who stays, all that time believing
their cheek once felt a kiss.


## Incomer
Judith Taylor


You can play that cello all you like
to the cool, thickening dark
– nothing will answer.
The woods at the end of your garden
are low and leaning, shaped by gales
and gripping stone for their footing.
They are never heady with wild flowers.
This isn't nightingale country.

Take in your elaborate music-stand
– the dew will rust it –
close the patio doors, and light the light.
Don't be disheartened. You've been out
asking the wrong questions:
everyone does, at first. But listen later
when your neighbour makes
another midnight effort to get finished

whatever ramshackle thing
he's building now.
A tawny owl will come to a nearby tree
and hoot the noise of his hammer back
in the same rhythm precisely, blow for blow.
Though whether in love or mockery
or to warn him off ancestral ground
I doubt we'll ever know.

John Humphries: "Welcome to Mastermind. First contestant, your name?
Contestant: Joe Bloggs
Humphries: Your occupation?
Contestant: Novelist
Humphries: And your specialist subject?
Contestant: Myself of course

# Bride from Lahore

**Rizwan Akhtar**

Buffed with filigree
holding the rustling *gharra**
ears and nose
reined-in by golden trinkets
the bride steps out
from a glossy car
wobbling on the pointed heels
smile-collector she walks
with a market-logic
the photographers
land on her with cameras
like octopus's tentacles
lips slicked with lipstick
eyes clogged with mascara
she blinks at the camcorder
the post-box mouth
swallows the greetings
amidst clank of crockery
and velvety drizzle of guests
face-lowered she goes on
waiting.

*ornamental wedding dress worn by women in the sub-continent.

# In the Flood

**Brian Johnstone**

*for Andy Góldsworthy*

These stupa-like cairns that punctuate the gorge
are Goldsworthy's in spirit, if not
in name. We add to them

a stone, a pebble, waymarking the route
to lead those that the coming autumn will permit
the better down the course

of what will be a river come November
with the start of winter rain,
a torrent from the snow-melt in the spring.

The permanence of what resemble Henry Moores
in all their form and bulk,
shore up every fly-by-night route marker

stacked upon these eddy-sculpted rocks
but subject to the coming wash
of water Goldsworthy might welcome, were he here

in more than spirit, when the force
now dormant in the gorge sweeps
all – direction, art, intention – before it in the flood.

# What the young films of Man Ray dream about

**Sarah Neeley**

The arch of the lip
as smooth as the hip
over which the camera rolls
then settles on like dust
loves symmetry
as graceful as doves' wings,
puzzled tight like piston rings.

# Four Poems from *Anderson's Piano*, a work in progress
Sally Evans

### CRUACHAN: DERAILED TRAIN

A rare red rose bloomed for a week in June.
Perhaps it saved the lives of those
who came unharmed from the rock-tripped train
high above the deep water in Argyll
where the long loch is death's wake deep
and the wild rose blooms in a canyon,
the rare red wild June rose.

Late light of June, lasting almost
all night, they file at evening's end
in a forced trudge to Cruachan,
tracks empty and safe as houses,
this desolate dedicated railroad
five miles or more from all houses

but how lucky, here's Cruachan,
power station under the mountain
of caves and a visitor centre,
bread and soup and a small first aid box,
a flare of yellow light in the dusk,
sweet tea for the shaken driver.

## ANDERSON'S PIANO (I)

No myth, but strange reality,
those eerie sounds that sing to the dark,
symphonies for foxes, scavengers,
seabirds come too far, misled by lochs.
Muffled in slumber, intensified by mist,
atmosphere its own instrument,
the last traveller's last lullaby.

Tracing the perilous railroad,
over the bare bouldered terrain
through the terrible Pass of Brander
where the water is black and deep,
the glen-long fence-wire sleeps on guard,
instinctive harp of the high wood.

The train brings commerce to a coastline,
bridges this pass of bleak landscape
to the islands beyond poverty,
runs safer thanks to Anderson's trick.
If rock falls, the harp's wire
signals, a bell is struck.

## ANDERSON'S PIANO'S FIRST SONG

My wordless story
is music's preparation
for the crux of a journey,
its unknown value,
the strains it will put on you,
gains it could make for you
if you strive.

Do not listen for me if
you would not know the truth,
though I can be a comfort
to the comfortless,
I do not place you
above the animals.

Unmoving, untended,
my undisturbed century
forgotten and superseded,
I need no sleep.
I am what you choose to start,
can never stop.

ANDERSON'S PIANO (2)

Single-track, trespass-hostile,
through steep soft leafmould, thorns, saplings,
fern and fleas, the railroad runs.
Protective piano poles,
rakish and rusting, hold their wires
invisible across the landscape,
seen from below against the sky.

Wires, tensioned, Aeolian, respond
to caresses of the wind,
their primary purpose as signals
of rockfall, failed strikingly.
Their actual, airborne singing
seeps to the earth like lore.

We heard their message by day, by night
we recounted it, our flat tones
inadequate. Go no nearer, stay away
unless you have all the strength
of the interpreter, a halfwit walking
a deadly forest the awkward way.

# The Wedding Flowers

Wayne Price

IT WAS A slow, hard climb through the Muslim graveyard. There was no path between the graves and the way was steep and shadeless, but it was a shortcut to the ruined chapel, saving at least half a mile, the English boy reckoned. Besides, he was desperate to escape the main route, winding and dusty, that followed the stream to the springs at Ras el Ma. All along the river, under the old town walls, gangs of brown, half-naked children had crowded the shallow pools, splashing and shrieking and begging when they noticed him; and above them, lining each pocket of shade above the path, lounged the older youths, interrupting their endless conversations to call out tirelessly as he passed, *Hey, mon ami! Amigo! Hashish? Hey! My friend – good hash! Very cheap. Si? Hey, venez ici! Sit here. Yes? Hey!* And always one or two standing and following until he reached the next strip of shade and the next gathering, the reek of *kif* heavy in the hot air again, and in every brittle tree and bush the invisible cicadas screaming as if on fire, and then a new volley of offers, and another stranger stalking behind him, dropping away only when the path twisted out of the shadows and into the painful glare of the sun, leaving him to the next link of shade and waiting smokers in the long, watchful, murmuring human chain. It was exhausting and he had chosen the shorter, steeper climb as soon as he'd noticed it though it took him away from the river where he'd been able to drench his burning face and neck. His bottled water was already running low, but he could pace his drinking more carefully now that he was alone at last. He'd had to drink wastefully

as he walked the gauntlet of the local youths, sucking from the bottle when they called out so that he'd seem preoccupied and purposeful. It was the same in the souks and markets of the medinas. In Tangier, Marrakech, Fez, and now here: always the bottle ready to seal his mouth though he knew it was probably exactly that which singled him out as a tourist and brought him the attention he was warding himself against.

He stopped, wiped the sweat out of his eyes with the linen sleeve of his shirt and for the first time noticed properly the scattered, whitewashed graves surrounding him. They were almost identical: just narrow troughs of stone, around four feet in length. Even the largest were shorter and narrower than any adult coffin. The newest were dazzling under the late morning sun. At their ends they were stepped or arched, sculpted very simply and set low to the ground, many of them nearly hidden by the clumps of parched, wiry mountain grass that lay matted in between. A few carried short Arabic inscriptions but most were plain and there were no flowers, nor any other kind of offering, just pale gravel or more of the tough hillside grass inside the shallow walls of each rectangle. He wondered idly how deep the graves could be dug in the rocky soil. It looked unpromising: knuckles of grey Rif limestone jutted through the grass in every part of the burying ground. The clean, wordless graves were pleasing, though. Blank headstone after blank headstone, blocky and white, as if the blazing sun had bleached even their meanings away.

But Christ, it was hot. Too hot to linger in the open. The high sun seemed focused to a single, burning cone on the crown of his head and the glare and repetition of the white graves was making him dizzy. Just a few hundred yards further on, at the highest boundary of the graveyard, a skirt of trees fringed the last steep rise before the chapel. He could make for their shade or turn back and face the hustlers again at the river. With his left hand shielding the top of his head, he squinted up at the ruin and started to climb again.

The hunched figure sharing the shade of the trees, a little way above him and to his right, was silent, though the boy knew he was being watched as he dried the streams of sweat on his face, took a little water and recovered his breath. Behind them both, from the ruin, drifted the sound of cheerful Spanish voices. Eventually, two young couples carrying small, bulging day-packs on their backs came picking their way down a stony path between the shrubs and olive trees. The figure in the shade called out to them familiarly in Spanish and the two boys answered with laughs and a few fragments of conversation. It seemed to be the continuation of an earlier exchange, the English boy thought, though he could understand none of it except the *adios* the figure finally called out as they vanished into the scrub. Other than the endless background sawing of the crickets and cicadas there was silence for a while, then the sound of a match being struck. As if on cue, the stranger called over to him: *Amigo. Español?*

He turned and shook his head, examining the other man for the first time. No, he called back. The stranger was small and wiry, clearly a local. Older than the youths at the river, the boy decided – his scant goatee beard had streaks of grey in it, though the rest of his face was youthfully smooth and sharp-boned. He was staring again now, knees drawn up almost to his T-shirted chest, and smoking a black wooden sebsi. The smell of the struck match rolled by the boy, then the aroma of *kif*.

English? Yes?

The boy nodded.

The stranger grunted and puffed on the short pipe.

The boy turned away, ignoring the rattle of pebbles behind him as the Moroccan rose to his feet and made his way to the boy's side, settling himself on a rock close by.

From London?

No. A smaller place. Nottingham.

Ah! Nottingham Forest. Brian Clough!

Despite himself the boy laughed. You've heard of him?

The stranger grinned toothily. All great coaches famous in Maroc!

The boy shook his head, still smiling. Dead now, he said.

Yes. You have smoke?

No thanks. I'm fine. He toyed with the cap of the bottle but resisted the impulse to open it and drink. The water was warm through the plastic and his fingers were slippery with sweat.

No smoke?

No. No smoke. I'm here to see the mountains.

Good. Very good. Many fine mountains here in the Rif. He cleared his throat. My name – Ibrahim, he announced abruptly, and reached over to offer his right hand.

The boy hesitated, then shook it. It was slender but the grip was strong. Hello, he said flatly.

For smoking I ask just once, said Ibrahim. In town, they say hash, hash, hash, yes? Always the hash. Me, I ask once.

Okay, the boy said. All around them the cicadas were deafening: an endless, grating chirr. It set the boy's nerves on edge the way a baby crying always did when he was a child.

Very hot, yes? Ibrahim went on. Rest before more walking.

Very hot, the boy agreed. Too hot.

Yes. Even for August – very hot.

They fell silent for a while. A calm, watchful immobility seemed to settle on the stranger's face whenever he stopped speaking. It gave him a detached, superior air. You live in town? the boy asked at last, uncomfortable with the silence. Without speech as a distraction, the uproar of the cicadas was maddening.

In Chouen, no. My village – that way.

Ibrahim pointed with the stem of his sebsi towards the broad stony valley running east from the town and the chapel. Sometimes, I stay in Chouen, he added, and shrugged. You travel far in Maroc?

The boy nodded. I was in Tangier to start, then Fez and Marrakech, then headed back north. I was hoping it would be cooler in the mountains.

Ibrahim listened with a tilted head, as if straining to catch the words. He paused for a moment after the boy had finished speaking, then straightened his neck and grunted. Marrakech – too hot, he said. In Marrakech now, fifty-five degrees, maybe more. Centigrade, he added ominously. Very bad. Better here. But today, not so good. Very hot in Chouen, too. He took several quick puffs on his pipe. Then, as if suddenly struck by the idea: I show you the mountains, yes? Show you the spring – cold water. Very clean. Good to drink. I know all the ways in the mountains. Good places for photographs. Very high up.

A wave of weariness and irritation ran through the boy but he fought to keep it from his voice. I don't know. I was planning on that anyway, you know? Walking in the mountains. You understand? I was going there anyway.

Of course, of course, said Ibrahim, smiling.

Well, okay, the boy finished lamely.

Of course. Ibrahim tapped the debris from his pipe. You see my village too, yes? I show you the farms where they make the kif and the hash. Tourists not permitted, but I take you.

The boy yawned helplessly. It was suffocatingly hot, even out of the sun, and being hustled always made him feel strangely drained. Ever since arriving in the country and breaking up with his girlfriend who had taken an early flight home, he had become more and more aware of a weakness in himself, like a painless but sapping wound that each hustle opened up afresh; now, sensing it opening again, he felt a wave of despair. He closed his eyes, remembering his first night in Tangier. Within minutes of strolling onto the palm-lined Corniche he'd been cajoled by two guides into buying his evening meal at an empty beach restaurant where they'd promised he could find cold beer. They'd plied him with fresh sardines, American beer and pipes of kif until well past midnight, then pretended to collect the bill from inside the bar before presenting him with a crudely scribbled note in Arabic demanding more money than he'd set aside for a week's accommodation. When he'd tried to reason with them they'd called the big, taciturn waiter to the table and the boy had understood, suddenly fearful, that all three of them were in on the scam. The most bewildering part of it though was that once he had paid, defeated and furious, the two guides had acted as if nothing untoward had happened. They'd insisted on escorting him back to his hotel, making friendly, broken conversation and the younger one had been completely at ease jostling at his shoulder, even showing off the creased scraps of paper, scrawled with names and addresses of various foreign girls, that he kept stuffed in a bulging nylon wallet. As they'd approached his hotel a café-owner, watching the late night stragglers along the Corniche from his doorway, had called a greeting in Arabic to the guides and the older hustler had answered in English, calling back over his shoulder with a barked laugh: ai, like a hambourger!

Afterwards, in his hotel bed, he'd lain awake, humiliated, for most of the airless night and every shout and commotion in the back street below his window seemed to be the raised, impatient voices of his guides, waiting for him to slot neatly between them again in the morning. He had learned his one word of Arabic that evening, at the older guide's insistence: Shukran. Thank you. Shukran.

Since then he'd used silence more or less successfully in navigating the streets and souks of each city. In Marrakech he'd even found a source of hash without having to deal with the local sellers: a ravaged, middle-aged Frenchman called Pierre who seemed to be living year-round all alone on the shared balcony of a cheap hostel.

Still, he thought, conscious again of Ibrahim stirring beside him and relighting his sebsi, what was happening now wasn't so much a hustle as a kind of bargaining. If he wanted, he could simply fix a small price for a hike in the mountains. It would be just a hundred dirham, maybe, for the whole afternoon – easily affordable and probably worthwhile, especially if he got to see the huts where they processed the local hash. Pierre had told him that in the huts, when they beat the resin out of the plants, you could get high for free by breathing the thick golden dust that hung in the air. Yawning again he fought the impulse to drop his head to his chest, sensing Ibrahim's watchful eyes on him.

Is it dangerous? he asked abruptly.

Alone, yes, of course. Alone, not permitted. But with me – not dangerous.

For a short while the boy considered the offer, but underneath his curiosity the prospect of Ibrahim's company all afternoon, of any company in fact, repulsed him. Just the effort of listening seemed to chafe at his brain. *Centougrade, August, of coorse, pourmitted. Like a hambourger,* he recalled again, and felt the sweat come fresh to his face and scalp. He waited grimly for the bitterness to pass, listening to his tormentor puffing patiently at his *kif*. Well, this Ibrahim could go with him into the mountains if he wanted. It wasn't his problem if he expected to be paid at the end of it. It would be useful to get fresh water at the spring, and if some local bum insisted on keeping him company – fine. They needn't speak to each other. He hadn't hired him and he wouldn't pay, even if he had to give him the slip somehow. It was a strangely satisfying thought in fact and a new liveliness, a feeling of strength and self-righteous resolve, lifted the boy to his feet.

A good rest, said the voice at his side, as if to praise him. Ibrahim rose also and began immediately to climb the slope ahead of him, quick and sure-footed. Come. See the chapel, he called back. Very old. Many visitors.

The boy followed him slowly, up through the trees and out into the glare of the hilltop.

The ruin was roofless and in the main cavity of the building the remains of its white stone walls seemed to magnify the sun's heat from all sides. It's like an oven in here, the boy said, more to himself than to Ibrahim. On his exposed forearms, pin-heads of white blisters were rising and prickling even as he watched, and when he rubbed them they flattened into smears of clear liquid.

Ohven, yes, said Ibrahim non-committally.

The boy looked around him. How old is this place?

Very old. Very old. First Mosque, centouries ago, then Spanish – *Católico* – then Mosque again, then ruin. See – the crosses. They are broken to make Mosque again. He pointed to one of the small, deep-set windows above their heads. It was clear that the arch had been bricked in at some point to form a cross, but at some later date again knocked through leaving just the extremities of the arms. Framed by the oddly shaped opening the hard, bright blue sky glittered like a gem.

The central tower of the Mosque was also ruined but its windows had not been blocked in; their shapely Muslim arches looked west towards the town, north and east to the tall, jagged Rif and south to the distant, hazy foothills of the Middle Atlas, rounded and blue-green. Without another word, Ibrahim disappeared inside the tower's crumbling narrow stairway. Emerging near the top he called the English boy up after him.

On the narrow balcony where the stairs opened out the boy took photographs of the town and the sharp grey horns of the Rif beyond, Ibrahim offering advice on the views and then, finally, pointing out the graveyard.

I walked up that way, the boy said.

Yes, said Ibrahim. Before, I stand here – he tapped the stone parapet in front of his stomach – and watch you walk there. Grinning, he made a walking motion with his fingers, then turned to climb back down the tower steps.

A qualm of distaste passed over the boy as he watched the narrow shoulders dropping from view. He imagined himself as he must have appeared from the vantage point of the tower, toiling up through the white stones and tussocks of grass like some tiny, noiseless insect. From the far-away white bricolage of the town the long, faint cry of the midday call to prayer drifted up to him. It carried to the chapel in unpredictable fragments, the stretched, sombre

➼

phrases arriving or failing depending on the faint breeze. For a while he enjoyed the last of his solitude, then picked his way carefully down through the tower.

They left the chapel in single file, following a narrow path that wound steeply up towards the broken slopes of the nearest peaks. Here and there, stands of thorn and cacti hid rasping crickets, their dry clamour rising up around the walkers like a protest as their feet crunched past. Soon, the boy was too parched and winded to speak even if he'd wanted to, and when Ibrahim stooped to gather up a handful of brittle herbs – good for the hort, he said earnestly, slapping his narrow chest – all the boy could do was nod, bow his head dutifully over the fistful of dusty stems and breathe in the pungent, eucalyptus scent. Very good for the hort, Ibrahim repeated before scattering what he'd gathered and once more clambering on ahead.

After an hour or so they reached a tree – the first of any size since the slopes beneath the chapel – perched incongruously on a narrow terrace of rubble. Ibrahim waited in its shade for the boy to join him, then pointed out the deepest patch of shadow for him to rest in. Obediently, stunned by the high sun and the steepness of the climb, the boy sank down on the spot. When he closed his eyes tightly, squeezing the burning sweat from them, liquid lights writhed behind the lids. He reached out for the rough trunk of the tree to keep his balance.

Cooler here, he heard Ibrahim murmur, as if from behind a barrier of some kind that muffled the words. Good shade. A little water now, yes?

He drank to the last inch of fluid in the bottle, then offered it to Ibrahim, who refused with a smile and a shake of his head. Closing his eyes again the boy finished the water off and then leaned back uncomfortably against the tree's rough bark, still gasping from the climb. Even in the shade the air felt scorched. Each ragged breath seemed to parch his body further, as if he were being stripped of moisture from within. How long had he been exposed to

this heat now? he wondered dazedly. It was at least four hours since he'd left his hostel and set off wandering through the quiet alleys and dead ends of the medina. He thought of the drinking fountains, their stone bowls painted white and powder blue, which he'd found from time to time on street corners and drunk greedily from. One of them had been jammed open and a gang of small children had been splashing and laughing in the cool mud around the overflow. Everything about the water – the noisy spatter of it onto the packed dirt of the street, its cool touch on his bare legs, its almost salty limestone flavour – tormented him now.

Ibrahim was moving about under the tree. There was a rustle of dry leaves, the scrunch of footsteps on scree and then a tap on his forearm. The boy opened his eyes.

Taste, said Ibrahim, offering him a green pod. Carob, he said.

The tough husk was bitter and seemed to parch his mouth even more. He grimaced and spat the fragment away.

Not ready, Ibrahim agreed. Very... he made a puckering motion with his fingers in front of his mouth.

Sour, the boy said curtly.

Yes – soor. He flung away a second pod and stared wordlessly down the big, rock-strewn valley they had climbed up from. Very high, he said at last.

The boy nodded. To the side of the path a dry gulley had followed their course all the way from the chapel, its floor filled with a long, winding column of close-packed, pink flowers. For the first time now the boy stared over at them, curious. They seemed to grow without moisture or soil, not just in the gulley at hand but in every distant scar and parched streambed as far as he could see on the many mountainsides round about them.

Wedding flowers, said Ibrahim, noticing his interest. He waved a hand towards the massed shrubs. When they first come, it is the season to marry.

Oh, said the boy absently. Under the fleshy blossoms the dark, straight stems stood stiff and fairly tall – at least throat high – and grew as dense as maize. They would be easy to hide amongst.

Ibrahim said something in Arabic, naming them properly, the boy guessed.

You have a wife? asked Ibrahim.

The boy laughed. God, no – I'm too young for that. I'm just a student. He tossed away the bitten carob pod. It bounced high off a rock, like rubber. You? he asked.

Yes, a wife. I have five sons.

Five! How old?

The oldest – ten and four.

Fourteen?

Yes. Fourteen. The oldest.

The English boy looked again at the flowers. Their dark leaves and pale blossoms seemed oddly solid in the brightness and heat, like china, or enamel. How much farther to the spring now?

Not far now. Not even one hour. Rest more, yes? Ibrahim advised, and began filling his sebsi. When it was lit he offered it to the boy.

No. Mouth too dry, he mumbled.

Ibrahim nodded. Water soon. There, he said – pointing out a sharp stone ridge high above them and to the north.

That's where it is?

The spring, yes.

This spring – it never dries up, yes? It always has water?

Yes, yes. Summer, winter. Under the rocks – always water. He pointed to the flowers lining the gulley again. For the flowers, in the hot summer – always water. God provides, he announced.

There was silence for a while. Ibrahim smoked one pipeful, then lit another.

You guide many people up here?

Many visitors, yes. This year, not so many. Spanish, French, South African – still many. American, English – not so many. He streamed smoke through his nostrils. George Boosh, he said, and shrugged. To me, all visitors welcome.

The boy laughed. But Americans and English not quite so welcome?

Ibrahim laughed in return. To me, Americans, English, all welcome. My English – not so good. But very welcome, still. To me – yes. Always – as-salam wa alaikum, peace be upon you. Christian, Muslim – as-salam wa alaikum. Welcome.

Well, I'm not anything, the boy said.

Yes, not anything, Ibrahim repeated cheerfully. All welcome. He shrugged. Many visitors, they ask me to hire mules for journeys in the mountains. A thousand dirham every day. Sometimes, gifts too. All welcome. Two South Africans, a man and a wife, they come many years for seven days and nights in the mountains. The man, always photographing. The wife, always – he mimed writing, scribbling a ghost pencil over his palm. Many gifts from them, he finished.

The boy nodded and fell silent again while Ibrahim smoked. The mention of money and gifts was vexing, but now as he rested it fed his determination to be alone and at peace again. He glanced across at Ibrahim. His round, stony, close-cropped head was turned away towards the gulley. Okay, I'm ready, he announced, and eased himself upright. A cooler breath of wind was stirring – he could feel it on his face when he stood up though it was too gentle to move the compact leaves of the carob tree. Now that he was on his feet he could see the Spanish chapel again, white and tiny, its square tower like a stick of sugar or salt in the distance below them. They'd climbed a hell of a way, he thought – much higher than the mountain had seemed from its foot. And they still had almost as far again to go.

Ah! said Ibrahim, also noticing the breeze. Grinning at the boy, he spread his arms wide to embrace it. Alhamdullillah, he said. Thank God, yes? When there is a gift from God: alhamdullillah.

Alhamdullillah, the boy repeated dully.

Ibrahim nodded approvingly, then turned and left the shelter of the tree. Come, he said.

The boy had no idea how long they had been climbing before Ibrahim next stopped and led him, almost reeling with dizziness, into a narrow strip of shade. Very close now, very close, he could hear Ibrahim saying, but his mouth, even the deep connections in his brain, felt too clumsy and numb to master any words

➡

of his own.

Gradually, after what felt like many minutes, he realised they must be in the shade of the ridge they'd been aiming for. The path was nothing more than a goat track now, littered here and there with their smooth, pebble-like droppings, and the gulley with its long river of flowers was just a stumble away to the left, its sides almost sheer and its bed shrunk to a narrow cutting, though still packed tight with the tall, stubborn, pink-headed stems that had lined their long climb. Ibrahim was smoking again, but peering anxiously at him as he puffed his *kif*. Very close now. Five minutes, then water, very cool, he urged.

The boy shook his head. Listen, can you fill the bottle and bring me back some water? I need to rest. No more sun. He dug the empty water bottle out of his satchel and handed it to Ibrahim. The spring – it's just along the path, yes? Easy to find?

Yes – very easy. I come here many times for water. Many times. Always water here.

Okay, said the boy thickly. That's good. He rested his head on his knees, hiding his face. Already he felt a little stronger at the thought of escape.

He listened until the sound of Ibrahim's footsteps faded completely, then stood and checked that he was out of sight. Not far ahead, the track curved sharply around a bulge in the ridge. Quickly, his heart pounding, he scrambled down from the path into the steep-sided gulley. Within minutes he was buried deep amongst the stiff-stemmed, waxy-leaved flowers, ducking to keep his head below the level of the blossoms. The going was noisy and difficult – his feet slithered and twisted on jagged stones and the stems gave way reluctantly – but he forced himself to climb through the undergrowth for another hundred yards or so before stopping breathlessly. If Ibrahim searched for him, he would probably assume he was heading back down the mountain, the boy guessed, and anyway, from the point he had worked up to he could, if he needed to and if he dared, stand straight and get an overview of the path. Weakly he settled himself on a burning slab of rock and waited.

The flowers provided much less shade than he had imagined – the spearing sun was still too high to be blocked by the stems and leaves – and he cupped his hands around the back of his head. There was no sweat on his palms, he realised then, a ripple of nausea sweeping through him; they burned like cinders on the back of his neck, but both neck and palms were completely dry. He frowned and tried to swallow, feeling his throat grip unpleasantly on nothing.

The first shout was a much longer time coming than the boy had anticipated and, confusingly, there seemed no urgency or anger in it. The long, wavering call was calm – almost mournful – and weirdly penetrating, though he could make nothing of the words. It was like the call to prayer, he thought hazily, and remembered the narrow balcony of the tower again – Ibrahim's lookout – the bleached town and graveyard spread out below, and himself, watched from above, floundering up the slope, each movement tiny and ridiculous in the shimmering heat. Time after time, more times than he could keep count of in his exhausted daze, the long, wailing call rang out, sometimes nearer, sometimes farther.

Then, abruptly, it stopped, and when he struggled to his feet, swaying, all feeling gone from his legs, there was no sign of Ibrahim anywhere on the path. He forced his way out of the undergrowth with far more difficulty than he had entered, his head swimming now as he stumbled on the rocks underfoot, stiff leaves cutting across his lifted hands and flushed face. The final effort to clamber the steepest few yards back onto the track was beyond him at the first attempt, and as he slid helplessly backwards into the gulley he felt the first glimmerings of real horror at his vanished strength and coordination. It took a great effort of will not to call fearfully down the mountain after Ibrahim, and only the knowledge that the spring must be very close now persuaded him to rest on his knees, silently and re-gather his energy instead.

Working more slowly and attacking the slope at an angle, he finally made the shade of the path, panting, almost sobbing with weakness and thirst. He would have to rest again, he realized, no matter how parched he was, and he slumped against the jagged wall of the ridge. When he closed his eyes he had the sensation of a giant oval pupil opening wetly at the back of his head, dilating and contracting with the rhythm of his pulse, black and glossy, and cool maybe, if he could just fall back a little, slip backwards into it, away from the pounding heat. If he opened his eyes, the ranks of flowers he had come from seemed to ripple and sway, though there was no wind to move them. They snaked away like a carpet of upturned faces, flat and naked to the sun.

Two days passed before Ibrahim was able to find more business at the chapel. A friendly, talkative young Dutch couple asked if they could hire him, very much wanting to see the view from the mountains and then to visit the cannabis farms. He had to speak English with them, which was tiring, but the girl spoke a little French, too, and even claimed to be learning Arabic. She had fallen in love with Chefchouen already, she said. She would like to learn Arabic and buy property there. It would be very cheap compared to Holland. Did the mountains around the town have names? she wanted to know.

Both the boy and girl had long, matted blond hair and they were dressed almost identically in loose cotton trousers and linen blouses. They held hands even in the worst of the heat, kissing and touching without embarrassment whenever they rested in the shade. When they were not whispering or caressing one another they were happy to share Ibrahim's kif, though the boy had a sebsi of his own which he passed sometimes to the girl. They could be twins, Ibrahim thought, watching them sidelong, amused and a little uncomfortable.

They found the body just beyond the tiny spring where they had stopped to rest and drink. For a moment Ibrahim was simply startled and angry at the thought of some other guide bringing tourists to his spring; then he saw the boy's spoiled face and understood. He heard a loud, wordless shout, and realised it

had come from his own mouth. Behind him, the girl too seemed to recognise suddenly what she was looking at and shrieked once, sharply. The English boy had come looking for the water and missed it, Ibrahim guessed at once, perhaps passing it again and again, not realizing that it was nothing more than a palm-sized, shallow pool hidden in the shadow of a flat rock. There was no running stream to give it away.

The boy's scorched forehead was open where he had collapsed onto a sharp stone and the blood had encouraged mountain dogs to take the eyes, ears and lips. A dark line of large, glossy ants was streaming in and out over the exposed white teeth. The ants were quick and purposeful, but here and there they reared up and wrestled where they collided, their long black forelegs rising and waving. They seemed like moving symbols when they stopped and jostled, as if a line of script had come evilly to life. Ibrahim suddenly recalled listening as a child to his grandfather's stories of the ruthless jinns of the mountains and a swelling panic began to knock his heart against his ribs. The ants could be the language of the jinn, he thought, and had to look away for a long moment before he could reassure himself that it was only the kif in his head making a child of him. The girl was at his side now, stooping and shaking one of the boy's stiff bare legs as if to try and wake him, moaning and babbling something – the same few words in her own unpleasant language – repeated over and over. Finally, the boyfriend took her free arm and pulled her roughly away.

Ibrahim was careful not to show any sign that he recognised the body, and he made sure that the Dutch couple, when they were calm enough to walk again, stayed with him to confirm his story when he reported to the authorities in the new quarter.

The police captain interviewed all three of them together, took written statements from the boy and girl and then interrogated Ibrahim alone. When they finally released him after the body had been examined on the mountain and a report radioed in, it was

➤➤

dark. The Dutch couple were gone and when he asked the guards on duty at the station door they laughed out loud and denied that either of the young foreigners had left the money they had agreed to pay him. What about the girl? Ibrahim insisted. Are you certain she left nothing? Not even an address? A message? They laughed again, insulted him, and pushed him out into the night.

He felt nothing more than annoyance at being cheated of his fee by the empty-headed Dutch boy, but walking towards his cousin's house at the foot of the medina where he planned to smoke and tell his story and sleep off the disastrous day, he felt strangely bitter towards the girl who had seemed friendly and had known a little Arabic and had asked him questions all the way up the mountain. It was foolish; an over-reaction, he knew. Allah provides. But still, he felt bitter. He would tell his cousin about the girl and about the ants, too. It had been like a dream. Why were they still in his mind, troubling him? He had the feeling that if he could speak about them it would be like brushing them away.

Wayne Price's debut story collection *Furnace* will be published by Freight Books in 2012

# Hello! Hello!

An extract from the novel *Bring Me the Head of Ryan Giggs*

Rodge Glass

IT'S THE 21ST of November 1992 and at this precise second in history all in the world of Marky Wilson feels good, well, happy. You're an up-and-coming United SUPERSTAR in the making, about to make your first dramatic impact on the field of play. In the film of your life this is the beginning of that crucial Second Act: the mood of the piece is dark and mean, it's a typical, rainy, miserable English day, and the action starts – bam! – right in the middle of a league game. First, there's a close-up of you sitting on the bench, waiting. Then a close-up of the Gaffer's face. He's chewing gum, fast. So fast he looks like he might just chew his jaw right off. Then there's another close-up, this time of Ryan Giggs, the team's fresh young inspiration, winner of last year's Young Player of the Year Award and already favourite to retain it. (But not if you've got anything to do with it, right?) Ryan's running down the wing like his life depends on reaching the touchline and putting in the perfect cross. The camera cuts from his face to his feet – nimble, quick, and so speedy his legs are just a blur, scissoring back and forward like a ballerina on a grassy green stage.

Here's the situation as the camera zooms out from Ryan's boots to the action on the pitch: Manchester United, fallen giants, title-less for 25 years, struggling in mid-table mediocrity and already out of Europe, need a win (or perhaps some inspiration from a certain local lad?) You're in the match day squad for the first time. So far, you've been sitting there all quiet, hands deep in oversized jacket pockets. Brain buzzing. Hands shaking. Toes numb. Things

must be happening – you've heard cheers go up behind you, big guttural roars of excitement, encouragement or insult – but you're not really following the game. All that matters is if you're gonna be part of it. If, after seventeen years five months and twenty eight days of being a man-in-waiting, a pretend-human-being, if after all those years of pointless meaningless NOTHING existence, you're FINALLY gonna GET ON THAT FUCKIN PITCH AND PLAY.

And then it happens. The REAL beginning of your life.

With a twitch of his head and a wave in the direction of the battlefield, the Gaffer tells you to warm up. *O fuck,* you think, *O fuck O fuck O fuck fuck fuck.* You're so nervous you can hardly run straight. You feel drunk. Maybe you are. You focus on the white paint down below and try to block everything else out, but it's shit-your-pants exciting, this moment. Life-flashing-before-your-eyes stuff: your tiny football-obsessed mind pulses with memories, in burst after dazzling burst, of everything that's ever meant anything: *first kick in the garden – in the playground – first goal for the school team – first time watching United – moving to a better team – moving to an even BETTER team – getting noticed by the scouts – Fergie at the front door – the world changing and twisting – through the gates at Old Trafford – work work work – hope – more work – more hope – wait wait waitwaitwait and now READY.*

Your new best mate Nicky Butt is ready

➡

too, looking up at you each time you cross as you warm up, stretch, sprint. That bright look in his eyes meaning *Hey it'll be us soon! Fuckin hell! We're gonna be real United players!* And he's right: nobody's gonna take it from you. You take every bad thought you've ever had and imagine yourself screwing it up into a tight ball and kicking it into the stands. Way up into Row Z. Out of sight. You try not to think about the last week at all. The note on the fridge: 'DEAR WORLD: I'M LEAVING YOU BECAUSE I'M BORED' The police round till all hours, asking endless questions with no answers as Mum paced the kitchen, offering to make more tea for the pigs every five minutes, then forgetting she'd done it, then asking again. *What do you think it means? Do you think this might be a suicide note? Son, do you think your Dad might have done something stupid?* You won't let yourself think about all that. Why would you? On today of all fuckin days! This moment he's prepared you for your whole life! You clench your fists tight, then unclench them. Up in the stand, you imagine Guy putting an arm around your Mum and whispering in her ear: *Aren't you proud of our boy?*

Butty gets his debut first (with a cheeky look your way and a wink as he goes on – you're basically blood brothers now), then a few minutes later your time comes. You get the call to go over the top. Saddle up and ride. Put on your armour, strap on those shin pads and come join the war *against the mighty Oldham Athletic*: not historically a *major* foe, but not one you're about to underestimate either. Not after all this time. You're shaking, standing there waiting for the board to go up with your number on it. (HA! YOUR NUMBER!) Right there you want to just say SCREW IT ALL and KISS THE GAFFER RIGHT ON HIS RUBY RED LIPS to say THANK YOU for picking you up out of the Salford dustbin, taking you far from the sad fucked up madness at home and making you a real person, in PARADISE. From now on, you'll be away mostly. On the move, with the team. This is the start of it all. The banter. The practical jokes and nicknames. Buddying up in bunks. Hotels, planes, buses, press conferences and interviews. Sitting in

comfy chairs in front of all those cameras saying things like: *We're just taking one game at a time... the three points was all that mattered today.* And the best thing is, it'll all happen away from home. But apparently your debut isn't a big moment for Alex Ferguson. It isn't the big speech you've been imagining. There's no great inspirational touchline talk. No real instruction or Churchillian call to arms. He just says, *That's you, son. Five minutes left, on the wing. See what ye can do.* Then you're nearly, very nearly, ON. A Manchester United player at last. Like Bobby Charlton. Like Bryan Robson. Like Ryan bloody Giggs. As your mouth is saying, *Yes Boss,* your brain is thinking: *If I piss myself in these shorts, will it be obvious on Match of the Day?*

It's mental, the way the mind works: you remember everything about that moment, the complete scene, right down to the details, like you're Mum's all-seeing all-dancing God looking down on the pitch from his great seat in the sky, not a scared young lad standing on the touchline.

- *Weather: light rain, slight Easterly wind*
- *Temperature: bloody freezing*
- *State of Pitch: muddy as fuck*
- *Footwear: brand new boots, not yet broken in*
- *Underwear: lucky boxer shorts (happy Red Devils holding pitchforks) and*
- *Overwear: a shirt too big for you. Number 14. Tucked in.*

(*That morning you looked at yourself in the bathroom mirror, and even though you felt like a twat, you actually said out loud: YOU WON'T BE A SUB FOR LONG, MARKY!*)

You know the whole United team for the day as well, off by heart. You know the names of the opposition. A statto's always a statto, on the pitch or on the couch, right? You'll never forget any of these things you notice as you step over that white line onto sacred ground. They're gonna be the first notes in the scrapbook, after all. The *senior* one. (So far there's one from school and three jam-packed Youth Career Commemorative Books which Mum keeps by the trophy cabinet in the front room, easy access for whenever she wants to show you off to visitors.) United have already won this particular battle by the time you put toe to turf – that's why they've brought you on. Coz it's 3-0, the game's nearly over, and nothing's at stake. One of your old poster heroes, Choccie McClair (who's already scored twice and is being rested) jogs off the pitch and slaps your hand with his, without saying anything. The Gaffer barks an order, moving Ryan up front. You think to yourself, *Good time to make a cameo.* You think to yourself: *Where the fuck is Dad?* And then you start running like hell.

For the first minute you're on the pitch Oldham are looking for a consolation goal. They have a corner, and you try to impress the gaffer by defending instead of hanging around up field. So you hover at the edge of the area, wishing the ball towards you, wishing, wishing, then watching as it fizzes past your ears. Everything happens so fast you can't clear your head and THINK. The ball flashes into the box then right out again, getting punched away for a corner on the other side. Then, the opposite: everything's in slow-motion now.

They seem to take forever to put it back into play, these Oldham lads.

What are they waiting for?

Don't they know how important this is?

When the ball finally gets flighted in, you hover and wish again, just for a touch.

For the first time in your life, you talk to God (Sir Matt Busby).

You ask him for a favour.

He answers instantly.

This time the keeper catches it, rolls it out of the United box and after a few passes side to side in defence the ball gets threaded through to Ryan Giggs out on the left side of the pitch. Along with thousands in the stands you shout out his name, then your own, then leg it as fast as you can. All the time shouting your names. *Ryan! Marky's ball! Ryan! Marky's ball! Pass it! Pass it! Over the top!* You're behind the chasing defender but put your head down and pump your legs, so hard and high that you pass him, easy. Everyone in the crowd can see how much it means to the new local lad, and

they're bound to remember you for the next game. Halo glowing, boots sparkling, Saint Ryan attempts a lob – it should be beautiful, exquisite, gorgeous, just right – but he's only a human being so even he makes mistakes, and he gets the pace of the pass all wrong. People in the stands groan, yell, roar advice. The ball bounces once, twice, three four times. Bobbling nowhere, slow. About to go out for a goal kick at the other end of the field. But you know that whatever happens you're gonna get to that fuckin piece of air and leather before the Centre Back shepherds it out of touch.

And you do. You sneak in and steal the ball from between his legs, turn and trap it, ready to look up and head for goal. Just like you did for the Rezzies. (You're already seeing the screamer you're gonna score and considering celebration options. A tribute to the Gaffer? A novelty dance? A serious pout, hands on hips, to show YOU HAVE ARRIVED?) At that split second in time, thousands of people have their eyes watching you. Cameras record you, and if something happens they'll magic you into the homes of millions more on *Match of the Day* tonight. This is your chance. And what if you don't get another? So when the defender whips the ball away from you and turns to take it away, you chase. You chase because you don't want everyone to see what you are: a boy among men. In your head the challenge is perfect – you slide in dramatically and take it away from him, safely, skilfully, as the crowd start up into wild applause.

But it isn't perfect at all. It's the opposite of perfect. You break the defender's right leg with a clumsy flying two-footed challenge from behind, and break one of your own too. The heavy bastard crashes down on top of your left knee and lets out a quiet cry, like a baby, as the high-pitched SNAP of your bone sounds like a tiny twig coming apart. As you hear that sound, Sir Matt hits the pause button on time, and that sound reminds you of one autumn day, years back, maybe ten years, when Dad took you and Guy walking in the local park. A rare thing. A one-off. The three of you, racing each other through the forest, seeing who could make it to the gate first, hearing lots of little SNAP sounds

→

going off like fireworks beneath your feet, embedded deep in clusters of crackling leaves. You wonder if, wherever he is, Dad has heard that SNAP and thought of the same thing.

Back on the pitch, in the match, even the referee is stunned.

Seconds pass.

More seconds.

And more.

Still dazed, he looks down at you for what seems like forever before he reaches into his pocket, draws out a red card and holds it up. You look away to avoid seeing it and ball up in agony, next to the defender, who does the same. The stretcher comes to take you both off. No applause. Not even any boos. The crowd are in shock, people checking with each other: *What happened? He did WHAT? Who IS that kid anyway?* Your debut lasts exactly one hundred and thirty three seconds, from the moment you see Guy and your Mum clapping and crying in the old family seats and tag with Brian McClair, to the moment you're back off the pitch asking the physio what's happened and wailing about how you can't feel your foot.

Later on, a nurse asks you if that's a record. If it is, you don't want it. You're hoping that somewhere in a land far away, an alternate universe maybe, there's another match going on against Oldham Athletic, at that exact time. Maybe some *other* dickhead is making his Manchester United debut, lasting a hundred and thirty *two* seconds before making his poor long-suffering kind supportive good soft sensitive Mum WHO DESERVES NO MORE PAIN IN THIS LIFE OR THE NEXT leak tears and tears and tears onto her cheeks, that will probably carry on for all time and spread, flooding the pitch, the whole stadium, all Manchester. Maybe if it was all happening to someone else as well, the sensation of sharing would make all this feel that little bit better. Maybe not.

And your big moment? On *Match of the Day* they run a feature about the worst debuts ever. Meanwhile, the Gaffer shocks the entire world of sport (and probably a few in other worlds too) by admitting that one of his own players has ACTUALLY MADE A MISTAKE.

He says to the interviewer, *It's not like the lad. Madness, pure madness, that's what it was. I'll be speaking to him, there's no question aboot that, but for now our thoughts should be with the boy Tredwell and his family. I know I speak for everyone at Manchester United when I say we all hope he gets better soon. Awful, so it is. Just awful.* The boys in the box love it. They can't get enough. They smell blood, drool, ATTACK. But if there's one thing worse than that lot, it's the press – so you know what's coming. Loads of stories about famous nightmare debuts in the history of the game (own goals, gaffes, goalkeeping errors), every last one with pictures of Muggins Wilson right there in the centre of it all, being carried off next to the man he nearly murdered.

YOU nearly murdered.

When Mum comes to visit you in hospital the following morning, she's carrying her usual paper under her arm. And yes, the back page is a close-up of the guilty party. You're staring out at yourself in horror (at the pain or at something else?) The first thing Mum says is: *I wish your father was here. He'd know what to do. Gregory was always good in a crisis.* Talking like the fat bastard is dead already. As it happens, you're pretty sure your Dad would be useless in this situation. Forcing yourself to sit up in bed, you feel your leg throbbing, making you dizzy, like maybe that delicate head of yours is gonna fall off. You wonder, quietly, if Danny Tredwell's Mum reads the same paper as yours. Then you consider sending flowers to Mrs Tredwell. You reject that idea. Then you remember who passed you the ball.

A month later everyone else on planet earth has forgotten that pass except you – according to the TV there's *no stopping the Welsh boy wonder* after he scores a screamer against City in December 92, the year the brave new world begins. Year One of the Premiership.

But you aren't going to forget that easy.

Are you?

*Bring Me the Head of Ryan Giggs* will be published by Tindal Street Press in April 2012

tindalstreet.co.uk

# The Minotaur of Pollokshields
R W Mosses

AH HEARD IT out the back of the close, stampin and snortin. It musta thought the gardens at the back ay the tenements was a maze. Ah widnae a minded but ah needed to put the bin out.

Ah crept down the stairs, ma slippers scuffin on the stone, ma heart speedin, until ah could peek round at the back door. Ah couldnae see it, but ah heard it clatterin about. Ah got to the door, sleekit like.

It towered up against the sky, a shadow in the dark. Its horns curved around the moon. It smelt me and turned its red eyes on me.

Ah jumped back inside and ran back up the stairs. The binbag in my claw, batterin my legs, tins clankin. Ah got back to ma door, ma breath behind me. It didnae follow me in, but ah didnae feel safe. Ah couldnae go back in though as I still had the bin to put out.

Ah stood shiverin in the close outside the door until ma Ma came out and asked me what was ah doin still standin there, ma tea was gettin cold. Ah telt her there was a Minotaur down by the binsheds. She telt me to stop talkin rubbish and get back in fur ma tea. Ah left the bin bag by the door. Ah promised to take it down later. Ah forgot all about it after the fitba came on the telly.

The bag was still there when ah left for school. Ah wanted to hurry down with it before ma Ma noticed ah'd no done it. Ah peeked out the back, all the grass was turned to mud, marked deep by hooves.

It was a long way to the bins. Open. Full of fences, broken walls, jaggy nettles and tall grass.

Nothin happened when ah stepped out. Ah walked a wee way along the path, keepin low. Nothin happened. Ah reckoned ah could make it back from there if ah needed to.

Ah went on, so close to the bins now there was nae way back. Ah kept lookin round, tense, expectant. Ah felt like a soldier, about to be ambushed. Ah threw the bag on top of the big stinkin pile and ran back. It could be hidin anywhere.

Ah stopped runnin when ma breath ran out, halfway to school. Sunil waved to me, his bag slung low on his back. Ah walked over.

You wudnae believe what ah saw last night, ah telt him. He didn't. Come round after school, you'll see, ah said.

News got out. Ah got the piss taken out of me all day. Ah was used to it, but ah liked Sunil. Ah thought we were friends. He telt me it wasnae him, that someone heard me telling him. But ah don't remember anybody else bein close by.

Still, by home time there was at least ten ay us all marchin down to ma bit tae see the proof of the Minotaur of Pollokshields.

The closer we got to ma house, the more nervous ah got. What if ah was wrong? What if the footprints had all gone? Ah'd have the piss taken forever.

We all trooped through the close and out the back. Mr Woods rapped on the window and telt us to bugger off or keep the noise down. We laughed at him, but ah had hoped he'd chase us off.

The mud was still ground down, hoof

marks everywhere. Bobby even found some black hair in the grass. Ah'd gone from an eejit to a hero.

Ma called down to see what all the fuss was about. There's nae usually so many kids in our back close and ah think she was worried ah was getting trailed again. She telt me to get in and do ma homework. Ah telt her we was looking for the Minotaur and ah'd be in in a minute. Ah still got laughed at.

A few weeks later it was getting lighter at night and ah liked watchin the bats swoop through the back garden. Ah heard it snuffling and stompin behind the bins. Ah thought about runnin in, but ah wanted to see it properly. So ah crept over, hidin in the grass.

Ah didnae know where to look. It was nekkid. Bits dangling, like mine, a man's body and arms. Its head was a bull, thick red furred shoulders, two massive curving horns, and its legs turned to hooves. It must have been freezin. It was tryin to eat. Bent over awkward while its mouth chewed at grass or somethin spilled from a bin bag. A short stick was comin out of its side where the man skin was purple around it. Ah didnae see blood, there shouldae been loads.

Ah got closer, as it gave up eatin and collapsed heavily. It moved until its back was up against the brick wall around the bins. The smell was sweet and sour at the same time. It stayed in the back ay ma nose. It made me boak. The bin men hadnae been yet, but this was way worse. The heavy head slumped forward, the horns nearly scrapin the dirt. Its breath still steamed, but came in short random spaces.

Ah didnae know what to do. It had never hurt me, but ah was still scared. It was hurtin, but ah knew nothing that could help. Ah came a wee bit closer and it opened an eye. It tried to struggle up, but slipped in its own mess and gave up tryin.

It started to get cold and ah needed to go in, but ah didnae think it was right to leave it. We just sat watching each other as the light disappeared. Then ma Ma called out the window for me to go in.

# GAP
## Ewan Morrison

THIS TIME IT'S for real. No more exercises or excuses, lads. This time it's a life-challenge. Are we going to do it in a pub, in a nightclub? Nah, that's the loser's way. You're going out there to the mall in broad daylight, and I'm giving you one hour to get an N-close. Not a K-close, which means kiss by the way, or an F-close, which I'll leave to your imagination gents, but a number. You gotta close the deal with a real girl's phone number, over the road in SilverDale. I picked up most of my top three hundred chicks in malls, dunno why, but it's a fact. So, I want you to form pairs again, cos picking-up is sixty-five percent easier in twos. Right then, no time for losers cos we are the champions, right lads? It's just across the car park, under the flyover. Remember the Ten rules – get out of your comfort zone – A ninety-nine percent failure rate with a hundred girls-a-week is still one brand new lay every seven days – warm up with some ugly birds to get the confidence up before going for that ten-girl. It's all about numbers gents. OK, see you on the ground floor between Gap and La Senza, one o'clock. The guy that scores highest wins a pass to the Platinum Plus Workshop in Los Angeles, December. May the best man win!

Dave stays seated as the others surge out of the conference suite. My God, this place, these people. This is so not Dave.

A hand on his shoulder. It's Raj, the six-footed acne-faced business start-up guy from Milton Keynes who, at the Who-We-Were-session, before the coffee break, talked at great speed about how this Neuro-linguistic-programming life coach saved his life by curing his stutter. Dave thinks Raj has probably never had a girlfriend or maybe even sex and it's a bit weird that he should go from being a virgin to a pick-up artist, by-passing what normal people do, but Dave kind of likes Raj, because although he hasn't got a stutter anymore, something even stranger has replaced it. Raj takes a deep breath before he starts and his face is usually blue by the time he's finished.

You-alright-mate-you-look-knackd-gotta-get-pumped-up-man-face-the-day-man-you-ready-gotta-get-over-approach-anxiety-man-you-know-what-I-mean-we-gonna-win-ready? Dave looks up at Raj's gasping face; it is maybe that and Raj's extended hand and the foresight that Raj may turn suicidal if Dave doesn't help him, which makes Dave rise from his seat to the challenge.

You're probably wondering what the hell a nice quiet guy like Dave is doing on a Pick-Up-Artists weekend boot camp with twenty sharp-dressed single men, run by a man who has re-named himself after a type of weapon, looks like Brad Pitt's bodyguard and is 'bestselling author' of 'PPP' (Pussy Pulling Power) and 'FFF' (Find Fuck Forget) – well so does Dave. Dave is not what you'd call an ambitious or sexually active person, in fact I don't think he's had a girl since Sally in 1993; he prefers to sit at home and collect old blues records from the 1930s and to walk dogs for house-bound geriatrics. Personally, I think he's got this kind of hidden genius, but most folk think that in the soccer-game-of-life he's the kid that always gets put in goals.

How it started? Well, it was Dave's thirty-third birthday and all us Facebook buddies got together and asked some fundamental questions like: is Dave seriously going to be alone forever? I feel kind of bad about it but about thirty of us chipped in and paid the six hundred quid – his mum even gave us fifty. She's wild, her name's Tricia, but she calls herself Tree; she was a wild child in the 60s and fried her brains. She wants Dave out of the house, because that's where he's still living. A guy your age, she says; you should be out there, up to your neck in pussy.

I dunno, said Dave. Saying I dunno is just so Dave. Cos when he doesn't know he admits it, cos he's got a thing about truth. I think it's admirable, but it's probably why he used to get called *Rain Man* at school.

Anyway, it started as a kind of joke but Dave didn't want to let his mates down, plus it cost a lot and Dave worries about money, probably cos he's the only person who's been a Barista for over twelve years, and we're talking, by choice. I mean you got to look at the irony of the words, like Baristas and Barristers – and more than a few of us are in law now, and Dave – well, personally, I put his stunning lack of ambition on all fronts down to Starbucks. They have this weird flexi-working rota thing that means you have to be on call practically all week even if you're part time, we're talking like eighty hours on call to get thirty-two. Go do the math. So you can't really plan anything social or hold down another job or study, and dating is kind of tricky too. Dave doesn't complain, it's not like he even wants promotion or a date, he's just happy serving coffee, drinking coffee, he even hangs out there when he's not working. In fact coffee, it's probably his chief passion in life, he probably drinks about twenty cups a day. Maybe that's another reason, actually, why he accepts the challenge, cos he's thinking there must be a Starbucks in the mall and he could get a Frappe or a grande cappuccino, cos the craving has started.

Raj and Dave are standing outside GAP and it's been fifteen nervous minutes since Stealth left

them alone with their POA, or Plan Of Attack. They have to stop random females in their tracks and 'force an opening' and 'split-up the set'; they are to 'isolate' one girl and 'accelerate' using the chat techniques and Kino, which as I might have said before is nothing to do with cinema and means touch. I know, the lingo is kind of hard to get. Lingo is so not Dave.

Don't worry if you can't think of anything to say to the chicks, Stealth smiled – Use one of the 'canned openers' I taught you, if you can't remember them, they're in the info-pack. Then he turned away swiftly leaving Dave with this unusual visual image of trying to undo a woman's head with a mechanism designed for tins of beans.

There were three canned openers from the second morning session and Dave remembered them almost word for word, due to their high absurdity quota. The first went something like this:

'Hi girls, I'm looking for my friend, have you seen him?' As Stealth explained, this makes women ask, 'What does your friend look like?' At which point you get the 'hook' in and make 'the joke'. You lean down to your ankle and say, 'he's about this size and has red hair.' This technique is called 'the squirrel' – for some reason Dave cannot fathom, there are supposed to be squirrels in shopping malls.

Then there was this one that baffled Dave.

'Hey girls, my mate gave me two hundred pounds to buy a birthday present for his girlfriend cos he's stuck at work. Any ideas on what she might like?' According to Stealth this was ideal because it showed that you have both money and friends, and there's nothing chicks distrust more than guys with no friends and no money. Stealth's lack of irony in saying such things made Dave's left shoulder twitch involuntarily (which is another thing he does that is 'just so Dave').

At least a hundred girls have walked past with their shopping bags and extremely intimidating push-up bras since they started and Raj is getting quite frothy around the mouth. You-gotta-believe-in-yerself-gotta-think-out-of-the-box-man-you-gonna-go-first? Eh?-eh? You-go-first-eh?

Well, I dunno, shrugs Dave.

Got-to-fight-it-man-approach-anxiety-man-it's-a-killer-gotta-just-jump-in-I'm-just-warming-up-here-man-I'm-gonna-do-it-I'm-gonna-do-it-it's-only-chicks-man-don't-fear-rejection-man.

Dave stares out over the forecourt: The Hugh Grant look-alike guy and the cop-looking-guy from the workshop are chatting with a group of four girls, each one with a different hair colour, like the *Spice Girls* or *Girls Aloud*. Hugh Grant is pointing to one of the girl's shoes, he's touching her arm. There was this thing Stealth had shown some of the other guys, before, some dance move. Hugh Grant is twirling a girl in his arms, now. Jesus.

Further down the court Dave can see the short bald man and the skinny guy stopping three young Latina-looking girls. One of them shrugs away from the outreaching hand of baldy, then all three move swiftly away, laughing. Over by the pillars, outside GAP, Stealth is standing, judging all, arms crossed over his steroid chest. He makes these big arm movements as if to usher Dave forward; mouthing big slo-mo words like GO-FOR-IT. BREAK-UP-THE-SET. Raj taps his shoulder, nods to an approaching set.

Quick-the-canned-openers-man-we-need-the-canned-opener-give-em-the-lines-stop-em-isolate-ask-em-about-themselves-keep-em-there-accelerate.

It's pointless, Dave thinks, it's the same Latinas that ran laughing from baldy man. Didn't Raj even notice?

Now! Raj, shouts, make-a-move-make-a-date-no-no-I-mean-get-an-Nclose-yeah-an-Nclose-wow-she's-a-seven-an-eight.

They do this, they rate women – it's like that self-monitoring performance form Dave has to fill in every month at work. He only ever gives himself a six.

I dunno, Dave says. But it's too late, Raj has leapt forward.

Hi-girls-I've-got-this-girlfrend-nah-nah-I-mean-my-mate's-got-this-girlfriend-and-she's-got-this-phone-ah-I-mean-she's-got-this-birthday-and-I've-got-two-hundred-pounds-and...

Their faces – as if accosted by a leper. Raj accelerating, getting louder, all the words in a glue. We-need-yer-help-yeah-yeah-that's-right-cos-I've-got-this-text-she's-gave-him-this-text-for-his-birthday-and

Dave has to do something, Hi, we're looking for our friend, have you...

The girl laughing, the tallest, in the purple top, speaks in this Latina-way that Dave finds rather lovely.

We have already... your friends, over there, they ees looking for friend also. Ees thees market research? She points over to baldy man.

From the corner of Dave's eye he can see Stealth gesticulating vigorously to keep on, intercept, chat, Kino, Kino! Raj is starting, it seems, to stutter and the girls are wanting to move on.

Sorry, Dave says, actually we don't have a friend. In fact we're just doing this because we need to get one, like a girl, I mean two, one each, maybe... or something.

This is so Dave.

You want me to be girlfriend? And this sends the girl's friends into hysterics. She is speaking to them now in Spanish.

Dave shrugs, he went to Madrid once with Sally Carter; Sally had a couple of secret addiction issues and that's maybe why Dave turned out so square, but that's a story he'd rather I didn't repeat.

Raj is giving him frantic facial indicators, much like Stealth's.

Sorry, Dave blurts out, My friends made me do this cos I haven't had a girlfriend in thirteen years. I dunno.

Thirteen years? The tall girl laughs, No sex?

He shrugs, nods. I dunno. She strokes his cheek.

You are joker with me, you are funny man!

Raj is nodding for him to move to Kino, she's touched his face, it's fair game. But Dave can't think of anything to say. Jeeso, he could really do with that coffee, straight Americano, three sugars.

Bye-see-bye, the tall girl says, we have to go for shoppings now, see you, bye, you are very

➵

cute, these ees wonderful country, I hope you have sexy times soon, ees very best, Adios.

And they run off in hysterics.

Hey, that was nice, Dave says to Raj.

Nah-man-we-got-to-get-their-number-the-N-close-man-you-was-close! I-was-shit-I-froze-man-fuckin-approach-anxiety-man-I-was-shit-you-got-style-you-was-good-you-believe-in-yourself-man-you-got-what-it-takes-man-you-were-that-close-to-an-Nclose-what's-yer-secret-man?

I dunno, Dave says, how about we break for a coffee to celebrate, and maybe a choco muffin? My treat.

JESUS! It's Stealth shouting, he's run over, hands on both their shoulders – That was fantastic, gents! You held them, you accelerated, you almost had Kino dude. Stealth is slapping him on the back. Dave isn't into back-slapping.

Look lads, I don't know what you've got going here, the geek thing, yeah some girls are into that, good cop – bad cop, the sensitive types, I dunno, but you've got to escalate to Kino, no point telling you, look...

He leads Dave to one side, by the doorway of GAP.

What's that on your shoe? Stealth says to him.

Dave is perplexed, chewing gum, dog-shit? He stands on one leg to look at the sole, just then, off balance, Stealth offers his hand to support him and Dave takes it. In a flash, Stealth has locked Dave's hand, twisted it over his head. Dave flashes back to many humiliations in high school, but this is not that, Stealth is not going to force him to kiss feet, to eat dirt. No, Stealth spins him round, once twice in his arms, as if in a tango. Stealth takes his waist, and sets him back on his feet.

Didn't expect that did ya? And Dave cannot reply.

Kino, Stealth says, Adrenaline, did you feel that? I'm talking about setting off subliminal trust triggers in a woman in seconds. I'm talking about accelerated intimacy that it'd take a bloke in a pub three hours and three rounds of drinks for her to even get close to. This is primordial, this is cave man stuff, you get a woman's adrenalin going, she'll feel it in her dark wet cave.

Raj stands, dumfounded, almost applauding, his enthusiasm growing inversely to Dave's embarrassment as shoppers pass.

Once you've hooked them, pull the shoe trick, or one of the hand tricks from earlier. You think you could pull off that move, Dave?

I dunno, says Dave.

Stealth backs off. Hey, Dude, you want out, go join the masses, be a loser for the rest of your life. You want to go?

Dave is about to say – Sounds fine to me. He's thinking that Americano with three sugars would be the answer to just about everything. Then he sees Raj's face, Raj's future – once he's abandoned him, back in the conference suite with nineteen strangers, an odd number and no partner; Raj will be paired up with Stealth, jabbering his way through the rest of the day's exercises and the final nightmare night-game test, as outlined in the info-pack: the exclusive, high end nightclub where 'real models' hang out, where, rumour has it, Beyoncé was once seen. He has this image of Raj, drunk on the dance floor, trousers round his ankles, doing the only move he knows.

I'm cool, says Dave, I'm going nowhere.

Excellent, so what's your strategy? Says Stealth. You got twenty mins, max, before we head back to compare scores. What you gonna do?

Get-an-N-close, Raj shouts.

We're gonna... Dave forces himself to say it... get an N-close.

But do you believe it, do you believe in yourself?

Raj's face says he'd like to have a self, one day, whatever they are.

Sure, Dave says.

Stealth puts his hand in the air. Hi-five! Raj hi-fives him. Dave puts his hand up and it stings when Stealth hits, hard, deliberately.

Great-man-fab-man-tastic Raj shouts to Dave, all fired up on Neuro Linguistic Programming. We're-gonna-do-it-man-gonna-throw-away-the-script-man-no-canned-openers-man-just-gonna-do-it-yeah!

OK, just for Raj, Dave tells himself. He scans the mall for girls and his eyes come to rest on two with baby buggies – they're all wrong, in many ways: the shell-suits, the babies most of all. He gets wondering if girls that young, that poor, ever had any romance, then he gets thinking that romance is probably outdated by now, and maybe it's just best to skip all the hoo-hah and make babies when you're fifteen and not have to be picked up by Pick-Up-Artists.

LA SENZA! Raj shouts. She's-an-eight-man-maybe-a-nine-man-nine-at-nine-o'clock-man. Dave looks up and locates the pair of busty high-heeled mid-thirties types coming out with bulging shopping bags. Raj nudges him and heads over.

I dunno, Dave calls after him. I really dunno. What the hell is Raj going to do? Stop them and rant about their choices of intimate lingerie.

No way Raj, just, let it go.

It's too late anyway, Baldy has intercepted first and in the seconds that follow Dave catches sight of Stealth, head in hands, as Baldy gets it all in the wrong order and goes straight for Kino before chat and the girls must think they're being accosted by a store detective. One of them whips her hand round and almost slaps the guy.

Jeeso, Dave is craving that Starbucks, a mochachino, an espresso with three shots. But Raj is heading towards the shell-suits. A quick flick of the head tells Dave that they've left their baby buggies with another teenage mum outside Mothercare. Raj is already running before Dave can stop him. When Dave gets there, this is what he hears:

Oy!-hi-by-the-way-I'm-not-making-you-feel-nervous-am-I?This-isn't-market-research-if-that's'-what-your-thinking-sorry-I-can-talk-a-bit-fast-my-name's-Rajesh-by-the-way-and-I-used-get-approach-anxiety-you-know-but...

The girls move from fear to scorn by-passing pity as Raj accelerates into verbal oblivion. It's-cool-I'm-cool-I'm-just-wondering-what-two-babes-sorry-girls-sorry-ladies-are-doing-like-you-in-a-place-like...

Raj! C'mon.

Raj's eyes flash years of frustration. He unleashes it and strikes Dave, sending him flying across the tiles. It's fine, Dave tells

himself as he tries to right himself, it's maybe from the stutter, understandable. Girls push past Raj, eyes spitting disgust, while others stop and stare. It's cool, he says to Raj, extending his hand to shake and to ask for a help-up but Raj is already raging away, towards Stealth.

Dave checks for broken bones, he's taking his time to stand because he's actually a little portly. Something strikes his chin and a voice yelps Fuck!

He scans around and there's this girl lying on the ground, with this heavy rucksack on her back.

Jesus fuckin' Christ! She's shouting, rubbing her forehead. It's only then that Dave feels the pain. Jees, he says, I'm really sorry.

Her eyes are anger, her hair is cut like a boy, but dyed purple, she's got these big army boots on, and they're sort of in the air, as she tries to kick herself back upright.

Ten minutes in this fucking country and... She sounds Canadian or Aussie.

He knows his apologies sound lame but he stands there offering a hand.

No fuckin' ta, she says as she reaches back and tries to lug the back-pack back in place. Fuckin', fuckin'... He stands there as her hands struggle with the straps.

Can I?

Take your fucking hands... But after tying herself in knots, she agrees and so he helps her up, gets her bag strap over her shoulder. Already there's a cluster around Stealth, laughing and pointing. Jeeso, as soon as he's said sorry he's gone, forever. Before that he has to make it all OK.

As you know, when Dave feels stressed Dave tends to crave coffee, which is not good for stress but it's very Dave. In such situations, he has also found it's a good idea to try to get the offended party to join you in the thing you need. So, it just slips out. Jees, sorry can I buy you a coffee or... he says, D'you know if there's a Starbucks in here?

What, she say, fuckin' what?

Now he feels selfish, You fancy a coffee?

What are you a fucking spaz?

I dunno, he says and thinks he should probably walk away, but she's laughing.

Fuck, I only came into this shit hole to get a cappuccino anyway, what a fucked up country, they kept me for an hour in immigration, pulled all the shit out of my sack like I was a fuckin' dealer, thought they were gonna strip me and get their rubber gloves on. Fascist fucks.

He was kind of shocked by her language.

So where's this fuckin' Starbucks, anyway?

He didn't know and that was what he said.

Fuckin' fascists, she said again as she shifted the weight of her rucksack. Beyond in the doorway of GAP Stealth was amassing the troops, motioning to Dave, pointing at his wrist where a watch might once have been.

Dave didn't fancy the conference suite now that Raj was pissed at him and he really did need that coffee. Must be round here somewhere, he said, you can usually smell it before you see it, it's usually near the entrance, or close to Magic Muffins.

You're weird, she said, then smiled.

So they were walking, not quite together, as his eyes scanned the shops and she was ranting behind him about the UK, how it looked just the same as Oz, and why did she even fuckin' bother.

He didn't really have anything to say about the subject that people hadn't said before so he kept walking, past the phoney fountain thing and there it was.

Cheers, she said as he set her grande skinny cappuccino with soya milk on the table in front of her. She had her ruck-sack on the next seat like it was a person. She was putting her hair back in a headband, she was pretty pretty, not pretty-pretty, but pretty much the OK-est looking girl Dave had seen in a hell of a long time, in a kind of fucked-up grungy way, what with her nose piercing. He caught himself staring and sipped his Americano. It was hot and good like it should be. She was staring at him.

Sorry, I'm a kind of total junkie, he said.

You take smack?

No, no, he held up the coffee, nodded at it, twenty a day – keeps the doctor away. She nodded, a slight smile.

I had a boyfriend that did crystal meth, she said, Toby Spencer, back in Melbourne, he's in rehab now, that's kind of why I'm here.

Wow, thought Dave, maybe it was an Aussie thing, not the drug thing, but that she was one of those folk who always told you the full names of people they knew, like you were supposed to know who they were, which was something he did too.

So you just going to stand there or what? she said.

Oh, was I? Dave said. Of course he was standing. She patted the other seat beside her.

Weird fuckin' country, she said again. And he sat.

Well Dave, she said, I'm Daisy by the way; she put out her hand to shake.

He wondered how the hell she knew his name. She smiled and pointed to his sticky badge that he must have forgotten to take off. Jeeso.

Oh that. He fumbled with his cup and took her hand, her shake was vigorous, Yeah, it's a long story, he said. Stupid fucking name, she said then laughed, mine not yours, my mum was a hippy.

Wow, Dave said, well so was mine, sort of, actually.

No shit, Daisy said, it's fucked up right? World Peace, I mean, look at all this shit, she said, motioning out to the mall, Yeah right.

He could have told her about his mum and asked about crystal meth but he didn't want to pry. He was just savouring the good hot black coffee and her face and the way she'd go sort of nuts when an idea shot through her, a bit like this dog he knew – you could tell when it was going to bark because this kind of power started in its belly and few seconds later a bark came out, and it was always really funny, like the dog wasn't even in control of its own bark. Sal it was called, she was old Thompson's dog. It would have been nice to tell her these things but he kept quiet and just kind of smiled at her.

So what you doing here in hell? You got a job, here? She had a frothy bit of chocolatey milk on her top lip.

Yeah, Starbucks, but not here, another one.

Fuckers, she said, every cup goes to a kid in Africa or shit, I dunno, I dunno, she said, and that made him smile. So, are you just... she paused to add some sarcasm, which seemed to be her thing – shopping?

Well, he could have said 'yes', but that would have been a lie; he could have even come out with that old canned-opener about shopping for a present for his best mate's girlfriend, but no. Out through the glass he saw Stealth and the guys looking round for him. They were heading towards Starbucks. He bent down behind her ruck-sack.

What the fuck?

Are they there? He tried to cover his head.

You are a fuckin' junkie, she said, did you steal something? I don't want to get fuckin' deported!

Nah, nothing like that, the guy with the tan and the stripe shirt is he...

Shh, she said, yeah, he's snooping round, slimy lookin' motherfucker. She put a hand on his shoulder, Stay there a min. He did as she said, crouched. Beyond, he could see the staff staring.

OK, It's cool, she finally said, Coast is clear.

He exhaled and got back up; he'd spilled some coffee on his trousers.

Why do I always end up with Junkies, she said exhaling loudly, I must have a fuckin' sticker that says co-dependent. Jesus.

I'm not, he said, brushing the coffee from his crotch. Honest to God.

Through the glass he saw Stealth and the team heading back in the direction of GAP, away from the main doors, Stealth checking his mobile. He sat down next to her again, cautiously looking over his shoulder.

So, why don't you stop fuckin' me around and tell me why the cops are after you?

He apologised, trying to hold in the laugh but it farted out the sides of his mouth.

I'm, I'm... he said.

What? What the fuck are you?

OK, she was freaked and she'd been so honest with him so he had to level with her. I'm on this dumb course, he said, and, after her initial shock, it was funny when he told her the details, she was all eyes and they were incredible eyes, like a locked door that suddenly opens and she laughed like hell when he told

her about the N-close and Kino and NLP and 'the squirrel'.

No fuckin' shit!

He really liked her accent; the swearing seemed part of it, not something put on for show. So he went on.

Yeah and you do this thing where you get this girl to show her your foot then you spin her round and you touch her but she doesn't notice, I don't get it but she's supposed to feel it in her 'primordial cave.'

She roared like old Thompson's dog when it got barking, Wait, she said and went into her rucksack to look for something but couldn't find it. It was this book called *The Rules.*

It's totally fucked up, she said, I mean, what if all guys have to read *The Game* and all women read *The Rules,* there's like books to tell you how to have sex and how to have babies, it's fucked-up. Anyway. My friend got it for me, it's crap.

Who's your friend? Dave asked.

Debbie, Debbie Carter, she's like this uptight career chick now but she's sweet, she has these weird teeth she's going to get fixed but I think she's probably nicer with them the way they are.

Wow, said Dave, I can totally see Debbie Carter. I used to know this girl just like her, with braces, called Sharon Mackay.

Really, Daisy asked and there was this moment when they both could have been trying to imagine Debbie Carter and Sharon Mackay but not quite making it.

Anyway, Daisy said, She thinks I need to get some self-esteem and believe in myself.

Self-esteem, I dunno, Dave said.

She says self-belief makes you a winner.

Weird, Dave said, I mean, but how can everyone be a winner, when there's like gazillions of people in the world.

Here's to losers, Daisy said, toasting him with her cup.

She drained her coffee, then stood, Yup, I think it's time...

Sure, he said, though he wanted it to go on and he could have done with a second double shot. He set his cup down and stared at the floor, Well, it was nice...

➤➤

Nah, hah, she said and stretched her arms, I want to try out this fuckin' Kino shit. Seriously, so what you say – nice shoes and...

Dave couldn't help but laugh.

Yeah, well, I say, nice heels or something, or I could neg you, women are supposed to like being put down, like I could say – you've still got the price sticker on your sole.

For real! She roared then put on a funny face, he thought maybe she was pretending to be Debbie Carter, she did a funny voice and stood on one leg, reached out and balanced on his arm.

My God, you're right, she said, with the funny voice, I'm never shopping in Shoe Shed again, I'll get my stilettos from Dolce in future. And it was funny, what with her Army boots.

So, she said, aren't you supposed to take my hand. So he did, and then she nodded, and he raised it above her head and with a bit of pressure from her, leading the way, he spun her round, like in those old fifties dances, like in Grease. People were staring.

Again, she shouted, laughing like mad, so he spun her again and she looked like she was going to fall, so he took her waist and balanced her.

Just then there was a knocking behind them, Dave didn't care. Her laughter took on whole new devilish quality like she was laughing at someone, not him, but not with him either, and now she was pointing to the window. Dave turned and there were Stealth and Raj and all the gang staring back. Stealth holding up his mobile to take a photo and Raj giving a hi-five to the cop-guy.

OK, OK, OK, Kiss me, Daisy said, and Dave sort of really did want to but not in front of those guys. C'mon, just to fuck them off.

She took her hand from his and held his face and planted her lips on his. It went on for a long time and all the folks in Starbucks and the pick up artists were forgotten in the smell of her Patchouli and sweat. She took his waist and held him tight and it was arousing in an uncomfortable way but she didn't seem to mind. She whispered to his neck, Shhh, they're still staring, looks like you've got your K-close, after all eh?

Dave didn't want to open his eyes, but when he did he saw her waving away Stealth and the gang. Then she gave the gang the finger. Dave tried not to look as she went up to the window and mouthed FUCK OFF and finally they sloped away. Fuckin' retards! She shouted.

When they were gone from sight she said Hey-ho and got her rucksack on her back and had the same as before trouble with the last arm, so he helped her, hundreds of question in him, but none for the asking. And this sick feeling. He probably shouldn't have had the coffee on an empty stomach, should have had a blueberry muffin to soak it up.

Cheers matey, she said, turning to face him. What the fuck is there to do in your country anyway? I just got the stupid flight cos it was cheap.

Well, he said, I dunno. There was a whole bunch of tourist stuff she could do, but it was all pretty much the same stuff you'd get anywhere. He was thinking he could show her around the city but she'd not asked and, probably, it'd be too hard for him to get time off work anyway. He was thinking of the solitary walk back across the car park, under the flyover, the entrance to the conference suite, and the round of applause he'd get, and the slaps on the back, and Stealth handing him the gift voucher for the Platinum Plus Executive Workshop in Los Angeles.

She paused, as if waiting for him to say or do something and when he didn't she said, have a good one. An Australian expression maybe that probably meant life, and she probably did have major problems with addicts and she may even have been a junkie herself – these were the things Dave told himself. She took the weight of her bag, I hope you find your friend, she said.

My friend?

The little guy, and she bent down, and made a sign, at about ankle level, tricky with the weight of her ruck-sack – You know, with the red hair and the fluffy tail.

Oh, right, he said, feeling himself smile.

She didn't stroke his cheek or kiss it goodbye. He had to step out of her way as she passed so as not to get knocked over by her rucksack.

See ya, she said, and she walked out of the

door into the mall.

So, he calls me, and I'm telling him, this is so great, good for you Dave, and he's asking me, So what should I do? And I'm like, Wait, did this just happen, like right now? And I'm telling him run after her Dude, but he's saying we'll I've been on the phone to you for half an hour, so she'll be long gone by now. And I'm like Jesus, Dave, why the hell didn't you run after her, why d'you waste all this time telling me? And why the hell didn't you ask for her number, she kissed you for chrissakes! And he's like, I dunno, I dunno. And I could weep with laughter or just plain weep cos this is all just so Dave.

# Hive
Jim Stewart

*hex*

Against the attacks of cold or heat
there are no sure spells;
but the thrumming
grubs in their dreams
love this muggy thraldom
where, charmed and mothered
in their wax curbs
they curl and fatten;
unfold, then break the seals
of their stills
with first impressions.

*dance*

They'll trip it among the further blooms,
if the sun's humdrum curve
is rejigged in the steps
of their ceilidh's measures
as trigonometry.

Hungry for the unlearned moves
they'll summon a star's angle,
and by its numbers
figure how close they've come
to stripping the willow-herb.

*mind*

Flicks of their mother's tongues
slurp and mix the nectar with the spit
in their guts' cul-de-sacs;
and to get it they've dredged,
drugged with her pheromone,
the beds of flowers
for licks of that bliss
disgorged in tubs.
Her sweet talk's pledged
a loving-cup from the comb,
once her hungers relax.

*agon*

Among the hexagon stacks,
each side one of a further six
where the burden of space is felt
and a surplus packed in store,
the destined brood
that curdles in great pods
dreams of being stung,
as a young queen grudges
the means and ends
not in her keep.

*queen*

What must she be for whom
pollen mulch and the spat nectar
of a dozen honey drums
are not enough; for whom
the flux of glands must ooze elixirs
so that within six days
her prospect burgeons from weeks to years,
the urgent flesh, itself, times thirteen hundred?
What is she to terminate the cells
and forestall population;
she who'll castrate
the judged sex
of a big-balled drone for his milt?

*swarm*

A dance is the rumour of farewell.
The old cummer's shrieks
hurry her hundreds
of daughters and drones
as the warm wax threatens to melt.
The cleft or tree that's home
is well known when it's found.
Her bag of bees veers here and there
and bristles in the bush,
gathers and seethes, adoring its source
– her delirious, honey-dosed
bundle of joy;
her drudges of the combs.

# A Raincoat, A Spell of Rain Ago

Ryan van Winkle

An incompleteness ago
my fingers and turpentine nails,
laser hairs standing cold.
The market of twilight,
horse left on the monument,
six legs, one raised as a rifle,
his man like an apple in a barn.
  Red on red on red on red.
An incompleteness ago;
the earth and a terracotta cup,
the earth a finger of whiskey,
the earth a freezer of corn.
  An incompleteness ago:
a mint melting in the bath, a mint
in pubic hairs and fingered dust,
a mint of dimes, pennies, nickels.
  A quarter a quarter a quarter –
call it an incompleteness ago.
When the foundations opened,
the words were all magnets.
  An incompleteness ago
a baby almost ate a banana. Small
  spoons, small spoons small
incompleteness ago.
The sinks are still buildings,
the counter a revolution,
the gorillas in the kitchen
the coal train – an incomplete
the bruised boy – an incomplete
the candy shop – an incomplete
the tractor trails – an incomplete, no
incompleteness ago. No grief ago,
no moons ago, no alone ago,
no tires ago, no buzzard pond ago,
no dream ago, no Freud ago,
no pickled vans ago, no cherry ago,
no pits, no canyons, no shaved rocks
of ice from an incompleteness ago.
  No red no red no red no
water for boil, no bottle,
no bottle for punch.
No gum. No shoe,
no shoe detective for my life.
No narrative, no born
  lived then died.

No tomb, no ash, no clay.
　　　　No bones, no dice
no smoke, no fire. No ants
on the way to mango.
　　　　No incompleteness,
no raincoat for the rat-ta-ta,
　　　　a raincoat ago. A dog ago.
A hat ago, a love ago, a week ago
　　　　there was only no.
No gas, no trucks, only tunnels.
Only pavement. No food,
only smell.
No song in my voice.
　　　　No voice.


# St Anthony's Fire

*advice to a young hermit*

John Brewster


First the pig sweat comes, when grunts drown out
the desert-song of God; then semen,
thick as milk and honey, roasts the snout
of Adam to a purple demon.
Hell, my son, is ecstasies of doubt.

# Light
## Leela Soma

'He is never born, and never dies.
He is in Eternity...
he does not die when the body dies'
(The Bhagarad Gita c. 500 BC)

A road, a path unknown, a familiar quest
in the inroads of our being, not in rest
sea breeze salt laced on mourning faces dark
still night, words unspoken, sobs distilling, mark

flesh, bone, cremated ashes from dust to dust
reincarnating life anew, the shadows sieved
Maya* released, the product of yesterdays lived

In darkest sorrow we desire pain- the impression of life
a mother, father, a child, love and strife
by material things are memories made
a sari, a thumbed book, an unopened satchel's shade
a life unfulfilled in our mind's eye

while bright Consciousness, the Light Eternal
moves on to the ether world upstanding
we mourn, not ever understanding.

Life continues.

* Unreal/Illusion


# Describe to me the Post-war
## El Gruer

This is how it will be.
Scene one – the re-entrance –

I will be wrapped naked-legged
in a damson throw, draped
across the window chair.
There will be a crumpled newspaper
napping beside an afternoon coffee cup.

As you enter, you will bring in
the fresh scent of chopped wood.
The kindling will splinter to the carpet
as we re-kindle fire that the enemy stole.

With a new season on our lips
we will kiss reunion into each other.
And it will be as if there was no war. Almost.

Scene two – the re-awakening –

When you awaken
you will find me on the dock
dripping my feet in the morning chill,
the peel of an orange still between
my fingertips. We will spend sunrise
gazing into the eyes of the loch.
Out with words you will hold me. Moments
that the enemy stole are re-born in us.

With a new season in our eyes, we see
images of lifetimes in each other.
And it will be as if there was no war. Almost.

Scene three – the re-dreaming –

As time begins to darken
we will spend days in the sigh
of a wicker chair. With creators'
hands we will trace promises on
each other's faces.
With eternal bread that the enemy could
not steal, we will entertain angels
as dinner guests.

With a new season in our hearts,
we will memorise the word 'future' in each other.
And it will be as if there was no war. Almost.

# Prayer/Fasting/Almsgiving
## Iyad Hayatleh and Tessa Ransford

*IYAD HAYATLEH AND TESSA RANSFORD*
are working together on a project to write a
series of poems inspired by The Five Pillars
of Islam: creed, prayer, fasting, almsgiving
and pilgrimage: (أركان الإسلام: الشهادة، الصلاة،
الصوم، الزكاة والحج). They are each writing
from their own experience and perspective
and are translating each other's work.
Ransford describes their process as follows:
"In my case, Iyad prepares his own first
translation into English and I work on that
with him, to try best to convey what he wants
to say. Iyad asks me about anything he needs
clarified in my poems while seeking the
Arabic for them."

Iyad's perspective is that of a Muslim from a
Palestinian Refugee Camp in Syria who has
lived in Glasgow for ten years now. Tessa's
is from a Christian, church and Quaker
background, with links to India and Pakistan,
but now with no formal attachments of a
religious kind. They want to explore the
deeper meanings in their traditions and
how they can be understood in the modern
interconnected world. Through this they
hope to gain new insights and understandings
in the process of translating, itself a deeply
integrative activity.

## Prayer
### Iyad Hayatleh

صلاة

الشاعر إياد حياتله

إلهيَ
ربُّ السَّماء البعيدة عنّي هناك
القريبة منّي هُنا
إليك أصلّي هُناك، إليك أصلّي هُنا
هُنالك من قبل خمس عقود سمعتُ رخيمَ الأذان بأذني الشَّمال
وقبل ثمان شدوتُ بعذب الأذان بأذن وليدي الشَّمال هُنا
وأغدقتُ دمعاً على وجنتيه، غريبٌ يُواسي غريباً هُنا
وأمٌّ تُراقبُ خلف ستار الدموع وتأسوعلينا هُنا
وقابلةٌ تفتحُ الثغرَ مشدوهةً: ما الذي يفعلونَ هُنا؟
وماذا يُتمتمُ ذلك في أذنِ هذا؟
نداءُ الصلاةِ
صباحاً وظهراً وعصراً
غروباً عشاءً،
وفي كلّ وقتٍ أصلّي لزبِ لنا الخيرَ حُبّاً، عطاءُ وهبْ
وفي نُسغنا النّورَ والمعجزاتِ، حياةً سكبْ
أصلّي، لتَغشى السكينةُ روحي
لهديٍ يفيضُ على العالمين بكلّ الدُنا
أصلّي، لِيَملأَ قلبي الوداذ
و يُشرقُ من مقلتيّ الهنا.

هُنالِك في جامِع الحيّ أبصرتُ بعضَ الوجوهِ التي وَدَعتني قبيل سنينٍ
وَما كان وجهُ أبي بينهمْ، ولكنّ رُكناً تَعوَدَ أنفاسَهُ العاطِرات دعاني
سَجدتُ، وَمَرَغتُ وجهاً غلى ما تَساقطَ مِنْ روحِهِ في المكان

وأهديتُهُ دمعتينِ
ورتّلتُ دهراً على قبرِهِ الفاتِحهْ،
بكيتُ عليه وأيضاً بكيتُ على روحيَ النّائِحهْ.

هُنا
في مساجِد أرض الصّقيع التقيتُ أناساً أتوا مِن جميعِ الجهات
كسجادةٍ لونُها ألفُ لونٍ، بها مِن كلّ حقلٍ وُرودٌ مُدِدْنا وراء الإمام
لكُلٍّ لسانٌ، وصوتُ الصّلاةِ لهُ لُغةٌ واحدهْ
فكبّرَ وهلّلَ على أمّةٍ ساجدهْ
لربٍّ تربّعَ عرشَ السّماء هُناكَ
وأيضاً تربّعَ عرشَ السّماء هنا.

# Prayer

## Iyad Hayatleh

translated with Tessa Ransford

My God
Lord of a heaven far away from me *there*
near to me *here*
I pray to you *there*, pray to you *here*.
Five decades ago *there*
it was tuneful *Athan* rang in my left ear
and eight years ago *here*
I chanted the same *Athan*
in my new-born baby's left ear
and showered his cheeks with tears -
one stranger *here* comforts another.
Mother watches behind a curtain of tears and feels pity for us *here*
and an astonished midwife with an open mouth gasps:
*What on earth are they doing here?*
*What is he mumbling in the baby's ear?*
dawn, noon, afternoon
sunset and night
each time I pray to the Lord who granted us love, grace and blessing
and poured the light and sap of life into our bodies.
I pray for tranquillity to overwhelm my soul
for the right guidance to flow over all the people in the world.
I pray for mercy to fill my heart
for happiness to rise from my eyes.

*There*
I returned to the neighbourhood mosque
and recognised some faces that bid farewell to me years ago
and my father's wasn't amongst them;
but a corner where he used to pray, perfumed with his breath,
invited me.
I knelt down low and repeatedly pressed my forehead
on what fell from his spirit there
and offered him my tears
and recited the opening verse of the Holy Quran by his grave
for a long time.
I cried for him and also cried for my mourning soul.

*Here*
in the mosques of the land of frost
I met people who came from all over the world.
Like a rug of a thousand colours
we've been unfolded behind the Imam,
a flower from each garden, each has their own tongue
But there is only one language for prayer.
Glorify, saying *God is great*
for the nation praying to the Lord
who sat on the throne of heaven *there*
and who sits on the throne of heaven *here*.

# Fasting
## Tessa Ransford

To go without food by choice is like
driving a car without fuel.
Is what matters the work to be done
or proving, improving ourselves?

Much harder for me
to give up working or caring,
to let go my longing to know,
to share, to love

*You need to be needed*
they say accusingly.
*You always ask exactly what happened*

# Fasting
## Tessa Ransford
translated by Iyad Hayatleh

تيسّا رانسفورد

أن تمضي بدون طعام طوعاً
كأنّك تقودُ سيّارةَ بدون وقود
الأهم، أن يُنجزَ العمل
أن نثبتَ، ونطوّرَ أنفسنا

الأكثرُ صعوبة بالنسبة لي
هو أن أتوقّفَ عن العمل أو الرعاية
أن أفقدَ فضوليَ إلى المعرفة،
إلى المشاركة والحب

"أنتِ بحاجةٍ لأن تكوني مطلوبةً"
قالوا متّهمين:
"دائما، تستفهمين عن الذي حدث بالضبط"

I could forsake that need, that asking
only by force of will, by unwilling consent,
by continual heart-wrenching effort

أستطيعُ أن أتخلّى عن تلكَ الحاجة، عن ذلك السؤالُ
بقوّة الإرادة فقط، بالموافقة على مضض
بالجهدِ المتواصل الموجع للقلب.

ترجمة الشاعر إياد حياتله

# Almsgiving
## Tessa Ransford
translated by Iyad Hayatleh

تيمّا رانسفورد

( قيمةُ الشيء تُقاسُ بقيمة الحياة التي نمنحها له، وبقدرته التبادليّة ) ثورو *

ساعدني الآخرونْ
ولمْ أستطع أن أكافئهم على ذلكُ
ولكنّي بدوريَ أعطي
أعطي كينونتي
وأشارك ما أملكُ مع الآخرينْ

كميّةُ الحياة التي أمنحها
تُكلّفني، ما يُستهلكُ ويُلتهم
من الوقتِ والفكرةِ والنيّة

لكنّ الحياةَ كلّها لم تُستهلكْ بعد
فالذي يُعطى، يُردُ بقوّةٍ،
ليسَ تماماً، ولكن بما يكفي للإستمرار
حتّى يُؤخذ الشيء الأخيرْ

لذلك، آملُ عندما أموت
هذا وذاك، هو وهي
أن ينذروا أنفسهم للصدقات
تماماً كما كنتُ أنا.

ترجمة الشاعر إياد حياتله
*دافيد هنري ثورو : شاعر أمريكي عاش بين عامي 1817 و1962

# Almsgiving
## Tessa Ransford

*The cost of a thing is the amount of 'life' we give to it,*
*that is required to be exchanged for it*
*(Walden – H.D. Thoreau)*

Others have supported me
and I could not repay them
but give in my turn
give what I am
and share what I possess

The amount of life I give:
time, thought, intent
absorbed, devoured
is what it costs

Yet life is not consumed
for the given is returned
in strength, not fully
but sufficient to continue
until the last is taken

So when I die I hope
this and that and he and she
will be endowed, as I have been
by this 'in person' charity

# Soldier II
## Andrew F Giles

Brooke, R., *1914 & Other Poems* (Complete Press,
28th impression, 1920). Restrained, a story of memory,
navy-bound with a firmament of stains, the mess
of years, paint, ink, dust and detritus. Unfortunately,

page 25 to 26 is missing. An enigma. A code of
ruptured spines and dark mottled centres, *have*
*taken out a favourite page for constant use, J.G.*
written in pencil, bound in yellow paper and saved.

A hard treasure to read upside-down, try to eke out
its mysteries. On earth or undersea an icy corpse
with a face like J.G.'s remembers the late-night rout
that took the tattered page. His favourite. He morse

coded it, bewitched it with blue pencil, hieroglyphed
it with newspaper cuttings. He was its second or third
owner, and like me J.G. lightly lifted the shroud of tissue
paper that covers R.B.'s beautiful profile, his last word,

one word, crouched in a trench. A US soldier, Iraq, Turner,
called it his *clavicle-snapped wish*. What a phrase. Yes.
It made me think, a rarity, being more of a slow learner
these days. I blame all things except myself, more or less.

Turner's page 25-6, present: *the droning engines of midnight.*
Should I remove it? *For constant use, A.G. etc.* The wind
took J.G., page 25-6 in his pocket (it was Brooke's *The Great*
*Lover*, the last two pages), with this sound on his mind

perhaps as he died. As soon as *Here, Bullet* arrived at home
I was on the phone to M, whose father built R.B.'s tomb
on Skyros. I dreamt of snapped skeletons, whiteness, bones,
and the history of violence – unburied because it died too soon.

M gave a talk to the R.B. society on her father, Lieutenant
Colonel Stanley Casson, who wrote: *Let anyone but me be hit.*
I like the way her eyes sparkle when she sifts through remnants
of Casson, like a bird's. Papers thickly inked, room gloamy, unlit

except for page 25-6 in slow looping letters. Slowly, through
suspended dust, it's clear that death is J.G.'s equal friend,
and this is his epitaph. The re-appearance of a lost book, I knew
it was strange, came later. Turner, Casson, my father's laugh

as he came across J.G.'s book. Weird. Owners past scrawl
their dedications on the inside cover: Marie Jaux or Joux, scored
out in someone's heavy blue pencil, wrote *With gratitude for all
the good you have done me* dated *Londres Juin 1921* in words

of the most delicate form, slightly slanted with g's like scythes;
J. Gwinnell is written centrally with a scruffy marching column
of favourite pages in blue pencil on the left, Pages 20, 24, 25
doubly underlined. For constant use. J.G., History's son,

foresaw some horror (and what about the scrap of diary marked
Saturday 26 [207-158]? New writing this time: *Garden
Party 20 wounded sóldiers. 70 altogéther*) and cloaked
it in a strange synchronicity of numbers, a coal-blue distance

in his eyes. J.G. – my friend – with your page 25–6 in hand,
R.B. is singing *sét them as a banner, that men may know*
in your brain! Starlight, engine sputters - here lies man,
his fray-edged secret and the million bony faces of ghosts.

# Against the Grain
**Jim Carruth**

What for hard labour, tractor's strain when slope's
steep so little gain, blight and crows are hardships
plain, acid clay, driving rain strangles the barley
we start again: days all working against the grain.


# Twins
**Jim Carruth**

twin lambs
in a hollow

head to tail
tail to head

yin and yang
coughed up dead

sling them
in the back

there's the living
to be fed

# Held And Held In Place
Gordon McInnes

(Coatham Dunes & The German Charlies)

           cormorants duck amongst the iron-slag
              dumped into the sea
                 scuttled ores spent of metal
                    coastal defence turned mussel beds
                    awash with the sediments of dredging
                     buttress for the fragile dunes
                      that ridge inland
                       defilades of knitting shoots
                       strand line vegetation
                        patchwork spots of lyme and marram –
                     sea sandwort, marsh orchid, oraches
                    the first colonisers
                 clustered scrub
              huddling into wind-breaks
           digging down to be
        held and held in place
     resistance accumulating
  establishing new roots

# The Black Art
Marion McCready

*The black art of the shore*
*strokes the gills behind my ears*

The black art of the shore
rises around us.
Mussels crackle-comb the air,
rocks jostle with sea drift,
our conversation takes place
in my hair.
I am a lampshade of a girl,
I light up the rocks
with the whirl of my skirt.
You may think I am a sort of fish, you may
stroke the gills behind my ears.

# Vision
William Bonar

From the top of The Rocks, blue miles
of Clyde, river flaring to firth,
hills, mountains. Here we would stockpile
sods of moss howked from crevices, earth
grenades hurled in ecstatic war games;
we would stone tin cans on the quarry side,
or finger and toe the rock face
hauling out, gasping, quivering, landed.

Here on one of those hot July days,
gazing at Argyll's mountain shuffle,
there was a tilt and the earth laid itself
open in true colours beneath my gaze,
as if in turning, it dawdled, forgetful,
its dingy pelt sliding from hidden pelf.


# A Surplus of Possible Reintegrations
Dorothy Alexander

Waves fract stone and shell.
Together, waves and these fragments make sand: the littoral.
Threads of water sparkle
in dry grass where discarded voices chi-chick
and chirrup in imitation of birdsong, cling to winds
that plunge into the corners of sea-pinks
and wait.
The waves' long hiss crumbles
and drags along the shore, where
approximations duned on the horizon waste
before the not so foolish, who advance;
who want to advance.

# Extract from a memoir in progress
## Fiona Montgomery

EXTRACT 1

Submerged.

Slight ripples on the surface.

Then little hands burst through, escaping, reaching up.

I'm leaping skywards out of an imploding splash. Cascading water all around me is being sucked back down into the open-air swimming pool. Above is endless blue sky and the scorching Sudanese sun.

The real me blinks as the rewinding cine film tracks my skinny six-year-old self up the twenty feet to the top diving board. A few children stand at the side of the pool looking up. Arms outstretched, I zoom past a grown man, watching from the lower board, clearly impressed at my confidence. Landing gracefully on the very edge, I quickly pinch my nose tight.

'Grandad, excuse me please! I need the toilet.'

The request fast-forwards me to December 1994. Julie, aged four, had been sitting cross-legged on the carpet by Dad's baby grand piano, in the front row of our impromptu family cinema. Now she's scrambled up beside Dad, who's on a stool next to the projector, blocking the door.

'Julie, look at your Auntie Fiona,' he urges, pressing a button to send me plunging into the pool again. 'Isn't she brave to jump from so high up when she's just a little girl? She learned to swim when she was your age, you know. We used to go every day when we lived in Khartoum.'

He runs the film backwards and forwards once more, oblivious to the real little girl at his side. She is jumping from foot to foot, chanting, 'I need a pee', paying no attention to the stunts he's putting me through on-screen. Up and down. Frozen in mid-air limbo. Then up and down I go again. I glance over at Jane and Karen. My girls have seen this a few times, but still seem to like it.

'Grandad!' Julie insists loudly, tugging on his trouser leg. Lorna looks over from the couch. Julie's toddler brother is asleep in her arms or she'd get up to help.

'Dad,' I start, and Lorna smiles gratefully at me.

'Michael!' says Mum, exasperation in her tone. 'Will you let Julie go to the bathroom?'

'What? Oh.' Dad switches the light on, pulls the stool out of the way, pats Julie through, shuts the door, puts his seat back and re-starts the projector. Mum tuts loudly. He doesn't seem to notice. I feel sorry for him, as usual when she is annoyed.

'Wait for Julie, Dad,' I say gently. 'She will want to see it. And you'll need to move again to let her back in.'

'Yes, sorry,' he apologises, standing away from the door.

At times like this he seems like an overgrown schoolboy, anxious to please and not sure what he's done wrong. I want to tell him it's okay.

And yet... something is not okay in me. I shiver, looking at the photo on the piano. Dad, his arms around Mum and me, standing in a courtyard area at Buckingham Palace. He was thrilled to be awarded an OBE earlier this year and, as the eldest, I made up the fourth place, with them and my grandmother, to see him being presented with it by the Queen. Mum had recovered enough from her depression to attend.

Then there was his retirement do last month, with various speeches, teasingly highlighting foibles, alongside his integrity and principles. I organised a mocked-up *Evening Times* front page, with my byline on it. Probably everyone saw that as a lovely touch, but I felt hollow, as if just playing the part of affectionate daughter.

Ever since, I've had a constant painful sore throat. I can't afford to be off any more. The managing editor questioned my sickness record last year. The editor, when he promoted me to political reporter, seemed willing to put it down to my children being ill. It wasn't that at all, but now I really must justify his confidence in me. The devolution debate is headline news once more, with daily developments. First thing tomorrow, I'll need to speak yet again to George Robertson, the shadow Scottish Secretary, and to SNP leader Alex Salmond.

At work today, before dinner and the cine show with all the family, I arranged a lunch with Salmond for January, part of spending more time getting out to talk properly with politicians rather than being so deadline driven. I want to be able to concentrate on the new job and, hopefully, move on to *The Herald* or *The Scotsman* at some stage.

As soon as is polite, I make my excuses and leave with the girls.

A few weeks later, the persistent sore throat finally lays me low. When it won't shift, despite being off work resting, I succumb to floods of tears at my obvious incompetence. My GP diagnoses depression.

It will be more than a year before I'm back at work.

*Rewind*

January 1992. Dad and I are eating dinner in my parents' Loch Rannoch timeshare chalet. They have bought several holiday weeks in Scotland and Spain in recent years. Good investments it now seems, despite our fears they were being conned by aggressive sales reps offering free tellys.

'Mum and I are so delighted, and proud, that you and Craig and Lorna have really successful, happy marriages,' he says. Not mentioning, of course, that the weddings all followed unplanned pregnancies. David and I were the bad example that started it all, shocking my parents to the core. Me just seventeen, in sixth year at school. At least the other two scraped into their twenties.

'Of course we're proud of Alistair too and all our wonderful grandchildren.' He beams lovingly and pours more wine.

I pick at my food, ashamed to feel resentful when Dad's being so generous. I think about my youngest brother, who at twenty doesn't have a love life that we know of. No wonder. We all joke that Alistair must be scared to even look at a girl in case she gets pregnant.

I can't think what to say about my marriage and don't really want to try. While it would be good to be closer to Mum and Dad, if attempting it, I would start with Mum. A hard task, as she nearly always is polite and pleasant, rather than engaging emotionally.

It was only because they said they were working and couldn't use their January week, that I agreed to the offer of this time away. I'm exhausted with far too much going on in my life. I want to be on my own, not uncomfortable in Dad's company.

But last week he phoned. 'Hello darling. Happily I am going to be able to get away from work for a couple of days. So, like you, I'll drive up on Monday.'

I could hardly ask him not to come. I smiled into the receiver, then complained bitterly to David.

At lunch on Tuesday, since Dad is here, I use the opportunity to raise something my cousin recently revealed.

'You told us that Mum's mum died when she was a little girl, but you never actually said what from.' I take a deep breath. 'Susan told me that it was suicide.'

He looks up sharply.

'Auntie Sheila told Susan years ago. She was surprised that I didn't know.'

Dad chews for a long time.

'I didn't want to upset Mum by asking her.'

He puts his knife and fork down.

'We felt it best not to tell you all when you were younger.'

'What happened?'

He relates the same facts that Susan did. She put her head in the gas oven. Your mum was just four, Sheila a baby.'

It will be another year before I learn from Sheila some of the complex and rumoured background and that my grandmother killed herself in a far more horrible way. 'I think I inherited the affairs gene and your mum inherited the depression gene,' Sheila will say, bravely trying to lighten the mood, as I wonder where that leaves me.

'Was Mum ever suicidal?' I ask Dad.

'I did find a suicide note in her handbag once,' he says quietly.

My breathing almost stops.

She had several lengthy episodes of depression as we grew up. She would retreat to her bedroom for weeks or months at a time: weepy hair unwashed, unwilling to see friends, often shouting at my brothers and sister for making too much noise. That angered me, as they were just playing. Dad explained she couldn't be her normal self, in the way it is impossible to walk with a broken leg. Because we couldn't see what was wrong, it was harder to understand, but it wasn't Mum's fault.

'When?'

'It was when we'd dropped all of you off for a summer school week in the south of England and she and I spent a few days touring, staying in guest houses nearby. I put the note back in her bag and never asked her about it.'

A picture comes into my head of a small blue and green bag made of intertwined wicker-like strands of hard plastic. I think she lost that, putting it on the car roof while strapping Alistair in, then driving off. Does he mean that bag?

Thursday. He's gone. I can breathe.

But my head's all over the place.

I run a bath, steaming hot, overflowing with bubbles. I've really needed this day to myself. It feels like I've got two full time jobs just now, my main one at the *Evening Times* and all the evening and weekend work for *Harpies & Quines*, the new Scottish feminist magazine. Next week I plan to try and persuade the collective to postpone the launch until after the general election in April. And I must finish writing up interviews with child sex abuse survivors for the paper. Plus, I hope to do some fun things this weekend with Jane and Karen.

I smile, remembering the girls laughing at the foam neck collar I had on when they arrived home with David on Thursday. Thankfully, my neck improved enough for me to drive here. Sitting up, I try moving my head from side to side. Out of the blue, I'm sobbing and sobbing at memories of Raymond, our creepy former lodger, with his neck collar. I need to blow my nose. Dripping onto the tiles, I climb out, wrap a towel round me, grab some loo roll, blow hard, then scramble onto the bed. I'd wanted to relax and instead am a blubbering mess. Some break this has been.

Raymond had the small room upstairs when I was doing journalism at Napier College in 1987. Tim, tickly Tim as our girls called him, was in the big room. Their rent paid for childcare while I studied. We slept in the living room, with the kids in the main bedroom, just off it. We'd never have managed it in a smaller flat.

I was already uneasy about Raymond. He appeared unkempt for a seemingly erudite middle-aged man. He was at university in Glasgow, embarking on a career change. One day in his second or third week he came downstairs, unshaven, with a neck collar on. Apparently some ongoing problem meant he often had to wear it. The grey covering repulsed me. It seemed grubby, almost sleazy.

Shifting on the bed, I realise I'm shivering. Seeking heat, I slip back into the bath, turning the hot tap on full.

The tears have subsided, but the collar images won't go.

The one the GP gave me was a pristine white. I couldn't turn my head with it on, but the pain did ease. What hurt was that Gavin was inexplicably cold when I called to tell him. Upset, I had mentioned his part in it, details I couldn't tell David or the doctor.

'It happened in the car on Tuesday when you pulled me round to kiss you. I felt a twinge then. By last night it was agony.' We'd been out for a quick drink after work, the first time since before Christmas.

Silence. Maybe there was someone with him in his office.

'I needed that kiss Fifi,' he said, clearly alone after all. 'You can't blame me. I wouldn't hurt you. If you were here, I'd kiss it better.'

He knows I hate being called Fifi. It makes me sound like a poodle. I splash water on my face to banish Gavin, leaning back into the lovely warmth – only to be disturbed again by the awful lodger.

David alarmed me when I mentioned not liking Raymond. He said that several times, when he'd gone to the toilet in the middle of the night, he'd found Raymond standing in the hall for no apparent reason. Or wandering in the kitchen. Not making tea or anything. Just there. I remember being so glad that the girls' room was only accessible through ours.

One day, soon after, Jane was at school and I was in the flat alone with Karen when Raymond arrived back. Hearing the door, I stopped putting clothes away in the bedroom and rushed through to the dining part of the kitchen, now in use as our living room.

He was squatting down chatting to Karen, who'd been sitting playing with her toys. She was looking up at him, seemingly fascinated by the collar. As she reached to touch it, naturally inquisitive, I decided we must ask him to leave. Usually I give people the benefit of the doubt, don't trust my own gut feeling. For once I did and acted quickly. We told him that evening to find somewhere else and he was gone within a fortnight.

Sinking further down into the bath, I suddenly connect that image of him and Karen with a photograph of my father and Jane, when she was about two. He's sitting leaning forward on a couch. Jane is standing on it beside him, cuddling into him to whisper in his ear.

Everyone remarks on what a lovely intimate picture it is. I don't like it.

Gavin comes back into my head. No, don't phone his house, I lecture myself in vain. I've memorised the number yet have never called him there.

'Hello?'

A woman, presumably his wife. I quickly hang up. He's maybe working late. There's time to try again before leaving.

At seven pm on the dot, 'Hello?' A young girl. He has a son and two daughters. Putting the receiver down, I give it ten minutes and try once more. Even if he answers, I'll not dare say it's me when they're all around. I just want to hear his voice.

'Sorry we can't...'

I click the message off. His wife is the voice on the answering machine. If it had been him I'd have listened some more.

After a quick dinner and packing up, I go to pay the electricity and phone bills.

The receptionist thinks she has good news. 'Your father has arranged that we just send him the itemised bills.'

It takes some time to persuade her to let me cover it and promise she won't send Dad anything. I don't want any questions about my shameful silent calls.

In the car, I turn on the headlights and push in a cassette – Tina Turner's *Break Every Rule* album. Foot to the floor, I should be home before midnight.

Silence from Caroline. My stomach is noisy. Not from hunger. It's from telling her about my churning emotions around a sexual abuse case I've been reporting on. That and my fury about the politics of how it and some far higher profile cases, such as Orkney and Cleveland, or some from America, have been covered in the media. Too many journalists seem to think it is more likely that social workers would invent abuse than that some men fondle or rape their own children. My counsellor, as in all our six or seven sessions to date, hasn't said anything about what she thinks. I may as well have done a Shirley Valentine and told the wall.

I change the subject. 'I've been considering speaking to my mother, telling her I might be depressed,' I venture.

Her face is unreadable. Maybe she thinks I should. Or shouldn't. Why did I imagine counselling might help?

'I might ask about her experience of anti-depressants.'

Still nothing.

My parents were always very anti-drugs, but Mum eventually ended up taking them. She's still on lithium to prevent a recurrence. I say to Caroline that perhaps pills would be a good idea. I'm worried that I'm going to be off sick if I don't do something.

'Maybe you will end up unable to keep going at work,' she says.

Thanks for nothing, I think.

Tears soak my face as I drive home, wondering when might be best to catch Mum alone.

A fortnight later, Caroline ushers me in, unsettling me by remarking, 'You're glowing.'

'The paranoid part of me instantly worries that you mean you can tell I've seen Gavin today. And if you can see it, then can David?'

'I only commented because you do seem radiant. I didn't know you had seen Gavin.'

The glow must be from feeling loved. We managed to meet up today and Gavin kissed me all through lunch. 'I love being held and kissed by him,' I tell her, smiling at the memories. 'I love David but he won't talk to me. Not about emotions. Whenever we argue about me wanting more, he just dismisses my feelings.'

Tearful now, I sit quiet for a minute, then add, 'But he doesn't deserve what I'm doing to him.'

Reciting a favourite quote, I tell Caroline that it's from Jill Tweedie's In the Name of Love, my mother's book.

*Lies ruin everything, leaving nothing but rubble behind, because what you thought happened didn't happen, what you thought didn't happen did and the person you thought you loved wasn't that person at all. And in that case who the hell*

*are you?*

At home later, I sit with David. He's watching football.

I pick up a book from my current pile. *The Girl Within. A Radical New Approach To Female Identity,* by Emily Hancock.

One line in it stops me dead. She writes, about a woman contemplating problems in her marriage:

*The confrontation that mattered, however, was not with her husband. It was with herself.*

One day in September Mum comes looking for me.

The previous weekend David and I had stayed overnight at my parents' house for the first time in years. In the middle of the night I threw up repeatedly in the downstairs toilet, blaming too much wine. I don't know whether Mum and Dad heard.

She turns up at my front door midweek, saying she's glad to catch me before David and the girls get home. In the living room, she sits down and asks, 'Are you alright? You've been very overworked and I'd hate to see you become ill.'

My eyes fill up.

'You're not feeling depressed are you?'

I reach for a tissue. Mum moves from the chair to sit beside me on the couch, but that's too much. I stand up to put the used tissue in the bin.

'A little. Nothing like you had, I don't think. Probably I'm doing too much, like you said. I am pulling back a bit from *Harpies* now. Don't worry about me. I'm seeing a counsellor, who is helping a lot.'

'I didn't want to go for counselling,' Mum says. 'Our GP was against it. Also, I was always worried it would make you change your views of people.'

'What do you mean?'

'That it might make you have a different view of the people around you.'

I can't think what to say in response. To that, or to her next comment, made out of love, wanting to spare me the pain she has suffered.

'Perhaps you should think about taking lithium.'

EXTRACT 2

On a trip to London I decide to steal another woman's multiple personalities. I only briefly wonder if this makes me one of those hypochondriacs who feel the symptoms of any problems they read about. I don't care. More than anything just now, I want that woman's inner teenage rebel. Her name is Fuckit and everybody should have one. Within minutes of realising it is possible to just magic up your own, I'm moulding her in my image. CND earrings of course, and the kind of big heavy Doc Martens I could never have afforded as a teen. Though I can also see her in a stunning red ballgown, wild curly hair with a scattering of little ribbons, sat on a wall with friends, drinking straight from a bottle of Cointreau.

It's early 1994 and I'm down south to stay with my friend Carol. She's been in a psychiatric hospital for three weeks and needs support for the first few days back home. She doesn't know that I've worried about whether I too might end up hospitalised. I'm certainly not telling any doctors about the strange sensations of wanting to drag my wrists over broken glass.

Those feelings scare me, although I'm not suicidal – I have a desperate fear of death for God's sake – and doubt I would ever actually cut myself. *Fake! Hypochondriac,* whispers Sarah, my newly nicked and instantly on message inner nag. Although internal criticism has been there so long it seems part of my very being, it's good to picture the enemy at last, to put a name to her as an identifiable entity. My Fuckit hates her already and they've not exchanged a word.

The original Fuckit is the star turn in *The Obsidian Mirror,* my latest purchase from Silver Moon, the women's bookshop that I always head for in London. There was no warning about the various sparring personalities, but I took to them all after the first few pages of this magical, heartbreaking memoir. Now they're mine. Just like that. One day I'll write to the author, Louise Wisechild, and confess. Maybe if I give mine different names, apart from Fuckit of course, she will be less angry.

Carol is out seeing her GP. I'm lying on the fold-down sofa in her sunny living room, reading voraciously. Wisechild (presumably another wishful, creatively chosen name) relates her difficult adolescence, dropping out of university, her struggle with enveloping sadness and isolation. The mood is lightened by Fuckit's antics, which make me laugh, although I could never speak my mind the way she does. I'm too goody-goody. She's glorious in her anger. I've never touched a cigarette, while she's a heavy smoker, but I really want part of me to be like her. Irresponsible, carefree. To not worry about being in trouble, being bad, telling the truth.

'I'm fucking sick of studying,' she declares. 'I don't give a flying fuck about the definition of a definition.'

I read on. Fuckit yells some more, then spends nights in cafes talking to prostitutes and men she should be scared of. Maybe I won't try that.

Turning the pages, I'm entranced too by Wisechild's Sure Voice, who is intuitive, wise, calm. How I long to have a Sure Voice instead of that fear of being so very wrong and a silent panic that often threatens to overwhelm me. But she doesn't come as readily as Fuckit. Either that or I'm not listening hard enough. Too used to the family and work demands back in Glasgow to hear a wise woman creating a room of her own in my cluttered head.

Carol arrives back and flops into the armchair next to me. 'I'm sorry I've not been much company. But at least I managed going to the doctor by myself, thanks, and he's happy with how I'm doing. So far. Hey, have you been crying?'

'No,' I lie. 'And don't worry about me. I've been reading and...'

My heart trips suddenly as she bends down to see the book. The subtitle is *An adult healing from incest.* Will she jump to ridiculous conclusions about me? But she doesn't have her glasses on and just glances at the nondescript cover, then stands up.

'I'm going to have a quick shower to wake myself up.'

'Shall we go for a walk after that?' I ask, relieved. 'Or do you feel up to the pictures or something else? I'll cook dinner to fit in with whatever you fancy.'

She shrugs. 'I can't really decide much about anything. I probably should be sociable, but can we leave it until tomorrow, just watch some light telly tonight?'

Nodding, I put my book and journal away and lock up Fuckit and Co in a secure inner ward so I can pay full attention to Carol. She seems really low. I don't want weeFionas, my versions of Wisechild's YoungerOnes, running about distracting us, or, worse, crying when I'm meant to be here for Carol.

Sure Voice – my very own I realise – points out that the children will be distressed to be shut away again, just when they thought they'd been rescued from my long-term efforts to ignore them.

'Good,' says Fuckit, plugging in her earphones in case their crying gets too loud.

Soaring above the posh houses, my smile couldn't be bigger, revelling in sunshine and the music on my bright yellow Walkman. I'm high enough to see the castle ruins and the Clyde. Flying, arms outstretched, swooping, surfing in the air like Raymond Brigg's snowman. Except the soundtrack is Bruce Springsteen not Aled Jones.

Now I'm bopping and rocking forty feet up. Below, my heavy body walks along the pavement, no hint of the joyful cavorting up here. In that baggy jumper, old tracksuit trousers, worn trainers, it is going through the dark part of the woods near the castle. The trees block out the sun, their top branches almost meeting way above the road, just below me as I look directly down. We're off to collect Karen from school.

Down at ground level I bring flying Fiona back down to earth, feeling myself reeled in like a kite. We turn up the volume to enjoy a slower favourite, *My Home Town*. No wonder I fancy the guy. His voice is sex itself.

On days like this, walking to school can be a pleasure, although, of recent, a lingering dread marks the quiet parts of the road.

Blasting Bruce into my ears has helped today. But now I think back to a couple of weeks ago, on this same stretch. I had been walking along, no earphones that day, feeling low about being off sick, labelled with the D-word, depression. A white transit van with three guys in it slowed beside me. Instantly on alert, I then chided myself, thinking maybe they knew me through David, or they simply wanted directions.

No. The driver rolled his window right down. All three looked big and bulky. One shouted 'hello darling' and another wolf whistled.

'Cheer up love,' the driver said, going past slowly, sticking his tongue in and out in crude display. His friends laughed, blowing kisses.

I looked straight ahead, walking faster, fists clenched by Fuckit. Crossing around the roundabout, I tried to look back nonchalantly, as if checking the traffic. The van was turning and coming back, no other cars or people in sight.

I turned swiftly off the main road into a cul-de-sac and walked up to the front door of the first house. They didn't follow and I slowly retraced my steps to the road. But I was fighting back tears all the way to the school as my thoughts ran riot. If they'd got out and grabbed me, I'd have crumpled in a terrorised heap. But Fuckit was boiling with rage. She would first have looked with scorn at the wreck on the ground. Weak and useless baby, she'd taunt. I knew she would then have softened. I could see her kneeling down, whispering that she wouldn't have let them lay a finger on me. She would have killed all three or been killed in the process, though there's no way she'd tell weeFiona7 that last bit.

Today, remembering it all, I curse them, but am determined to keep walking.

Bastards, Fuckit spits out. But she cheers instantly at a change of tempo in our earphones. Tina Turner's *Paradise is Here*. I love the way music can change your mood so quickly. In my early teens I used it to help me get over boyfriend break-ups. Probably got the idea from somewhere like *Jackie*. Playing three sad songs, then three happy dancing ones. Over him now! If only.

To my shame, I once used music utterly inappropriately.

A team of us had covered the murder of a young girl. We'd spent hours knocking doors near her Glasgow home. I'd interviewed the couple who found her body and I felt hugely stressed all morning. After filing everything for the second edition, we went to a nearby pub for lunch. A song I liked came on and I jumped up, trying unsuccessfully to pull one of the photographers up to dance. There weren't many people in the place, but my colleagues just looked on, shocked as I bopped about.

John, the crime reporter, who I'd thought of as one of the least sensitive guys I knew, quickly stood up, came over and whispered in my ear.

'Not really a good idea Fiona.'

I flushed and sat down, appalled and imagining complaints to the editor.

My face burns again at the memory but even so I can barely stop my feet jigging along the pavement to *Paradise*, all thoughts of the van men banished. Pushing away the murder too, I can see myself leaping into the air, clicking heels together Gene Kelly style. Then some sexy moves, à la Turner. Though that immediately slows me, thinking of *Private Dancer*, the men, the sexism, the exploitation. Dancer me disappears back into dowdiness.

Nodding to some of the other mums as we gather at the school gates, I almost laugh out loud when Four Non Blondes' *What's Up?* comes on. I'm remembering driving Jane and Karen home from swimming in David's work transit van last month. Me and my girls having fun. People we passed looked round in surprise at the big van, with us screaming happily out of the windows 'What's going on?'

Those creeps wouldn't harass me driving that, I think, picturing myself and a friend or two driving slowly past one of them, trying to scare him. But of course there's no comparison, even if there were ten females to one guy.

Only as Karen comes running out, thrusting her schoolbag at me and jostling affectionately with her pals, do I make a connection between the van men and a frightening experience in France. I'd worked near Cannes, aged sixteen, between fifth and sixth year at school. Just two weeks into the three month summer stint, I was walking down a lonely bit of road heading to the beach, when a guy driving a small red car pulled up beside me. He was naked and playing with himself. When I tried to run off, he drove after me, first down, then back up the hill as I panicked. I stumbled into a farmhouse yard shouting loudly 'où est le patron?' The red car followed me in but drove off when I went to enter an open barn door, ready to scream. I never told anyone, scared I'd be sent home, the last thing I wanted.

Today, walking to the bus stop, I realise that Fuckit's anger was also about that French flasher.

In a couple of years I will decide to go back to the south of France, to that road, that farm, testing in case some flashback might tell me that it was worse than I remember, that I've blocked out something too frightening to deal with all by myself.

On the bus now, as Karen chatters happily away, I try to focus on her, but can't help spotting that Fuckit, chain smoking on the back seat, is casually sticking two fingers up at a white transit van behind us.

NB: Some names and identifying details have been changed.

# Pleasureland
Anna Stewart

THE DAY WE went to Pleasureland I told Mum t' piss-off-fuck-you-fuck-off-out-my-life, after we got off the bus. She said she wis only tryin t' fix my collar coz it wis twisted under my coat. I wis like it's okay dinnae worry aboot it let's just get inside.

We'd come on the 73 aw the way fae Dundee t' Arbroath, me and Mum sometimes go on daytrips coz we dinnae live the'gither anymair and I dinnae like it when she comes t' mine.

Mum told social services she'd had enough so I got my own flat. I had to wait fir ane fir ages. She said she couldnae cope wi my bitin and hittin anymair. I said I'd try t' stop it but I'd said that loadsa times and she kent I couldnae help it.

She said we'd do a compromise, I'd stop hittin people and she'd stop fussin. At Pleasureland when she touched ma collar I tried really hard to rein it in, she didnae touch my skin though so she wis on pretty safe groond.

Some people've said my Mum's highly strung. She's got really deep wrinkles, she ayways looks in pain and her hair's just loadsa straggly bits hangin on her face.

If Mum wis in a Francis Coppola film he would say, 'Fir fuck sake Jean, stop hidin behind yir friggin hair!' Coz he's an American he would say friggin instead o fuckin, 'Grow some balls before yi next come on my set. Time means friggin money Jean and you're throwin my money down the friggin drain. That's it I'm dockin yir wages. Until you get a mair hard ball attitude yir on half pay and nae amount o wingin t' the Guild of Italian American Actors is gonnae change that fact, on my set Jean, Unions mean jack shit.' Italian American actors can be in their own union if they want, I saw it on Wikipedia and Mum's got Italian family so she would be in that ane.

Mum wis totally cryin when I moved out o hers. She wis cryin even though she knew she wis comin ower my flat the next day t' help uz unpack.

She wis smilin and cryin at the same time so I thought she wis dead happy I wis leavin. Some people cry when they're happy.

She said any Mum'd do the same and that I wis a man now and it wis time fir me t' stand on my own two feet. I screamed in her face then got in the van wi this man wha wis rollin his eyes and winkin at my Mum, he wis laughin a bit too. Then he said, 'See yi Jean, dinnae worry, I'll get him settled in' and Mum smiled and wiped her eyes wi her sleeve and said, 'Thanks Frank, thanks.'

Then me and that Frank bloke went in his van t' my flat and he helped uz unload ma stuff and we did things like read the gas meter and light the pilot light in the boiler and he showed me the corner shop whar I could buy electricity on a piece o plastic that's actually a key. I do that every week now but it's pretty expensive.

Anyway the day we went to Pleasureland wis good coz I won twa pound on the puggys. I wis really happy jumpin aroond and athin and Mum wis happy too. But then I spent it tryin t' win a cuddly toy on ane o those crane machines wi the metal claw. I caught Donald Duck but then the claw let him go and I had to tip the machine to get him oot. Mum told uz t' stop it. She said those toys hud been there since the eighties and they wirnae supposed to come oot. I wis like, well how come they pretend that yi'll win a cuddly toy and then no let yi hae ane? But Mum said it's the way o the world, so I kicked the machine and shouted, 'Fuck the way o the world' and the manager looked ower and Mum wis like, 'Let's do somethin else then' coz she wis tryin t' change the subject as usual.

We went on the bumper cars even though we were both too big fir it. We were the only anes on the track so we just kept bumpin intae ane another, I got a bit carried away and Mum had to tell uz in a serious voice to stop it.

Pleasureland wis totally empty apart fae us and it wis good coz there were nae queues or anythin but we got a bit bored efter a while and I wanted t' go home.

Mum said that Frank bloke wha helped me move hoose would come and pick wi up so we wouldnae hae t' get the 73 back tae Dundee. I thought this wis totally excellent coz I felt tired and that 73 bus sometimes makes me sick. I thought Mum must be payin this man loadsa money t' come and pick wi up aw the way fae Arbroath.

Arbroath smells o fish, that's coz in the auld days they used to make loadsa fish there. Now no that many people eat fish coz we're no very religious anymair and it used to be that people ate fish on fridays coz jesus said we should.

Jesus said we hud t' eat fish coz fish dinnae really mind bein ate coz they've only got three second memories, so they wouldnae ken if yi ate them or no. Yi could probably eat a fish when it wis alive and it wouldnae even remember yi were doin it, even when yi were doin it. That's because fish hae small brains.

Sometimes people at school used to say I hud a wee brain but I can remember loadsa things other people dinnae ken coz I get loadsa information fae aw the documentaries. Yir brain's a muscle and that's how I've got such a big heid, coz my brain's dead muscley.

TV is well better than books and even computers fir information coz people in Telly just tell yi things aw the time in a really cool way.

Yi get to see aw the things happenin, it's no just borin like in a book when yi huv to read it first and then see the pictures in yir heid, or on the computer when yi hae to think o things to look up or ken the questions.

Telly just tells yi stuff and then it makes it intae people yi remember. Like Arnold Schwarzenegger he's a person yi remember coz he's on telly and now he's a really powerful person in America coz he's a Governor.

Governors get t' make loadso decisions aboot what happens, so Arnie's totally in control and that's only coz he wis the Terminator and ane o the twins in that film, The Twins wi Danny Devito wha wis the small ane coz he wis the afterbirth.

That's how I found oot aboot aw the fish, coz Auchmithie village wis on a telly programme called Coast that goes roond aw the different places that hae coasts in them and then interviews people and asks them what's happenin. Anyway there wis this wifey on Coast and she said she lived in Auchmithie and that she liked eatin seaweed fae the beach. She said people in Arbroath ayways used tae eat fish and that's why it stinks.

That Frank wha helped me move beeped 'is horn aboot a million times ootside Pleasureland, he looked dead happy and I thought it wis probably coz he'd had the sea air. That's what happens when yi huv the sea air yi get dead happy and then in aboot five minutes yi fah asleep.

But he didnae fah asleep coz he said he would take wi fir fish and chips and I wis like, yes! This is well cool coz fish and chips in Arbroath's dead expensive and I knew he'd probably pay. Even if he didnae I hud some change left ower that I wis usin on the puggys and maybe we could aw bunce in.

I didnae huv fish coz I kept thinkin aboot their three second memory and then thinkin maybe I'd bite them on like one second or somethin and they'd ken aboot it. So I had a sausage supper instead. Mum said I wis missin oot coz the fish in Arbroath's dead good so I tried t' tell her aboot the three second memory thing but got distracted coz my pickle fell oot my paper and I had to get doon under the seat

➤➤

tae find it. Mum got annoyed coz I wis blockin Frank's view but he didnae seem t' care, he just kept laughin and sayin I wis a rare lad.

I thought he must fancy me or somethin and thought I better tell Mum later he wis a bit o a weirdo coz he wis really tryin it on comin aw the way through t' Arbroath to buy me a sausage supper.

That Frank asked me what my favourite things are, I told him my favourite colour's definitely orange coz I'm a Dundee United supporter and we're total winners coz we won The Cup Final.

He said he supported Dundee and then I knew he wis a protestant.

Dundee supporters are protestants and United supporter are catholics, a lot o people dinnae ken that and they end up wantin t' support United coz it's a better team and then findin oot they cannie coz their Mums dinnae go tae proper church.

My Mum doesnae go tae church. My granny did but she's dead now so me and Mum are probably agnostic.

Agnostic means yi dinnae believe in anythin and yi cannie be arsed arguin.

There's this man cawed Richard Dawkins wha wrote a book cawed The God Delusion that I saw on telly.

He's well annoyed at people wha believe in god and wants a'body t' stop goin on aboot it aw the time and tellin wee bairns to believe in god when we dinnae even ken if there's a chocolate teapot in the sky.

He's an atheist coz he's dead angry aboot it and wants to go on aboot it aw the time like the jehovah's witnesses do.

The driver wis like that's good, but what's yir favourite film? I said it's a pretty hard question coz I totally love aw the Godfather movies obviously, except Three's a bit o a disappointment coz it's got Coppola's daughter in it and she's well rubbish. And I love Taxi Driver and I really like the film K-Pax wi Kevin Spacey.

That driver Frank said he hadnae seen K-Pax. So I told him it's this film whar a man comes doon tae earth fae ooter space an a'body thinks he's totally mental and even you'd think he wis mental but actually he's really an alien and tellin a'body the truth.

My Mum started the cryin game when I told Frank aboot that film and he said, 'It's awright Jean' and I thought my Mum wis probably just bein sentimental coz she thinks I'm an alien from ooter space or somethin.

Frank said aw the films I like are aboot men findin their way in the world. I thought maiste films are probably aboot that though.

I read this book cawed Screenwritin fir Dummies aboot how tae write a film, coz I'm writin a film aboot this... well, naw it's actually no oot yet so I cannie really say what it's aboot. But yi'll see it at the cinema when it's finished.

Anyway this book is aboot how yi huv t' write the story in a line and yiv got t' hae some problems t' overcome and stuff. So that's probably why loadsae films are aboot men findin their way in the world coz that's what yir supposed to write a film aboot, like life's a big problem or somethin.

After I read that book, well I scanned it actually coz it wis pretty samey, anyway after I scanned that book I watched aboot a million films t' test if it wis right and aw o them followed the line even though they were different films, aw o them had a problem.

I didnae just test Action or Horror or anythin like that, I properly cross referenced so it wis a real test, that's what yir supposed to do when yir doin a test. We got told that in science but yi can do it wi other things like films if yi want, it's no just fir borin stuff like cells.

When I told Frank aboot Screenwritin fir Dummies aw he could think aboot wis this film I wis writin. He wis well excited. I told him I couldnae tell him what my film wis aboot, but I did tell him I wis totally stuck wi The Problem.

Its like coz aw my characters get on really well and athin and are aw best mates they just dinnae hae any arguments and that. And even though Frank tried t' interrupt and say loadsa scenarios where I could make arguments and problems and stuff I had to tell him straight – look Frank yi dinnae ken these guys they're totally tight, they'd never fah oot. That's how their friendship's so good, there's nae problem so I'm totally stuck.

Then Frank wis like, why dinnae yi make it that nane o them fah oot but they fah out wi someone else or someone dies and they aw hae tae get ower it or somethin. I wis like yeah – okay Frank I could write it like that if I wis writin a chick flick or somethin but this is a serious proper gangster film. I mean I'm no gonnae hae subtitles or that, but it's pretty serious.

Anyway my Mum wis well bored wi me and Frank's chat so she got oot the van and it wis a bit weird just me and him so we went in Mum's fir a cuppo tea.

When we got in Mum's, Frank put the telly on and athin and it wis dead good coz Match o The Day wis on. I wis like yes! Frank asked if I liked Match o The Day and I wis like, totally, obviously.

Frank said he wanted a tinney instead o a cuppo tea and he took 'is shoes aff and put his feet on Mum's favourite pouf.

I thought I better gie him a wee word tae the wise and I said, 'Here Frank yi better make sure my Mum doesnae see yi on her favourite pouf coz she'll go mental.'

Frank just started laughin and Tennent's came oot 'is nose.

Then he started goin on and on aboot how I wis a rare lad again and I thought, wait a minute he's takin it a bit too far, I'm no leavin Mum on her own wi this weirdo.

When Mum came through she sat next t' Frank and she didnae say anythin aboot his feet on her pouf. I thought that wis pretty weird.

Then somethin really creepy happened, my Mum took her shoes aff and put her feet up next to the drivers and their feet were touchin and I wis like yuck this is disgustin!

I said, 'Mum yi cannie just go roond puttin yir feet on van drivers, yi shouldnae be touchin like that!'

And then Mum wis like, 'Frank's my friend he's no just a van driver Derek' and then that Frank he put 'is hand on my Mums arm and he wis like laughin and rubbin it and sayin they were mair than friends.

I wis like, what the frig is goin on here? This is totally sick, are you a sicko or what?

And then that really sore breathin that happens when I feel angry came on. Mum wis like, calm doon Derek but I hud t' push past her an' run oot.

I ran doon the streets fir like-ever, just to stop my chest pain.

But then I got that other pain from when yi run too much.

When I got t' the flat I hung on the door handle fir ages til ma heart stopped beatin so much coz aw the runnin and my hand stopped shakin so's I could get the key in the lock.

I felt dead sweaty. Runnin makes yi feel like that if yi really run fir ages. And then when yi sweat it gets aw kindae salty in yir eyes and mouth and yi just want tae drink loads but yir belly is like – nae way am I takin aw that liquid and then yi start wretchin and athin.

It wis a really weird day coz it hud been dead good at Pleasureland and then wi the fish and chips and aw the movie chat. But then I found that oot and it wis like, huge. It wis like, yi ken when yi huv those dreams that yir fallin, and when yir droppin yir stomach flips ower and yi wake up? It wis totally that feelin.

I think it's really weird that auld people start goin oot wi each other when they're auld, it's like what's the point yir awready auld so what's goin on?

Then the maist weird thing happened, that Frank bloke came bangin on ma door and I wis like there's nae way I'm lettin him in so I hid in the bog.

He came in anyway and he wis sayin, 'Derek, Derek...' in that really creepy singsang way that's like what the baddies do in the horror films, like Jack Nicholson in The Shinin when he's lookin fir Wendy except I wisnae Wendy and Frank has too much o a gut tae be Jack Nicholson.

Then he mustae known I wis in the bog coz he starts thumpin the door really slow wi his foot, like thump... then wait aboot a minute and then another thump.

I wis well-freaked oot and I thought em no sayin anythin.

And then he wis like, 'Derek I ken yir in there' and aw that usual stuff fae the films.

➼

Then he says, 'Now listen you, yi wee shite. Me and yir Mum just want a quiet life and if that means you fuckin aff oot the equation then that's fine. Yir welcome tae come roond and visit but yi'll no be doin yir usual pushin roond. If anybody's doin any pushin roond, it'll be me fae now on d'yi hear me?'

Then he kicked the door and I wis like, 'Yeah' coz I thought he might break it doon. I wis pure greetin and athin but I dinnae think he could hear me.

And he wis like, 'Yir Mum's put up wi yir shite fir far too lang. There's fuck aw wrang wi yi a good kick up the arse wouldnae fix. And fae now on expect tae feel my foot right up arse pal coz yir no gettin away wi yir capers anymair. Tomorrow yi'll be doon that jobe centre an I'll be roond in the mornin tae mak sure o it. Nae mair Pleasureland fir you pal.'

Then he banged on the bog door twice wi 'is fist and athin went quiet. I waited fir ages before I came oot just t' make sure he'd gone.

Then I went in ma bedroom and started packin up aw ma stuff coz I thought, this maniac's totally after uz and he kens whar I live so I better get oot o here.

But then I must've just fallen asleep on the bed mid-pack, coz when I woke up the next day I still had my Pleasureland clathes on and my bag wis only half full and loadso ma stuff had fallen on the flare.

I wis waitin in aw day fir him to come roond and make uz go doon the dole office t' give up my benefits and say I'd work fir the bins or the berries or somethin. But he never came.

Next time I saw him wis at Mum's when I had to go and do my washin. He wis aw dead nice like and he gave uz a beer and told uz tae sit doon an watch the match.

Sometimes even now when I go roond and my Mum goes oot the room, he makes snidey wee comments and says how he'll make uz do stuff and that I'm a total waster. But then when ma Mum's in the room he's dead nice and really pally.

Mum's started askin me roond loads t' watch the game wi Frank and hae tea and stuff. Mum's totally cheered up and she's got a new haircut and is like laughin and jokin aw the time.

Frank said he's gonnae take us on a wee holiday when he gets his next wage. He said I could come if I helped lay some patio fir Mums garden so I've been helpin wi that.

Sometimes I think now how it's dead good I fell asleep that night efter Pleasureland coz otherwise I couldo been like ane o those guys yi see ootside the chippy scabbin fir money.

Frank says when we go on holiday, we'll go t' this place he's been wi his ex-family cawed The American Adventure that's actually a place in England. He says it's got loadso really big rides, and that Pleasureland's a total hole in comparison.

My film's nearly finished now coz I've managed t' come up wi a well cool problem. I cannie let yi know what its aboot yet, but let's just say it's pretty brutal.

# William John MacDonald
## Carl MacDougall

*THE MOTHER*

He's usually back by one.

When he didn't come in, I phoned Peter.

He'll be fine, he said. He'll be getting a lift off Lachie John.

But Lachie's car passed without stopping, so I phoned again.

I'll have a look, he said.

*The Brother*

He was at the side of the road, two miles out of town and six miles from home. He was on a bend and at first I thought he'd been hit by a car, but when I saw his face I knew it was different. He'd taken a doing, a really bad doing. He was unconscious, lying in blood and vomit.

I was lucky. I got a signal and had some credit, so I phoned the ambulance and waited till the paramedics came.

*The Paramedic*

There wasn't a lot we could do. We took him to hospital and waited till the doctor came. She took one look at him and said, Glasgow. Right away.

I don't know how he was alive. I was afraid to look at his head. His skull was almost lying open. He must have been kicked, but it was more than once. I think they kept stamping on his head. And his eye was out. I've never seen anything like it and can't imagine how anyone could do that to another human being.

*The Girl Friend*

I know Billy MacDonald. His Mum works in the Co-op. I think his Dad was lost at sea, something like that, an accident. We were in the same class right through primary and secondary; he stayed on and I left. I heard he was going to university, but I don't know what happened.

I know there was a fight and they said it was Andy. He'd left the pub and I didn't know where he was; but he was in the house, sitting by the fire when I got in. I asked and he said, No. But his shirt and jacket were soaked in blood and there was even blood on his boots.

Don't tell anyone, he said. Please don't tell anyone.

I don't need to tell anyone, I said. Everybody knows it was you. They told me.

*The Driver*

I usually give Billy a lift home right enough. But he was in a fight. I don't know what happened. But I heard he fancied Kelly Ann Mathieson. He must've said something to her for Andy wouldnae've done that unless he'd said something, even though he can be funny, mind.

Anyway, I never saw him and thought he must've gone to Wilma's party. He usually says, but I hardly spoke to him all night, so when I never saw him at the end I just went home. It was next day I heard.

*The Boy Friend*

I don't know. I don't remember. I don't remember what happened.

I was drunk and don't remember.

➤

## The Barman

Billy was drunk. He gets drunk most weekends, falls about the place but doesn't cause any bother. He gets drunk, sometimes he sings that country and western thing about *Crazy*, then he sits and is quiet. He usually gets a lift off Lachie John.

I didn't think there'd be a problem. That happens up here, then they sort themselves out when they leave to go to university at the end of the summer, or they get a job in Glasgow or someplace. There's no work here. The fish farm. That's it.

## The Barmaid

I did, I saw a bit of it. He was at the bar and he was talking to Kelly Ann, nothing in it, just talking. He asked if she wanted a drink and she said no. He asked how she was doing and she said Fine and asked how he was and he said he was going to university in Glasgow.

Andy had been in bother at work. I don't know what for and Kelly Ann took the boss's side and said he was in the wrong, which everybody knew would be the case anyway.

Andy was sitting by the door, watching Billy and Kelly Ann and he followed Billy out when Billy went for a smoke.

I was over by the door, collecting glasses. Next thing, I heard Billy scream.

## The Helicopter Pilot

The weather was bad. We couldn't get up there. The call came in the middle of the night, about twenty to four and it was well after ten when we got up there. A lovely run. Lovely. Up there in just over an hour and back to Glasgow in the same time, maybe a wee bit more because a wind got up, but the sun was lying low over the water. Magical. Just magical. Gorgeous it is, absolutely gorgeous. Imagine living there and waking up to that every morning. It's a dream really.

## The Barmaid

Billy did nothing to defend himself.

He went outside for a smoke.

I said something about him getting cheap fags because his mother worked in the Co-op and he said she didn't even know he smoked.

Then Andy came out. Billy was lighting a fag and Andy said, What the fuck were you saying to her?

Billy said, What? Saying what to who?

And that seemed to rile Andy. Saying what to who, he said. Saying what to who. Do you think I'm fucken daft.

He had something in his hand. It could have been a knife. I'm not sure, but he lashed out and the next thing Billy's let out this scream and put his hand up to his eye. Then Andy shoved him and started kicking into his head. Billy couldn't even defend himself because he was holding his eye.

They pulled Andy off, but he got away and jumped on Billy's head, fucken jumped on him with both feet, then jumped again. I don't know how many times he jumped on.

Jesus.

We got him off and Billy was just lying there.

You stupid fucker, someone said. Get you to fuck out of here. Get off home.

Andy knew. He looked at Billy and he knew. He never said a word, never even went back into the pub, just went off home, ran down the road. It was the last thing I saw, him running down the road like a wee boy.

## The Driver

I'll tell you what I heard. They took Billy and left him at the side of the road.

As if we didn't know.

As if anything's a secret here.

I think they thought the police would think a car had hit him.

I don't know for sure, but I can well imagine who did it.

## The Mother

They told me Billy'd had an accident and I said what kind of accident and they said he's had a bad accident and he's in the hospital. Our Peter had told me they'd found him and he was in an awful state, so we went down to the hospital, but they wouldn't let me see him.

I spoke with the doctor, just a girl really,

and she told me he was going to Glasgow and I could go in the helicopter with him if I wanted, but I asked how would I get back and she said she wasn't sure, so I said would I be able to phone Glasgow and she said she'd be sure to let me know what happens and she'd give me the number.

So I just waited.

*The Police Sergeant*

The paramedics have to tell us and we investigated. Waste of time. We knew what happened; but if you ask anybody, they saw nothing and heard nothing. We spoke to Kelly Ann Mathieson, Andrew MacLeod and Lachlan John MacKinnon and they all said they knew nothing. We spoke to the barman, Michael Smith, and the barmaid, Sarah Ann Campbell. She said nothing, though we know she saw what was going on, and he more or less confirmed what we already knew.

We could tell MacLeod was lying. Anybody could tell.

People saw you leave the bar after Billy.

I went for a piss, he said.

Who saw you in the lavatory?

And he just looks at us and said, Nobody.

The case is still open and will be open for some time. It'll come out. We know what happens up here. It'll come out.

*The Doctor*

No matter how many times you see this, you never get used to it. I got the call around half ten on the Sunday. I was told a serious case was coming in from the north and to get ready. It was an emergency.

I asked for the notes and there weren't any. They come with the patient, so I phoned the local doctor. She told me what I needed to know. A fight, severe fracture, internal bleeding, brain probably pierced with skull bone, eye almost certainly lost, cuts to the face and the paramedics had done a good job. No idea how long he'd been lying out on the road, but he had definitely been moved and could have lost consciousness when they moved him and after that he just drifted off.

I had the theatre ready; the anesthetist

and nurses were waiting. They wheeled him in and I opened his eye to see if there was any sign and of course there was none, but there was something about the boy, the look on his face, or maybe just the face itself, a soft face, a sensitive face. It could have been an intelligent face. There was certainly no harm in it.

I don't often do that and I don't know why I did it then. I don't do it because I was advised not to; it can distract you, personalises the thing, makes it a person rather than a patient. But I'm not sorry I did it. He looked as if he'd been a nice lad.

I did what I could, of course. Things might have been different if we've got to him sooner, but that's always the case.

*The Mother*

I don't know how I heard. But it didn't take long.

Billy was hit on the Saturday and I heard on the Monday.

Tell the truth, I don't know how I heard, but when he came in for cigarettes I told him.

My Billy's in hospital in Glasgow, I said. Do you know anything about it?

He never spoke, never said anything. Just looked at me and walked out.

*The Nurse*

We do everything for William. Three years he's been here, we wash and dress and change him, we feed him and try to give him exercises, move his arms and legs, sometimes we try and speak to him.

Sometimes he might respond to music. If a tune or a song comes on, country and western usually, you see something like a smile, as if he's trying to smile.

*The Brother*

It's done something to her. I don't know what it is, but I can see it. It's as if it's given her a purpose, as if her life has a meaning.

Ever since my Dad died and I got married, Billy was everything, absolutely everything to her. And since his accident, what else can you call it, she's taken on a new lease of life, a new

➼

spirit, as if she's fighting to bring him back, as if somehow doing what she does will restore him.

It's sad, such a shame. What can you do?

*The Local Doctor*

You never know, difficult to say. I've seen them survive if they're left alone. The kicking was the cause, but him being moved probably did more damage. He'd been put in a van and driven and left at the side of the road like a dead dog. Moving him could well have been as bad as kicking him, worse maybe. You can't tell one from the other. If I was asked, I'd have to say the place, really. No one's to blame and they're all to blame.

*The Mother*

My Billy still can't talk, I told him. He was going to university and now he can't talk.

He never came back.

So I told her, the Kelly Ann one. I told her. You can tell that useless waster who sleeps with you that my Billy still can't talk. I hope what happened to my child never happens to your child, even though he's the father.

She stopped coming in as well.

So I told his father and mother and her father and mother and none of them said anything. Enjoy your grandchild, I said to them. I hope he's happy and well and a clever baby and I hope nothing happens to him like what happened to my Billy.

I put up a poster, reward for information leading to the conviction of the person or persons who harmed William John MacDonald. No response. Not yet.

None of them come in now. They've a round trip of more than eighty miles for their shopping. I was told to stop driving customers away and I told them I'm not driving customers away. They're perfectly free to come and go as they please. I'm only making conversation.

I hear he's going to Glasgow. But I'll find him. I go to Glasgow to see Billy and I'll find him when I go there.

It won't take long. Somebody's sure to know Kelly Ann.

*The Police Sergeant*

Not much more we could do.

It's an awful thing to say, but if the laddie dies and it becomes a murder inquiry, everything's different then.

We can subpoena witnesses, bring them in for questioning and eventually the truth comes out. But while he's still alive, there's not much more we can do.

*The Nurse*

It's his Mum I feel sorry for. She's a lovely woman, always cheery and she comes down here as regular as clockwork. Mrs MacDonald's due today, we say without thinking.

There's no point in feeling sorry for William. His life is more or less over. But his Mum comes every two or three weeks. She brings crisps and sweets and juice and feeds him and she sits and holds his hand and strokes his hair and asks him to tell her who it was.

She brings new clothes for him, tracky bottoms and good shirts.

But he keeps putting on weight. He's over 24 stone now.

We tell her, Please stop feeding him rubbish. It's bad for him.

I have to do something, she said. I can't leave him like this.

# Toothless Towards the Grave

Steve Cashell

IN THE EARLY 1970s Hallam must've felt a little sympathy for us. He tried to distract us from the terror he caused. He got his niece, an art-college student, to paint along the surgery wall a mural that was high up enough to see even when he had us tilted back in the chair.

Sally Hallam produced a detailed and realistic-looking mural showing part of our town's high street – the section you saw across the road from the steps of the Powsail Hotel. She painted the two and three-storey buildings that formed an uneven terrace there, with shop facades jostling one another at street level, and flat-windows lining the floors above and more windows jutting as cornices from the roofs. She painted townsfolk too, walking along the pavement in front.

Did it work? Did the high street mural prove so fascinating that we forgot about Hallam while he bent over us and squinted into our mouths?

With me, I suppose it helped. I appreciated having something to look at other than the dentist and his tray of instruments. In fact, by the time he poked the sickle-probe and the mouth-mirror towards me, I was more than looking at the mural. I thought that by concentrating on it hard enough I could transport myself out of the chair and into it. And maybe behind the doors of those two-dimensional shops, or among the folk on that two-dimensional pavement, I could hide from the sadistic bastard.

I thought so, and tried to do it, but never succeeded.

Through those bouts of intense concentration I came to know the shops and businesses in the mural very well. Indeed, I learned far more about the features of Mason's the Newsagent, Hegarty's Grocery and Off Licence, the Soulis Bar, Harmony Records, Rob Fleet the Barber and Palacci's Tearoom than I would've done by merely walking past them every day on the real high street.

I ended up knowing the exact hue of paint used for each façade – for example, the verdant green of Hegarty's and the waxy white of the Soulis, though the latter also had yellow streaks running down from the ends of its windowsills and from points along its spouting. I knew that the frontage of Mason's had three square sheets of glass with red sills while Rob Fleet had small casement windows with brown roll-up blinds behind them. I knew the style of lettering used in each sign – how, say, Palacci's was written in capital letters but Tearoom was written in lower-case ones, whereas Harmony Records was transcribed in italics along five parallel lines that began with a g-clef.

While I absorbed these features Hallam talked above me. Mostly, he talked about the big political issues of the times – the three-day week, the oil crisis and the Northern Irish troubles, and later the Lib-Lab pact, the Winter of Discontent and the devolution vote – though as I was a kid and had a steel prong hoking around in my mouth, he was obviously thinking aloud and didn't expect discussion. Occasionally, however, he'd say something that was directed at me. Never did he say anything good.

'Well. Don't like the look of that second molar on the left mandible. If I've ever seen a tooth *begging* for a filling, that's the one.'

'Discoloration already? How old are you? Ten? What have you stuck in your mouth to make those central incisors the colour of cheese?'

'Good news. If you maintain this standard of dental hygiene you won't need to see me for much longer. Bad news. That'll be because you won't have a tooth left in your sweetie-munching wee head.'

Often there'd come a point when the nurse wheeled over the drill and its attendant machinery and I'd stare at the mural more desperately than ever.

The figures on the pavement weren't anonymous. Sally Hallam had painted real townspeople. For instance, stepping from the door of Harmony Records was a young man in a purplish jacket, with black curly hair covering his shoulders and great shirt-lapels tapering out from his throat. I recognised him as Ronnie Sterricks, who seemed to spend all his free time in Harmony, pestering its staff to play David Bowie or King Crimson or Mott the Hoople on the shop hi-fi. And I saw a woman who was short but very broad, so that her greatcoat looked like it'd been hung over a drying rack. She carried a wicker basket – the real basket, I knew, contained a purse, brush and hairbands, stuff other women kept in handbags. This was Mrs Mason, who ran the newsagent's.

Meanwhile, two men stood by the entrance of the Soulis Bar. One was burly and wore a shirt and flannel trousers that were kept up by braces. He held a glass of stout in one hand and a cigarette in the other. The other was a tall skinny man in a black duffel coat. Only a few wisps of hair saved his head from baldness. These were the proprietor of the Soulis, Sammy Knox, and Willie Maxwell, whose son Drew was known at school as Maxie the Bully and was the only person in my childhood who inspired as much fear as Hallam did. Because I'd seen Willie Maxwell teetering about in real life, I suspected that in the mural Sammy and him weren't having a sociable blether. Sammy was likely saying, 'Ye cannae come in here, man. Ye're foo awready. Eff off!'

By now Hallam had taken the drill and lowered it into my mouth. It began its noise and made contact. Not even the characters in Sally Hallam's mural could divert me then. Suddenly the only sensations I had were of the drill gnawing through my tooth and shrieking in my head.

Later I'd stumble along that part of the high street, past those half-dozen shops, maybe even seeing some of those people – Ronnie Sterricks inside the window of Harmony Records nodding his head along to Space Oddity, or Mrs Mason clutching her wicker basket in a hand blackened with newspaper ink, or Willie Maxwell smelling of the Famous Grouse though it was only the early afternoon. My jaw throbbed with pain and I wondered where I was really, if my body was in the high street proper or if it remained in Hallam's chair while in delirium my mind wandered amid the daubs of paint on his surgery wall.

By the time I reached my teens, it wasn't just my diet of chocolate, chewing gum, liquorice, toffee and Irn Bru that was ravaging my teeth. I'd started playing in the most junior of the high school's rugby teams and my stocky shape made me ideal for the front row of the scrum, where my mouth and its 32 tenants could easily collide with heads, shoulders, elbows and, occasionally, fists. I'd graduated to playing for the second junior team when a collapsed scrum left my head pressed against the turf while above me a blundering second-row forward stepped on my upper jaw. One of his rugby-boot studs broke through the teeth there.

'Left canine on the maxilla,' sighed Hallam later. 'I'll splint it to its neighbours and see if it re-attaches.' I contemplated the picture on his wall and after a moment's puzzlement I realised what was wrong about it. Rob Fleet had sold his barber's shop the year before and the premises, completely refurbished, were home now to a unisex hairdressing salon.

It didn't re-attach and my upper left canine passed into history just as Rob's barber's shop had.

My next visit to Hallam came a few years

later, following a Friday-night disco at the Drill Hall where I'd got into a fight with Drew Maxwell, formerly known as Maxie the Bully. It wasn't much of a fight. Beforehand, round the back of the hall, I'd drunk three cans of cider and a half-bottle of Southern Comfort and after throwing one punch I lost my balance and landed on the floor. Drew was in a ferocious temper – his old man had died two months earlier and he was still screwed up about it – and while I was down he kicked me four, five, six times in the face. With the last of those kicks came an agonising snapping in the gum above my central-right incisor. For some reason it was another fortnight before I went to Hallam. By then the tooth was swivelling in its gum as drunkenly as Drew's Dad had often swivelled on the high street. The dentist removed the dead root, filled the cavity with cementing material and splinted the tooth in the hope that it'd find anchorage again.

'If you'd come to me *immediately*,' sighed Hallam, whose hair was iron-grey now. 'But the longer you wait, the worse the prognosis.' Then he started speaking about how Margaret Thatcher was making good on her election promises and was turning round the country's fortunes. By now I was old enough to understand his ramblings and felt confident enough to argue. But there was so much dental apparatus in my mouth that I couldn't tell him I thought he was talking shite.

On Hallam's wall the late Willie Maxwell hovered like a ghost beside Sammy Knox outside the Soulis Bar. And in real life, I realised too, you no longer saw Ronnie Sterricks at Harmony Records. Ronnie had given up on music, possibly in disgust at the advent of punk rock. In fact, he'd moved away and was reportedly married and working in Aberdeen.

I should've gone to Hallam earlier. The incisor was a lost cause. He rigged up a mini-set of dentures for me, a false canine at the side for the rugby injury, a false incisor at the front for the Drew Maxwell injury – though for the set to fit in my mouth he had to remove a *third* tooth for it, at the *other* side.

For many years I didn't bother with the dentist. As my father had done before me, I took a job in the town woollen mill. I continued to play rugby and eat sweet things, without always bothering to brush my teeth, and in addition I smoked and drank heavily with my rugby-mates and mill-colleagues. Then sometime in the late 1980s a molar in my left lower jaw became painful. The tooth was badly decayed. Underneath, the gum swelled up and oozed pus. So I made an appointment at the surgery again.

I got a surprise. Hallam was no longer there – that I hadn't known about his retirement showed how negligent I'd been of my dental health during those years. His replacement was a man who didn't look much older than I was. His voice had the same disdainful tone as his predecessor's, though.

'Dear me,' he said, 'what a dreadful mess. Beyond repair, I'd say.'

So out it came.

Ironically, a major reason for the crap state of my teeth had recently disappeared – the high street had lost Hegarty's Grocery and Off-Licence, which I remembered neither for its groceries nor for its alcohol but for the trays of sweets and chocolate bars on its counter. In the mid-1980s Fine Fare opened a big supermarket on the outskirts of the town, causing Hegarty's and the other local grocery shops to go out of business. The Hegarty family rented the premises to a cancer research organisation, which turned them into a second-hand fundraising shop. Now the only reminder that they'd been a grocery was that façade painted on the surgery wall.

Occasionally during the ensuing years I returned to the dentist, though only when I was in pain and *had* to return. My later rugby career brought more crazings and chippings of enamel. An inflammation of the gums, difficulty chewing and complaints about my halitosis – which I got on the rugby field whenever we locked heads together for a scrum – sent me back, to be told by Hallam's successor that I was suffering from something called periodontal disease. For the condition to stabilise, he warned, I had to take *meticulous* care of my teeth in future.

➥

I didn't. More of my teeth disappeared.

And more things on Sally Hallam's mural went the way of those teeth. Harmony Records closed its doors, a victim of economics even before downloading music from the Internet became popular, and was replaced by an estate agent's. Marcello and Marisa Palacci retired and headed back to Italy and their tearoom turned into something called the Box of Delights. It was a place of chintzy wee ornaments and figurines that few local people bothered with, although it was popular with the tourists who were visiting the town in growing numbers.

The Soulis and Mason's the Newsagent soldiered on, though the latter stopped its paper-rounds and got rid of its paperboys, and apart from two racks of papers and magazines inside it didn't resemble a newsagent any more. Instead, it stocked books, especially tourist guides and volumes of glossy photographs taken by a man called Colin Baxter that depicted the Scottish countryside in glorious colours and light-tones. I lived just ten minutes' walk from the Scottish countryside but I'd never seen such colours and light myself.

I eventually became too old to play rugby, but by then I seemed to be losing teeth at an unstoppable rate and I no longer needed the odd thump or kick from a Gala or Kelso or Jed-Forest player to aid the process. At some point Hallam's successor retired too, much to my bemusement. The woollen mill where I'd expected to spend my life working had closed several years ago and since then I'd drifted, doing whatever I could find – laying bricks, serving drinks, washing dishes, stacking shelves in Fine Fare. So this guy who was hardly any older than me had retired while I hadn't *found* a proper job yet.

Hallam's replacement's replacement was a little Welshwoman who didn't say much. She removed the final teeth from my lower jaw and fitted me out with a complete bottom plate of dentures, to go with the partial plate I had in my top jaw. What saddened me more than the loss of those mandible teeth was the sight of old Mrs Mason bustling along in the high street mural, wearing her greatcoat and carrying her basket. In reality she'd died the previous week at the age of 84. She'd worked behind her shop counter until the end.

Recently the little Welshwoman removed something from my upper jaw and informed me, 'Well, that leaves just the one.'

My eyes were fixed on the mural. I knew that Mason's had lately been replaced by a Help The Aged charity shop, a neighbour for the Cancer Research shop that'd taken over Hegarty's twenty years earlier. I didn't reply.

She continued, 'I can take that last one out too if you like. So you can get a full plate of dentures for up top as well.'

An hour later I made my way along the high street. Past two charity shops, an estate agent's, a gift shop and a tanning salon – that last one had replaced the unisex hairdresser, which had replaced Rob Fleet's barber shop. People milled by me but I didn't recognise any faces until I got to the entrance of the Soulis Bar, where Sammy Knox spent even more time these days on account of the smoking ban.

Poor Sammy was in bad shape. His trademark braces seemed ready to slide off his slumped shoulders and his face was a swollen mess. A similarly-swollen hand clutched a pint of Guinness while his cigarette was almost hidden between the pudgy fingers of his other hand. He peered across the high street, to where some workmen were carrying out renovations on the Powsail Hotel.

'Okay, Sammy?' I asked.

'No okay,' he mumbled. He nodded across to the Powsail. The construction company had put up a wall of boarding along the front of it. 'Thir's rumours aboot that place, ye ken. Supposedly it's Wetherspoon's whae've acquired it.'

'Wetherspoon's?' I gasped. 'The pub chain? *Here?*'

Sammy shuddered – he was feeble now, so it was a violent shudder. Froth lapped over the edge of his pint-glass and splattered down on the pavement. 'Gies me the willies jist thinking aboot it.'

'Sammy,' I said, rubbing my tongue against the stub of my last remaining tooth, 'take good care o yerself.'

I put a hand on his shoulder and was

shocked at how insubstantial it felt – as if it consisted of two dimensions rather than three. Meanwhile, his face was so misshapen it looked like a big, crude smudge of paint.

Then from the direction of the Powsail, from beyond the wall, there came the sound of a drill.

# The Custodian

**J David Simons**

THERE WAS SOMETHING satisfying and manly in the sound of bristle against blade. He twisted his chin from side to side, made sure he'd got the shaving sharp and clean. Then he poured some balm into his palm, rubbed it into his cheeks, along his jaw-line, into his neck, marvelled at the immediate soothe to his skin. He only ever used the stuff on special days. And this was a special day. This was her death day.

Some say he looked like her butler. He often thought it was the reason the Trust had given him the job. Almost everyone who stepped off the tour buses commented on the resemblance, asked him to pose for a photograph, made some joke he'd heard a million times before. It was the eyes that did it. He could see that as he pushed his face up close to the mirror. That trusting, pathetic, sad-eyed look of the dutiful retainer. Of the loving servant. He slapped his cheeks. 'There you go, Brian,' he said. 'Special day.'

On any other day, they only visited her mansion down in London, with never the desire to come all the way up here to see where she had grown up, to view the place that had really moulded her. Only the truly dedicated fans made the pilgrimage to this council estate, the women sporting her hair-do and the mock-ups of her famous dresses, the men because they had been a little bit in love.

He took a sip of his tea now gone cold. At the London house, his custodian counterpart, Roger, greeted everyone at the door with a double-handed clasp, a solemn air and the pious smell of talc as if he were welcoming them all to church. 'Thank you so much for contributing your energy to this wonderful place,' he'd heard Roger tell visitors as they marvelled at the marble pillars and the gilded panelled ceilings. 'She would have been so very happy to know you have come here to pay your respects.' How the bloody hell did Roger know what made her happy? He slurped down the rest of his cold tea, tossed the tea leaves into the toilet.

He closed the door on his tiny bathroom, made up his bed, tidied away his clothes. Once this had been her parents' bedroom, long gone they were now, slept together here for forty odd years, thought he could smell her mother's lavender perfume still lingering. They wouldn't move out the place when their daughter offered, didn't want to uplift to London, or even a bigger house in the area, happy where they were, God bless them. They lived in a world after the war when the real things in life were appreciated. Like community. Like loyalty.

He'd grown up himself in the area, another reason why the Trust might have employed him, a local lad. He'd even met her once, years ago, when she was but a child, out walking in the park with her mother. He'd had his dog with him then, a black Labrador, skin as shiny as shoes newly polished, Ringo he'd called it, after the Beatle, that's what he'd wanted to be back then, a drummer. Always with a pair of sticks in his hand, rattling on the bins, the fence posts, the bollards and the flower pots, banging out his frustrations. Ringo was the one who'd sniffed her out, must have known the lass was going to shine. He could see her now, swirling around, clapping and giggling as the mutt poked his wet snout around her ankles. He knew straight away there was something special about her. It was as if she kicked up a magic dust with her feet, lit up his boring teenage life with that smile. How that simple gesture with those ample lips had penetrated his adolescent heart. Her mother had made a simple comment, a shy, thin woman she was, battered down by the war, she said: 'Your dog seems to like her.' 'She's like a little princess,' he heard himself reply, talking as if he were a local housewife rather than a pock-marked teen with a Beatle haircut. To which her mother snapped back, quick as a wink, like she could see the future: 'It's a film star she wants to be. Like Audrey Hepburn. But a Princess Grace would do fine too.' They had laughed at that. It was funny that out of all the millions of forgotten memories piled up since that simple encounter, he should be able to recall that one. As if it were preparing him for this job to come. Or maybe it wasn't even a memory at all. And he had just made it up to spite Roger.

He locked the door on his bedroom, tested the handle just to make sure, it was the only room in the house they didn't have access to. He wiped his sleeve along the banister as he stepped down the narrow stairway, poked his head into the front room, a step back into his own teenage years that would always cause his breath to shorten. Everything in its place, the armchairs and the sofa, the Dansette record player in garish red leatherette, the wireless set, the musical cigarette box that played The Blue Danube Waltz, one of those silver-plated ash-trays you pushed down on so the ash spins to the base. He remembered as a child mercilessly playing with one until it broke, felt himself flinch even now to his father's leather belt slashed across his naked thighs. Put him off cigarettes for life.

In the kitchen, he took down his clothes from the old-fashioned pulley, boiled up an egg, made himself a cup of tea, watched the rain pouring down, at least there would be no showing them out to the garden to see the swing. That photograph of her playing on it remained the iconic image of her childhood. It must have been taken about the same time

he'd come across her in the park for she was even wearing the same pair of sandals and the cardigan with a pretty posy of flowers embroidered on the front. Her little white socks, her bare legs kicking away, her head hung back, that Looby Loo doll from off the telly wedged in her lap, so innocent she was and unspoiled. The swing used to be hung up with ropes but too many fat-arsed visitors had jammed themselves onto it until the fibres had frayed and snapped. Health and safety meant chains held it now.

There had been seven mini-bus loads. Three in the morning. Three in the afternoon. Then the Trust phoning him up late on to see if he could take one more. He'd rather be going down to the pub but the overtime was too good to miss. The demand to visit too great. After all it was ten years to the day since the accident. He met them at the gate. 'Oh, doesn't he look like...' 'He's the spitting image of...' 'Could we just have one photo before we go in?' It usually took him a couple of hours to warm up, so it was the early afternoon crowd that got the best of his patter, the jokes, the Ringo story. He'd herd them around from room to room, showing them where she performed her party pieces on Sunday afternoons as she danced to The Blue Danube Waltz, the banister she loved to slide down, the bits of framed needlework, the gilt-edged certificate for winning a baby photo contest. Then he'd leave them to wander. No mobile phones or photographs allowed inside. That would drive them mad, especially the Yanks and the Japanese, usually they'd try to sneak one in anyway. Some had even brought black-bordered memorial cards. He generously displayed them on the mantelpiece beside the photograph of her on the swing, he'd get a decent tip for that. One woman from Tucson, Arizona, had even got down on her knees and kissed the kitchen floor.

It was after nine before he got down to the pub, swigged down a couple of pints quick to ease his throat dried up from all the talking. He managed a game of darts with Billy from behind the bar, felt a bit wobbly on his feet from all the drinking on an empty stomach, so he just plonked himself down in a quiet corner with an evening newspaper and a double whisky. The print was all a bit hazy before his eyes, he patted his pockets for his glasses but he'd left them back at the house. He'd just lifted up his gaze from the page when he thought he saw her. Not directly but through her reflection in the long bar-mirror. That famous blonde bob, the smudge of dark around the eyes, the cornflower blue dress she'd worn on the night of the accident. He could have sworn it was her, just flashing by between the snug and the ladies' loo, the mirror just catching the space. His chest went all tight on him, the taste of stale beer washed back from his stomach, thought he might throw up there and then. He looked around the bar, Billy drying the glasses, giving him back a quick smile. 'All right there, Brian?' 'Yeah, I'm fine', he stammered, the fruit machine winking and flashing its too bright lights, the empty tables, his own hand shaking as he reached out to pick up his glass. He'd keep a watch on the mirror. If she'd gone in to use the loo, then she'd have to come out. Which she did about five minutes later. He pushed himself out of his chair, stood up quick, his head feeling all empty and dizzy, he stumbled against his table knocking over the pint glass. He heard Billy shouting after him but he was up at the swing doors of the snug with their brass fingerplates, fancy patterns on the glass, pushed them open, expecting to see her there at one of the three small round tables. But the room was empty.

He was soaked through by the time he got back to the house, decided to let himself in round the back, didn't want to leave his wet footprints all over the carpet in the hallway. As he fussed and scraped with his key in the lock, he could hear the garden swing creaking away on its chains in the wind, had a flash of her sitting there, bare legs kicking away, but he daren't turn round. He took off his shoes in the kitchen, draped his coat over a chair to drip dry on the lino, he'd worry about mopping up in the morning. Up the stairway he tiptoed like he used to do as a

teenager with his parents asleep, thought about checking in on her room but decided against it. He unlocked his own bedroom door, didn't even bother putting on the lights or closing the curtains, just threw himself down on the bed.

A loud banging and a rattling woke him, his first thought being he must have left a window open. He turned over, squinted at the clock, two o'clock green-glowed in the darkness, he threw back the blanket, he was still in his clothes. He sat up at the side of his bed, knuckled his eyes open, his head still woozy, but clear enough to realise it wasn't the window rattling but someone downstairs at the front door. He staggered out into the top landing, he could see the outline of a figure beyond the smoky glass. He switched on the light. Christ, it was her.

'Come on,' the voice teased through the letter box. 'You can open up now.'

He let himself down the first few steps. She rattled the door hard.

'I can see you in there,' she said. 'Come on, let me in.'

He reached the bottom of the stairs, flicked on the outside light. He could see her instinctively shield her eyes. The blonde bob. The cornflower blue dress. He slid back the chain, turned the handle. She pushed open the door hard and fast. He felt her hand pat his cheek as she passed. He grabbed her wrist, smothered her palm with kisses.

'I'm sorry, I'm so sorry,' he said, the familiar hint of lavender on her skin, he wanted to suck it in.

'Too late for that now.'

He tightened his clutch on her wrist, that so slender wrist.

'Let go. You're hurting me.'

He dropped his grasp and she paraded into the front room.

'So this is where you ended up. I should have guessed ages ago.' She turned round to face him, clutched her dress at the hem, fanned out her skirt, gave a twirl. 'What do you think? Do I look like her?' She screwed up her mouth, leaned over in a pout at him. 'Ooh, Brian. Don't you just love me?'

'I think you should leave.'

She looked around the room. 'I grew up in a place like this. So did you. And I'm not going anywhere. It's taken me all this time to find you.'

'How did you find me?'

'Your picture was in the evening paper. Outside this very house. Kind of them to give the address.'

He watched as she plucked the cards off the mantelpiece, had a quick read, sniggered, threw them into the empty grate.

'Please don't do that.'

She picked up the cigarette box off the sideboard, opened the lid. The Blue Danube Waltz. She smiled. 'Pretty.'

'It's just for show.'

'No fags then?'

'You can't smoke in here. Against Trust rules.' He pointed to the sign on the wall. No Mobiles, No Photographs, No Smoking. He felt stupid doing it, withdrew his arm, shoved his hands in his pockets, fingers gripping tight. 'Just go.'

'The little girl got a bedroom then?'

'You can't go there.'

'I'm going to do whatever I want, Brian. Just like you did. Walking out on me.'

She waltzed through into the kitchen, tripped slightly on that one step down, it was something he usually warned the visitors about.

'Bloody weird,' she said. 'Living like this. In the past. It's like being trapped in a bloody mausoleum. Makes me shiver.'

'A living history,' he said, annoyed to find himself having to defend this place against her. 'She touched all our lives.'

'She touched your head more like it.' She took one of the china teacups off its hook above the sink, let it drop, smash on the floor. 'Pity about that.'

'Stop it.' He crouched down, scrambled about for the broken pieces. A shard cut into his finger. He sucked the spot, looked for blood. Another cup fell, broke beside him. 'Please stop it.'

'What? The Trust wouldn't like it?'

He followed her back into the front room.

'Look at you,' she said. 'Just like a little puppy. Sniffing around after me. Here, doggie, doggie. Here, doggie, doggie.'

'Please go. I want you to go.'

She had reached the Dansette record player, plucked the record off the spindle. 'Summer Holiday' by Cliff Richard. She had loved that record. Made her want to go places.

'What's this then?'

'Summer Holiday.'

She laughed in that too loud way of hers, like she wanted to pretend to everyone how happy she was. It made him want to cover his ears.

'Well, you never took me on any summer bloody holidays.' She tossed the record across the room like a Frisbee. They both watched as it hit the curtains, fell to the ground.

It wasn't a conscious thought. Just like when he had walked out on her all those years ago. One minute he was at home, the next he was on his way for the interview. She should have known. After all, she always said he looked like her butler. But there it was. The musical cigarette box in his hand. Solid wood. Needed a full spread of his fingers to hold it. He struck it hard against the side of her head. Her knees buckled, she fell on to the sofa. She lay there quite natural, her head against the arm of the couch, her limbs loose, her dressed pushed up a little on her thighs, the blonde wig fallen half-off. She could have been asleep really, watching the telly, her tongue slobbering a little over her bottom lip. He had a notion to check if she was still breathing but he didn't want to touch her. He threw the box onto one of the armchairs. The lid must have opened for it was still playing The Blue Danube Waltz as he left the room.

At the top of the stairs, he pushed open her bedroom door. The milky moonlight cut across the made-up bed, the magazine photo of Princess Grace thumb-tacked to the wall. He picked up a couple of her combs that lay on the child-dresser, started to tap out a beat across the back of a chair, across the dresser itself, the top of the window sill, the tiled shelf above the fireplace. 'Da, da, da, da, da – da,' he muttered to himself. 'Da, da, da, da, da – da.' He felt very tired now, a heavy weight pressing on his

➼

shoulders, his thighs, sucking the strength from his legs, forcing him to lay down on the pink candlewick spread. He picked up the Looby Loo doll that lay against the pillow, clutched it to his chest, felt the roughness of its yellow-wool hair against his chin, the cool silk of the red ribbons, the coarse cloth in the stroke of his fingers.

'I love you,' he said. 'I love you.'

'If you don't have anything to say
don't write.

Ivan Klíma, *Love and Garbage*

# The Whip Hand
Brian Johnstone

Believing in the possibility of showtime
on the move,
that the sound of circus music blaring

from the speakers on the roof
means more
than silver in my pocket, pegs to hammer home,

I stake out another pitch and flatten grass:
for what?
The cheers, the hollow gasps, the silence

as I place my head inside each
lion's mouth.
It's not the teeth, the jaws I fear but seeing

deep into their eyes, each pupil blank
as every pitch
we quit, lifeless as the ground we pack so hard.

# Parable
Owen Gallagher

When the priest stood in the pulpit, the congregation's
prayers gathered speed like the engines on a Houston rocket.
We prayed that he be thrust to Heaven, cast down
for siding with the shipyard owners. He denounced
as Communists those who aided the striking workers.

God moves hands in many ways. The collection plate
was empty for weeks. Part of the flock moved to graze
on an ungodly plain. The priest, with a bishop and a live-in
housekeeper to keep, spoke no more on these Earthly matters.

# The Pope & Saint Marx
Owen Gallagher

Back then, every Catholic home possessed a picture of Pope John
XXIII. Some had lights that flashed, it was said,
to the rhythm of his heart. Most men in these households
were thankful for the light this cast which aided them
during the night to empty their weak bladders.

Mother's brother, Hugh, had two pictures, side by side:
one was the Pope, the other Saint Marx as Hugh called him.
Both were leaders of millions, he said. One was to assist us
into Heaven, the other to enable us to take what we were due
on Earth. This, the priest informed me at confession

was a mischievous notion. We prayed God would give me
extra guidance as I encountered such people as Hugh.


# The Bitter Fruits
Brian Johnstone

Something persuades the bitter fruits
that sweetness must be bought
with more than tears,

more than patience in the tending
of their needs, more than tasks
as endless as the seasons

still demand of those
who cut the stem to grow the shoot,
who risk the thorn

that worms into the flesh,
the gout of blood
that berries on the surface of the skin,

who cradle in the hollow of their palm
the thought of ripening,
something provable with time,

a certain knowledge
                    of vitality, of zest.

# Art School 1 & 2
Allan Harkness

## 1. UNTITLED (OR, WASTED EFFORT)
'There's not much there', but it is philosophically compact, controlled. Three
times untitled contains *untitled-ed*, at one point. White void abjection
in a feeble hand makes me think of Twombly, Fontana, Bataille...or Beckett.
I reckon he tosses off-references (minus lyrical, miracle-wracked Twombly).
On the bracketed metaphor/paradoxical title, gather this into both worlds,
sharing 'Untitled' with every materialist, self-referencing title-that-
isn't (the modernist's <u>Untitled</u>), whilst playing ennui, anomie, cool despair
to a gallery of poets. Of course, Waste Matter would be a better phrase
than 'Wasted Effort' because we poets had to squat to see this piece
and paint always reminds us of... shit. Just there, precisely there, it came
late as a perfect *drain-hôle* for Fine Art. From Untitled (or, Wasted Effort)
to the wall is a significant move too, as if this piece is an internal organ: *Ceci,
c'est un* exhausted *pipe, non?* All in all, a neatly deconstructed painting
addressing failure, in the land of Samuel Beckett – 'I can't go on. I will go on.'

'Go on! Do one!', cried the Liverpudlian in protest.

Colour's dance of infinity, heart's hope in narrative, both are missing.

So, **A** for pensive cleverness, **E**\* for denial of joy?

Fail, big style? Write 'Dip tha' thong' in red.

*What?*


## 2. FLOOR PIECE – 16 TITLES
for those who don't like titles

Magic Square

Jupiter Square

Untitled (From Saturn to Jupiter, a Navigational Device)

Untitled (Homage to Carl Andre)

Modern Ambiguity

Grid of Grids (Non-Priapic Piece)

Reason Blocked

Key Code

Pibroch at Marfa

Thick Black Blood : Evening is Particularly Dangerous

Un-Tiled (Glasgow Glottal Stop Version)

Understanding/Getting Lost

Self Text (To Be Deciphered)

Purity and Beauty of Failure

Untitled (Tiled)

Secret Name

# Unthanks
*for MD*

Andrew F Giles

'I wish, I wish, but it's all in vain. / I wish I was a maid again, / but a maid again I never can be, / 'til apples grow on an orange tree. / I wish my baby it was born, / and smiling on his Daddy's knee, / then I would go to yon churchyard / and let the long green grass grow over me.'
*Trad* arranged by the Unthank sisters

Between the piano keys, a tiny gap, the starless space unseen in a filament, hush, the music jumps up, gushes through it, well – it is not a gap, it is a maw. It is not a door. The same lippy mouth that gulped Lanark down, dragonscale and all. But there is a present of light there, this is important, a tiny present of light that can be sung in words. There are two worlds, more or less (like Donaghy's two kinds of folk it is not one of them but *un*-them, sort of neither within nor without, shivering on the borderline, the dragonstar meridian, where MD drank a cup of booze by the fire and told tales with his fiddle.) The two worlds are: i) a world that believes in the future, ii) a world that does not (this, all after MD, but that is something that had to be done personally. Perhaps you can see.) Unthank,  you may have read about it in the Scots folk novel that attaches itself to your arm and slowly grows up it like vine, or galloping trenchfoot, or twittering, glittering rigor – there are other names for it – it's a language, you learn it. I offered up my present of light to the dawning day, I scoured the dark planet for fiddles, drums, the last whistle of my ancestors, really I was just looking for a name or somebody to give me a name. The name I gave him was Uncle Mikey, he took it with him to a different meridian, a phantom-plane with a gunpowder sack on his back. Years passed. I had a blast. I followed everybody down the rabbit-hole and reached the nexus of two worlds, panting. Then, out of nowhere, these sisters, singing like 1000-year-old witches, tap-tap-tap, that fiddle, plumbing Lanark's interstices, the gap, the lilting volume between worlds. They unmake you, the clenched fistful of words that take shape in song and deliver you to the open mouth, the faceless maw. That is the door.

# Far Field

Jim Carruth

## I.

Because he knows, has always known
that a time will come in the near future
when he will have no say in the matter,
will not decide the date or time of departure
but be taken from here silent or screaming,
today he commands the collie to stay home
and one more time makes this journey of choice
leaving the farm for a couple of hours,
setting off from behind the old byre,
walking over the hill to the far field,
spending time away from the needs
of family and herd.

## II.

When he gets there the field will welcome him,
its gate open for that is how he leaves it
for anyone who'd take the time to travel here,
find as he does a space for thought,
safe for a moment in its heart,
the rough ground by the whins.
He disturbs a flurried brace of pheasants
then stands awhile, watching his childhood
and all the years since rise like the smoke
from the valley to drift in the wind.
However much he wants to.
he cannot shake the hands
of all those loved, buried or burned.

## III.

He searches for fragments and clues
and finds them in the marks he's left on this land,
cultivated grasses, fence and dyke;
the dry stane wall built up and fallen down
and raised again throughout his life.
He marks his herd, stamped through generations,
his decisions on their breeding, his choice
of bloodlines. He marks his family, his children
inheriting his weak heart, his values.
He marks himself,  branded
from a lifetime on the hill.

IV.

Does his life echo others in the valley,
their days sliced through with tarmacadam?
How many down there have never found their fit
and place? For them he offers up a prayer,
a promise of belonging. He offers up this field
but does not sense a bond with the valley and beyond
content to mark them like members of his herd.
All he feels is a greater pain, a loss
that he cannot name or comprehend. He falls
on his knees, rolls onto his back and cries out.
Who will tell him where the healing starts?

V.

Looking straight up into the sky
he follows one cloud, slow moving,
a thought with direction and purpose.
His ears fill with finches, a single peewit
and closer, the meanderings of industrious bees.
He turns his head, chants a litany:
timothy ragged robin cocksfoot common sorrel
meadowsweet bracken dock.
He is the witness to their survival from shared soil;
the celebrant to their community offering up
fistfuls of soil before closing his eyes

VI.

opening them on a vision – all seasons in one,
sun and moon together, birds circling
in endless migrations without destination,
smoke rising from the forests where each tree
is brought down. And hunger is the great harvest
as ripe barley shrivels back to the seed
in ploughed furrows. One field remains
a last acre without grass cloaked in the bellow
of black bullocks tearing at each other,
a surging mass of bloodied hides and flesh,
until knees buckle, stinking bodies
pile up in shrouds of flies.

**VII.**

He cries out, his body shudders
and he wakes not to one perfect answer
offered up in the blast of the west wind
but to questions that lie in the chill
of his bones, the roar of his herd,
the constant hum of the city in the valley.
Releasing his grip on this earth,
he rises to return home across the hill,
the light already failing.

# Husbandry

(for David)

Jim Carruth

Happens
   the farmer

to calve
   the cow

bring cow
   to calf

raise calf
   to cow.

Happens
   the farmer

to calve
   the cow.

# Laidlaw

## Jim Carruth

They say that some just end up bad
as though that should suffice for this:

the eldest of the brood, a black angus
fed from childhood on festering bales;

a mad beast uneasy in enclosed spaces,
heavy with dung, each breath's a wound.

His wide-eyed stare's a barley field on fire;
his muscled haunches thunder the night.

Circling the air with butt and bellow
his anvil thick skull puts out the stars.

*


Her slow brother came to visit one day,
followed a trail of red spots into the house

found the buckled belt, her sobbing body
a bloodied shield trampled into the carpet

uncovered beneath her a shaking son
offering up his stolen egg unbroken.

*


He charged them but was downed with a shovel.
Her brothers dragged him roaring to the pen.

They took castrators and pulled out his tongue;
in the end left him chained, neutered and mute.

Across the sharp stubble of harvest fields
the family carry their sister home.

Publisher to writer: "So you have 3000 people following your weekly blog, you have 8000 friends on Facebook, you have 4500 followers on Twitter and you podcast to 2000 subscribers. Excellent, excellent... oh, by the way, one last thing... Can you write?"

# Playing Dead

Ever Fallen In Love
Zoë Strachan
*Sandstone Press*, RRP £8·99, 350pp

Zoë Strachan's eagerly awaited third novel, *Ever Fallen In Love*, resonates with themes of identity and sexuality that have come to characterise not only her own writing, but that of the new wave of Scottish novelists who have emerged in recent years. The dual narrative, with one half set in a remote village in the Highlands and the other half in an unnamed Scottish university town, describes the student days of Richard and his shady but desirable friend Luke. While we become aware of a tragedy looming on the horizon for the student version of Richard, the second narrative shows us Richard ten years on, retreating from life and living as quietly as he is able.

The central relationship between Richard and Luke develops familiarly into that between the impressionable young student and the idolized bad-boy, complete with his scruffy hair, endless cigarettes and flamboyant sexual conquests. The stakes are upped regularly, with Luke leading Richard into drink and drugs, through joy riding and beyond, with Richard's interest in him moving through lust towards something approaching love, and his boundaries, moral and sexual, shifting ever outwards as a consequence. Meanwhile, the older Richard's sister comes to visit him in the Highlands, shaking up his hermit-like life and prompting recollections of his student days.

Following on from *Negative Space*, a debut filled with brutal emotion, and the weirdly intriguing cast of her second novel *Spin Cycle*, *Ever Fallen In Love* is Strachan's most accessible novel to date. That's not to say there are no challenging scenes here – as ever, Strachan is unflinching in her depiction of humanity's more questionable impulses – but with the students, the sex, the drugs and the dead girl, there is also a recognition of where we're at. The plot is carefully paced to keep the reader gripped and the well-placed hooks are effective. This is a tight and well-constructed novel. Chapters alternate between the two narratives, a device that keeps us reading fast, but Strachan surprises us with a matter-of-fact summation partway through the book when Richard tells his sister: "I was at uni, with Luke. There was a sort of accident. Somebody died. We both got chucked out." Except, of course, that's not all that happened, and this book is about more than a page-turning plot.

It is clear how the Scottish landscape influences Strachan's writing. The setting is vivid, with drenching downpours and wild seas mixing with beautiful shores and panoramas. The contrasting university town has its fair share of atmosphere too, with its abandoned castle and student digs, not to mention the simmering antagonism between the locals and the 'Yahs,' with Richard and Luke stuck somewhere in the middle. Older Richard works as a morally aware and sometimes morally compromised programmer for computer games, designing *Somme*, a WWI shoot-em-up with a conscience of sorts and a woman in the trenches pretending to be a man. That, combined with the subplot between Richard, his sister and his sister's friend Lauren, adds another level to the story and allows for some interesting asides.

*Ever Fallen In Love* doesn't quite have the red-raw emotion of *Negative Space*, or the unusual characters of *Spin Cycle*, but Strachan's maturity and insight shows through the beautifully constructed pages. The tempo stays effortlessly high and the tension keeps building along with Richard's desire. While Strachan's first two novels never quite achieved the levels of success they deserved, *Ever Fallen In Love* might be the one to catapult her into the mainstream.
**Golden Monkey**

# Questions or Answers

Gillespie and I
**Jane Harris**
*Faber, RRP £14·99, 528pp*

Is the heroine of Jane Harris's second historical novel a dangerous psychopath or a misunderstood spinster? That one could so easily be mistaken for the other is part of the fun Harris has with her readers – her first, massively popular work, *The Observations*, offered us a spirited young Irish maidservant's involvement with the wackier elements of nineteenth-century gentility. How will readers care, though, for the possibly deluded, certainly lonely Harriet Baxter? That question matters because Harris's work depends on making the strongest pact possible with her readers and she uses characterisation to do it. If John Fowles's *The French Lieutenant's Woman* alerted us to the postmodern possibilities of history – the general unknowability of sources – and Michel Faber's *The Crimson Pétal and the White* thirty years later cocked a snook at such artificiality with eye-wateringly authentic detail, where does Harris come in?

Well, she gives a nod to the postmodern ploy of the unreliable narrator, and plays around with 'official' testimony in the form of court records (and as they are presented in Harriet's narrative, how do we even know these are 'true'?). But Harris likes solidity in details too, and this book is a testimony to that effort to getting things right. We begin with a 1933 narrative, as the elderly Harriet looks back over the events from 1880 to 1890 when she arrived in Glasgow for the International Exhibition. An orphan with an independent income, she is in her thirties and unmarried. She is a classic Victorian autodidact, keen on self-improvement, and has even learnt first-aid – handy for the moment a middle-aged woman, Elspeth Gillespie, faints in front of her and swallows her false teeth. Harriet prevents the woman from choking to death and is duly invited to tea, where she meets Ned, Elspeth's son.

Ned is a painter struggling to gain acceptance into the small world of professional Glasgow artists. He has a beautiful but somewhat frail wife, Annie, and two daughters: the surly, elder Sybil, and the adored, angelic Rose. Harriet soon becomes acquainted with his sister, Mabel, and brother, Kenneth. Living only round the corner, she finds excuses to visit and eventually asks Ned to paint her portrait. He has no time, but Annie agrees to do it. Harriet is either a nuisance, inveigling her way into another household, or a great helper, keeping an impoverished family afloat. But as she gets to know them, Sybil's behaviour worsens, Annie becomes distraught, and when Harriet and Annie are poisoned at a New Year party, matters reach breaking point. A fatal catastrophe ensues, and Harriet finds herself remanded in prison on charges of kidnapping and murder. Is she a truly malevolent soul, or did she simply try to help, out of a need to belong? Her voice is appropriately uptight and prissy, yet this is a woman who knows about homosexuality, who walks through the city at any time of day or night, who rents out rooms for herself and engages staff. There is a hinterland to Harriet that suggests she is not quite the prim spinster she seems.

Harris's tale is a character-driven mystery thriller and she uses Harriet with great skill to woo us all. And yet when I turned that last page, I found myself wanting to know what it was all for. To inform about the Glasgow art scene at the end of the nineteenth century? Portray women's lives in the late Victorian world? To entertain? Perhaps we only ask these questions of historical fiction and perhaps that is unfair, but justification beyond being a 'rattling good read' seems necessary. This is historical fiction that merges the unreliability of the postmodern with the authenticity of the detailed doorstopper: but for what purpose? At the end of a hugely enjoyable read, I was, alas, no nearer to answering that question.
**Argos**

# Breaking the Rules

Can The Gods Cry?
Allan Cameron
*Vagabond Voices*, RRP £11·00, 256pp

In the afterword to *Can The Gods Cry?*, the author states, "As I reread these short stories before publication, my principal emotion was one of disappointment at their inability to live up to the original idea. The reasons for this failure probably lie in that original concept itself and in my limitations as a writer." Whether this is all meant as ironic humour or deliberate misrepresentation, there are some aspects of this afterword that ring rather too true. Even the back page blurb reads as a review of the collection (attempting to override actual reviews), mentioning how "The plot in one story stands out from the others." Hold onto your hats readers, your challenge is to wade through the rest until you find it.

Cameron tries to work innovatively in this collection, with awareness that he is covering previously trodden ground. He counteracts this with weighty but convoluted prose that suggests it might lead somewhere if the reader can just persevere a little longer. Too many false promises of pudding will leave readers with gurgling tummies. Bypassing Cameron's tendency to veer towards sententious dialogue and poorly hidden polemic is difficult.

Cameron makes no apology for breaking the accepted ground rules for writers, using adverbs ("... a lot of the academicians, the prescribers of good English don't like you doing that."), italicisation and capitalisation to convey meaning (as in the final dramatic climax of 'Escaping the Self'.) It is refreshing to read a book so adamantly written in a way that flouts the rules whilst still aiming to attain literary status. Cameron wants it both ways: he roots his stories in the everyday, readers meet familiar types in Scottish locations; then the net is thrown far from home.

Easy postmodern tricks ("That's right. I'm the Narrative Voice and I'm telling a story about you." – 'The Narrative Voice, Litter, Dog Turds and Sundry Other Things Most Base and Foul' and "Let me take time out from these short stories to speak as the author in an imagined dialogue..." – 'The Essayist') meet with stories written in experimental forms ("...entirely written in iambic / trochaic meter" says Cameron of the shortest story in the collection, 'This'). 'The Difficulty Snails Encounter in Mating' takes the form of an eighteen page letter and 'A Dream of Justice' incorporates half or full-page sections of narrative heavy dialogue, then reverts to narrative proper when back story or context is required. This mix and match approach could work but *Can The Gods Cry?* is a clunky collection, lacking a clear sense of what links the stories within.

A reader who makes it through the mishmash will be met with a commentary on the collection. The Author's Afterword raises questions about whether this book should have been published in its current form, undermining any editors who were involved with the work, the publisher (Cameron's own Vagabond Voices) and the author. While it might have been intended as a Nabokovian joke, ultimately it is an accurate misrepresentation that exposes an unhappy author and haughty publisher of an unsatisfactory collection. As a final 'dear reader' message it conveys an egotistical tone and in ending his afterword, Cameron references George Orwell's 1984 then quotes from his own work. The pompous finale sums things up well: this collection is too big for its boots. A brief afterword to a tightly edited collection, a mention of how dedicated the writer was and a mature approach – if it doesn't work, pull it and tweak it until it does – would have been much better received.
**Fantastic Mr Fox**

# Feeling Blue

Pack Men
Alan Bissett
*Hachette Scotland*, RRP £12·99 192pp

If Scotland's father of working class consciousness James Kelman had a literary son it might be Alan Bissett. Doubtless the uncompromising Kelman would dismiss his offspring's fey metrosexuality, a capitalist affectation. He'd be exasperated at the love of naff MOR, U2 and 'The Floyd': opium for the masses. Would he appreciate the hedonism – the hash and coke – that litter Bissett's books? I doubt it. But as Bissett matures as a writer the more like the old man he gets.

*Pack Men*, Bissett's fourth novel and notional sequel to his cult debut *Boyracers*, follows the misadventures of Alvin and his Rangers supporting mates on a once-in-a-lifetime trip to the UEFA Cup Final in Manchester in 2008.

Like Kelman's Kieron Smith, Alvin has gone to "the good school", in this case Stirling University, escaping from hometown Falkirk but losing touch with his pals and his roots in the process. The trip to Manchester is an opportunity not only to re-bond with Dolby and Frannie (Brian having flown the coop to California) and a motley crew on the bus they travel in, but to re-engage with the working class identity he so easily shed.

Alvin is horrified by the ugly sectarianism of his companions but is soon put in his place by The Cage, a man-mountain of Sectarian prejudice: 'I'm sickay this "Scotland's Shame" business. Ye're allowed to rip the pish out the English all ye like, but the minute it's the Old Firm there's a steward's enquiry. I'll stop singin "The Billy Boys" when them Tartan Army wanks stop singin "Floweray fuckin Scotland"'.

While Bissett is no apologist for bigotry he probes at the heart of the problem: "Ye can jump up and doon in a pub in the Gallowgate glorifying IRA atrocities and folk'll pass it off as "the craic"... But the second anyone sticks "The Sash My Father Wore" on the karaoke, a folk ballad... ye're as popular as Freddy Krueger in a primary school." This isn't about perceived inconsistencies in treatment across the Clyde but about the absence of accurate representations (warts and all) of Protestant working class life. While immigrant Irish Catholicism has always been articulate, Bissett is rare in his loving but balanced portrayal of bluenose culture.

But for those with no interest in sectarianism or fitbaw, *Pack Men* is much, much more. Bissett's real focus is the dichotomy in Alvin's personality, his repulsion / attraction to everything the Manchester debacle represents. His working class identity equals misogyny, homophobia, bitterness, paranoia, powerlessness; but also honesty, camaraderie, defiance of authority, acceptance, a tension mirrored in his equally confused sexuality.

For Bissett, like Kelman in *Kieron Smith, Boy*, language is the heart of the struggle. Young Alvin speaks in unfettered "Fawkurt", while adult Alvin flits between middle class R.P. and his childhood brogue, unable to locate his true voice. As in his previous novels, and doubtless part of his burgeoning success as a playwright, Bissett's command of the rhythms of vernacular is pitch perfect, his dialogue whizzing and exploding like beer bottles thrown through the air.

Kelman consistently refers to himself as a post-colonial writer, giving voice to a working-class ignored and oppressed by an imperialist literary establishment. In *Pack Men* Bissett creates an unsentimental, honest and wholly believable working class consciousness in crisis. But this is no worthy piece of agitprop, it's also funny, irreverent and moving. Let's hope it gets the readership and recognition it deserves.

**Behemoth**

# Desire has a coast

Terrific Melancholy
**Roddy Lumsden**
*Bloodaxe Books*, RRP £8·95, 79pp

Such is the diversity, bawd and shimmer of the language on offer, it is hard to know where to start this review of Lumsden's sixth collection since 1997's critically acclaimed *Yeah Yeah Yeah,* and which carries the baton of good form onwards from 2009's *Third Wish Wasted*.

In reality this book is a bumper annual of four pamphlet-sized collections in one: beginning with the reflective, wistful-yet-mischievous mortality of the eleven poems that make up 'From the Grave to the Cradle' – with its juxtaposition of mundane and fabulous imagery ('A localised history of dry precipitation'), raw metaphysical musing ('Sakes', 'Yeast', 'Alsace') and sheer wit 'Bowdler in Heaven', in which the eponymous hero has: "One hand lost in the mane of Aslan / the other fingering a virgin cocktail". I was even able to overlook the looming anachronism (Bowdler having died seventy-five years before CS Lewis was even a dirty thought in his lawyer father's mind).

This is followed by the main central sequence 'Hair and Beauty', dominated by the lengthy poem of the book's title, which is one of the few good contemporary long poems that I have read of late. A verbal kaleidoscope in which lines and words fract and reflect, 'Terrific Melancholy' is a work of great beauty and innovative formal consistency. Written from the perspective of a middle-aged actor musing on his unrequited crush upon a younger colleague, Lumsden avoids the easy territory into which a lesser almost-middle-aged poet might have strayed, and instead allows a delicate game of phrasal tennis to take place within the bounds of the court he has constructed. This delicacy nicely suits the uncertain certainty of the narrator's predicament, and creates some beautiful encapsulations of the social boundaries of love and infatuation: "Desire has a coast /... / I fancy black boats / sail your coast, crewed by sweet-smiled apes".

The next segment, 'Six Ripple Poems' is an aquatic wave-propagation from Syd Barrett to Arthur Russel via Percy Shaw (this reference to the Yorkshire-born inventor of the Catseye belying Lumsden's *alter ego* as a quiz composer and master of trivia.) 'Six Ripple Poems' makes much use of what Lumsden styles 'fuzzy rhyme' (e.g. Aprils/pillars, slicker/slacker, colours/corals), a concept that is also much beloved of this here reviewer-poet (who himself christened it sqyme) and which perfectly suits the slant, tangential way-of-looking in this sequence.

The book ends with the slack-jawed poems of 'Steady Grinding Blues' – probably best described as Tom Waits getting drunk with Kenneth Koch and Paul Blackburn while listening to the bar band performing alt-country covers of Howlin' Wolf songs. It is tempting to regard this US-set sequence as Lumsden's own pause for reflection, in his mid-forties and the author of six well-regarded books of poetry, yet still with a wanderlust in him. He touches on many familiar tropes of the blues, as in Freight Train Interlude, where stopped at a level crossing, he muses 'and only I am having for the first time the old 'shall I jump into one empty car' thrill" then checking himself "the locals on Princes Street do not gawp up at the Castle; /.../ I *am* the man they think I am and I *am* the man I used to be."

Once again, Lumsden proves himself a poet worth spending an evening with – and not "just for the dirty thrill of it" either.
**Moby-Dick**

# High Sights

The Echo Chamber
Luke Williams
Hamish Hamilton, RRP £18·99, 384pp

Early in Luke Williams's wonderful new novel *The Echo Chamber* there are two scenes that are telling of the writer's attitudes towards authorship and literary construction. The first is a delicious piece of mock gothic where the heroine's father meets his own soon to be father-in-law for the first time, "He saw nothing at first, or nothing tangible, since the room was filled with smoke. As it dispersed, Rex made out a figure bent over a large wooden table, a broad, round-faced semblance of a man with unkempt hair and black shiny eyes." This is Mr Rafferty who is working on "a woman, or rather the likeness of a female form, white bloodless, prostrate on the table, parts of her covered with a sheet, others simply missing..."

The father-in-law is a kind of Victor Frankenstein who is employed by the British Government to build emotionless killing machines from old body parts. Earlier in the novel he has attempted to build a clockwork heart to bring his dead wife back to life, a brilliant satirical riff on the Romantic notion of the author, one who brings immortality through finely wrought trinkets.

Williams's book itself is a kind of Frankenstein's monster. He has used large sections of text from other writers – Perec, Grass, Schulz – in its construction, and a whole section was written by a collaborator. The novel is an attempt to debunk the notion of authorship. In interviews he has said that his ultimate aim is to write a novel in which not a single sentence is his own, which brings us to the second scene: a storyteller within another story within the central story of the novel (there are a lot of stories in this book, it is after all called *The Echo Chamber*) says: "To write is to substitute living words for empty scrawl. It is to filch and deceive. There is nothing natural in it – a parasitic, masturbatory art." Which has more than an echo of Beckett about it.

Like Tom McCarthy's Booker nominated *C*, this is a novel that engages with the legacy of Modernism, and like the central character in *C* the heroine of this novel, Evie, is involved in an act of hearing, trying to build a narrative from fragments and transmissions from the past. Evie has a bionic capacity for hearing, she hears everything from the scurrying of mice in the ceiling, to her parents embracing in Oxford fifty years ago, to the streets of Lagos where she grew up. She is writing down what she has heard aided by a few trinkets around her, a fake Mappa Mundi, a pocket watch, both items which attempt to record something and fail. Although a book about the failure of memory, the failure of the creative act, still like Beckett it says 'on.'

This is a novel full of wonderful stories imbued with a wealth of beautiful images. Williams's prose is dynamic and flexible, able to change register at will and employ a wealth of different styles – from the icily clear to the wildly lyrical. There is a great tension at its heart between its theoretical pinnings and its linguistic and storytelling exuberance, but that is certainly no bad thing.

It is deeply satisfying to find a novel as ambitious as this in both scope and style from a contemporary Scottish novelist. The book has a cosmopolitan swagger missing from a great deal of contemporary writing in Scotland. It sets its sights high and in almost every department delivers. The fact that it is a debut is even more impressive. Luke Williams is most definitely one to watch.

**T. Tyger**

# Melancholic Humour

The Immaculate Heart
Andrew Raymond Drennan
*Cargo Publishing*, RRP £11·99, 232pp

There is an inuring line of melancholic humour that runs through *The Immaculate Heart*, a compelling new novel about the nature of love. Starting and concluding with a funeral – one a depressingly done-on-the-cheap affair that nearly crashes into a late-running wedding; the other a somewhat larger affair that somehow manages to keep a curious media at bay – it's the book's smile-inducing weariness that bizarrely powers the reader onwards.

Central character Maggie is 14 years old – nearly 15, as she keeps reminding anyone who will listen. She is literate and thoughtful, and so disliked by her peers, or at most rated as a 'second-best' shag. She is obsessed with love; about what it is, and whether she will ever experience it, given that the local boys always fail to live up to her expectations when it comes to romance, or even their ability to make her pregnant (so she can experience the true love she believes can exist between a mother and her child). "Maggie's romanticism was never outdone by her optimism," we're told at one point. Just as well, as there's little of what anyone would call love at home.

Maggie's the younger – adopted – daughter of Bill and Jean Burns, a couple long ago separated emotionally by alcohol, depression, concepts of manhood and (at least for Jean) fantasies of being rescued by Humphrey Bogart. The novel starts soon after the death of Maggie's older sister, Trish, in a road accident for which Maggie partly feels responsible. With Jean taking up a guilt-fuelled vigil on the roadside where Trish was killed, and Bill losing himself in drink and long sex sessions with a well-to-do housewife, Maggie turns to her only friend, 80 year old Bertrand Mantis. Now living alone in a soon-to-be-demolished part of the same estate, a youthful Bertrand had experienced the purest love imaginable with a young woman called Rose, but when separated from her by his soldier stepfather, he was forced to spend many years in a host of mental institutions undergoing ECT and other 'treatments' to cure his supposed 'melancholy'. It's through Rose's numerous letters to Bertrand (sent from a remote Scottish island where Rose had planned to escape the Second World War), that Maggie senses the kind of true love that she herself dreams about. Coming to the letters afresh, she decides to track Rose down, to not only prove that Rose survived but also convince herself that such a kind of pure love is possible.

There is a lot to like about this novel; both the modern-day teenage world Maggie inhabits and Bertrand's oh-so-distant childhood on a small Scottish island are grounded in a sense of truth, while the portrayal of a mental health institution is chilling thanks to its vigorous bludgeoning of the imagination. "With a little help from Mr Benjamin Franklin here," says one of the staff, applying the ECT, "we'll get you back to normal. Seeing normal things. Get you better."

Drennan's expert turn of phrase is lean and nuanced, telling much with few words, and doing so in a way that's memorable but not false: such as his early description of Billy with "a cigarette stuck to his bottom lip, as limp as his penis would be when he tried to corral Jean into having sex later." Yet, despite being an accessible read, *The Immaculate Heart* is a book that takes its reader into some pretty dark and frightening areas; this is especially the case with Maggie's cousin Dee-dee, whose own search for love and meaning has – combined with excessive drug taking – left her in the same hospital in which Bertrand was once incarcerated, constantly flicking through an old newspaper in search of some message from the man of her dreams. In the end, this is a mature and accomplished study of heartbreak, loss and the drive we have to survive them.
**Yeti**

# Adland Politics

Killing the Messenger
Christopher Wallace
Freight Books, RRP £12·99, 272pp

*Killing the Messenger* is the latest offering from Christopher Wallace. A political conspiracy based around the idea of "an extraordinary formula, one that could truly change attitudes, behaviours and buying habits, all that and more. Oh yes, things changed in adland when governments realised they could sell policy like any product, change social behaviours by creating the craving for change." In a *Mad Men* meets *In the Loop* political satire, the power of governments and methods of communication are explored.

Set in the final days of the Labour government the 'wellbeing' of the nation becomes the new priority for the government. With striking parallels between the Conservative-Lib Dem coalition's Big Society and the theory of 'Broken Britain' it is the job of rising star Greig Hynd to implement and market the new policy. A policy of 'togetherness'. A cohesive, happy society which can share its problems with the government and work towards improving the wellbeing of its members. The benefits? Less crime, more productive industry, happier people and less strain on the health system. Can anyone really stand to lose?

The only way to achieve such an ambitious policy is to call on the services of the admen. And advertising executive Calum Begg has the solution; "the formula... Accidental alchemy, magicking up the stuff of dreams. Ads that have the audience salivating with an unbearable yearning, yet serve up the meal to be devoured then and there, all in the same communication... Together Now!" And so ensues the unorthodox subliminal programming of society though the channels of the mass media.

But who is working for who? In Kafka-esque style the characters embark on endless meetings, encounter endless middlemen and endless struggles for power. The government needs the admen to achieve more power, and the admen need the government to bring in the work. Together they are a machine, ready to fix the problem no matter what the cost. Yet just like Cameron's 'Big Society', 'wellbeing' is hard to fix because no one can say exactly what the problem is. A solution is offered, but a solution to what? The flagship policy is an airy-fairy confusing cloud that keeps expanding and contorting until it eventually bursts.

In the age of the mass media and the Facebook generation the power of advertising is clear to see. The tangled web the government weaves with campaigns and spin doctors, super-injunctions – the fictional conspiracy in this book can be seen as a critique of today's government and certainly does beg the question: who has the power? According to the admen all you need to do is "show people coming together and you've got something powerful. Show it fast with all kinds of colour-coding, background noise and ambient cues and you add an exponential element of force. Put it together; test it, fine-tune it so you know where it kicks hardest, and you can sell anything. Happiness. Compliance. Anything." Yet the enormity of the situation, the struggles and the confusion – all integral themes of the book – do not make the first few chapters easy reading. It is only as the campaign launch approaches that the situation is revealed to both reader and characters.

Despite this, *Killing the Messenger* is very of the moment. Wallace creates a plausible conspiracy with all the farce, stress, power-chasing and scandal that is part and parcel of government. The novel questions the motives of those who seek power and those who advocate change. The issue of mental health and who knows best is also raised in an interesting context. But the message surrounding the control of society through the media is clear – "it comes with its side-effects, many as yet unknown."
**Bagheera**

# Fargo and Family Life

The End of the Wasp Season
Denise Mina
*Orion, RRP £12·99, 416pp*

Exploring family life, justice, gender and class, Denise Mina is in recognizable territory in her ninth novel *The End of the Wasp Season*. This foray into the intricacies of a murder investigation based in Glasgow and Kent is the second to feature no-nonsense female Detective Sergeant Alex Morrow, although readers won't have to be familiar with her first outing in *Still Midnight* in order to understand or enjoy what's on offer.

Mina's heroine is reminiscent of Marge in the Coen brothers' *Fargo*: the fact that she's five months pregnant with twins won't stop her from capably sidestepping the petty power plays and social prejudices of her own staff and witnesses alike as she susses out the motivations of people around her in order to collar the perpetrator of an especially brutal crime.

This crime – the murder of a young woman called Sarah Erroll in her home in a wealthy suburb of Glasgow – opens the novel. The action begins from Erroll's perspective, so the tension of the tale comes not so much from attempting to work out whodunit, but rather from whether Morrow will be successful in rooting out the culprit, despite trying circumstances.

Tied up in the unravelling mess are a number of contrasting families: a brood of four living in Castlemilk brought up by single mother and friend from Morrow's past, Kay Murray; the exorbitantly wealthy but unhappy wife and children of vicious, failed Kent banker Lars Anderson; and the shady side of Morrow's own criminal family roots, from which she is seeking an escape.

Unlike *Fargo*, there is little to laugh about here. Suicide, theft, madness and murder all feature. We're taken into the callous world of instantly disposable sex workers and shown family life that's at best brutal, at worst indifferent, as Mina weaves comparisons between the way the murderer literally stamps the life out of his victim and the way egocentric banker Lars Anderson has been able to trample all over the savings and dreams of strangers, as well as the feelings of his own family. But there are also moments of love and hope to be found. "The babies were leaping hard on her pelvis," Morrow notices at one point, "cheerleaders for life, telling her not to give up, not to get sucked down." Strong women, with their capacity for unselfish love and a day's hard toil – the examples of Morrow, Kay Murray and perhaps surprisingly, Sarah Erroll herself – are all held up as worthy of admiration in a damaged, greed-driven world.

The danger is that this can all become rather simplistic and moralising: with women being declared the good guys and men the bad; wealth the sure sign of a hollow heart and slender means the lot of the honest and true. Fortunately, Mina throws in just enough exceptions to the rule in order to keep things ticking over and so the marriage of a reasonably suspenseful plot with social commentary as well as a degree of realism is largely a success. She has a skill for character too, deftly moving between a trio of quite distinct perspectives – DS Morrow, her old friend Kay Murray, and Thomas Anderson, the son of banker Lars – in order to build pace. Add to these accomplishments her ability to turn a phrase, and it's easy to see why Denise Mina's work is held in high regard by many.

**Brer Rabbit**

# This is Glesca

### Where the Bodies are Buried
**Chris Brookmyre**
*Little, Brown & Company, RRP £17·99, 304pp*

Revenge, drugs, violence, Glasgow hard men and a tough but weary cop. So far so familiar. *Where the Bodies are Buried* starts with a gangland revenge killing and proceeds with a plot about missing parents told from the perspectives of Jasmine, a drama student turned trainee private investigator who has lost her own mother and doesn't know her father, and Catherine, an ambitious police woman with a normal home life and a troubled past.

Chris Brookmyre has written thirteen previous novels largely set in Scotland and this novel is billed as a departure from his usual style, being placed more firmly in the genre of crime fiction than that of 'satire with a few dead bodies' for which he is known. We are reminded several times that "this is Glesca... we don't do subtle, we don't do nuanced, we do pish head bampot bludgeoning his girlfriend to death in a fit of paranoid rage induced by forty-eight hours straight on the batter" and sure enough there are no real surprises as we are taken through a competent crime thriller to a fairly predictable twist at the end.

There is a lot of strong writing here, though, and the main characters are well drawn. Brookmyre has the rare ability for a male writer to write female characters well. But the fact that he can write complex characters makes it all the more disappointing that, for the baddies, he just doesn't bother. A wee ned who is happy to kick people to death ? Check. A gangland lord with steely charm who has moved to the suburbs and gone legit? Check. A bent cop with a guilty conscience? Check. Tanning salons used to launder drug money? Again, check.

Unfortunately *Where the Bodies are Buried* lacks the wit of the Dadaist bank robbers in *The Sacred Art of Stealing* or the gleeful political intrigue and send up of Catholicism, sectarianism, and Scottish parliament of *The Country of the Blind*. Catherine and Jasmine, too, are not as engaging as Palabane or Angelique de Xavier, the main characters of several of his previous novels.

In this, like all of his novels, there is often the sense that the author is using his characters as mouthpieces to make his opinion known, regardless of their relevance or their suitability to the character. He can also torture a joke until it hurts. Take for example the sentences "The Organised Crime Unit Special Task Force was often decried as having a name longer than its list of convictions. It was officially known as Locust, a quasi acronym that ignored the final F and added an L at the front to accommodate a work invoking parasites and pestilence, presumably to describe its targets rather than itself." Or "McGroarty had a younger brother, Charles, who had been known pretty much from birth as Chick. Which is a shame, as Charlie would have been a serendipitous choice of name for a Class A dealer specialising mainly in the eponymous." Tell me you didn't have to read them twice. Tell me when you'd read them the second time you weren't sure why they were necessary. There are enough examples like this to become irritating.

Does Glasgow need any more depictions of two-dimensional gangsters selling drugs and carrying out revenge torture? Does it need any more bent cops or criminals with good hearts volunteering at a women's refuge to make up for their past? If it does then I think Brookmyre should return to the satire that he is good at and leave someone less imaginative to do it.

**Aslan**

# A Newcomer's Guide to the Culture

Surface Detail
Iain M Banks
*Orbit*, RRP £8·99, 640pp

DISCLAIMER: Fans of Iain M Banks may want to look away now. This review is aimed at those readers who come to Banks's work as neophytes, without having read his earlier works. I won't be telling you how this book compares to the last one, but for diehard fans, there may be a little sentimental pondering on why they liked Banks in the first place.

I was drawn straight in by the opening scene, where Lededje, an intagliate or slave identified by a kind of whole-body tattoo, is being hunted by her master, rapist and the most powerful man in her Enablement across an opera house (note the sneaky nod to the concept of a 'space opera'). This meant it was a bit of a blow when she was killed off at the end of the first scene, but then, you see, comes the complicated plotting of a Banks book. The novel is based around the concept of death in the universe Lededje inhabits, so a character's death doesn't mean the end of the line for their plot thread. I was reunited with a 'revented' Lededje a few chapters later, when she, in her new body, is making plans to find her killer and return the favour. Meanwhile, factions of the Culture are seriously considering the matters of life after death, specifically, what to do about Hell.

*Surface Detail* is the 9th novel set in the Culture, a civilisation far more advanced than ours, and than many of the surrounding civilisations sharing its universe. In this progressive world, wars are carried out as super-high-tech video games, with both sides agreeing to accept the outcome as binding in the Real. A war is being fought over the necessity of hells, which some civilisations still desire as methods of keeping their citizens in line, or as religious necessities, but which the more enlightened see as being horrible forms of torture and unnecessary barbarism. Unfortunately, the anti-Hell side are losing the virtual war – the only solution seems to be to break the moral codes of the virtual battle chambers and, as one might say, make it Real.

What comes near to being didactic morality in the novel is carried off with a fantastic depth of imagination and an exuberant glee in the futuristic world that gives the subject a lightness of touch and an originality beyond anything I've read in a long time. That said, it was sometimes hard to follow all the nomenclature of the Culture, and this occasionally made the plot drag. There's an exchange between Lededje and Demeisen, an avatar of the Falling Outside The Normal Moral Constraints, a battleship, in which she accuses him of thinking like a teenage boy and expecting girls to get all moist at arcane language. This struck an immediate chord with me, as there was a point about a hundred pages in where I was struggling to remain interested. On the other hand, the ships have great names – there's The Usual but Etymologically Unsatisfactory, and the Fractious Person, and the hierarchy of the battleships ranges from Demeisen's Abominator class ship, to Torturer, to Deepest Regrets class.

This is a really smart, wonderfully written novel with a lot of humour. I might not advise you to start an Iain M Banks journey with the ninth book in a series, and there were a couple of sub-plots that seem rather incidental to the story and interfered with the pacing. However, if you haven't read any Iain M Banks because you don't usually like science fiction, or you just haven't got round to it, you're in for a treat. I'll be spending a lot of time with backlist Banks from now on.
**Maltese Cat**

# People and Places: Collections and Pamphlets of New Poetry

In terms of poetry collections, size does not matter. Both pamphlets and full collections share equal opportunity to delight and disappoint their readers. This is due, perhaps, to the haphazard process in which devoted readers of poetry approach a new book: flipping back to front, front to back, or starting at the middle and reading their way out. Readers of both short and long collections have only one objective in their hunt – to locate the best poem of the lot.

The following works are of varying sizes and styles and range from established poets to ones just starting out. Some poets fill their book with pieces about day-to-day life; others base their collection on a concept.

Graham Fulton's latest collection *Open Plan* (Smokestack Books, £7·95) describes the perks and quirks of office work. In this collection, over sixty poems (which are, naturally, reminiscent of a certain hit TV show) describe a generic office environment and the bizarre personalities of the workers within.

Some poets would find it difficult to produce volumes on one topic, but Fulton has created his own tiny world. His poems feature a wealth of characters: Loony Tony, who brightens the day with impressions of Gollom; John, the 'fount of knowledge' who spouts useless facts; Prince John, who entertains the office with his severe eye twitch and the much-feared 'Huge Head', the boss of the operation.

Comedic happenings are Fulton's main reportage and these appear in the form of employees scanning their faces for fun, fighting for the first look in mens' magazines and turning the fire extinguisher into a makeshift penguin. Though the collection mainly focuses on toilet humour and shows of office bravado, occasionally Fulton produces poems that explore the ephemeral nature of such an environment, such as when the lights go out each night.

In these vignettes, Fulton adopts a swinging beat with his consistent structure of short lines arranged with varying indent. This particular pattern illustrates the pace and breath of the narrator's voice. It can be said, however, that *Open Plan* requires a deeper narrative. Since Fulton created an entire cast of characters, the reader looks for a climax that brings them together, and there is none to be found.

\*

Edinburgh poet Colin Hind's slim debut collection shares Fulton's use of lower case lettering and a casual register, although his observations on human behaviour are not quite as honed as Fulton's. The title of the collection, *Too OK* (Blazevox Books) is perhaps an example of Hind's tendency to overstress emotions, and a simpler approach might have more impact. In his poems Hind can be accused of being self-conscious hip or having the intention to shock, as in the short poem:

> 'unsimulated sex':
> i thought i should warn you that
> this poem is just one in this book
> that features unsimulated sex. though,
> don't be alarmed because you might
> not even notice...

Though attempting to be clever, this poem lacks purpose; Hind hides behind cheap talk instead of developing a poem that contains nuanced phrases about intimacy. When Hind is being honest, however, his work smacks of e.e.cummings-ish wonderment. The poem 'poetry is love in action' uses a line heard at a conference as the foundation for an intricate progression of observations. The arrangement of the text as a series of short and long waves illustrates the narrator's wavering thoughts:

i
was at a poetics
conference
and heard michael
golston say in a paper
on clark coolidge 'poetry is
love in action'. i jotted it down.
i desperately want that formula to
be true, like bubblebaths make you
sleep well...

This poem illustrates that Hind's talent is
not in the short poem but in longer verse,
where he has the space to present protracted
conflicts.

*

Jenni Fagan's *The Dead Queen of Bohemia*
(Blackheath Books) shares Hind's youthful
tone in her eclectic pamphlet. Her work
illustrates a desire to find drama in foreign
places, as the settings of these poems can be
found in America, China and Mexico. 'The
Bob Conn Experience', presented in long,
descriptive lines, illustrates an outlaw's race
across North America on a Harley. 'For Wang
Wei' contains an unhurried pace and lyrical
similes, beginning with the opening verse:

lanterns' brilliance
recedes,
clogs clatter
on ancient
stones

The poems' remaining images, such as 'hair
shiny as oil', are presented simply and slowly,
like a fan opening. Fagan has a similar
approach in the poem 'Tree House', where
a series of three-line stanzas deftly depict a
sombre outdoor scene:

An owl called Esme
hoots, her eyes
yellow as dawn.

River of leaves
whorl, currents
too strong to sail on.

When writing of people and places, Fagan's
work shines. However, poems of a domestic
nature could require more clarification of
the conflict at hand. 'The First Time I Met
My Dad' feels as though it is lacking in
content. The poem begins with the suspicious
comment 'I don't trust your hairline', but the
narrative softens with the closing line '[you]
tell me I look like the Mother I've never met
/ but more beautiful'. The poem leaves the
reader feeling as though more should be said
about such a momentous event. However,
in the magic realist poem 'The Dead Queen
of Bohemia', it is a case of the less said, the
richer. The poem captures the fiery nature of
Elizabeth of Scotland:

She cut the engine
stole in Mexico
wearing yesterday like a veil
wearing a black mask
fire for hair
the silver flash
of scales on rattlesnakes
shaking out there in the desert
shaking with rage.

**Puss In Boots**

# The Girl from Ipanema

### The Secret's in the Folding
**Fiona Thackeray**
*Pewter Rose Press*, RRP £8·99, 182pp

This collection of stories is a bit like finding a Brazilian restaurant lurking in some dank lane in Inverness: unexpected, original, exciting, and best of all an opportunity to whisk yourself to an exotic place in the skin of one of your own tribe. For the author, Fiona Thackeray, is Scottish to the core. She brings her ruthless yet compassionate eye to bear on Brazilian homeless, maids, famous mistresses, carnival dancers, and just about everyone else she comes across. Her observations are the kind one often finds with expats – detached, philosophical, meticulously honest, and full to the brim with curiosity and heart. As if to combat some homesickness running through her days, the stories are written with a kind of passionate sadness.

Some of her best stories involve British characters who find themselves being affected in varying degrees by immersion in Brazilian culture. In 'We are All Cut from the Same Cloth', a slightly smug British wife has her complacency rattled, when her husband takes a little too easily to Brazilian morality. She gains some insight into non-British sensibility when her maid helps her learn how to keep her husband faithful. This note of humility and willingness to change yields an optimist ending, but often her stories end on a more plaintive note.

In the title story, 'The Secret's in the Folding', we meet the mysteriously elegant Dona Celestina. She comes into town with haughty airs and a fancy parasol rolled up under her arm, but proceeds to the riverbank where she builds a rough hut to live in. As the story progresses, we learn more about the town's inhabitants, and how they move from dislike and suspicion, to eventual respect for Celestina. It is one of the most moving stories about the redemptive potential of pride I

have ever read.

In 'The Girl in the Song', we get to indulge a universal nosiness of the *Héllo* variety, for the story concerns the famous song 'The Girl from Ipanema'. This song is so culturally embedded, just the title is enough to set the tune rolling in most people's minds, and yet of course that inspirational girl really did exist, and the narrator claims to be her. She has exploited her role in this song which made the singer a millionaire, and she now owns a clothing shop called Girl from Ipanema. It is a short story, read in ten minutes, yet lingers in the mind delightfully long.

Fiona was shortlisted in the Neil Gunn competition, with 'Forgotten Tigers of Rio de Janeiro'. My first response was that this was a great title, and really great titles are rare. How could the story live up to the title? It is set in the past, and the narrator is the daughter of a slave. At first, I found the dialect too clumsy to follow, but after a few paragraphs there was no obstacle to understanding. What emerged was a picture of a man stripped of all dignity, who nevertheless clung to his own humanity. He was a tiger, because his dark skin was bleached from the mistress's urine and faeces dripping down his body as he carried them. But he was also called a tiger because he had integrity, courage and honesty. He was a hero. The tone is fable-like, but I was totally riveted. It should have won first place.

'The Darling of Brazil' is my favourite story, and I won't tell you much about it. I will tease you like the lovely Elena who stole men's hearts right, left and centre. Who was born a slum dweller and became a fabulous carnival dancer. She symbolised the common man achieving hero status, and was loved by all Brazil, until... buy the book!
**Doc Raccoon**

# World Enough and Time

Andrea Mullaney

'I'VE WANTED YOU for so long,' she said, five and a half minutes after we met. We were at a dismal drinks reception on the opening night of the conference: cheap wine in plastic cups and a few bottles of half-decent beer stashed behind the podium.

She took me straight up to her room. But she wanted me to know that she wasn't easy: 'I haven't had sex for a very long time,' she said, her eyes burning into mine. 'That's okay,' I said.

It was brief but intense, a condensed shock of sensation. Afterwards, she lay back on the bed and told me about her home, a system far away in the constellation of Cancer where two white dwarf stars circled each other so closely that their gravity pulled energy back and forth across space. They move so fast, she said, that the orbit takes only 321.5 seconds. Her people had the shortest year in the universe but as the distance between the stars narrowed and their mass leaked away by fragments, it was becoming ever so slightly shorter with every rotation.

'One day they will crash into each other and merge,' she told me, stroking my leg, her face glowing. I wanted her fire. We made love again, almost as quickly, but with less passion, more tenderness.

Hungry now, we raided the mini-bar: peanuts, two cookies, a mouthful-sized can of Coke each. I liked how she gathered up the wrappings and rolled them into a neat ball before dropping it in the bin. I made up a little song for her, to a familiar tune, and made her laugh: *Crab girl, pinch me with your pincers, Crab girl, give me a sideways glance...* She danced around, clicking her fingers above her head. 'I'm so happy!' she called out, spinning wildly, but somehow I was the one who felt dizzy.

In the bathroom, I splashed water on my face and wondered what I was doing there. When I came out, she tried to pull me back down onto the bed; I let her, but it wasn't as good the third time. As I started to sober up she looked older than I'd thought. Worn out.

'Listen, maybe we ought to go back down,' I said. 'You know, network. It's what we came here for, after all.'

'What?' Her face distorted into a frown. 'I don't understand.'

'This was nice,' I said, 'really nice.' She started to cry. I wondered if those stars near her home would ever break their orbits and spin apart. I wondered if that was possible.

As I left she said softly: 'You've taken the best years of my life.'

Downstairs there was still some of the good beer left. Later I saw her across the room, talking to someone. She looked like a stranger.

# The Mast

Extract from a novel

Kathrine Sowerby

## 1. KILKIVAN

At the shout, Helen ran. They all ran, bumping and knocking into one another until it was air that Helen grabbed in front of her instead of a coattail or apron string. Her feet slipped on the uneven ground and voices came and went but she kept going until something scraped against her side. She paused to run her hands over the cold stone; the damp moss growing in the engraved letters and the voices became distant. Helen opened her eyes but fabric pressed against her lashes and the solidity of the darkness scared her even more. If she pulled the blindfold off now she could run over the hill to the shore or back into the woods but as soon as they noticed they'd be after her and how far could she get in that time anyway? With her eyes shut she could picture the churchyard, its graves dotted across the hilly slope and the gable ends of the chapel. She ran again in the direction of the voices disappearing ahead of her.

Someone caught her hand. The fingers were slim, smooth, a woman's. She shook it away and ran faster, the night air biting on her cheeks, catching her throat as she breathed harder. The slope was getting steeper which meant she was nearing the top of the chapel and she needed to turn to her left. Her foot slid on the grass and her ankle turned. She crumpled to the ground, her skirt gathering in folds around her. The grass was wet with the first beads of dew and she could feel the material growing damp under her. Something hit hard against her shoulder and she heard

herself whimper.

'Helen, is that you?' A whisper.

Hands patted her back, her head and her face. She caught them and traced the ring she'd pushed on the finger herself.

'Graham?'

'Ssh, get up.'

'I can't.'

She felt his hands hook under her arms and pull her to her feet. A sharp pain shot up her leg when she tried to put her weight on it but a push from behind propelled her forward.

'Graham?'

He was gone.

He could have pulled the blindfold from her eyes but he hadn't. Wasn't he as scared as she was? Maybe he wanted to be doing this. She heard giggling pass by on her right and she hit hard ground. The path. She had come full circle. Twice more and it would be over.

The incline was easier this time. Behind her, waves broke against the shore reminding her of the vast ocean that she longed to be swallowed up by. If just one of those waves could reach up as far as the hilltop and bite this tip of land clean off, her problems would be gone.

The number of times she'd stood at the roadside by the chapel listening to the sermon on crisp clear days and days so overcast with drizzle that even the wind couldn't shift the cloud. The crowd would gather and huddle together to hear the words that gave them hope in harsh times or gratitude in times of plenty but now here in the pitch black, this was something else altogether. Something she hadn't agreed to.

Again the idea of running off, changing direction, escaping what was coming came to her, but what would she live on. She had no money. There were berries. She could catch and skin a rabbit but what kind of life would that be and where would she end up? What was coming would be worse perhaps but maybe it was meant for, maybe her life really was in the hands of someone who knew more than she ever could. Was it greed that made her want something different? Hadn't she been happy enough with Graham, hadn't she worked hard on their land and in their home? Was this her punishment for not bringing a baby into their first year of marriage, for not giving him the son he so wanted? But she wanted it too and he had been patient when she lost the first and the second. It had been so early that it wasn't yet a baby, they'd agreed. And they'd loved each other.

She felt the hard stones under her boots again and knew she was twice round the chapel. The others were surely faster and the shout would come soon. She knew this time to go left to miss the gravestone that had given her the smarting graze under her ribs, to veer right to avoid the slope down to the chapel walls, to keep her strides short and low to the ground. There were others and she heard their curses when they tripped, their laughter when they bumped into the gravestones or each other and once she heard low sobs escape from someone she passed but still it seemed she could be the only one out there on the hillside. Her last hope was that she might find Graham in the final minutes and without a word they would join hands and run together, not stopping until the silhouette of the chapel was out of sight. They would crouch in the rocks until sunrise when they would find a hidden fishing boat and sail out and away, find another shore where they knew no one.

Her head was beginning to ache. The scarf had been knotted so tightly at the back of her skull to squeeze any possible source of light from her view. The slope was at its steepest and the back of the chapel to her right. Instead of going higher and round she took small steps down to the back wall. She pressed her face against the stone. Curls of algae flicked against her skin and she thought of the butterfly kisses her mother had given her, fluttering her eyelashes against her cheek. She wished for a back door into the building, a way into a corner that no candlelight could find. She walked the length of the wall until she reached the corner. Wind belted her in the face and she ran now, ran to whatever waited for her, picking up speed as she ran down the hill and the shout came. She stopped.

It was the moment she'd been dreading, the signal to grab the nearest man or woman. She heard drumming in her ears and realised it was her own breathing, her own heart thumping. For a second she imagined an impenetrable seal around herself that nobody could break through and in that time she felt lighter than ever, as if the wind could pick her up and fly her away, then thick arms were around her knocking her to the ground. Stubble rasped against her cheek and she struggled to breathe under the weight that pinned her down and, when she did gasp for air, her lungs filled with stale smoke and warm fish stuck between the rotten teeth of the person she most feared. A mouth pressed against her neck then her ear, drooling and gulping as blunt fingers pulled at the ties on her blouse and a knee worked its way between her clasped legs.

'Get off me,' she hissed.

Everything stopped and her chest rose then she winced as the blindfold was yanked from around her head taking a tangle of hair with it.

'I don't want you,' she said.

The face hanging over her own was laughing, dripping beads of sweat from its forehead onto her face. One landed on her lip and she licked it away, tasting the salt on her tongue. Curls of black hair fell around the eyes she knew, she'd always known, dark and heavy lidded.

'You've got me,' it said. 'For a year, you've got me.'

The knee forced its way between her thighs and a hand was there, fighting its way under

➡

her layers of clothes. Helen tilted her head back. The moon was high above the hilltop and the sky was the colour of ink but a light blue bleed from the ocean promised light. She lay quite still. Had everyone gone? She could hear nothing. The first birdcall perhaps or did she imagine that? No voices, no footsteps, no hands reaching out to pull her from under this body that covered her with the weight of a house. But nothing hurt. Not in the way she was expecting. She shut her eyes and tried to find herself between what was on her and what was under her while the wind licked her bare legs and a feather light touch drove her into the ground.

# The Mothers
Sandra Alland

THEY WERE ALL lined up – all the mothers of all my friends from my whole life. There was Florence's mother, part Chinese and part Jamaican, who people just called 'tanned'. There was Leslie's mom who used to feed me sushi and teach me her best dance moves. There was Lisa's stepmother, who'd shamed me at age three for peeing in her garden after she'd said not to step foot in her house in my wet bathing suit. In the centre of the line was Laura's mom, a black woman people mocked for not shaving her armpits. She killed herself one white suburban Sunday.

The terrible mothers were all at one end of the line together, holding hands and clucking. Emily's mother who fed her porridge with cockroaches in it. Jen's mom who made her eat soggy cereal for lunch if she didn't finish it for breakfast. Ronnie's who molested him. Trudy's who beat the shit out of her. Judy's who put cigarettes out on her vulva. Tina's who called her fat and made her wear frilly dresses, when all she wanted was to be one of the boys.

There were a lot of bad mothers – they stretched so far that my aunt Martha's head was just a dot in the distance. She'd enjoyed telling my cousins how worthless they were. Even then, in the line, I could see her telling Johnny's mother that not sending him to school with a change of clothes would teach him a lesson for wetting his pants.

The mothers looked at me expectantly – the sad, the good, and especially the bad. I think they wanted me to tell them something important, to judge or absolve them. Most of their eyes said, 'I did my best with what I had.'

Or, 'I was only 17.' Or, 'We didn't know any better then.'

But I didn't have time for them. I had my own mother, and she was nice and had cancer. I feel a bit bad about it now, but I honestly just wasn't interested in their bullshit.

# Mind Furniture
Jim Ferguson

SUMMER. INSIDE. MATTHEW Deen's heid. Therein, forever, the eternal present. That process. The process of the eternal present. The tense? Still in the past. The back of beyond. The Wild Parochial Boy. How was he to know? How was anybody?

Throughout the summer he nursed the furniture of his mind. Let it arrange and re-arrange itself. Mostly he focused upon his body. His brain developing to better control his body. His boyhood was over. He was on the threshold of being a man.

He learnt to swim. It turned out much easier than he'd thought. Flipper Deen, the underwater man, Matt Cousteau, observer of rare species and behaviour below the waves.

Matt loved swimming, the isolation of it, yet at the same time folk were there, round about you while you swam: if you needed them. If you were drowning, somebody would try to rescue your body before it had a chance to die. He was there, a being, in the world, movin through, through the water, the rhythm, the strokes the breath, the breath in your body, his body, the breath in, out, in, out, in, the breath out, and going through the water, the fluid, the strange sensation, the everydayness of it. This thing he'd been feart of too, feart for so long when there was nothin to be feart of, just breath and rhythm.

It was aw there, it had been, waiting inside, waitin for the man-boy to take it into his control, to exercise his strength of will. Exercise his limbs and swim through it, the water, the fluid.

The man-boy's mind furniture too rumbled about his brain whilst he swam. The regular deep rhythmic breathin, the depth, the pull of the arms, the kick of the legs, the way of walkin in water, of transporting himself, there but not there, the mind furniture, the heid furniture being in a state of removal, of decan'ture; then there's the bearings and lack thereof, and the demeanour and general state of being whilst attired in swimmin trunks, the vulnerability of it, the bare naked truth of it, the body complex and the complex body.

Deen wisny troubled by that nor by the shifts and rumbles of the mind furniture. In a sense it was all subconscious. Unconscious even. He was relaxed. In a state of release from the normal apparatus required whilst navigating the world through air, the earth's atmosphere, the gases, the gases and the fluids and the movement through such being different, in the extreme and in the mainstream, the mad and the moderate. And through all this, the movement of the body through a body of water, hemmed in a hole in the world tiled up and grouted, through all this the mind furniture was takin care of itself. Rumbling and shifting and healing, without the effort of conscious thought.

Matthew Deen's heid enjoyed the physical exertions of his soon to be adult body. The physical pleasure. The mind furniture thrived on physical exertion. Developing away, in different ways too: the auld young mind was moving, moving to the rhythm of his body, the chemistry of it all, the neurotransmitters sparkin away. All the presently correct states of messaging, forward and back and over and through the labyrinthine, spherical prawn beast of a brain that contained the mind furniture, that which registered the eternal present, that which made up the personality of man-boy Matthew Deen: the whole organism, body and soul moving. Rhythm. Swimming. Watery rhythm of cerebra-spinal fluid, rhythm of heartbeat and lungs, strong and true, everything moving smoothly.

Then there was the occasional missing floor-board where an item of mind furniture would land awkwardly. But the sheer physical pleasure, and the body relaxed. Relaxed, relaxed, relaxed, tense, just now and again, but – relaxed, relaxed, relaxed and travelling in a calm sea, only the tiniest of eddies. The mind furniture stored in a sea-worthy vessel, gettin ready for voyages further afield, away out, beyond these waters now navigated safely.

*

Matthew looked at his face in the bedroom mirror. A spot was starting to sprout on his chin. He noticed the shape of his face; it was changing, not so much a child's face: it was getting longer, his nose sharper, eyes deeper blue. The chin more pronounced. Lips fuller and softer while the rest of his face looked harder, cheeks red with the sun, and the freckle on the right cheek being very alive and strawberry. He'd taken a stretch too, stood at the grand height of five feet and one inch tall.

He put on T Rex's *Metal Guru* and continued gazing into the mirror, not thinking about anything, just looking at his face, the spot, the freckle. Letting the furniture of his mind quietly rumble away, letting the cells do their work, while all the while Matthew Deen himself remained unconscious of it all, but somehow knowing too, feeling the changes. The settling and movement of that conscious muscle, and the information contained inside. Inside. Deen's heid. Therein, for ever, in there, the eternal present. Summer.

# A Visit
## Natasha Soobramanien

OTHER PEOPLE'S EVERYTHING. It's always less interesting than your own. This is what he thought, walking to the station to meet the brother. This was the brother's first visit to the city. He himself had moved there five months previously. This city is built on several hills. For convenience there are steep flights of steps carved into them. Crooked, narrow steps. He walked down a flight of these to reach the station. 'New Steps' they were called. This was the first time he had come across the New Steps. In this sense, they are new, he thought. New to me. Though actually they are very old.

He and the brother climbed the New Steps. They walked on towards the Old Town, where he lived. We've got an Old Town and a New Town, he said to the brother. But the New Town is quite old and the Old Town is so old it looks fake. They were walking through it now. The brother said, This whole town is new to you. They passed a bagpiper in ceremonial dress. He was playing for money. That guy. I pass him every day, he said. I'm ashamed for him. *Ashamed for him.* The brother had not heard this expression before. On the way to his flat he had plenty of things to say to the brother about the gift shops, tourists, the landmark buildings they passed. The brother got the feeling he had been walking around these past five months thinking things and storing them up for a visitor. The brother asked if he had friends here. A few pals, he said. You know. From the pub. The pub, said the brother.

The brother asked if he missed home. Not *miss*, he said. But you don't know what something is until you see it next to something else. An orange on its own. How do you know it's one orange until you put it next to another one and can count *one, two...* I never realised what the place was like until I moved away. Big-shouldered buildings knocking you about. You come up here and there's sky. You can breathe. They were in his flat now. The brother looked outside. The slopes of a greenish black mountain pressed up to the window. It was like looking at a wall. Breathe? The brother thought, turning his back on the view. You take yourself with you, you know, he said.

Later they went for a walk across a park and saw the greenish black mountain from a distance. It's much easier to see things from a distance, the brother said. But you miss the detail, he said. They could never allow themselves to agree. Even if they were thinking the same thing, essentially. The brother asked if he had found work yet. I have my work, he said. But a job? No. He was poorer than many of the people here but felt much richer, having moved from a bigger city. A richer country. Like them. He nodded at a group of young people passing. One of them was wearing pyjamas. He did not say they had the same effect on him as the big-shouldered buildings from home. The brother must have felt the same because he turned round after them and swore. What's wrong, he asked. The brother would not have been angry if he could have said that it was the boy wearing pyjamas. The brother was angry because he felt that it was not so very important to that boy to be wearing pyjamas, but that the boy didn't care that it might be important to other people that everyone else should be dressed in clothes and not pyjamas. But the brother just shrugged. And he himself thought This city feels unreal to me. But to wear pyjamas is to let everyone know you think that. That you think the place a joke. So again they were essentially thinking the same thing, but could not bring themselves to agree, as though to disagree were in essence to distinguish themselves from one another.

It was time for a drink. He took the brother to his favourite pub. It smelt of sweat. Sweet and yeasty like a stable. At the bar, everyone leaning up against each other for the warmth. In the corner, a group of folk musicians. Students, the wholesome type in traditional jumpers and one old man. But he looked boyish. Girlish. They started up a song, all the young people looking to the old man for a lead. First he played a violin, but played it like percussion. Then he played a double-bass but played it for the tune. They went to another pub the next day, before the brother went home. They went to watch the football. The city felt its most foreign to the brother then. The only place they found that was showing the game was the basement bar of a restaurant where the beer was served in long frosted glasses. Sitting on club chairs in something like a corridor near the toilets. Not the sort of place where they would usually watch the game. Then they went to the station. After seeing the brother off he walked back home. He thought the only reason the brother had come to see him was so he could say he had visited his brother. He stopped at a shop to buy some potato pancakes and a tin of beans for his tea. As he was cooking it occurred to him that the brother had taken no photos of his visit. Shortly after eating he went to bed, where he read until he fell asleep.

Most nights here he sleeps well and seems so far to have outrun the same feeling that the brother got on looking out of his living room window. The feeling that usually keeps him awake at nights wondering what does a life amount to, what does he have that amounts to a life. But on the other hand since moving here it always takes him, on waking, a good

five seconds to work out where he is. Like the habitual liar who is losing her powers and can no longer keep track of the stories she has told.

# The Weight
Craig Lamont

THERE'S A SILENCE that comes to a house when no one can sleep. But not when you're alone. The wooden furniture contracting in the cold like someone creeping, calm, determined in the hall; the next-door neighbour's wind chimes, swaying like earrings; the foxes outside barking their dry cough.

I picked one once, imagined its past: someone's pet dog that got lost and just happily wandered, living off the food people bin, sleeping under cars or in hedges. Its once brown fur tinted orange under that damp glow of the street lights. This might well have been a dream; the kind you don't tell people about. You can't even tell if you're still fully awake, or if it's only possible to think like that when you're asleep. This has been my routine for a long time. How long, I can't tell. Something feels like it's broken.

A voice plays on a loop in my head. I only met George once, at the new pub that opened where the road splits into two at Farmecross. One leads you over the Clyde into town, the other takes you away to the newer estates. In the middle is a tiny pub, shaped like a triangle inside, with the door at the apex, the bar at the base and the thirsty regulars leaning there. George was one of three people drinking that day. The way his grey hair poked out the side, all matted, you could tell he never took off his bunnet. I got myself a drink and sat between George and the other two: a young couple who were all smiles and shopping bags. This was a pit stop for them.

I can't remember how we started talking.

It's like we already knew one another, how familiar it was, the way there didn't seem to be an introduction. His eyes were like spoiling lochs, closed off from their flow. A pale blue pool of wisdom remained here and there in specks. When I think about it now I wonder if he was like me, and it makes me dread looking in the mirror.

'It was one of those days, son, one of those days,' George said. I nodded, knowingly, and looked at the mahogany bar through the bottom of my pint glass.

'Did you see much of the war, then?' I said.

'More than enough,' George said. 'I was on the receiving end of things.'

He tapped his heart, put his finger to his eye and sniffed.

He went on, and it was as if he was describing a bad taste the way he summed up the Blitz.

'It wisnae nice,' he said.

George was a union official for the Clyde shipbuilders. He took a drink, as they say, and sometimes he took the next man's as well. 'Some of the boys didn't take to the medicine,' explained George. 'Oh no; they were newly married with fresh-faced weans. It would take them a couple years to get the taste for him. They all smoked like chimneys, mind. All except one lad. Lenny Alexander was his name, and he didn't have a vice to it. It was a shame seeing him end up yon scattered way, torn at the seams. Face all red, liver all shot. He didn't have a choice in the matter after those two days. All he could do was stay up late and breathe in the smoke the Germans left behind. He lost everything he held dear, son, so he did. I don't like talking about it. It wisnae nice.'

'Did you see any action yourself?' I said.

'Listen, son, I've been a working class man all my life. If you gave me a winning Euromillions ticket here and now I wouldn't move house or buy a car. My family are from here, all of them within two miles of this wee town.' He tapped the side of his glass and checked his watch. 'And "Those who take to the sword shall perish by the sword". Kirkwood said that in '35 and not a thing has changed, ne'er it has, not one thing.'

George must be a fair age, I thought, though I almost missed it; common sense sometimes passes me by, it slips through my fingers like rain, and we get so much rain.

When he stood up to leave he gave me a trailing look that said *what are you waiting on?* I got up and we both left the pub and headed towards town. The traffic was crawling with funereal respect and a light fog was rolling low. You couldn't miss the Tesco Extra, massive and bright across the road, in front of the railway station, the red and blue letters already lit at six o'clock. George went on to explain how things were before the Tesco was built, the slice of land it sits on, how people accepted it for what it was – just land, not potential, except for maybe hanging your washing out for a quick dry.

'That shop ay makes me laugh, so it does', said George, nodding at Tesco.

'You've obviously never been inside,' I said.

'Never stepped a foot inside,' he said, 'but it's that look on people's faces coming out. Like they've seen a ghost. Too busy for their own good. The old becomes new and nobody notices.'

*

One of the things that keeps me awake, or that I hear because I can't sleep, is a dull and distant echo. I think it's the nightshift steel works, but I never bother to ask if there are even any steel works left, and if so how far away. It's nice though, to hear activity when most people are sleeping. I once read in the Bible that 'the Lord will come again like a thief in the night.' That dull sound: it's like some lost

giant stepping on a bridge. Probably just people working away, away into the night. Busy little foxes chasing their overtime. The only thing I have in common with them is being awake.

George was whistling with his hands in his pockets. 'I bet you didn't know Rutherglen had a castle, son,' he said. For a second I didn't realise he'd spoken. This is something that happened from time to time since the insomnia kicked in. I would hear words, or read them, and instead of taking them in I questioned why they sound and look the way they do.

The word 'moon', for example, who decided on the word 'moon', a funny sounding word with a sad face. I sometimes think about how sad it looks.

'Come to think of it,' I said, 'I didn't know there was a castle. Where?'

'Guess,' he said.

'I don't know – where the park is?'

'Oh, come on. The castle! Guess!' he said, his voice getting higher at 'castle', his eyes getting younger.

'Main Street?' I said.

'Warm.'

'King Street?' I said.

'Toasty.'

'I don't know...?'

'Castle street, ya numpty! Where else? Open your Eyes, will ye. Built in 1264. The English kept ransacking the place till Robert the Bruce got it back, and it went back and forth like that for years. When it fell to bits we used the stone for houses and walls, so we did, to keep the fuckers out. A lot of good it did. Nobody thought of planes then. Or Germans. And poor Lenny Alexander. He lost the lot.' George spoke like he witnessed it all, from The Wars of Independence to The Clydebank Blitz. Like he actually moved the ancient stones himself.

But I was glad when he didn't notice my skin as it paled to a chalky white.

When you live in a place so long you forget what it means. And I've never seen a monument or a plaque or anything. Not even a stank or something less obvious, trodden on daily by rushing feet. Maybe I've just never really looked.

We were walking on the bridge over the Clyde. When I looked at George his eyes were waiting, and he winked.

'That's me son,' he said. 'I'll be on my way. Take care now.'

We had stopped on the middle of the bridge and he was leaning on the metal barrier, watching the fog spiral over the river like smoke. He didn't seem ready to move anytime soon. I wondered if he knew by my silence exactly where I lived. House number, everything. I gave him a wave, turned round and walked home.

That night I couldn't sleep. I felt the past.

The weight of it.

The light from the hall was dim and glowed like a dying fire through the open bedroom door. I could see shapes in the shadows, ghosts of objects like crowns and candles from watches and pens, a passing glance, nothing more, that I held as long as I could, picturing the stone, dense with the spirits of the dead between peeling wallpaper decades thick, time was crawling through the air, slow as fog until a fox, crying like its throat was cut, snapped me out of it.

My brow felt heavy, strained, like I'd never slept a day in my life, like it had always been this way and I was just now realising it.

Maybe it has.

I still can't look in the mirror – can't bear the idea that I'll see George's stagnant eyes where my own should be.

# Translation
Chris Wardhaugh

It's Tuesday
and some cunt's having
at me with a baseball bat
I'm thinking where
do you get a baseball
bat in Cumbernauld
so maybe it's a softball
bat is there a difference
anyway in the naked
space between the top
of the backswing
and contact there is
that moment of silence
like the one they say
precedes the explosion
of an atomic bomb
and in which you're meant
to be able to hear
the metal casing crack
before the black rain falls
and while I know that
a man tumbling from his
horse has enough time
to beg for absolution
before he hits the ground
I lie with my face pressed
to the sweating earth
waiting for my stillness
to end my throat
embraces silence

# Fragment 2
Arno Camenisch
Translated by Donal McLaughlin

ich gewöhne
mir das Hinken
an sie meint noch
etwas unbeholfen und
gibt mir Feuer ihrer Brille
fehlen Gläser

I'm getting used
to limping
Am still a bit clumsy
she says  giving me
a light  Her glasses
don't have lenses

sie liegt
am Strand ich grab
im Sand mit einem Holzkeil
um das Rad vom Wagen lege
Steine drunter der Abend kommt
und geht wir stecken fest es ist
mein Werk ich mag das Meer
heut nicht besonders

She's lying
on the beach  I dig
in the sand with a wedge
round the wheel of the car  put
stones under it  Evening comes
and goes  We're stuck here  It's
my doing I don't much like
the sea today

die Stadt
behauptet sich
am Rand die Grenze
ist nicht fern die Lampen um
den Parkplatz werfen unsere
Schatten an die Innenwand sie
tanzen schwach der Wagen
schwankt die Stille ist die gleiche
kurz danach das Unbehagen kommt
verzögert und für Schlaf sorgt
nur der Brand

The town
asserts itself
at the edges  The border
not far now  The lights round
the car park cast our
shadows on the wall  They
dance weakly  The car
sways  The stillness is the same
It's not long before unease arrives
delayed and only alcohol
passion bring on sleep

ans Meer
gelangt man hier
nicht mehr zu dicht
stehn kühn die Monumente
aus Beton das Hirtenlied
kommt aus den Boxen
und gewacht wird hier
auf Rädern

You can't get
close to the sea
any more  Too bold
tight is the line-up
of concrete monuments  The shepherd
sings from the speakers
and keeping watch here's
done on wheels

die Strasse
schlängelt sich
den Berg hinauf den
Höhepunkt erreichen wir
bei Tag nicht mehr es lockt
dafür zu oft ins hohe Gras ob's

The road
meanders
up the hill
We won't get to the top
before light fades  The long grass is
too tempting too often for that

| | |
|---|---|
| Schlangen hat im Unterholz | Could there be snakes |
| schrammt's einem erst | in the undergrowth? |
| am nächsten Tag | It's only the next day |
| am Kopf vorbei | it even occurs to you |
| | |
| weiss | White |
| in weiss | and white |
| verschachtelt | interlocking |
| liegt das Städtchen | The little town |
| in der Bucht | in the bay |
| | |
| landeinwärts | Inland |
| ein Motorradfahrer | a biker |
| überholt uns trägt nicht | overtakes us  He's |
| einen Helm ist barfuss | no helmet on  is barefoot |
| einen Korb mit einem Igel | Behind him a basket |
| hinten drauf im Mund | with a hedgehog in it  In his mouth |
| die Zigarette | his cigarette |
| | |
| den Kopf | The head |
| der Blume reisst | of the flower |
| sie weg versucht ihn wieder | she tears off |
| drauf zu tun | Tries to put |
| | it on again |
| | |
| wer's | Those |
| sich leistet | who can afford to |
| forstet auf die | re-timber  The steppe |
| Steppe folgt auf | takes over where the forest |
| Wald und kündigt bald | fades and is soon announcing |
| die Wüste an Geisterdörfer | wasteland  Ghost villages |
| säumen hier die Gegend | hem the region |
| wer's sich leisten kann notier | Those who can afford to  I note down |
| ich mir der bleibt nicht länger stehn | don't hang around long |
| denn Gras wächst hier schon | it being a long time |
| lang nicht mehr | since grass grew here |
| | |
| eine Tankstelle | Shimmering |
| taucht im Flimmern | on the horizon  Up pops |
| auf am Horizont und dämmt | a petrol station to dam |
| die Leere zweiundvierzig Grad am Mittag | the void   42 degrees at noon |
| sagt der Wirt im blauen Überkleid | the pump attendant |
| die Sonne brennt der Tankwart | in the blue overalls says |
| lächelt ich beneide ihn um | The sun's burning  The attendant's |
| seine Fröhlichkeit | smiling  I envy him |
| | his cheerfulness |
| | |
| der Bauer | At first light |
| treibt im ersten | the farmer |
| Morgengrauen seine | |
| Schafe still vorbei es rauscht | |

im Kopf das Meer ist fern
mit ihm kommt etwas Kühle
auf er blickt zurück es
scheint ihn nicht zu stören
liegen wir auf seinem
Feld auch seine Schafe
schauen nur und schweigen
und entgegnen erst dem
Glockenschlag
vom Kirchturm her

träumte in
der Nacht ich träumte sagte
mir im Traume aufzuwachen
wachte auf und war
zurück im ersten
Traum

ich reiche
ihr die Flasche
lache ab dem Fisch
in ihrem Mund er
schwimmt ihr durch
die Wörter

der Onkel
lief mit einem Ziegelstein
in der Tasche durch die Gegend
man sei sich niemals sicher ob
man plötzlich einen
bräuchte

die Ebene
scheint zu enden
ich blicke in den Spiegel
und da vorne steht die nackte
Sierra auf sie schläft ich
denke mir zwei Zeilen
für sie aus bis uns der
Wald einschliesst und wo
man nicht viel weiter sieht als
bis zum nächsten Baum

sie zeigt
ins Dunkle
da steht der Fuchs
jetzt seh ich ihn sie
sagt er hat mich
angeschaut ich habe

herds his sheep
past quietly  My head's
booming  The sea a good bit away
It would be cooler otherwise
He looks over his shoulder
Doesn't seem bothered
Are we lying in his
field  His sheep too
just look  say nothing
take on only
the carillon
the church tower

Dreamt
during the night I was dreaming
told myself to wake up
Woke up  And was
back in the first
dream

I hand
her the bottle
Laugh at the fish
in her mouth  Way
it swims through
her words

My uncle
walked round with a brick
in his pocket
You could never be sure
he said  when you'd suddenly
need one

The plain
seems to be ending
I look in the mirror
and up ahead the naked sierra
is rising  She's sleeping I
think of two lines
for her before the forest
closes in on us and
you can't see further
than the next tree

She points
into the darkness
There's the fox
I see him this time

seinen Blick gespürt
im Nacken

allmählich
wird die Strasse
breiter in die Stadt
die in der Nacht den Hut
aus Licht hoch überm Haupte
trägt der Fluss aus Blech
er reisst und zerrt und
frisst auch uns

He looked at me  she says
I could feel his eyes
on the back of my neck

Slowly
the road broadens
heads into the town
that by night wears
its hat of light
high above its head
The river of tin
tugs and pulls and
scoffs us too

# Walk With Me, Anne*

Ginna Wilkerson

If I found you in a dream,
would I find the silent and
intense Darke Ladie,
stopping with my cries of terror
with sonorous voice?

Or the perilous, beckoning
Mermaid, claiming presence
with a sea-sent alarm?

Maybe – for me – you would
Appear in the forlorn shape of
the Perjured Nun. We would
recognise death together
with the candle's flickering end.

I would take your fragile fingers
in mine, giving comforting warmth
through the slanted sense
oddly perceived in dreams.

Poet to poet – woman to woman –
my delicate mentor with sinew of steel.

Hold tightly and you elude death.

Walk with me, and I'll never wake.

*Anne Bannerman, Scottish poet (1765–1829)

# Helen Doing the Crossword in Bed
Graham Fulton

beside me, this second,
the one
just gone, the pen in her hand,
her hands, mouth, mind
stretching from clue to clue,
across, down,
the newspaper page,
dust on the lampshade,
down, across,
glasses on the tip of her nose,
creating sense from empty air,
an answer, inside, filling these boxes,
filling in what's wrong, right, dark, light,
down, across,
the curl of her hair, heart of her eyes,
curve of her shoulder, furrowing brow,
perfect, in time,
her cheek, neck, strap
of her nightdress, seconds, hands,
the sounds of her thoughts, pen
in her hand – and now
the song of words being churned,
whispered, rolled, sifted, alive,
shadows in corners,
books on the shelves,
all of our words, the ones just gone,
no other,
no other,
down, across,
a pillow, soft, behind her head,
the permanence of what is gone,
unmeasured distance of what will come,
everything left is
going to come,
her thoughts, gracefully, stretching
through time,
its rhythm being, completely, filled,
down, across, one
by one,
there's nothing wrong – my gaze, our bed,
a pen in her hand, her hands, the seconds,
all of it being, perfectly, turned, one, by one,
everything, every thing
is being perfectly filled.

# Two Gaelic Translations by Kevin MacNeil

## Construction

Tom Petsinis

God tinkered in darkness an eternity
On the construction of time, space, light -
Creating an admiring audience last.
I glance backwards through the cut-out in boards
Indifferent to the building going up:
An architect unfolds his quartered plans
And enters a doorway not yet drawn;
Rods suspended from the silent crane
Move in an imperceptible arc;
A youth in an orange vest yawns wide
Directing a reversing concrete truck;
A carpenter puts his helmet on, thinks,
Then tests his hammer for sound –
The site's depth impresses me most.

## Togail

translated by Kevin MacNeil

Tom Petsinis

Rè na sìorraidheachd anns an dorchadas bha dia
ag obair air tìm, fànas is solas a thogail –
's air a' cheann thall e a' cruthachadh luchd-amhairc
làn ionghnaidh. Bheir mi sùil tro na tuill gheàrrte sna bùird
-coma leotha mun togalach a tha dol suas.
Tha ailtire a' fosgladh pasgadh de phlanaichean
is e dol a-steach doras nach eil fiù 's air a' phàipear fhathast.
Na slatan a' crochadh bhon inneal-togail sàmhach
tha iad a' gluasad ann an cearcall do-mhothaichte;
tha fear òg ann am peitean orainds a' mèaranaich
is e a' stiùireadh làraidh làn concrait an comhair a chùil;
tha saor a' cur air a chlogaid, is e ri smaoineachadh;
's an uair sin a' feuchainn an ùird aige airson an fhuaim.
'S e an rud as motha a tha cur iongadh orm,
cho domhainn 's a tha an làrach.

# Now That We Are Parting
## Lidija Šimkutė

rain has returned

I want to be nothing
only the fragrance of some
       scattered rose
and pass like smoke

now that we are parting
the music will fall and settle
in the pages of your books
and wait to be opened

now that we are parting
my eyes follow invisible birds
      across the ceiling

hands become wind
and earth turns faster than
      a night ago

I leave a white cloud in your hand

now that we are parting
I will dress in rain and
watch the warmth
behind some distant window slowly
      take on your name

# Agus sinn a-nis ri dealachadh

translated by Kevin MacNeil

Lidija Šimkutė

agus sinn a-nis ri dealachadh

 tha an t-uisge air tilleadh

chan eil mi ag iarraidh càil
dìreach fàileadh ròs air choreigin sgapte
's mi dol seachad mar an ceò

agus sinn a nis ri dealachadh
tuitidh an ceòl, laighidh e
ann an duilleagan nan leabhraichean agad
far am fuirich e, a' feitheamh ri fhosgladh

agus sinn a-nis ri dealachadh
tha mo shùilean a' leantainn eòin do-fhaicsinneach
tarsainn mullach an rùim

tha làmhan a' tionndadh nan gaoith
agus an talamh a' tionndadh nas luaithe
na bha e a-raoir

tha mi a' fàgail sgòth gheal nad làimh

agus sinn a-nis ri dealachadh

bidh mi gam sgeadachadh leis an uisge
's mi a' coimhead air a' bhlàths
air cùl uinneag air choreigin fad às
fhad 's a tha e, beag air bheag,
a' gabhail air d' ainm fhèin.

# A Celebration
## Allan Wilson

I'M SITTING WITH Jack having a few beers when he eventually gets round to asking. He says, 'Tony will you... will you be my best man?' He says it like a proposal.

It's after that the two of us really get to drinking. The girls are out celebrating and me and Jack have all night. He says my sister cried when he asked her. That he was on one knee and she wept. He asks if I ever plan on making an honest woman of Eve.

At one point I suggest we hit the supermarket to get more drinks. But I don't say supermarket, I say *supermarché*. And I know I'm pretty much gone. That's when Jack tells me to wait a minute. He comes back from the kitchen with the good stuff.

'This is a celebration,' he says. 'If we're not meant to drink it tonight then we're never meant to drink it.'

Later, when the TV goes to static and we've started drinking the whisky slow, Jack tells me about when he was a kid and his Mum decided he'd be better off home schooled. 'Two months we lasted,' he says. 'But then my Dad found out and he got the courts involved. The funny thing is I loved school. I only put up with being at home for her.' He tells again about the time he met Quentin Tarantino. About how they stood side by side at urinals during the Monte Carlo Grand Prix. I've heard him tell that one a few times. He always uses the same punch line: 'I looked down. Then Quentin looked down. We made eye contact. I winked. Then Quentin went pale.'

I ask Jack if he's ever heard me tell about the time I got locked in a disabled toilet and

had to climb into the ceiling. He's heard it. I ask if I ever told him about my sister's friend I refused to kiss during school who's now a top model in Japan. My sister told him that one. I ask if I ever told him Eve's story. About the time someone left a puppy on her doorstep. 'Someone's told me,' he says. 'Maybe it wasn't you but I definitely know that story. How the puppy was just lying at the door wrapped in a blanket then they had that party and the puppy... Yeah, I know all about that one. It's a good one.'

'What about the time with the Doctor. Have I ever told you that story?'

'What's this?' he says.

'Man, this is a good one,' I say. 'If you think the puppy story is a good one, wait until you hear this.'

So I start to tell him.

'I was in the pub at the bottom of the road. Normally I go to the shit one cos it's quiet and cheap but I'd had a pretty tough week and decided to go to the nice one. You been in?'

'Only with you,' Jack says.

'Well anyway, they've split it into two sections so that the restaurant is completely separate from the bar. Means if anyone is eating they don't have to put up with the drinkers. And the drinkers don't have to... You know. So it's about lunchtime I go in and I walked right through the restaurant to the bar. The restaurant was mobbed but I went through the curtain and I was the only person. You can't hear a thing from the other side. It even smells different in there. So I go up to the bar and I

➤➤

order. I wasted my change on the puggy then grabbed a newspaper.

'A couple of minutes later a guy came in. Well dressed. He had a scarf on. Leather gloves. He went up to the bar and I looked over the top of my paper at him. He ordered a whisky. But then he looked over at me and said to the barman, "and I'll take a pint of whatever he's having." So naturally I thought here's some old pervert. But fuck it, a drink's a drink, right? Then he went and sat down in the other corner of the room, sipped the whisky then started on the pint.

'The next time I went up to the bar I ordered a pint but then I thought, I know what I'll do, and I said in a pretty loud voice, "And I'll have a glass of whatever whisky he's having as well barkeep." I said it so loud that the guy looked over. Then I took my drinks, sat back down and slammed the whisky in one.

'After that, if you want to know the truth, I pretty much forgot all about him. I was getting lost in the papers and with it being so quiet in there I was thinking aye, I could really get used to this place. Maybe it's worth spending that little bit extra for a classy joint like this. I was looking around thinking yeah, even just once a week as a treat I could come here instead of going to the shit pub. Now you've got to remember that I still had enough redundancy cash to last me another three months or so. I wasn't even worrying about that. But then what happened was we synchronised, you know. I'd be at the bar then he'd be at the bar. I'd be at the pisser then he'd walk in. The second time it happened I said something like, "fancy meeting you here," you know, something stupid and the old guy laughed. Then he said, "come here often?" And I laughed. But then he said, "no, I'm asking. Do you come here quite a lot?" I told him how I normally go to the other pub. "Is it always this quiet?" I said and he said, "I don't know. I don't normally drink in the afternoons." "Yeah, me neither," I said, then went like that, whoooooop, with my nose.

'By the time we sat down I'd worked out that this guy was pretty ruined. See, with the black curtain, it's really dark in that section of the place and even though it's lunchtime you always feel like you're one drink away from last orders. So I said to him, "how come you're in here drinking today then?" and he rubbed his eyes and went, "I finish up next week. Decided to take a half day. What they going to do? Fire me?" Then he started to laugh. This was the laugh to end them all. More to shut him up than anything else I said, "so what is it you do then?" and when he eventually stopped laughing, he said, "I'm a surgeon. At least I was. Now I'm a retired surgeon."

'"Surgery?" I said. "What type of surgery?"

'"Breasts mostly," he said. "Breast enlargements, breast reductions, breast uplifts, nipple corrections. Nipple tucks. That type of thing."

'"Shut the fuck up," I said.

'"I'm serious," he said. "Breasts have been my life's work."

'But he was smirking a bit and I said, "I wish it'd been mine."

'I started to imagine seeing them cut up and I said, "does the novelty not wear off though? Do you not sometimes get sick of tits?"

'He sipped the whisky and said, "would you?"

'I raised my eyebrows.

'"Well there's your answer then," he said.

'"And you're retiring man? I'd work that job to the death."

'"We all get old," he said.

'For a while we chatted about his retirement and I told him what had happened with my job. He said his name was Francis. That his Mother had named him after the Saint. He asked me if my mother had been religious and named me after Saint Anthony. I said she'd named me after my Dad. He went up and bought us a round then later I did the same thing. We were just chatting to each other. It was good. And that laugh. See when he got started. How contagious it was. I went up to the bar to get another round in and the bartender, he goes like that with his dour plum-sucking face, "yous two are going to have to keep it down or I'll stop serving."

'"Are you kidding on mate," I said, "there's nobody here to annoy."

'"Through there," he said, and pointed his

thumb at the curtain.

"'Och lighten up man," I said.

"'I'm being serious," he said, "I mean it right. I'll stop serving yous. I will, don't test me. You wanting to test me cos you'll see, I'll stop serving. Just you wait, I'll do it." Blah, blah, blah and all that crap.

'So I took the drinks over and whispered to Francis, "we've been ordered to keep it down by the drill sergeant over there." He looked over at the barman and said, "oh, right, I see." And for a while we stopped talking. Eventually I asked him, "do you like dogs Francis?"

"'I really like dogs," he said. "I love puppies."

"'Aye," I said, "I bet you do. In your line of work."

"'Funbags," he said.

'Then that laugh.

'The barman glared over and Francis held his hand up in apology. I ended up telling him how Eve made these posters describing the puppy. But stupidly, she named him. I said how she called him Rory cos she thought his growl sounded like a baby lion trying to roar.

"'Aww God, the worst thing you want to do is name the damn thing," the Doctor said. Then he went, "I do that with breasts sometimes. You see a lot of women. Some come in with lopsided ones. Paps with personalities I call them."

'I ended up telling the guy how she put the posters up three miles in every direction. He was leaning close in and I could smell his breath. It was that cheesy oniony way that old guys' breath gets. I told him how Eve put ads on the internet, called the local paper. Then I said how that night she had to go to a party and didn't want to leave the wee guy so she took him with her. I told him how everyone was fawning over the dog calling Rory, Rory, trying to teach him paw, trying to teach him fetch but the wee guy just wanted to stay with Eve and cuddle up in her chest.

"'It's a very nice place to curl up," the doctor said.

'I explained to him how one thing led to another and Eve ended up drunk. Rory was fine so she went mingling and eventually met this guy. Now this is a while before I met her and I don't mind admitting she ended up sleeping with the guy but I'm with her now, you know. As long as it was before my time.

'I told the Doctor how Eve met this guy. I said, "I'm sure I don't have to tell you Doc, but when you meet someone new like that and you both get those feelings you forget about everything else, don't you?" I told him how she claims she never forgot Rory, said she was just sure her friends would be looking after him, but for whatever reason she ended up in the bathroom with this guy, his name was fucking Colin or Charles or Clarence or something. Actually, why am I lying, his name was Craig. Just makes me fucking angry to say the guy's name out loud.

'Anyway, one thing led to another and they ended up shagging. So Eve says nowadays that she half remembers hearing scratching at the door. Half remembers hearing the little growl. But I said maybe she just thinks that now because of the guilt and she couldn't promise that wasn't the case.

'I was waiting on the doctor hugging me or something. Telling me that Eve was with me now so that guy didn't matter. That I must be much better if she chose me over him. That she must love me. But he didn't. He just said, "can you keep a secret Anthony?"

"'Aye," I said, "but gonna call me Tony, you're making me feel old."

"'I take photographs," he said.

"'You take photographs?"

"'It's standard procedure."

"'What is?" I said.

"'No, no, no," he said, "in private practices it can be standard procedure."

"'Fucking hell, you mean of the tits?"

"'What's not standard practice," he said, "is keeping the pictures of the girls that end up going in a different direction. The ones that decide surgery isn't for them or go to a different clinic. But I've not gotten to where I am by following standard procedure."

"'You want to see a few?" The Doctor said.

'Now, you know me Jack. You know how polite I am with strangers. I hate starting new relationships off on the wrong foot. So even though I'm feeling like a duty of care or something for these girls, that I'm worrying about all the times I've ever been to a doctor's, about all the times Eve has ever been. In the back of my head I'm thinking about what doctors must have whispered to each other about her after an examination, I don't say any of this to this Francis guy. I mean, you know how polite I get. Did I tell you about the time I got my haircut by a racist barber? Well yeah, I didn't want to upset him. I just let him carry on.'

'We ended up out the back of the pub. Lads together and all that. He had his arm around me and we were spilling pints everywhere. The doctor glanced about and when he was sure there was nobody around he opened his jacket and took a couple of Polaroids out his pocket.

'"Now these are the only ones I took today," he said.

'He showed me these photographs of women against a white wall and they were topless. One of the women was covering her eyes with her forearm but the other was just staring straight down the lens.

'"She was good," the doctor said. "A Mizzzz Symington. Divorced. Very much the entertainer. She wants to enlarge from a 34C to a 34DD."

'And there was me man, staring at this girl's tits. They were unbelievable. Anyway, he went on to tell me how he has a room in his house where he has albums. He said when he first started taking the photographs he would never capture the face. He'd focus purely on the breasts. Nowadays he tries to get in as much of the face and body as he can. He told me I should see the haircuts. That the funniest thing about it all is the change in hairstyles. He's got photos going back twenty years, he said, you should see some of the hairstyles, God.

'"Do you remember all the women?" I said.

'"Only the most recent. The most recent are always the best."

'We heard the door open and the Doctor stashed the photos back in his pocket.

'"Yous are still too noisy," the barman said. "It's carrying all the way through to the restaurant. This is the last time I'm warning yous then you'll be out."

'"Our apologies," Francis said. He smiled at the guy. He had that charming bedside manner, you know. "My fault," he said. "Not the boy's. I'm a retiree. We are having a retirement celebration. But we apologise. The noise will stop."

'"Well okay then. That's good then," the barman said.

'We sat on the bench beneath the smokers' heater and drank. Every so often I got a fit of the giggles and Francis shrugged or said something like, "just one of the perks," or, "it's a tough job but someone's got to do it."

'We finished our drinks and I said to him, "You want another one?" He looked at the glass for a while, checked his watch and said, "Afraid not young man, I'll have to be going."

'"It's still early man," I said, "have another."

'"It's late for me," he said, "but have a few more. My treat." He dipped into his pocket and brought out some cash and handed me it. Thing is, behind the note was one of the Polaroids. The one of the girl with her hand across her face.

'"You made this day bearable," the doctor said.

'"Thanks," I said.

'"Enjoy the gift," he said, "and listen, don't worry about your girl. Let me tell you, she'll make a great Mother. Keep that in mind. If she did that for a puppy then think what she'd do for a baby."

'And with that the guy was gone.

'I sat for a while and finished the dregs at the bottom of my glass. I was thinking about what he said. And then it started to dawn on me that maybe he was being sarcastic. Maybe he was telling me she'll sleep around. And I can't get this thought out of my head. That this Doctor, who has known more women than I'll ever know, he was saying that my girlfriend wants to fuck other guys. I started getting that watery feeling in my mouth, you know, the biley feeling that comes just before sickness, but I managed to calm it down. Instead of buying more drinks I took the guy's money and headed up the road. I stopped in at the Supermarket to buy a bottle of red and a couple of steaks so I could start making us dinner.

'When we were eating I started to tell Eve all about him. But obviously I didn't tell her everything. I just told her what he told me. About what he does.

'And Eve stood up. Said we should call the hospital and tell them, call the papers, call the police. I told her I didn't even catch his name. That he was probably just a janitor with a wild imagination. But she said, "no, we have to do something. This is big, it's sick. He's a sick man. What pub was it?" I told her I got the train into town and went to a pub near the station. The guy could be from anywhere.

'"I really can't believe this," she said. "I feel like I'm going to be sick."

'Later on, once I'd done the dishes, she was sitting with the laptop.

'"This is why I can't trust men," she said. "You hear stories like this and you know you can't trust men."

'"You can trust me," I said.

'"I can't trust you. You know fine well I can't trust you."

'"That's not fair," I said. "I'm actually fucking raging you're even saying that. That's fucking out of line."

'Eve walked away and sat in the kitchen. And you want to know what I did? I almost left. I almost went back down to the pub to try and find the guy. For a second I actually missed him.

Jack sits forward and shakes his head.

'Jesus Christ,' he says, 'what a fucking psycho.'

'I know man,' I say.

'Look listen,' he says, 'I was unfaithful once. It was ages ago.'

'What?' I say.

'I know, I know, sorry. But you're my best man now. I need to tell you this stuff. It was so long ago, I'm talking years and well, you know how it is.'

'But that's my sister, mate.'

I'm about to say something else when we hear a key in the door. We hear their voices in the hall and quiet laughter as they tiptoe about so as not to wake us. I hear Eve's whisper and her footsteps pad on the laminate. And all I want is to tell her I'm sorry. That I'll love her forever and I'm sorry.

Allan Wilson's debut story collection will be published by Cargo Publishing in October 2011

# Character sketches from the novel *Beat Versus Benoit*
## Toni Davidson

BEAT

Beat stared into the white distance. With both naked eye and strong binoculars he strip-searched mountain beauty looking only for movement; like an unexpected shadow across the alpine slopes or the suspicious fall in the windless twilight of snow from a tree laden with filmic tension. A rotten fruit. It was hard for him to separate the real and the performed. In his world it was lauded when there was no difference.

There were other incursions. Still more pugilistic memories surfacing for another round. Had he covered his tracks well enough? Once he had played a tense jangly murderer with weird sexual tendencies and he never understood why the script called for him to return to the scene of the crime, to cross the flickering tape and view the bloody mess of sexual organs still visible on the ground.

He could have played that part better now. You can never be sure.

As dusk slowly crept up the gorge, lengthening the shadows of the tall trees on either side of the valley, he peered like auld folk into the teasing moonlight, decoding nature, challenging the dark peaks to reveal a malicious presence.

When dawn revealed his rugged encampment on the balcony it might have been tempting to characterise the scene as one of abandonment, of encroaching destitution. If they ever found him it would be an obvious angle to take, such a great story with perfect backdrop. There he was, the Young Gun, Beat,

sensationally found, a ragged mess somehow surviving where many others had perished in the alpine killing fields. File footage would have frozen celebrities dug out of the ice, their beauty preserved better than Botox and would zealously catalogue an ungrateful list of the famous who wanted to disappear while contrasting crudely with lines outside the factory studios that showed those giving everything to appear.

But here he was and there was nothing of the refugee about him. Not in such a location, exclusive even for these gilded valleys of recluse and chalet; of money funneled into secret and secured investment. From one of the rugs covering Beat ran a thin flex that led to a power socket. When it was coldest close to dawn he was able to turn up the heat on the electric blanket. It could be argued that if he was suffering then it was not for want of anything.

Beat scrawled on his notepad a reminder for Sergio, the caretaker who slithered in and out of the chalet as required; *Get small but powerful searchlight.*

Once he had played a young conscript caught in no man's land lit by two flares one from either side of the war. He got a few of these roles early on, egged on by his first agent (short lived) who was keen for him to steer his career towards starring in popular mini-series or significant roles in up and coming soaps that would lather them both with success and recognition. In the film, Beat of course was required to make the right decision. He survived. The story ended happily.

The chalet normally rented for summer

seclusion or winter sports had been named with predictable ostentation as *Le Chalêt de la Bélle Montagne*. It gave its occupants an unspoiled view of the valley below, its acres, partially dedicated to a summer pool and terrace, also contained a walled garden, a children's play area and enough parking for several cars. The rest of the land went steep quickly and fell precipitously from lawn into soil and broken foliage; it was a slope treacherous enough for it to be fenced off from guest children and pets. If it was too dangerous for people then pines and elegant larches thrived; little had disturbed these slopes, the crack of branches in storms, the fall of fir cones in autumn of course as well as the scurry of critters but nothing else. Still, the chalet's often distinguished guests had on occasion intervened with balls and rubber rings thrown into the air then carried beyond the safe perimeter. Lost. Like the guest's car some years back with its handbrake carelessly left off so that some shimmering limousine careered through a party of the well to do, the type to rent such a place they liked to call La Belle M and fell with its oak lacquer effect unbarking as it headed into the abyss. Its chauffeur, red-faced and horrified, could only look on, his expression that of a man who had just lost his job. And once an old man, of hushed orientation, who dived for the cool rushing waters of the River Bors far below but ended up planted like a pine, withered before his time.

When Beat could no longer keep his eyes open, he pulled the brim of his hat down, adjusting the sunglasses on his face and sank further into his chair. Tiredness relinquished him of his vigilance, soothed with unlikelihoods and reassured that he had covered his tracks well. Beat had not played this particular part; however, he understood the worst that could happen, this was such fertile setting for the imagination, but in the end he was just another recluse with something to hide. They were ten a penny in this valley.

BENOIT

Across the valley layered with old growth and new, spindly saplings somehow clinging to the sloping earth, branches like taut fingers reaching for grip in the thin air, Benoit, in the same early dawn light, was drawing. He was sketching the figure of a woman, slim, almost curveless with hair length and style waiting to be applied. He had not dressed her nor had he anatomised her; like a mannequin she hung around waiting for someone to make her human. Benoit's pen hovered over her face and momentarily he filled in her lips, giving them volume, even a slight pucker.

Benoit smiled at his own invention but would not entertain it longer than it took to erase the figure with a storm of ink, a zig zagging bolt across her body. He was no artist and this was not a sketch book. He had a stack of these notebooks, cushioned covers with ostentatious gold lettering across the front, as though without a word being contained within they were already valuable. This was what he wanted. They were expensive just as everything else was – if necessary he wanted to be able to write on this balcony in the throes of a summer storm, just him, his tenacious words, the strong paper, the windproof pens. It would be a good way to complete his memoir, perfectly in situ, appropriately titled *A Rage In The Machine*. The timing was right for someone of his fame, renown and age. He was fond of saying that there would be no ghost writing only ghosts writing. Ha. It would have such pith. What would memoir be without memories?

Of course he was still a little drunk and the stupor held him like an old friend willing as always to put up with his rants, his anger, his tears, his surging desire, its inevitable detumescence. One moment he would be shouting at the night, letting his voice ring out across the valley, not a local tune, an alpine horn but a primal screech like he expected more than an echo, for some strange, muscular animal to clamber over the wall at the edge of the valley and crawl towards him rippling with menace. This would give way to whispers into the clouds which sank low at dawn, spreading out like a white canopy above the gorge and then he would finally close his eyes.

For most of the ten days he had been at the

➼

chalet this was how he fell asleep; rugged and comfortable, layers and layers of cashmere and merino on top of him, spread like a checkered picnic, everything he needed to hand. If the bottle on top of the table was emptied, there was another waiting below. He had sent ahead. A shopping list for someone who did not have to move for some time. He kept his phones close though. Benoit was not hiding. He told everyone who needed to know. The renowned academic and sex pundit – his description always depended on which media – was not being a recluse nor was he on the run as one or two newsfeeds liked to describe his departure from the University. This was a beautiful locale for a holiday. Ask anyone. Benoit was simply toasting the sunrise with the last drink of the night or possibly the first drink of the day. It didn't matter which.

To look at him now, no one would have thought him a stud. He was out to pasture of course, a pin up for the aging process with his body drooping gently like a leathery stalk bending to gravity, to inevitability. Where once there had been a man of distinctive attractiveness, of husky allure who had turned a few heads, licked a few lips, there was something crumpled about him. To look at him now, well not *now*, not in the chalet in the mountains but back in the brick of the University, he had merged with and given in to the incipient couture of corduroy; the languid blaze of subdued colours and loafers; the agreeable paunches and hunched shoulders of those who ate at their desks.

They, his colleagues of decades long, had not always been like that; their shared history that was no doubt still leaking into the present was startling evidence of that. They had been revolutionaries in an academic world, challenging the dumb status quo and there had been a shared verve. What was now the everyday of curt conversations, brief nods and rote teaching had once seemed something so much more challenging, the excitement of new territory explored. Such dulled collectivism had tried to avoid their controversial history by downplaying its role and their involvement. *We were young, idealistic, full of intellectual*

*bravado...* This was their cliché of matured rebellion, the belief that the past wasn't so much a foreign country but a once beautiful island that had now vanished because of rising tides. But everybody knew it was there beneath the surface.

Having staggered in from the balcony Benoit pushed his face into one of the twin basins in the bathroom, a room as opulent as the rest of the chalet with marble throughout, fine white porcelain fittings that whispered bespoke. The water was ice cold, straight from the mountains all around and his skin flushed with life as he gasped and then laughed. How could he possibly be here? He had been in some of the hovels of the world where restrooms were for anything but rest and where for hours on end he had only known the touch of enamel and skin, the intoxication of sex and smell. He had dived into research that most would have stayed away from and been with people in every sense of the word who few wouldn't have crossed the street to avoid. He met people he hardly knew, had nothing in common with and yet had some of the most intimate moments of his life. This was no secret although his colleagues were doing everything to make sure it remained one. Benoit was a loose cannon, always had been but now that things had blown up, they were afraid he would be the whistleblower.

When he asked them if they would stand by him, support him at this difficult time they looked away, stared at computer screens and changed the subject. This was their aim. To mute the past into loaded silence.

He stepped out of the bathroom and lay on a bed wide enough for three, laden with silk cushions and colourful draperies which he pushed off with a sweep of his arms, kicking the last cushion across the room, its tassels unable to cling on to the polished floor. His breakfast would be here soon. The hangover was beginning to creep up on him and when he reached for the notebook he kept beside the bed – another chapter, another time to recall – he knew it wouldn't work. Sure, the memories were all there, they were virile and vigorous but he was too tired to put them into words and

so instead he picked up the binoculars which
guests could use to watch soaring eagles or
floating hawks but which Benoit used to focus
on the chalet across the other side of the valley.
It had been his first choice but the agent told
him it had already been block booked for the
summer by a distinguished actor. Benoit would
have preferred the more modern interior of
that chalet and as he focused the binoculars, he
wondered what kind of man would do exactly
what he had done.

# Here Before
## Stephanie Brown

HERE SHE CAME. Rushing headlong into the world, from the warm wet darkness that was her home, through blood and bone and the meat of me. From the place before language and the mirror, from the time before time, from nothingness, from infinity, she came. A thing that should never have been. An abomination. I didn't want her, but from between my legs here she came anyway and I was her mother.

It isn't right to feel nothing, but I've heard it's very common. She reminded me in my arms of a new born piglet, blinking and looking out of her eyes for the first time. The eyes that appeared, with each effort, seemed to me very black. So black I almost shrieked and dropped her and felt the sweat on my skin go cold. I did turn her over to look for a tail. It isn't right to feel nothing, but if anyone had known the circumstances of her conception, they would have forgiven me.

My uncle ascended the stairs at night. I heard each step creak in his wake, under the weight of him. He held my face down to the pillow, and grunted at me to keep my mouth shut. Keep my mouth shut I did, but nonetheless I received the sort of black-hearted glares at the breakfast table that told me they knew, they knew and they hated me for it. My uncle came lumbering into the kitchen, pulling his belt buckle closed with great effort and hideous obscenity, and sat down to thank the Lord for his provisions. His wife's hands were clasped before her like claws stripped to the bone by the wind, and her head swivelled on its stalk to fix me with its most withering gaze. My uncle's eyes were closed in the blissful oblivion

of prayer while his children, my cousins, and their mother rained down accusations on me from their eyes. Under their gaze I grew pale, and my belly grew fat, and he kept coming, the fat stench of him, my nose squashed sideways so I couldn't breathe, until one day his hand fell on my stomach and he let out a cry and staggered backwards. Twelve, thirteen? Yes I could, I do, I did, I was. He backed out the room, a wild expression in his eye, and I sat up on my elbows and regarded my stomach, naked with the nightie lifted above it. It wasn't with horror, but more with mild surprise that I agreed with him. It was looking unusually rounded. If it was so, it was so, I thought. And this would be his punishment. But I didn't want it: the piglet would be his.

The family didn't speak of the disease till far after it was obvious. It became an unspoken fact. My aunt thrust open the door of my room one day and, looking down at me with derision, flung down a bundle of maternity clothes. The first I heard her speak of it was to her friend on the telephone. 'Gone and got herself into a state, hasn't she. Oh, some local scumbag, who knows?' My cousins made jokes about me with all their friends. Under their breath at every turn; *slut, whore*. They knew, they knew, they knew, but they would not countenance anything else. If it was God's will the child would be born.

And so my daughter was a piglet, but I began to love her all the same. Her eyes weren't black at all, but blue, the intense azure blue of the sky above some faraway beach, not the pathetic tired watercolour blue of even our best summer days. She wrapped her little hand around my finger and curled up to me. 'I'm only a child too,' I whispered, 'We can be children together.' She was only a baby, but she was on my side, I knew it. My aunt, whose maternal instincts were stronger than mine, would often try to take her and coddle her away from me.

'You're doing it all wrong,' she would snap venomously, and wrap her thin arms like tendrils around my baby. Lucy, for so I named her, would wail like a banshee and do her the wonderful discourtesy of vomiting on her shoulder, only quietening down when returned to the safe arms of her mother. In many ways, she was a delightfully rude baby. At mealtimes, when the family settled down to grace and closed their eyes in ostensible prayer, Lucy would gurgle and giggle loudly. When my uncle, losing his temper, roared down the expanse of the table for me to shut the thing up, Lucy released a globule of potato in his direction, with one of her many nonsensical noises of joy. My aunt turned and wished death fervently upon us for this blasphemy. Lucy blinked her little eyes at me like a baby orang-utan. I swear she knew I was pleased with her. I swear she was laughing at them.

Years passed and still he came to me in the night, wanting nothing but release, feeling nothing but loathing. Holding my head down hard into the pillow, so hard I sometimes thought he would suffocate me, half hoped he would. When he left me in the dark I would lay like that, not moving, and utter a low joyless laugh to myself, thinking of the magazines I read, the girls at school, their excitement, the mystery. I wished for my eyes to fill with self pity, but they remained resolutely dry and felt ancient in my head like the eyes of the sphinx, who has seen many lives. Sometimes Lucy would wake up. She made no sound at all, only looked at me through the bars of her cot, her eyes big in the moonlight but not surprised. 'One day you and I will be big enough to leave,' I would whisper to her, as though she was the one who needed soothing. 'We'll go and live somewhere nice. And we'll have a cat, I promise.' That way I could smile and comfort myself, and go to sleep.

Lucy and I grew, inexorably. I measured us both on the door frame. Lucy learned to talk, and with her words came a hush from the rest of the household, a hush and a silent tension, a feeling that we were rushing towards some unimaginable catastrophe. It cheered me, obscurely, to think of the house as the biblical one built on sand, sliding slowly into the sea. The family, held together by nothing but silence and ritual, so vulnerable to the new things I'd learned about paternity tests and the law. But it was Lucy who threatened, not I.

Of course I didn't tell her. She was too young to understand and to know such a truth about yourself was unbearable. But as we all sat in the semi-darkness of the living room one evening, the blue light of the television dancing on my uncle's fat cheeks and sending sparks of artificial life into my aunt's ferrite eyes, she burbled a single word, clear enough to send an arctic wind around the already cold room. 'Daddy,' she giggled, and pointed to my uncle. I froze in the midst of dandling her on my knee and looked frantically around the room. I saw my aunt's long finger, paused in the act of tapping itself on the armrest. I saw my uncle's face imperceptibly darken, his back hunch over like a huge silverback gorilla. 'Dadadablablabla,' I said to her cheerfully.

'Daddy,' she said back clearly with a self-satisfied and articulate air. I saw the side of my cousin's eyeball as he lay on the floor in front of the TV, his whole being concentrated on the sound behind him.

'Deedeelalala,' I said, and pressed her to my body to silence her as I ferried her from the room. Upstairs, she played happily, smashing a pair of bricks together. I sat with my head in my hands looking at her in disbelief. 'Yes, daddy.' I said. 'How did you know?' My little girl only smiled and hummed and smashed her bricks together and machinated quietly.

All I have learned is that there are more things on heaven and earth than we can ever know. 'Mummy?' Lucy asked me one day, when she had grown out of bricks and brushed the horse's hair of a doll's head with great concentration and love, 'When I was in your tummy, why did you cry?' I had tired eyes by then. I was fifteen. I had exams to complete, I had to get through school.

'I didn't cry, honey, I was happy you were coming.'

'No, mummy, I saw you, you were sitting at that window there and looking out and crying. I saw you.'

'Lucy, remember you were inside mummy's tummy so you hadn't opened your eyes yet.'

'But I remember it! I saw you.'

She started to cry. I felt my own eyes filling and fixed them to the wallpaper like bluebottles in the hope that they wouldn't. I could not have her see my sadness. But she was right, it was true, I had sat right there in the window box and cried for myself, for the life that I had lost, for the one I'd never been allowed to have. Her questions only worsened in time. Coming in from school one day in December, my nose red and my hands purple with the cold, I hurried to my room to find Lucy in there playing with Barbie and Ken. She was strangely quiet for a few minutes as I took off my coat and boots. With the ineffable sense we seemed to have, I knew she was looking intently at my back as I did so. I turned round to see her little feline eyes fixed upon me. Not with anger, nor with accusation, but with infinite calm and gentleness and understanding, she asked 'Mummy, why is Uncle Harry my daddy?' I stared at her like a guilty child while my mind stuttered through the various possible responses I could give her. My mouth opened and closed of its own accord several times while I tried to figure out if I should lie or tell her the truth, but eventually my eyes filled and I simply looked to the ceiling above her head, breathing hard, trying only not to break down in front of her. While I stood there like that, she crept over to me and wrapped her little arms around my legs. 'It's OK, mummy,' she said, 'I won't let it happen again.'

It was around this time that the house grew colder, and the shadows grew longer, and I lay awake at night, convinced of creeping fiends in the corner. A palpable fear had entered my veins and prevented me from sleeping at night, and although I pretended I didn't, I knew all

along what it was. I lay there, my ears pricked up for every little creak of the house, every little noise in the kitchen, thinking of ghosts and purgatory and demons, but when my eyes lighted upon my daughter they landed there like a leaden weight because the truth was I was afraid of her. She knew things she could not possibly know. I even imagined her eyes to open in the darkness and to look at me again, like she did when she was a baby and he was here. If I thought of her, she would hear my thoughts. Hysterically, I ran a tickertape monologue of good thoughts through my mind. *My lovely daughter,* I thought, *my lovely sleeping baby just you sleep on, don't wake up.* I crept up beside her bed, expecting what? To see the face of the devil, perhaps. Or a curled up little piglet, covered in amniotic fluid, turning and squealing 'mummy!' What I saw was my own little girl, with the covers half tossed off, looking pale and feverish. The sheen of sweat lay on her forehead, on her poor face which was the very face of innocence. I felt a hot flush of shame at my stupidity and superstition, my inadequacy as her mother, and my inability to save her from the circumstances of her birth.

The next day she wasn't well and lay tossing and turning in bed while my aunt and I fussed over her with thermometers and damp face cloths. When dusk came, most of her discomfort seemed to have died down and she lay exhausted, awake but peaceful at last. When my aunt had gone, she turned to me with bright feverish eyes and dry lips, her hair all stuck down to her forehead with sweat, and said, 'Once a long time ago when I got sick the doctor sucked blood out of me into a needle...' There was a long pause before I replied slowly, 'Is that right, honey? Have you been having dreams then?' As far as I knew, she had never had blood taken. She tossed to the other side of the bed and shook her head vigorously, then pressed her nose up against the wall and seemed to fall into a doze. When I had fallen to looking out the window at the bruise coloured sunset thoughtfully, she spoke again, suddenly and loudly, then trailing off, 'Then I grew up into a beautiful lady...' In an attempt to soothe and humour her, I bent down closer to her ear and whispered gently, 'A beautiful lady, eh? And did you ride a white horse?'

'No,' she said, quieter now, 'I walked along a dark road and a man pushed me into the ditch and did to me what Uncle Harry did to you.' Any words I would have used to respond were caught up and strangled by my tightening throat muscles. Into my vacuum of silence, she whispered expectantly, '...and I didn't get up again, Mummy.' She looked at me with wide eyes, just as she did when showing me a bird's egg she had found, and began to cry, and I could do nothing but put my arms around her. My hair was wet with her sobs. Eventually she pulled back and looked at me with shining eyes and wet lips. Earnestly, she took my face in her hands and looked into my eyes. As though telling me her deepest darkest secret, she whispered. 'I'm not going to let Uncle Harry do that thing any more.'

From then on I slunk around the house like a kicked dog, close to the carpet, nose to the skirting board, wishing I could hide under the couch, my eyes wide and fearful at all times with a terrible foreboding I had. Lucy had a sparkle in her eye and had discovered the joys of cheek. 'Lucy, pick up those toys now,' my aunt ordained one day.

'No!' she shouted back and went running from the room. Before my aunt's shocked mouth had even closed, bony hand still hovering at her throat, she ran back in, blowing a long raspberry. This was nothing, however, compared to the great maliciousness with which she turned to my uncle, eyes narrowed, and asked deliberately 'Uncle Harry, how do you get babies?' My uncle, unfazed and seemingly confident of his own innocence, had the insolence to *snort*, the bastard that he was, and say derisively, 'Ask your mother.' The suggestion that he wasn't to blame, that it was my fault, that it was down to my twelve year old sluttishness, that I had purposely and sadistically tormented him with my bare knees under my school skirt, that I had, with the dead eyes and open legs of an underage porn star, wanted him to fuck me so bad, caused the bile to rise in my throat and the blood to pump so tumultuously in my veins I thought

I might faint. The only thing that kept my lips pressed whitely together, vacuum sealed, was the genuine fear that he would kill me if I opened my mouth. I remembered his heavy hand on my face, his one gold ring cold on my cheekbone, his breath hot on my neck, and knew he could do it.

From that day onwards, Lucy began to follow my uncle around. Doggedly she would haunt him from room to room, sometimes playing with her toys, sometimes merely looking at him. When he went outside, she would go outside too, trailing her doll's hair in the dirt behind her. The last time I saw her she looked like a little rag doll herself, skipping down the path to the woodshed after my uncle, nothing but a silhouette in the sunset. She reminded me in that instant of a Victorian cut-out fairy, imposed onto the scene: the impossible made real. She turned and waved cheerfully at me in the upstairs window. And when the shed lit up the sky in one sudden huge exhalation of flame, roaring like a dragon, like the rage I had always felt, I knew she had meant goodbye. One of the gas canisters had exploded, and up with it went the wood and the shed itself, both of them inside. Now when I remember her waving cheerfully, I know she clutched in her other paw a little box of matches. I know she skipped mischievously with absolute intention to her own death.

So just as soon as she'd come, there she went. Like a magician, she disappeared in a puff of smoke. She waved her cloak over the scene like a tiny Houdini, vanquishing the devil. She turned herself invisible, she turned the clock back. She wound the spool of time right back and there I found myself, a childless child again, no longer a mother. Just as soon as she'd come, she returned to nothingness, to infinity. A thing that should never have been. An abomination. I didn't want her, but I look for her tiny bones in the ashes still; my daughter, the stranger.

# Yellow Polka Dot Dress

Dilys Rose

When their measurements were perfect,
wriggling in turn into its sharply-tailored curves
the daughters shrieked: How the hell could Mum –
who bought it in a thrift shop a million years ago –
have ever got into such a slinky thing?
How could she ever have been skinnier than them,
with a waist she could cinch between her fingertips?

In the style of downtown Louisiana, circa 1955 –
Was that when Mum and Retro were born? –
the dress and its itsy bitsy bolero shrug
has been around longer than they have:
souvenir from the old dear's youth; remnant
of the days she sashayed forth from cheap hotels,
turned heads – she says! – in London, Paris, Venice.

When it fitted like a snakeskin, the daughters
borrowed it, backpacked it to Delhi, Kandy, Bangkok
but it defied them, defeated their diet plans.
Crushed, torn, straining at the seams, it began
to smell of cumin, dope, drains. They shucked it off.
Mended and mothballed, snug in Mum's wardrobe,
the yellow polka dot dress awaits the granddaughters.

The black lace dress
This one smells of ragstore stour, of the dessication
Time brings to everything, of grit and brittle insects
A torn web of lace, crumbling/growing holes each time it's handled,

if you were rough, careless, impatient, thinking of other things,
the dress would crumble beneath your fingers.
It could give you new life as a vampire
It was, once, beautiful
Now disintegrating and yet a once lovely dress
The red dress: mmm, a mistake

# The M8 Gantry's Lament
JoAnne McKay

CAUTION SURFACE WATER

DON'T DRINK AND DRIVE

CHECK YOUR FUEL

CAUTION BREAKDOWN AHEAD

FULL CARS LESS QUEUES

STAY BACK STAY SAFE

DRIVE EFFICIENTLY

CAUTION BREAKDOWN AHEAD

      FACE

    DRINK

   YOU

        D      EAD

FULL

     AY    E

   I

    BREAK

WEAR A SEATBELT

KEEP YOUR WINDSCREEN CLEAR

CHECK YOUR LEVELS

SOFT TYRES WASTE FUEL

CAUTION BREAKDOWN AHEAD

RESPECT ROADWORKERS

DON'T TAKE DRUGS AND DRIVE

CAUTION BREAKDOWN AHEAD

  AR   SE

    YOU   IN      C  AR

     YOU

SO      WASTE FU L

                   D     EAD

       ECT    WORK  S

       TAKE  DRUGS

           DOWN

# Sitzpinkler
**Colin Will**

It's the German word
for men who sit to pee.
That'll be me then. It started
when I discovered the toilet lid
in our new home didn't stay up

That was ten years ago,
now I squat without thinking,
find it awkward to stand
for a piss in public urinals,
hate the spray it makes,
that damp stain on pale trousers
advertising where I've been

# Small Countries of Mother-of-Pearl
(from *Forget About Me* by Pablo Neruda)
**Olga Wojtas**

The best wee countries in the world are made of mother-of-pearl.
The bevvied punters cheer and whoop
as they birl along the glowing closes
and skite through shimmering middens.

# Contributor Biographies

Rizwan Akhtar divides his time between Aberdeen and Essex. He is currently a PhD student at the University of Essex. His poems have appeared in *Poetry Salzburg Review*, *Poetry NZ*, *Wasafiri*, *Postcolonial Text*, *Decanto*, *Poesia*, PAK, *Orbis*, *The Other Poetry* (forthcoming), *South Asian Review*, *tinfoildresses*, and *Poetry Forward Press*.

Dorothy Alexander is a creative writer and teacher who lives in the Scottish Borders. She is currently working on a long term project based on oral narrative tradition using original techniques derived from found poetry. Visual work will be exhibited at Patriothall, Edinburgh in October 2011. dorothyalexander.co.uk

Sandra Alland is a Scottish-Canadian writer, performer and intermedia artist. She has published two books of poetry: *Blissful Times* (BookThug) and *Proof of a Tongue* (McGilligan Books); and one chapbook of short fiction: *Here's To Wang* (Forest Publications). She currently collaborates with the multimedia performance troupe, Zorras. blissfultimes.ca

John Brewster is a poet, writer, creative writing tutor and musician. He has published work in a diverse range of books and magazines through the years. His poem 'am aa din' won the 2011 William Soutar Writing Prize.

Stephanie Brown grew up on a strawberry farm near Lanark and studied literature at university. Sadly she now administers Housing Benefit, but hopes to escape soon. If all goes to plan, she will be starting the Creative Writing MLitt at the University of Glasgow in September.

William Bonar is a graduate of the Glasgow University MLitt in Creative Writing and a recent St Mungo's Mirrorball Clydebuilt development scheme apprentice. His poems have appeared in numerous newspapers and magazines and on the BBC Radio 3 programme The Verb. He lives in Glasgow and works in education.

Arno Camenisch writes in German and Romansh and is one of Switzerland's most prominent younger authors. He has published three novels: *ernesto ed autres manzegnas* (2005), *Sez Ner* (2009) and *Hinter dem Bahnhof* (2010). An extract from *Sez Ner* will appear in November in *Best European Fiction 2012* (Dalkey Archive Press, USA). Arno read at Glasgow's Aye Write Festival in March. arnocamenisch.ch

Michael Cannon has published short stories in various anthologies and three previous novels: *The Borough* and *A Conspiracy of Hope* (both Serpent's Tail) and *Lachlan's War* (Viking/Penguin). He works at Strathclyde University and lives near Glasgow with his wife and daughter.

➡

Jim Carruth's first collection, *Bovine Pastoral*, was published in 2004. Since then he has brought out a further three collections and an illustrated fable. In 2009 he was awarded a Robert Louis Stevenson Fellowship and was the winner of the James McCash poetry competition. In 2010 he was chosen for the prestigious Oxford Poets anthology. jimcarruth.co.uk

Steve Cashell is an Irishman but has lived in the Scottish Borders from the age of eleven. His work has appeared, much of it pseudonymously, in a variety of magazines, newspapers and ezines, including *the Eildon Tree, The Honest Ulsterman, Groundswell, Roadworks* and the *Belfast Telegraph*.

Toni Davidson edited *And Thus Will I Freely Sing* (Polygon 1989) and *Intoxication* (Serpent's Tail of 1998). His first novel *Scar Culture* (Canongate 2000) was followed by the short story collection *The Gradual Gathering of Lust* (Canongate 2007). His novel *My Gun Was As Tall As Me* is to be published by Freight Books.

Brian Docherty was born in Glasgow and now lives in North London. He has published two collections; *Armchair Theatre* and *Desk with a View* (both from Hearing Eye). His third book, *The 'If' in California*, forthcoming from Smokestack Books.

Tracey Emerson is currently working on *The Trees Aren't Sad So Why Am I?*, a novel about abortion, as part of a Creative Writing PhD at the University of Edinburgh. She has previously published short stories in magazines and anthologies.

Sally Evans's poems included here are from her sequence *Anderson's Piano*, inspired by the train derailment near Cruachan, in the summer of 2010. It turns on the old system of wires to pull signals for falling rocks, which sings in the wilderness like an Aeolian harp. desktopsallye.com

Andrew C. Ferguson is a Fife writer, performer and musician. His work has been published by people who should know better. This issue's poem was inspired by reading *Ghosts of Spain*, a non-fiction book by Giles Tremlett, the *Guardian's* Madrid correspondent.

Jim Ferguson's early published work featured in *Tower of Babble* (Itinerant, 1987) with Bobby Christie, Graham Fulton and Ronald McNeil. More recent publications include: *Tannahill: The Soldier's Return* with an Introductory Essay by Jim Ferguson, *Read Raw Books* (Carluke, 2010) and *Sure 2b Braw: An Easterhouse Anthology* edited by Jim Ferguson, Easterhouse Writers, (Glasgow, June 2011). His work can also be found on *YouTube*.

Graham Fulton's collections include *Knights of the Lower Floors* (Polygon), *This* (Rebel Inc) and *Black Motel/The Man who Forgot How to* (Roncadora Press). A major collection *Open Plan* was published in February by Smokestack Books. *Full Scottish Breakfast* is on the way in 2011 from Red Squirrel Press.

Owen Gallagher is from Gorbals, Glasgow. *Sat Guru Snowman* was published by Peterloo Poets, England. His second collection is due from Salmon Poetry, Ireland. He has a third due to be published next year by Smokestack, England.

Andrew F Giles is a poet and translator who has work in or incoming in *Ambit*, JERRY, *Equinox, Paper X, Poetry Scotland, The Nervous Breakdown*, and *Collective Fallout*. He edits Scotland's online literary arts & culture journal *New Linear Perspectives*.

Rodge Glass is the author of the novels *No Fireworks* (Faber, 2005) and *Hope for Newborns* (Faber, 2008), as well as *Alasdair Gray: A Secrétary's Biography* (Bloomsbury), which received a Somerset Maugham Award in 2009. He was also the Editor of *The Year of Open Doors* (Cargo, 2010) and co-author of the graphic novel *Dougie's War: A Sôldier's Story* (Freight, 2010), recently nominated for Best Graphic Novel at the 2011 SICBA Awards.

Iyad Hayatleh, a Palestinian refugee poet, was born and grew up in a Palestinian refugee camp in Syria in 1960. He started writing poetry early and published his work in Arabic magazines, giving many readings in Syria, Lebanon and Yemen. He has lived in Glasgow since 2000, and he is now an active member of Scottish PEN and Artists In Exile Glasgow and has taken part in many events and translation and poetry workshops. His first collection *Beyond All Measure* is published by Survivors' Press. Recently he co-led two poetry workshops in Glasgow and Inverness sponsored by the Scottish Poetry Library and Oxfam.

Brian Johnstone has published two collections and two pamphlets. His second collection is *The Book of Bélongings* (Arc, 2009). His work has appeared throughout Scotland and in the UK, America and various European countries. *Terra Incognita*, a collection of his poems in Italian translation, was published in 2009. He is the poet member of *Trio Verso*, presenting poetry and jazz.

Craig Lamont's fiction has been shortlisted for several awards, including the Glasgow Student Short Story Prize and the Keith Wright Literary Prize. He is currently Assistant Editor at Cargo Crate Publishing and was recently Deputy Editor of *Valve*, a literary journal published by Freight Books in June 2011.

Kirsty Logan is a fiction writer, literary magazine editor, book reviewer, and arts intern. She is currently working on her second novel, *Rust and Stardust*, and a short story collection, *The Rental Heart and Other Fairytales*. Say hello at kirstylogan.com

Carl MacDougall has written three prizewinning novels, four pamphlets, three collections of short stories, two works of non-fiction and has edited four anthologies, including the best selling *The Devil and the Giro*. He has written and presented two television series and is currently working on too many things.

Anneliese Mackintosh has had short stories broadcast on BBC Radio 4, as well as published in various literary magazines and anthologies. Currently she is working on a 30-minute play for BBC Radio Scotland set on a train, and is writing a novel about terrorism and baked goods. She is also editor of Cargo Crate. Go to anneliesemackintosh.com, it's great.

Kevin MacNeil is a poet, novelist, playwright, editor and cyclist originally from Lewis. He is the recipient of a number of literary accolades and his books include *A Méthod Aĉtor's Guide to Jekyll and Hyde*, *The Stornoway Way*, *Love and Zen in the Outer Hebrides* and *Be Wise, Be Otherwise*. He recently edited *These Iŝlands, We Sing: An Anthôlogy of Scôttish Iŝlands Poétry*. He lives in London. His translations published in *Gutter 05* were commissioned for StAnza, Scotland's international poetry festival.

Robert Marsland is a writer living in the Southside of Glasgow. He has been writing for over ten years now and is the founder and editor of *Essence Poétry Magazine*. He has interests in philosophy and astrology, and volunteers for Oxfam books and music in his spare time.

➤→

R A Martens lives in Edinburgh, and should spend more time outdoors. She received a New Writers' Award from the Scottish Book Trust in 2010.

Brian McCabe was born in a small mining community near Edinburgh. He has lived as a freelance writer since 1980 and has held various writing fellowships. He is currently Royal Literary Fellow at the University of Glasgow and was Editor of Edinburgh Review 2005–2010. He has published three collections of poetry, the most recent being Zero (Polygon, 2009). He has published one novel and five collections of short stories, the most recent of which is A Date With My Wife (Canongate, 2001). His Selected Stories was published by Argyll in 2003.

Marion McCready lives in Dunoon, Argyll, with her husband and two young children. She has been published in a variety of magazines and anthologies including The Edinburgh Review, The Herald and Horizon Review. Calder Wood Press published her debut poetry pamphlet, Vintage Sea, earlier this year.

Gordon McInnes is a Glasgow poet, raised in the industrial heartlands of North East England. His work is an attempt to capture the dying culture and attitudes of the communities that grew up around, and evolved from the heavy industry.

Joe McInnes studied creative writing at Glasgow University. His poetry has been published in Gutter (01, 02) and his short stories anthologised in, In the Event of Fire (NWS 27), Let's Pretend and The Research Club. Joe has recently completed his first novel and continues to work on his short-story collection.

JoAnne McKay was born to a slaughtering family in Romford, Essex and subsequently joined the police. She now lives in a small Dumfriesshire village where she combines motherhood, work and a Masters degree with mixed success. Her latest pamphlet, Venti, was runner-up in the Callum Macdonald Memorial Award 2011.

Donal McLaughlin (An Allergic Reaction to National Anthems & Other Stories) will feature both as a writer and as a translator in Best European Fiction 2012 (Dalkey Archive Press). He is currently translating three books by leading Swiss writer, Urs Widmer. My Mother's Lover (Seagull) was published in June. donalmclaughlin.wordpress.com

Fiona Montgomery was a journalist with the Evening Times and was part of the collective behind the Scottish feminist magazine Harpies & Quines. She later taught news reporting at Napier University and currently works for UNISON Scotland. A graduate of Glasgow University's Creative Writing MLitt, she is writing a memoir.

Paula Morris is a novelist and short-story writer from New Zealand. She recently moved from New Orleans to Glasgow, and currently teaches creative writing at the University of Stirling. In 2011 she'll publish two novels: Rangatira (Penguin NZ) and Dark Souls (Scholastic US).

Ewan Morrison is the author of The Last Book You Read (Chroma, 2005), Swung (Jonathan Cape, 2006) and Distance (Jonathan Cape, 2008). Ménage, his third novel, was published by Jonathan Cape in July 2009. He lives in Glasgow.

Richard Mosses currently sells physics on behalf of eight Scottish universities. From writing scripts for school holiday zombie films, he is now on his fourth attempt at a novel. Other short stories are available in anthologies and mobile apps. khaibit.com

**Andrea Mullaney** is a journalist, tutor and writer who lives in Glasgow. She is currently a TV Critic for The Scotsman while working on a novel, *The Ghost Marriage*. andreamullaney.wordpress.com

**Philip Murnin** lives in the Pollokshields area of Glasgow. He divides his time between working as a high school English teacher and completing a Masters in creative writing at Glasgow University. Currently he is on his summer holidays and is using the time to finish his first novel. Mostly.

**Sarah Neely** writes poetry, prose and criticism. She is currently editing a collection of poetry and writings by the Orcadian filmmaker and poet, Margaret Tait (1918–1999). This will be published by Carcanet in June 2012.

**Tom Petsinis** is a poet, playwright and novelist. Born in 1953 in Macedonia, Greece, he immigrated to Australia as a child. Tom's published work includes six collections of poetry, five plays, three novels and a collection of short stories. He is the recipient of a number of awards, residencies, fellowships and short-listings. He presently works as a mathematics lecturer at Victoria University, in Melbourne.

**Wayne Price** was born in South Wales and now works at the University of Aberdeen. His stories and poems have appeared in many journals and anthologies and have won a number of awards including major prizes in the Bridport and Edwin Morgan International Competitions. His first collection of short stories, *Furnace*, will be published by Freight in Spring 2012.

**Tessa Ransford** is an established poet, translator, literary editor and cultural activist. She initiated the annual Callum Macdonald Memorial Award for pamphlet poetry in Scotland, now in its eleventh year. *Not Just Moonshine, New and Selected Poems* was published in 2008 by Luath. Tessa is working on a two-way translation project with Palestinian poet Iyad Hayatleh, who lives in Glasgow, for a book, *A Rug of a Thousand Colours,* and a new book *Don't Mention This to Anyone.* wisdomfield.com

**Dilys Rose** writes fiction and poetry and has published ten books, most recently *Bodywork* (poetry). Recent collaborations include *Twinset* (two poets, two graphic artists) and the libretto for the opera *Kaspar Hauser: Child of Europe.*

**Lidija Šimkuté** is a bilingual poet and translator based in Australia. She was born in Lithuania in 1942. Her parents fled from Soviet occupation during WWII and she spent her childhood in displaced persons camps in Germany before moving to Australia in 1949. Her books include: *Thought and Rock, Wind Sheen, White Shadows* and *Spaces of Silence.*

**J. David Simons** is a Glasgow-based writer. His first novel, *The Credit Draper* (Two Ravens Press, 2008) was short-listed for The McKitterick Prize. His second novel, *The Liberation of Célia Kahn* was published by Five Leaves in February 2011. He was recently awarded a Robert Louis Stevenson Fellowship.

**Natasha Soobramanien** was born in London and lives in Edinburgh. She has written a novel, *Genie and Paul* and is collaborating on a book with Luke Williams, author of *The Echo Chamber*, a section of which Natasha wrote.

Leela Soma was born in Madras, India and now lives in Glasgow, Scotland. Her work reflects the cultures of the two countries. Her first novel, *Twice Born*, was published in 2008 and her second novel *Bombay Baby* is due out later this year. She has also published a collection of poems *From Madras to Milngavie* in 2007.

Kathrine Sowerby is a graduate of Glasgow School of Art's MFA programme and Glasgow University's MLitt in Creative Writing. Joint winner of the Curtis Brown Prize 2011, she is working on a new novel, *The Mast*, and has recently finished a poetry pamphlet called *River Room*. kathrinesowerby.com

Anna Stewart has been working on a collection of short stories since completing the MLitt in Creative writing at The University of St Andrews. Last year she won The Dragons' Pen at Edinburgh's International Book Festival. She is a member of The St Andrews Playwrights Lab.

Jim Stewart was born in 1952; first published poems in 1966; and now co-teaches Creative Writing at the University of Dundee. His poems have appeared in such outlets as *RiverRun*, *New Writing Scotland*, *New Writing Dundee*, *InterLitQ*, *The Red Wheelbarrow*, *Gutter*, and other places.

Judith Taylor comes from Perthshire and now lives in Aberdeen, where she is a member of the editorial team at *Pushing Out the Boat* magazine. Her first chapbook collection, *Earthlight*, was published by Koo Press (2006) and her second, *Local Colour*, by Calder Wood Press (2010).

Eleanor Thom's novel, *The Tin-Kin*, was published by Duckworth in 2009. The novel won The Saltire First Book Award, and was recently chosen by BBC2's *The Culture Show* for a feature on new British novelists. Eleanor lives in Ayr with her husband and son. She is working on a second novel, and beginning a new project as a PhD student at The University of the West of Scotland.

Ryan Van Winkle's first book, *Tomorrow, We Will Live Here* is out now from Salt Publishing. He lives in Edinburgh.

Chris Wardhaugh recently returned to Scotland from a few years in New York, with his wife and their baby. Despite years of wandering, he considers Dumfries 'hame' and from Palmerston Park's forlorn stands watches Queen of the South play. As you read this there's every chance he's off wandering again.

Ginna Wilkerson travels between Tampa, FL and Aberdeen, Scotland, where she is pursuing a PhD in Creative Writing. Her poems have been published in such journals as *Gertrude*, *Chroma*, and *Causeway*; her poem *The Ocean at Dusk; to a Child* won third place in the 2010 Yeats Society Competition.

Colin Will is an Edinburgh-born poet and publisher who now lives in Dunbar. He is Makar to the Federation of Writers. His fifth collection, *The Floor Show at the Mad Yak Café*, was published by Red Squirrel Scotland in 2010. His own publishing house, Calder Wood Press, specialises in poetry chapbooks.

Allan Wilson was born in Glasgow. His first collection of short stories *Wasted in Love* will be released by Cargo Publishing in October 11, in 2011. He is currently writing a novel.

Olga Wojtas was born in Edinburgh to a Scottish mother and Polish father and attended the school immortalised by Muriel Spark in *The Prime of Miss Jean Brodie*. A Glasgow University psychology researcher has told her that, in one respect, she does not "behave abnormally relative to the population".